# Praise for *New York Times* bestselling author Diana Palmer

"Palmer proves that love and passion can be found even in the most dangerous situations."
—*Publishers Weekly* on *Untamed*

"You just can't do better than a Diana Palmer story to make your heart lighter and smile brighter."
—*Fresh Fiction* on *Wyoming Rugged*

"Diana Palmer is a mesmerizing storyteller who captures the essence of what a romance should be."
—*Affaire de Coeur*

"The popular Palmer has penned another winning novel, a perfect blend of romance and suspense."
—*Booklist* on *Lawman*

"Diana Palmer's characters leap off the page. She captures their emotions and scars beautifully and makes them come alive for readers."
—*RT Book Reviews* on *Lawless*

D1053818

Dear Reader,

I can't believe that it has been thirty years since my first Long, Tall Texan book, *Calhoun*, debuted! The series was suggested by my former editor Tara Gavin, who asked if I might like to set stories in a fictional town of my own design. Would I! And the rest is history.

As the years went by, I found more and more sexy ranchers and cowboys to add to the collection. My readers (especially Amy!) found time to gift me with a notebook listing every single one of them, wives and kids and connections to other families in my own Texas town of Jacobsville. Eventually the town got a little too big for me, so I added another smaller town called Comanche Wells and began to fill it up, too.

You can't imagine how much pleasure this series has given me. I continue to add to the population of Jacobs County, Texas, and I have no plans to stop. Ever.

I hope all of you enjoy reading the Long, Tall Texans as much as I enjoy writing them. Thank you all for your kindness and loyalty and friendship. I am your biggest fan!

Love,

*Diana Palmer*

NEW YORK TIMES BESTSELLING AUTHOR

# DIANA PALMER

## LONG, TALL TEXANS:
### *Callaghan*
### *Matt*

Previously published as
*Callaghan's Bride* and *Matt Caldwell: Texas Tycoon*

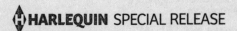 HARLEQUIN SPECIAL RELEASE

**H**HARLEQUIN® SPECIAL RELEASE

Recycling programs
for this product may
not exist in your area.

ISBN-13: 978-1-335-05997-0

Long, Tall Texans: Callaghan/Matt

Copyright © 2020 by Harlequin Books S.A.

Callaghan
First published as Callaghan's Bride in 1999.
This edition published in 2020.
Copyright © 1999 by Diana Palmer

Matt
First published as Matt Caldwell: Texas Tycoon in 2000.
This edition published in 2020.
Copyright © 2000 by Diana Palmer

This edition published by arrangement with Harlequin Books S.A.

For questions and comments about the quality of this book, please contact us at CustomerService@Harlequin.com.

Harlequin Enterprises ULC
22 Adelaide St. West, 40th Floor
Toronto, Ontario M5H 4E3, Canada
www.Harlequin.com

Printed in U.S.A.

# CONTENTS

A prolific author of more than one hundred books, **Diana Palmer** got her start as a newspaper reporter. A *New York Times* bestselling author and voted one of the top ten romance writers in America, she has a gift for telling the most sensual tales with charm and humor. Diana lives with her family in Cornelia, Georgia. Visit her website at www.dianapalmer.com.

### Books by Diana Palmer

#### *Long, Tall Texans*

*Fearless*
*Heartless*
*Dangerous*
*Merciless*
*Courageous*
*Protector*

#### *The Wyoming Men*

*Wyoming Tough*
*Wyoming Fierce*
*Wyoming Bold*
*Wyoming Strong*
*Wyoming Rugged*
*Wyoming Brave*

Visit the Author Profile page
at Harlequin.com for more titles.

# CALLAGHAN

# CHAPTER ONE

THE KITCHEN CAT twirled around Tess's legs and almost tripped her on her way to the oven. She smiled at it ruefully and made time to pour it a bowl of cat food. The cat was always hungry, it seemed. Probably it was still afraid of starving, because it had been a stray when Tess took it in.

It was the bane of Tess Brady's existence that she couldn't resist stray or hurt animals. Most of her young life had been spent around rodeos with her father, twice the world champion calf roper. She hadn't had a lot to do with animals, which might have explained why she loved them. Now that her father was gone, and she was truly on her own, she enjoyed having little things to take care of. Her charges ranged from birds with broken wings to sick calves. There was an unbroken procession.

This cat was her latest acquisition. It had come to the back door as a kitten just after Thanksgiving, squalling in the dark, rainy night. Tess had taken it in, despite the grumbling from two of her three bosses. The big boss, the one who didn't like her, had been her only ally in letting the cat stay.

That surprised her. Callaghan Hart was one tough hombre. He'd been a captain in the Green Berets and had seen action in Operation Desert Storm. He was the next-to-eldest of the five Hart brothers who owned the sweeping Hart Ranch Properties, a conglomerate of ranches and feedlots located in several western states. The headquarter ranch was in Jacobsville, Texas. Simon, the eldest brother, was an attorney in San Antonio. Corrigan, who was four years younger than Simon, had married over a year and a half ago. He and his wife Dorie had a new baby son. There were three other Hart bachelors left in Jacobsville: Reynard, the youngest, Leopold, the second youngest, and Callaghan who was just two years younger than Simon. They all lived on the Jacobsville property.

Tess's father had worked for the Hart brothers for a little over six months when he dropped dead in the corral of a heart attack. It had been devastating for Tess, whose mother had run out on them when she was little. Cray Brady, her father, was an only child. There wasn't any other family that she knew of. The Harts had also known that. When their housekeeper had expressed a desire to retire, Tess had seemed the perfect replacement because she could cook and keep house. She could also ride like a cowboy and shoot like an expert and curse in fluent Spanish, but the Hart boys didn't know about those skills because she'd never had occasion to display them. Her talents these days were confined to making the fluffy biscuits the brothers couldn't live without and producing basic but hearty meals. Everything except sweets because none of the brothers seemed to like them.

It would have been the perfect job, even with Leopold's endless pranks, except that she was afraid of Callaghan. It showed, which made things even worse.

He watched her all the time, from her curly red-gold hair and pale blue eyes to her small feet, as if he was just waiting for her to make a mistake so that he could fire her. Over breakfast, those black Spanish eyes would cut into her averted face like a diamond. They were set in a lean, dark face with a broad forehead and a heavy, jutting brow. He had a big nose and big ears and big feet, but his long, chiseled mouth was perfect and he had thick, straight hair as black as a raven. He wasn't handsome, but he was commanding and arrogant and frightening even to other men. Leopold had once told her that the brothers tried to step in if Cag ever lost his temper enough to get physical. He had an extensive background in combat, but even his size alone made him dangerous. It was fortunate that he rarely let his temper get the best of him.

Tess had never been able to understand why Cag disliked her so much. He hadn't said a word of protest when the others decided to offer her the job of housekeeper and cook after her father's sudden death. And he was the one who made Leopold apologize after a particularly unpleasant prank at a party. But he never stopped cutting at Tess or finding ways to get at her.

Like this morning. She'd always put strawberry preserves on the table for breakfast, because the brothers preferred them. But this morning Cag had wanted apple butter and she couldn't find any. He'd been scathing about her lack of organization and stomped off without a second biscuit or another cup of coffee.

"His birthday is a week from Saturday," Leopold had explained ruefully. "He hates getting older."

Reynard agreed. "Last year, he went away for a week around this time of the year. Nobody knew where he was, either." He shook his head. "Poor old Cag."

"Why do you call him that?" Tess asked curiously.

"I don't know," Rey said, smiling thoughtfully. "I guess because, of all of us, he's the most alone."

She hadn't thought of it that way, but Rey was right. Cag was alone. He didn't date, and he didn't go out "with the boys," as many other men did. He kept to himself. When he wasn't working—which was rarely—he was reading history books. It had surprised Tess during her first weeks as housekeeper to find that he read Spanish colonial history, in Spanish. She hadn't known that he was bilingual, although she found it out later when two of the Hispanic cowboys got into a no-holds-barred fight with a Texas cowboy who'd been deliberately baiting them. The Texas cowboy had been fired and the two Latinos had been quietly and efficiently cursed within an inch of their lives in the coldest, most bitingly perfect Spanish Tess had ever heard. She herself was bilingual, having spent most of her youth in the Southwest.

Cag didn't know she spoke Spanish. It was one of many accomplishments she was too shy to share with him. She kept to herself most of the time, except when Dorie came with Corrigan to the ranch to visit. They lived in a house of their own several miles away—although it was still on the Hart ranch. Dorie was sweet and kind, and Tess adored her. Now that the baby was here, Tess looked forward to the visits even more. She adored children.

What she didn't adore was Herman. Although she was truly an animal lover, her affection didn't extend to snakes. The great albino python with his yellow-patterned white skin and red eyes terrified her. He lived in an enormous aquarium against one wall of Cag's room, and he had a nasty habit of escaping. Tess had found him in a variety of unlikely spots, including the washing machine. He wasn't dangerous because Cag kept him well fed, and he was always closely watched for a day or so after he ate—which wasn't very often. Eventually she learned not to scream. Like measles and colds, Herman was a force of nature that simply had to be accepted. Cag loved the vile reptile. It seemed to be the only thing that he really cared about.

Well, maybe he liked the cat, too. She'd seen him playing with it once, with a long piece of string. He didn't know that. When he wasn't aware anyone was watching, he seemed to be a different person. And nobody had forgotten about what happened after he saw what was subsequently referred to as the "pig" movie. Rey had sworn that his older brother was all but in tears during one of the scenes in the touching, funny motion picture. Cag saw it three times in the theater and later bought a copy of his own.

Since the movie, Cag didn't eat pork anymore, not ham nor sausage nor bacon. And he made everyone who did feel uncomfortable. It was one of many paradoxes about this complicated man. He wasn't afraid of anything on this earth, but apparently he had a soft heart hidden deep inside. Tess had never been privileged to see it, because Cag didn't like her. She wished that she wasn't so uneasy around him. But then, most people were.

CHRISTMAS EVE CAME later in the week, and Tess served an evening meal fit for royalty, complete with all the trimmings. The married Harts were starting their own tradition for Christmas Day, so the family celebration was on Christmas Eve.

Tess ate with them, because all four brothers had

looked outraged when she started to set a place for herself in the kitchen with widowed Mrs. Lewis, who came almost every day to do the mopping and waxing and general cleaning that Tess didn't have time for. It was very democratic of them, she supposed, and it did feel nice to at least appear to be part of a family—even if it wasn't her own. Mrs. Lewis went home to her visiting children, anyway, so Tess would have been in the kitchen alone.

She was wearing the best dress she had—a nice red plaid one, but it was cheap and it looked it when compared to the dress that Dorie Hart was wearing. They went out of their way to make her feel secure, though, and by the time they started on the pumpkin and pecan pies and the huge dark fruitcake, she wasn't worried about her dress anymore. Everyone included her in the conversation. Except for Cag's silence, it would have been perfect. But he didn't even look at her. She tried not to care.

She got presents, another unexpected treat, in return for her homemade gifts. She'd crocheted elegant trim for two pillowcases that she'd embroidered for the Harts, matching them to the color schemes in their individual bedrooms—something she'd asked Dorie to conspire with her about. She did elegant crochet work. She was making things for Dorie's baby boy in her spare time, a labor of love.

The gifts she received weren't handmade, but she loved them just the same. The brothers chipped in to buy her a winter coat. It was a black leather one with big cuffs and a sash. She'd never seen anything so beautiful in all her life, and she cried over it. The women gave her presents, too. She had a delicious floral perfume from Dorie and a designer scarf in just the right shades of blue from Mrs. Lewis. She felt on top of the world as she cleared away the dinner dishes and got to work in the kitchen.

Leo paused by the counter and tugged at her apron strings with a mischievous grin.

"Don't you dare," she warned him. She smiled, though, before she turned her attention back to the dishes.

"Cag didn't say a word," he remarked. "He's gone off to ride the fence line near the river with Mack before it gets dark." Mack was the cattle foreman, a man even more silent than Cag. The ranch was so big that there were foremen over every aspect of it: the cattle, the horses, the mechanical crew, the office crew, the salesmen—there was even a veterinarian on retainer. Tess's father had been the livestock foreman for the brief time he spent at the Hart ranch before his untimely death. Tess's mother had left them when Tess was still a little girl, sick of the nomadic life that her husband loved. In recent years Tess hadn't heard a word from her. She was glad. She hoped she never had to see her mother again.

"Oh." She put a plate in the dishwasher. "Because of me?" she added quietly.

He hesitated. "I don't know." He toyed with a knife on the counter. "He hasn't been himself lately. Well," he amended with a wry smile, "he has, but he's been worse than usual."

"I haven't done anything, have I?" she asked, and turned worried eyes up to his.

She was so young, he mused, watching all the uncertainties rush across her smooth, lightly freckled face.

She wasn't pretty, but she wasn't plain, either. She had an inner light that seemed to radiate from her when she was happy. He liked hearing her sing when she mopped and swept, when she went out to feed the few chickens they kept for egg production. Despite the fairly recent tragedy in her life, she was a happy person.

"No," he said belatedly. "You haven't done a thing. You'll get used to Cag's moods. He doesn't have them too often. Just at Christmas, his birthday and sometimes in the summer."

"Why?" she asked.

He hesitated, then shrugged. "He went overseas in Operation Desert Storm," he said. "He never talks about it. Whatever he did was classified. But he was in some tight corners and he came home wounded. While he was recuperating in West Germany, his fiancée married somebody else. Christmas and July remind him, and he gets broody."

She grimaced. "He doesn't seem the sort of man who would ask a woman to marry him unless he was serious."

"He isn't. It hurt him, really bad. He hasn't had much time for women since." He smiled gently. "It gets sort of funny when we go to conventions. There's Cag in black tie, standing out like a beacon, and women just follow him around like pet calves. He never seems to notice."

"I guess he's still healing," she said, and relaxed a little. At least it wasn't just her that set him off.

"I don't know that he ever will," he replied. He pursed his lips, watching her work. "You're very domestic, aren't you?"

She poured detergent into the dishwasher with a smile and turned it on. "I've always had to be. My mother left us when I was little, although she came back to visit just once, when I was sixteen. We never saw her again." She shivered inwardly at the memory. "Anyway, I learned to cook and clean for Daddy at an early age."

"No brothers or sisters?"

She shook her head. "Just us. I wanted to get a job or go on to college after high school, to help out. But he needed me, and I just kept putting it off. I'm glad I did, now." Her eyes clouded a little. "I loved him to death. I kept thinking, though, what if we'd known about his heart in time, could anything have been done?"

"You can't do that to yourself," he stated. "Things happen. Bad things, sometimes. You have to realize that you can't control life."

"That's a hard lesson."

He nodded. "But it's one we all have to learn." He frowned slightly. "Just how old are you—twenty or so?"

She looked taken aback. "I'm twenty-one. I'll be twenty-two in March."

Now he looked taken aback. "You don't seem that old."

She chuckled. "Is that a compliment or an insult?"

He cocked an amused eyebrow. "I suppose you'll see it as the latter."

She wiped an imaginary spot on the counter with a cloth. "Callaghan's the oldest, isn't he?"

"Simon," he corrected. "Cag's going to be thirty-eight on Saturday."

She averted her eyes, as if she didn't want him to see whatever was in them. "He took a long time to get engaged."

"Herman doesn't exactly make for lasting relation-ships," he told her with a grin.

She understood that. Tess always had Cag put a cover over the albino python's tank before she cleaned his room. That had been the first of many strikes against her. She had a mortal terror of snakes from childhood, having been almost bitten by rattlesnakes several times before her father realized she couldn't see three feet in front of her. Glasses had followed, but the minute she was old enough to protest, she insisted on getting con-tact lenses.

"Love me, love my enormous terrifying snake, hmm?" she commented. "Well, at least he found some-one who was willing to, at first."

"She didn't like Herman, either," he replied. "She told Cag that she wasn't sharing him with a snake. When they got married, he was going to give him to a man who breeds albinos."

"I see." It was telling that Cag would give in to a woman. She'd never seen him give in to anyone in the months she and her father had been at the ranch.

"He gives with both hands," he said quietly. "If he didn't come across as a holy terror, he wouldn't have a shirt left. Nobody sees him as the soft touch he re-ally is."

"He's the last man in the world I'd think of as a giver."

"You don't know him," Leo said.

"No, of course I don't," she returned.

"He's another generation from you," he mused, watching her color. "Now, I'm young and handsome and rich and I know how to show a girl a good time without making an issue of it."

Her eyebrows rose. "You're modest, too!"

He grinned. "You bet I am! It's my middle name." He leaned against the counter, looking rakish. He was really the handsomest of the brothers, tall and big with blond-streaked brown hair and dark eyes. He didn't date a lot, but there were always hopeful women hanging around. Tess thought privately that he was probably something of a rake. But she was out of the running. Or so she thought. It came as a shock when he added, "So how about dinner and a movie Friday night?"

She didn't accept at once. She looked worried. "Look, I'm the hired help," she said. "I wouldn't feel comfortable."

Both eyebrows went up in an arch. "Are we despots?"

She smiled. "Of course not. I just don't think it's a good idea, that's all."

"You have your own quarters over the garage," he said pointedly. "You aren't living under the roof with us in sin, and nobody's going to talk if you go out with one of us."

"I know."

"But you still don't want to go."

She smiled worriedly. "You're very nice."

He looked perplexed. "I am?"

"Yes."

He took a slow breath and smiled wistfully. "Well, I'm glad you think so." Accepting defeat, he moved away from the counter. "Dinner was excellent, by the way. You're a terrific cook."

"Thanks. I enjoy it."

"How about making another pot of coffee? I've got to help Cag with the books and I hate it. I'll need a jolt of caffeine to get me through the night."

"He's going to come home and work through Christmas Eve, too?" she exclaimed.

"Cag always works, as you'll find out. In a way it substitutes for all that he hasn't got. He doesn't think of it as work, though. He likes business."

"To each his own," she murmured.

"Amen." He tweaked her curly red-gold hair. "Don't spend the night in the kitchen. You can watch one of the new movies on pay-per-view in the living room, if you like. Rey's going to visit one of his friends who's in town for the holidays, and Cag and I won't hear the television from the study."

"Have the others gone?"

"Corrigan's taken Dorie home for their own celebration." He smiled. "I never thought I'd see my big brother happily married. It's nice."

"So are they."

He hesitated at the door and glanced back at her. "Is Cag nice?"

She shifted. "I don't know."

A light flickered in his eyes and went out. She wasn't all that young, but she was innocent. She didn't realize that she'd classed him with the married brother. No woman who found him attractive was going to refer to him as "nice." It killed his hopes, but it started him thinking in other directions. Cag was openly hostile to Tess, and she backed away whenever she saw him coming. It was unusual for Cag to be that antagonistic, especially to someone like Tess, who was sensitive and sweet.

Cag was locked tight inside himself. The defection of his fiancée had left Cag wounded and twice shy of women, even of little Tess who didn't have a sophisticated repertoire to try on him. His bad humor had started just about the time she'd come into the house to work, and it hadn't stopped. He had moods during the months that reminded him of when he went off to war and when his engagement had been broken. But they didn't usually last more than a day. This one was lasting all too long. For Tess's sake, he hoped it didn't go on indefinitely.

CHRISTMAS DAY WAS QUIET. Not surprisingly, Cag worked through it, too, and the rest of the week that followed. Simon and Tira married, a delightful event.

Callaghan's birthday was the one they didn't celebrate. The brothers said that he hated parties, cakes and surprises, in that order. But Tess couldn't believe that the big man wanted people to forget such a special occasion. So Saturday morning after breakfast, she baked a birthday cake, a chocolate one because she'd noticed him having a slice of one that Dorie had baked a few weeks ago. None of the Hart boys were keen on sweets, which they rarely ate. She'd heard from the former cook, Mrs. Culbertson, that it was probably because their own mother never baked. She'd left the boys with their father. It gave Tess something in common with them, because her mother had deserted her, too.

She iced the cake and put Happy Birthday on the top. She put on just one candle instead of thirty-eight. She left it on the table and went out to the mailbox, with the cat trailing behind her, to put a few letters that the brothers' male secretary had left on the hall table in the morning mail.

She hadn't thought any of the brothers would be in until the evening meal, because a sudden arctic wave had come south to promote an unseasonal freeze. All the hands were out checking on pregnant cows and examining water heaters in the cattle troughs to make sure they were working. Rey had said they probably wouldn't stop for lunch.

But when she got back to the kitchen, her new leather coat tight around her body, she found Callaghan in the kitchen and the remains of her cake, her beautiful cake, on the floor below a huge chocolate spot on the kitchen wall.

He turned, outraged beyond all proportion, looking broader than usual in his shepherd's coat. His black eyes glittered at her from under his wide-brimmed Stetson. "I don't need reminding that I'm thirty-eight," he said in a soft, dangerous tone. "And I don't want a cake, or a party, or presents. I want nothing from you! Do you understand?"

The very softness of his voice was frightening. She noticed that, of all the brothers, he was the one who never yelled or shouted. But his eyes were even more intimidating than his cold tone.

"Sorry," she said in a choked whisper.

"You can't find a damned jar of apple butter for the biscuits, but you've got time to waste on things like… that!" he snapped, jerking his head toward the ruin of her cake lying shattered on the pale yellow linoleum.

She bit her lower lip and stood just looking at him, her blue eyes huge in her white face, where freckles stood out like flecks of butter in churned milk.

"What the hell possessed you? Didn't they tell you I hate birthdays, damn it?"

His voice cut her like a whip. His eyes alone were enough to make her knees wobble, burning into her like black flames. She swallowed. Her mouth was so dry she wondered why her tongue didn't stick to the roof of it. "Sorry," she said again.

Her lack of response made him wild. He glared at her as if he hated her.

He took a step toward her, a violent, quick movement, and she backed up at once, getting behind the chopping block near the wall.

Her whole posture was one of fear. He stopped in his tracks and stared at her, scowling.

Her hands gripped the edge of the block and she looked young and hunted. She bit her lower lip, waiting for the rest of the explosion that she knew was coming. She'd only wanted to do something nice for him. Maybe she'd also wanted to make friends. It had been a horrible mistake. It was blatantly obvious that he didn't want her for a friend.

"Hey, Cag, could you—" Rey stopped dead in his tracks as he opened the kitchen door and took in the scene with a glance. Tess, white-faced, all but shivering and not from the cold. Cag, with his big hands curled into fists at his sides, his black eyes blazing. The cake, shattered against a wall.

Cag seemed to jerk as if his brother's appearance had jolted him out of the frozen rage that had held him captive.

"Here, now," Rey said, talking quietly, because he knew his brother in these flash-fire tempers. "Don't do this. Cag, look at her. Come on, look at her, Cag."

He seemed to come to his senses when he caught the bright glimmer of unshed tears in those blue, blue eyes. She was shaking, visibly frightened.

He let out a breath and his fists unclenched. Tess was

swallowing, as if to keep her fear hidden, and her hands were pushed deep into the pockets of her coat. She was shaking and she could barely get a breath of air.

"We have to get those culls ready to ship." Rey was still speaking softly. "Cag, are you coming? We can't find the manifest and the trucks are here for the cattle."

"The manifest." Cag took a long breath. "It's in the second drawer of the desk, in the folder. I forgot to put it back in the file. Go ahead. I'll be right with you."

Rey didn't budge. Couldn't Cag see that the girl was terrified of him? He eased around his brother and went to the chopping block, getting between the two of them.

"You need to get out of that coat. It's hot in here!" Rey said, forcing a laugh that he didn't feel. "Come on, pilgrim, shed the coat."

He untied it and she let him remove it, her eyes going to his chest and resting there, as if she'd found refuge.

Cag hesitated, but only for an instant. He said something filthy in elegant Spanish, turned on his heel and went out, slamming the door behind him.

Tess slumped, a convulsive shudder leaving her sick. She wiped unobtrusively at her eyes.

"Thanks for saving me," she said huskily.

"He's funny about birthdays," he said quietly. "I don't guess we made it clear enough for you, but at least he didn't throw the cake *at* you," he added with a grin. "Old Charlie Greer used to bake for us before we found Mrs. Culbertson, whom you replaced. Charlie made a cake for Cag's birthday and ended up wearing it."

"Why?" she asked curiously.

"Nobody knows. Except maybe Simon," he amended. "They were older than the rest of us. I guess it goes back a long way. We don't talk about it, but I'm sure you've heard some of the gossip about our mother."

She nodded jerkily.

"Simon and Corrigan got past the bad memories and made good marriages. Cag…" He shook his head. "He was like this even when he got engaged. And we all thought that it was more a physical infatuation than a need to marry. She was, if you'll pardon the expression, the world's best tease. A totally warped woman. Thank God she had enough rope to hang herself before he ended up with her around his neck like an albatross."

She was still getting her breath back. She took the coat that Rey was holding. "I'll put it up. Thanks."

"He'll apologize eventually," he said slowly.

"It won't help." She smoothed over the surface of the leather coat. She looked up, anger beginning to replace fear and hurt. "I'm leaving. I'm sorry, but I can't stay here and worry about any other little quirks like that. He's scary."

He looked shocked. "He wouldn't have hit you," he said softly, grimacing when he saw quick tears film her eyes. "Tess, he'd never! He has rages. None of us really understand them, because he won't talk about what's happened to him, ever. But he's not a maniac."

"No, of course not. He just doesn't like me."

Rey wished he could dispute that. It was true, Cag was overtly antagonistic toward her, for reasons that none of the brothers understood.

"I hope you can find someone to replace me," she said with shaky pride. "Because I'm going as soon as I get packed."

"Tess, not like this. Give it a few days."

"No." She went to hang up her coat. She'd had

enough of Callaghan Hart. She wouldn't ever get over
what he'd said, the way he'd looked at her. He'd frightened her badly and she wasn't going to work for a man
who could go berserk over a cake.

## CHAPTER TWO

REY WENT OUT to the corral where the culls—the non-producing second-year heifers and cows—were being held, along with the young steers fattened and ready for market. Both groups were ready to be loaded into trucks and taken away to their various buyers. A few more steers than usual had been sold because drought had limited the size of the summer corn and hay crop. Buying feed for the winter was not cost-productive. Not even an operation the size of the Harts' could afford deadweight in these hard economic times.

Cag was staring at the milling cattle absently, his heavy brows drawn down in thought, his whole posture stiff and unapproachable.

Rey came up beside him, half a head shorter, lither and more rawboned than the bigger man.

"Well, she's packing," he said bluntly.

Cag's eyes glanced off his brother's and went back to the corral. His jaw clenched. "I hate birthdays! I know she was told."

"Sure she was, but she didn't realize that breaking the rule was going to be life-threatening."

"Hell!" Cag exploded, turning with black-eyed fury. "I never raised a hand to her! I wouldn't, no matter how mad I got."

"Would you need to?" his brother asked solemnly.

"Damn it, Cag, she was shaking like a leaf. She's just a kid, and it's been a rough few months for her. She hasn't even got over losing her dad yet."

"Lay it on," Cag said under his breath, moving restlessly.

"Where's she going to go?" he persisted. "She hasn't seen her mother since she was sixteen years old. She has no family, no friends. Even cooking jobs aren't that thick on the ground this time of year, not in Jacobsville."

Cag took off his hat and wiped his forehead on his sleeve before he replaced it. He'd been helping run the steers down the chute into the loading corral and he was sweating, despite the cold. He didn't say a word.

Leo came up with a rope in his hand, watching his brothers curiously.

"What's going on?" he asked.

"Oh, nothing," Rey muttered, thoroughly disgusted. "Tess made him a birthday cake and he destroyed it. She's packing."

Leo let out a rough sigh and turned his eyes toward the house. "I can't say I blame her. I got her into trouble at the Christmas party by spiking the holiday punch, and now this. I guess she thinks we're all lunatics and she's better off without us."

"No doubt." Rey shrugged. "Well, let's get the cattle loaded."

"You aren't going to try to stop her?" Leo asked.

"What would be the point?" Rey asked solemnly. His face hardened. "If you'd seen her, you wouldn't want to stop her." He glared at Cag. "Nice work, pal. I hope she can pack with her hands shaking that badly!"

Rey stormed off toward the truck. Leo gave his older brother a speaking glance and followed.

Cag, feeling two inches high and sick with himself, turned reluctantly and went back toward the house.

TESS HAD HER suitcases neatly loaded. She closed the big one, making one last sweep around the bedroom that had been hers for the past few weeks. It was a wrench to leave, but she couldn't handle scenes like that. She'd settle for harder work in more peaceful surroundings. At least, Cag wouldn't be around to make her life hell.

She picked up her father's world champion gold belt buckle and smoothed her fingers over it. She took it everywhere with her, like a lucky talisman to ward off evil. It hadn't worked today, but it usually did. She put it gently into the small suitcase and carefully closed the lid, snapping the latches shut.

A sound behind her caught her attention and she turned around, going white in the face when she saw who had opened the door.

She moved around the bed and behind the wing chair that stood near the window, her eyes wide and unblinking.

He was bareheaded. He didn't speak. His black eyes slid over her pale features and he took a long, deep breath.

"You don't have anywhere to go," he began.

It wasn't the best of opening gambits. Her chin went up. "I'll sleep at a Salvation Army shelter," she said coldly. "Dad and I spent a lot of nights there when we were on the road and he didn't win any events."

He scowled. "What?"

She hated having admitted that, to him of all people. Her face closed up. "Will you let one of the hands drive me to town? I can catch a bus up to Victoria."

He shoved his hands into the pockets of his close-fitting jeans, straining the fabric against his powerful thighs. He stared at her broodingly.

"Never mind," she said heavily. "I'll walk or hitch a ride."

She picked up her old coat, the threadbare tweed one she'd had for years, and slipped it on.

"Where's your new coat?" he asked shortly.

"In the hall closet. Don't worry, I'm not taking anything that doesn't belong to me."

She said it so matter-of-factly that he was wounded right through. "We gave it to you," he said.

Her eyes met his squarely. "I don't want it, or a job, or anything else you gave me out of pity."

He was shocked. He'd never realized she thought of it like that. "You needed a job and we needed a cook," he said flatly. "It wasn't pity."

She shrugged and seemed to slouch. "All right, have it any way you like. It doesn't matter."

She slipped her shoulder bag over her arm and picked up her worn suitcases, one big one and an overnight bag, part of a matched set of vinyl luggage that she and her father had won in a raffle.

But when she reached the door, Cag didn't move out of the way. She couldn't get around him, either. She stopped an arm's length away and stared at him.

He was trying to think of a way to keep her without sacrificing his pride. Rey was right; she was just a kid and he'd been unreasonable. He shocked himself lately. He was a sucker for helpless things, for little things, but he'd been brutal to this child and he didn't know why.

"Can I get by, please?" she asked through stiff lips.

He scowled. A muscle jumped beside his mouth. He moved closer, smiling coldly with self-contempt when she backed up. He pushed the door shut.

She backed up again, her eyes widening at the unexpected action, but he didn't come any closer.

"When I was six," he said with cold black eyes, "I wanted a birthday cake like the other kids had. A cake and a party. Simon had gone to town with Dad and Corrigan. It was before Rey was born. Leo was asleep and my mother and I were in the kitchen alone. She made some pert remark about spoiled brats thinking they deserved treats when they were nothing but nuisances. She had a cake on the counter, one that a neighbor had sent home with Dad. She smashed the cake into my face," he recalled, his eyes darker than ever, "and started hitting me. I don't think she would have stopped, except that Leo woke up and started squalling. She sent me to my room and locked me in. I don't know what she told my father, but I got a hell of a spanking from him." He searched her shocked eyes. "I never asked for another cake."

She put the suitcases down slowly and shocked him by walking right up to him and touching him lightly on the chest with a shy, nervous little hand. It didn't occur to him that he'd never confessed that particular incident to anyone, not even his brothers. She seemed to know it, just the same.

"My father couldn't cook. He opened cans," she said quietly. "I learned to cook when I was eleven, in self-defense. My mother wouldn't have baked me a cake, either, even if she'd stayed with us. She didn't want me, but Dad did, and he put her into a position where she had to marry him. She never forgave either of us for it. She left before I started school."

"Where is she now?"

She didn't meet his eyes. "I don't know. I don't care."

His chest rose and fell roughly. She made him uncomfortable. He moved back, so that her disturbing hand fell away from his chest.

She didn't question why he didn't like her to touch him. It had been an impulse and now she knew not to do it again. She lifted her face and searched his dark eyes. "I know you don't like me," she said. "It's better if I get a job somewhere else. I'm almost twenty-two. I can take care of myself."

His eyes averted to the window. "Wait until spring," he said stiffly. "You'll have an easier time finding work then."

She hesitated. She didn't really want to go, but she couldn't stay here with such unbridled resentment as he felt for her.

He glanced down at her with something odd glittering in his black eyes. "My brothers will drown me if I let you walk out that door," he said curtly. "Neither of them is speaking to me."

They both knew that he didn't care in the least what his brothers thought of him. It was a peace initiative.

She moved restlessly. "Dorie's had the baby. She can make biscuits again."

"She won't," he said curtly. "She's too busy worshipping the baby."

Her gaze dropped to the floor. "It's a sweet baby."

A wave of heat ran through his body. He turned and started back toward the door. "Do what you please," he said.

She still hesitated.

He opened the door and turned before he went through it, looking dark as thunder and almost as intimidating. "Too afraid of me to stay?" he drawled, hitting her right in her pride with deadly accuracy.

She drew herself up with smoldering fury. "I am *not* afraid of you!"

His eyebrows arched. "Sure you are. That's why you're running away like a scared kid."

"I wasn't running! I'm not a scared kid, either!"

That was more like it. He could manage if she fought back. He couldn't live with the image of her white and shaking and backing away from him. It had hurt like the very devil.

He pulled his Stetson low over his eyes. "Suit yourself. But if you stay, you'd damned sure better not lose the apple butter again," he said with biting sarcasm.

"Next time, you'll get it right between the eyes," she muttered to herself.

"I heard that."

She glared at him. "And if you ever, ever, throw another cake at me...!"

"I didn't throw it at you," he said pointedly. "I threw it at the wall."

Her face was growing redder by the second. "I spent two hours making the damned thing!"

"Lost apple butter, cursed cake, damned women..." He was still muttering as he stomped off down the hall with the faint, musical jingle of spurs following him.

Tess stood unsteadily by the bed for several seconds before she snapped out of her trance and put her suitcases back on the bed to unpack them. She needed her head read for agreeing to stay, but she didn't really have anywhere else to go. And what he'd told her reached that part of her that was unbearably touched by small, wounded things.

She could see a little Cag with his face covered in cake, being brutally hit by an uncaring woman, trying not to cry. Amazingly it excused every harsh word, every violent action. She wondered how many other childhood scars were hiding behind that hard, expressionless face.

CAG WAS COLDLY formal with her after that, as if he regretted having shared one of his deeper secrets with her. But there weren't any more violent outbursts. He kept out of her way and she kept out of his. The winter months passed into a routine sameness. Without the rush and excitement of the holidays, Tess found herself with plenty of time on her hands when she was finished with her chores. The brothers worked all hours, even when they weren't bothered with birthing cattle and roundup, as they were in the warmer months of spring.

But there were fences to mend, outbuildings to repair, upkeep on the machinery that was used to process feed. There were sick animals to treat and corrals to build and vehicles to overhaul. It never seemed to end. And in between all that, there were conferences and conventions and business trips.

It was rare, Tess found, to have all three bachelor brothers at the table at the same time. More often than not, she set places only for Rey and Leo, because Cag spent more and more time away. They assured her that she wasn't to blame, that it was just pressing business, but she wondered just the same. She knew that Cag only tolerated her for the sake of her domestic skills, that he hated the very sight of her. But the other brothers were so kind that it almost made up for Cag. And the ever-present Mrs. Lewis, doing the rough chores, was a fountain of information about the history of the Hart ranch and the surrounding area. Tess, a history buff, learned a lot about the wild old days and stored the information away almost greedily. The lazy, pleasant days indoors seemed to drag and she was grateful for any interesting tidbits that Mrs. Lewis sent her way.

Then spring arrived and the ranch became a madhouse. Tess had to learn to answer the extension phone in the living room while the two secretaries in the separate office complex started processing calving information into the brothers' huge mainframe computer. The sheer volume of it was shocking to Tess, who'd spent her whole life on ranches.

The only modern idea, besides the computers, that the brothers had adapted to their operation was the implantation of computer chips under the skin of the individual cattle. This was not only to identify them with a handheld computer, but also to tag them in case of rustling—a sad practice that had continued unabated into the computer age.

On the Hart ranch, there were no hormone implants, no artificial insemination, no unnecessary antibiotics or pesticides. The brothers didn't even use pesticides on their crops, having found ways to encourage the development of superior strains of forage and the survival of good insects that kept away the bad ones. It was all very ecological and fascinating, and it was even profitable. One of the local ranchers, J. D. Langley, worked hand in glove with them on these renegade methods. They shared ideas and investment strategies and went together as a solid front to cattlemen's meetings. Tess found J. D. "Donavan" Langley intimidating, but his wife and nephew had softened him, or so people said. She shuddered to think how he'd been before he mellowed.

The volume of business the brothers did was overwhelming. The telephone rang constantly. So did the fax machine. Tess was press-ganged into learning how to operate that, and the computer, so that she could help send and receive urgent email messages to various beef producers and feedlots and buyers.

"But I'm not trained!" she wailed to Leo and Rey.

They only grinned. "There, there, you're doing a fine job," Leo told her encouragingly.

"But I won't have time to cook proper meals," she continued.

"As long as we have enough biscuits and strawberry preserves and apple butter, that's no problem at all," Rey assured her. "And if things get too hectic, we'll order out."

They did, frequently, in the coming weeks. One night two pizza delivery trucks drove up and unloaded enough pizzas for the entire secretarial and sales staff and the cowboys, not to mention the brothers. They worked long hours and they were demanding bosses, but they never forgot the loyalty and sacrifice of the people who worked for them. They paid good wages, too.

"Why don't you ever spend any money on yourself?" Leo asked Tess one night when, bleary-eyed from the computer, she was ready to go to bed.

"What?"

"You're wearing the same clothes you had last year," he said pointedly. "Don't you want some new jeans, at least, and some new tops?"

"I hadn't thought about it," she confessed. "I've just been putting my wages into the bank and forgetting about them. I suppose I should go shopping."

"Yes, you should." He leaned down toward her. "The very minute we get caught up!"

She groaned. "We'll never get caught up! I heard old Fred saying that he'd had to learn how to use a handheld computer so he could scan the cattle in the low pasture, and he was almost in tears."

"We hired more help," he stated.

"Yes, but there was more work after that! It's never going to end," she wailed. "If those stupid cows don't stop having calves…!"

"Bite your tongue, woman, that's profit you're scoffing at!"

"I know, but—"

"We're all tired," he assured her. "And any day now, it's going to slack off. We're doing compilation figures for five ranches, you know," he added. "It isn't just this one. We have to record each new calf along with its history, we have to revise lists for cattle that have died or been culled, cattle that we traded, new cattle that we've bought. Besides that, we have to have birth weights, weight gain ratios, average daily weight gain and feeding data. All that information has to be kept current or it's no use to us."

"I know. But we'll all get sick of pizzas and I'll forget how to make biscuits!"

"God forbid," he said, taking off his hat and holding it to his heart.

She was too tired to laugh, but she did smile. She worked her way down the long hall toward her room over the garage, feeling as drained as she looked.

She met Cag coming from the general direction of the garage, dressed in a neat gray suit with a subdued burgundy tie and a cream-colored Stetson. He was just back from a trustee meeting in Dallas, and he looked expensive and sophisticated and unapproachable.

She nodded in a cool greeting, and averted her eyes as she passed him.

He stepped in front of her, blocking her path. One big, lean hand tilted her chin up. He looked at her without smiling, his dark eyes glittering with disapproval.

"What have they been doing to you?" he asked curtly.

The comment shocked her, but she didn't read anything into it. Cag would never be concerned about her and she knew it. "We're all putting herd records into the computer, even old Fred," she said wearily. "We're tired."

"Yes, I know. It's a nightmare every year about this time. Are you getting enough sleep?"

She nodded. "I don't know much about computers and it's hard, that's all. I don't mind the work."

His hand hesitated for just an instant before he dropped it. He looked tougher than ever. "You'll be back to your old duties in no time. God forbid that we should drag you kicking and screaming out of the kitchen and into the twentieth century."

That was sarcastic, and she wished she had enough energy to hit him. He was always mocking her, picking at her.

"You haven't complained about the biscuits yet," she reminded him curtly.

His black eyes swept over her disparagingly. "You look about ten," he chided. "All big eyes. And you wear that damned rig or those black jeans and that pink shirt all the time. Don't you have any clothes?"

She couldn't believe her ears. First the brothers had talked about her lack of new clothes, and now he was going to harp on it! "Now, look here, you can't tell me what to wear!"

"If you want to get married, you'll never manage it like that," he scoffed. "No man is going to look twice at a woman who can't be bothered to even brush her hair!"

She actually gasped. She hadn't expected a frontal attack when he'd just walked in the door. "Well, excuse me!" she snapped, well aware that her curly head was untidy. She put a hand to it defensively. "I haven't had time to brush my hair. I've been too busy listing what bull sired what calf!"

He searched over her wan face and he relented, just a little. "Go to bed," he said stiffly. "You look like the walking dead."

"What a nice compliment," she muttered. "Thanks awfully."

She started to walk away, but he caught her arm and pulled her back around. He reached into his pocket, took something out, and handed it to her.

It was a jewelry box, square and velvet-covered. She looked at him and he nodded toward the box, indicating that he wanted her to open it.

She began to, with shaking hands. It was unexpected that he should buy her anything. She lifted the lid to find that there, nestled on a bed of gray satin, was a beautiful faceted sapphire pendant surrounded by tiny diamonds on a thin gold chain. She'd never seen anything so beautiful in her life. It was like a piece of summer

sky caught in stone. It sparkled even in the dim shine of
the security lights around the house and garage.

"Oh!" she exclaimed, shocked and touched by the
unexpected gift. Then she looked up, warily, wondering if she'd been presumptuous and it wasn't a gift at
all. She held it out to him. "Oh, I see. You just wanted
to show it to me…"

He closed her fingers around the box. His big hands
were warm and strong. They felt nice.

"I bought it for you," he said, and looked briefly uncomfortable.

She was totally at sea, and looked it. She glanced
down at the pretty thing in her hand and back up at him
with a perplexed expression.

"Belated birthday present," he said gruffly, not meeting her eyes.

"But…my birthday was the first of March," she said,
her voice terse, "and I never mentioned it."

"Never mentioned it," he agreed, searching her tired
face intently. "Never had a cake, a present, even a card."

She averted her eyes.

"Hell!"

The curse, and the look on his face, surprised her.

He couldn't tell her that he felt guilty about her birthday. He hadn't even known that it had gone by until Leo
told him two weeks ago. She could have had a cake and
little presents, and cards. But she'd kept it to herself because of the way he'd acted about the cake she'd made
for him. He knew without a word being spoken that he'd
spoiled birthdays for her just as his mother had spoiled
them for him. His conscience beat him to death over
it. It was why he'd spent so much time away, that guilt,
and it was why he'd gone into a jewelers, impulsively,

when he never did anything on impulse, and bought the little necklace for her.

"Thanks," she murmured, curling her fingers around the box. But she wouldn't look at him.

There was something else, he thought, watching her posture stiffen. Something...

"What is it?" he asked abruptly.

She took a slow breath. "When do you want me to leave?" she asked bravely.

He scowled. "When do I what?"

"You said, that day I baked the cake, that I could go in the spring," she reminded him, because she'd never been able to forget. "It's spring."

He scowled more and stuck one hand into his pocket, thinking fast. "How could we do without you during roundup?" he asked reasonably. "Stay until summer."

She felt the box against her palms, warm from his body where it had lain in his pocket. It was sort of like a link between them, even if he hadn't meant it that way. She'd never had a present from a man before, except the coat the brothers had given her. But that hadn't been personal like this. She wasn't sure how it was intended, as a sort of conscience-reliever or a genuinely warm gesture.

"We'll talk about it another time," he said after a minute. "I'm tired and I've still got things to do."

He turned and walked past her without looking back. She found herself watching him helplessly with the jewelry box held like a priceless treasure in her two hands.

As if he felt her eyes he stopped suddenly, at the back door, and only his head pivoted. His black eyes met hers in the distance between them, and it was suddenly as if lightning had struck. She felt her knees quivering under her, her heart racing. He was only looking, but she couldn't get her breath at all.

He didn't glance away, and neither did she. In that instant, she lost her heart. She felt him fight to break the contact of their eyes, and win. He moved away quickly, into the house, and she ground her teeth together at this unexpected complication.

Of all the men in the world to become infatuated with, Cag Hart was the very last she should have picked. But knowing it didn't stop the way she felt. With a weary sigh, she turned and went back toward her room. She knew she wouldn't sleep, no matter how tired she was. She linked the necklace around her neck and admired it in the mirror, worrying briefly about the expense, because she'd seen on the clasp that it was 14K gold—not a trifle at all. But it would have been equally precious to her if it had been gold-tone metal, and she was sure Cag knew it. She went to sleep, wearing it.

## CHAPTER THREE

EVERYTHING WOULD HAVE been absolutely fine, except that she forgot to take the necklace off the next morning and the brothers gave her a hard time over breakfast. That, in turn, embarrassed Cag, who stomped out without his second cup of coffee, glaring at Tess as if she'd been responsible for the whole thing.

They apologized when they realized that they'd just made a bad situation worse. But as the day wore on, she wondered if she shouldn't have left the necklace in its box in her chest of drawers. It had seemed to irritate Cag that she wanted to wear it. The beautiful thing was so special that she could hardly get past mirrors. She loved just looking at it.

Her mind was so preoccupied with her present that she didn't pay close attention to the big aquarium in Cag's room when she went to make the bed. And that was a mistake. She was bending over to pull up the multicolored Navajo patterned comforter on the big four-postered bed when she heard a faint noise. The next thing she knew, she was wearing Herman the python around her neck.

The weight of the huge reptile buckled her knees. Herman weighed more than she did by about ten pounds. She screamed and wrestled, and the harder she struggled the harder an equally frightened Herman held on, certain that he was going to hit the floor bouncing if he relaxed his clinch one bit!

Leo came running, but he stopped at the doorway. No snake-lover, he hadn't the faintest idea how to extricate their housekeeper from the scaly embrace she was being subjected to.

"Get Cag!" she squeaked, pulling at Herman's coils. "Hurry, before he eats me!"

"He won't eat you," Leo promised from a pale face. "He only eats freeze-dried dead things with fur, honest! Cag's at the corral. We were just going to ride out to the line camp. Back in a jiffy!"

Stomping feet ran down the hall. Torturous minutes later, heavier stomping feet ran back again.

Tess was kneeling with the huge reptile wrapped around her, his head arched over hers so that she looked as if she might be wearing a snaky headdress.

"Herman, for Pete's sake!" Cag raged. "How did you get out *this* time?"

"Could you possibly question him later, *after* you've got him off me?" she urged. "He weighs a ton!"

"There, there," he said gently, because he knew how frightened she was of Herman. He approached them slowly, careful not to spook his pet. He smoothed his big hand under the snake's chin and stroked him gently, soothing him as he spoke softly, all the time gently unwinding him from Tess's stooped shoulders.

When he had him completely free, he walked back to the aquarium and scowled as he peered at the lid, which was ajar.

"Maybe he's got a crowbar in there," he murmured, shifting Herman's formidable weight until he could release the other catches enough to lift the lid from the tank. "I don't know why he keeps climbing out."

"How would you like to live in a room three times your size with no playmates?" she muttered, rubbing her aching shoulders. "He's sprained both my shoulders and probably cracked part of my spine. He fell on me!"

He put Herman in the tank and locked the lid before he turned. "Fell?" He scowled. "From where?"

"There!"

She gestured toward one of the wide, tall sculptured posts that graced his king-size bed.

He whistled. "He hasn't gone climbing in a while." He moved a little closer to her and his black eyes narrowed. "You okay?"

"I told you," she mumbled, "I've got fractured bones everywhere!"

He smiled gently. "Sore muscles, more likely." His eyes were quizzical, soft. "You weren't really scared, were you?"

She hesitated. Then she smiled back, just faintly. "Well, no, not really. I've sort of got used to him." She shrugged. "He feels nice. Like a thick silk scarf."

Cag didn't say a word. He just stood there, looking at her, with a sort of funny smile.

"I thought they were slimy."

The smile widened. "Most people do, until they touch one. Snakes are clean. They aren't generally violent unless they're provoked, or unless they're shedding or they've just eaten. Half the work is knowing when not to pick them up." He took off his hat and ran a hand through his thick hair. "I've had Herman for twelve years," he added. "He's like family, although most people don't understand that you can have affection for a snake."

She studied his hard face, remembering that his former fiancée had insisted that he get rid of Herman. Even if he loved a woman, it would be hard for him to give up a much-loved pet.

"I used to have an iguana," she said, "when I was about twelve. One of the guys at the rodeo had it with him, and he was going off to college. He asked would I like him." She smiled reminiscently. "He was green and huge, like some prehistoric creature, like a real live dragon. He liked shredded squash and bananas and he'd let you hold him. When you petted him on the head he'd close his eyes and raise his chin. I had him for three years."

"What happened?"

"He just died," she said. "I never knew why. The vet said that he couldn't see a thing wrong with him, and that I'd done everything right by the book to keep him healthy. We could have had him autopsied, but Dad didn't have the money to pay for it. He was pretty old when I got him. I like to think it was just his time, and not anything I did wrong."

"Sometimes pets do just die." He was looking at Herman, coiled up happily in his tank and looking angelic, in his snaky fashion. "Look at him," he muttered. "Doesn't look like he's ever thought of escaping, does he?"

"I still remember when I opened up the washing machine to do clothes and found him coiled inside. I almost quit on the spot."

"You've come a long way since then," he had to

admit. His eyes went to the blue and white sparkle of the necklace and he stared at it.

"I'm sorry," she mumbled, wrapping her hand around it guiltily. "I never should have worn it around your brothers. But it's so lovely. It's like wearing a piece of the sky around my neck."

"I'm glad you like it," he said gruffly. "Wear it all you like. They'll find something else to harp on in a day or so."

"I didn't think they'd notice."

He cocked an eyebrow. "I haven't bought a present for a woman in almost seven years," he said shortly. "It's noteworthy around here, despite my intentions."

Her face colored. "Oh, I know it was just for my birthday," she said quickly.

"You work hard enough to deserve a treat now and again," he returned impatiently. "You're sure you're okay?"

She nodded. "A little thing like a broken back won't slow me down."

He glowered at her. "He only weighs a hundred and ten pounds."

"Yeah? Well, I only weigh a hundred!"

His eyes went over her suddenly. "You've lost weight."

"You said that before, but I haven't. I've always been thin."

"Eat more."

Her eyebrows arched. "I'll eat what I like, thank you."

He made a rough sound in his throat. "And where are those new clothes we've been trying to get you to buy?"

"I don't want any more clothes. I have plenty of clothes."

"Plenty, the devil," he muttered angrily. "You'll go into town tomorrow and get some new jeans and shirts. Got that?"

She lifted her chin stubbornly. "I will not! Listen here, I may work for you, but you don't tell me what I can wear!"

He stared at her for a minute with narrowed eyes. "On second thought," he muttered, moving toward her, "why wait until tomorrow? And like hell I can't tell you what to wear!"

"Callaghan!" she shrieked, protesting.

By the time she got his name out of her shocked mouth, he had her over his shoulder in a fireman's lift. He walked right down the hall with her, passing Leo, who was just on his way back in to see what had happened.

*"Oh, my gosh, did Herman bite her?"* he gasped. "Is she killed?"

"No, of course he didn't bite her!" Cag huffed and kept walking.

"Then where are you taking her?"

"To the nearest department store."

"To the…you are? Good man!"

"Turncoat!" Tess called back to him.

"Get her a dress!" Leo added.

"I hate dresses!"

"In that case, get her two dresses!"

"You shut up, Leo!" she groaned.

Rey was standing at the back door when Cag approached it with his burden.

"Going out?" Rey asked pleasantly, and opened the door with a flourish. "Have fun, now."

"Rescue me!" Tess called to him.

"Say, wasn't there a song about that?" Rey asked Leo, who joined him on the porch.

"There sure was. It went like this… 'Rescue me!'" he sang.

The two of them were still singing it, arm in arm, off-key, at the top of their lungs, when Cag drove away in the ranch truck with a furious Tess at his side.

"I don't want new clothes!" she raged.

He glanced toward her red face and grinned. "Too late. We're already halfway to town."

This strangely jubilant mood of his surprised her. Cag, of all the brothers, never seemed to play. Of course, neither did Simon, but he was rarely around. Leo and Rey, she'd been told, had once been just as taciturn as the older Harts. But since Dorie came back into Corrigan's life, they were always up to their necks in something. All Cag did was work. It was completely unlike him to take any personal interest in her welfare.

"Leo could have taken me," she muttered, folding her arms over her chest.

"He's too polite to carry you out the door," he replied. "And Rey's too much a gentleman. Most of the time, anyway."

"These jeans just got broke in good."

"They've got holes in them," he said pointedly.

"It's fashionable."

"Most fashionable jeans have holes in them when you buy them. Those—" he gestured toward the worn knees "—got like that from hard work. I've seen you on your knees scrubbing the kitchen floor. Which reminds me, we bought you one of those little floor cleaners that's specially made for linoleum. They're sending it out with the butane and lumber we ordered at the same time."

"A floor cleaner?" she asked, stunned.

"It will make things a little easier for you."

She was delighted that he was concerned about her chores. She didn't say another word, but she couldn't quite stop smiling.

Minutes later, he pulled up in front of the downtown department store and led her inside to the women's section. He stopped in front of Mrs. Bellamy, the saleslady who'd practically come with the store.

He tilted his hat respectfully. "Mrs. Bellamy, can you fit her out with jeans and shirts and new boots and a dress or two?" he asked, nodding toward Tess, who was feeling more and more like a mannequin. "We can't have our housekeeper looking like *that!*" He gestured toward her faded shirt and holey jeans.

"My goodness, no, Mr. Hart," Mrs. Bellamy agreed at once. She frowned thoughtfully. "And we just received such a nice shipment of summer things, too! You come right along with me, Miss Tess, and we'll fix you up!" She took Tess's arm and waved her hand at Cag. "Shoo, now, Mr. Hart," she murmured absently, and Tess had to stifle a giggle at his expression. "She'll be ready to pick up in about an hour."

I'm a parcel, Tess thought, and Cag's a fly. She put a hand over her wobbly mouth as she went meekly along with the older woman. Hysterical laughter would not save her now.

Cag watched her go with an amused smile. So she didn't want new clothes, huh? They'd see about that! Mrs. Bellamy wasn't going to let a potential commission walk away from her!

AN HOUR LATER, Cag went back for Tess and found her trying on a royal blue and white full-skirted dress with spaghetti straps and a shirred bodice. Against her white skin the sapphire-and-diamond necklace was brilliant. With her freckled white shoulders bare and the creamy tops of her breasts showing, she took his breath away.

"Isn't that dress just the thing, Tess?" Mrs. Bellamy was murmuring. "You wait right here. I want to show you one more! Oh, hello, Mr. Hart!" she called as she passed him. She waved a hand toward Tess. "What do you think? Isn't it cute? Now where did I see that pretty black lacy thing…"

Tess turned as Cag joined her. His face gave nothing away, but his black eyes glittered over the soft skin left bare by the dress. It certainly made her eyes bluer.

"Is it…too revealing?" Tess asked nervously, because of the way he was watching her.

He shook his head. "It suits you. It even matches the necklace." His voice sounded deep and husky. He moved closer and one big, lean hand lifted involuntarily to her throat where the small sapphire lay in its bed of diamonds and gold. His hand rested there for an instant before it moved restlessly over the thin strap of the dress. His fingertips absently traced over her soft skin as he studied her, noticing its silky warmth.

Her breath caught in her throat. She felt her heartbeat shaking the dress even as she noticed his black eyes lowering to the flesh left bare by the shirred bodice.

His fingers contracted on her shoulder and her intake of breath was suddenly audible.

He met her eyes relentlessly, looking for hidden signs that she couldn't keep from him.

"This is the sort of dress," he said gruffly, "that makes a man want to pull the bodice down."

"Mr.… Hart!" she exclaimed.

He scowled faintly as he searched her shocked eyes. "Don't you know anything about dresses and the effect they have on men?" he wanted to know.

Her trembling hands went to tug the bodice up even more. "I do not! But I know that I won't have it if it makes you…makes a man think…such things!"

His hand jerked suddenly, as if her skin had burned it. "I was teasing!" he lied sharply, moving away. "It's fine. You look fine. And yes," he added firmly, "you'll have it, all right!"

She didn't know what to think. He was acting very strangely, and now he wouldn't look at her at all. Teasing? Then why was he so stiff and uncomfortable looking if he was teasing? And why keep his back to her and Mrs. Bellamy, who'd just rejoined them.

"Here, Tess, try on this one. I'll box that one while you're dressing." She rushed the girl off before she could say anything to Cag.

That was just as well. He was fighting a raging arousal that had shocked him senseless. Tess was beginning to have a very noticeable effect on him, and he was quite sorry that he'd insisted on bringing her here. If she wore that dress around him, it was going to cause some major problems.

He stood breathing deliberately until his rebellious body was back under control. He noticed that Tess didn't show him the black dress she'd tried on. But she shook her head when Mrs. Bellamy asked her about it. She was trying to refuse the blue one, too. He wasn't having that. She looked so beautiful in it. That was one she had to have.

"You're not turning that blue one back in," he said firmly. "You'll need something to wear if you're asked out anywhere." He hated thinking about her in that dress with another man. But she didn't date. It shouldn't worry him. "Did you get some jeans and blouses, and how about those boots?"

After Mrs. Bellamy rattled off an inventory, he produced a credit card and watched her ring up a total. He wouldn't let Tess see it. She looked worried enough already.

He took the two large bags and the dress bag from Mrs. Bellamy with thanks and hustled Tess back out to the double-cabbed truck. He put the purchases on the backseat and loaded Tess into the passenger seat.

She sat without fastening her belt until he got in beside her.

"You spent too much," she said nervously, her big blue eyes echoing her mood. "I won't be able to pay you back for months, even if you take so much a week out of my salary."

"Think of the clothes as a uniform," he said gently. "You can't walk around in what you've been wearing. What will people think of us?"

"Nobody ever comes to see you."

"Visiting cattlemen do. Politicians do. We even have the occasional cookout. People notice these things. And you'll look neater in new stuff."

She shrugged and sighed with defeat. "Okay, then. Thanks."

He didn't crank the truck. He threw a long arm over the back of the seat and looked at her openly. Her barely contained excitement over the clothes began to make sense to him. "You've never had new things," he said suddenly.

She flushed. "On the rodeo circuit, when you lose, you don't make much. Dad and I bought most of our stuff from yard sales, or were given hand-me-downs by other rodeo people." She glanced at him nervously. "I used to compete in barrel racing, and I won third place a few times, but I didn't have a good enough horse to go higher. We had to sell him just before Dad gave up and came here to work."

"Why, Tess," he said softly. "I never knew you could ride at all!"

"I haven't had much chance to."

"I'll take you out with me one morning. Can you ride a quarter horse?"

She smiled. "If he's well trained, sure I can!"

He chuckled. "We'll see, after the biggest part of the roundup's over. We'd never get much done with all the cowboys showing off for you."

She flushed. "Nobody looks at me. I'm too skinny."

"But you're not," he protested. His eyes narrowed. "You're slender, but nobody could mistake you for a boy."

"Thanks."

He reached out unexpectedly and tugged a short reddish-gold curl, bringing her face around so that he could search it. He wasn't smiling. His eyes narrowed as his gaze slid lazily over her eyes, cheekbones and down to her mouth.

"The blue dress suited you," he said. "How did the black one look?"

She shifted restlessly. "It was too low."

"Low what?"

She swallowed. "It was cut almost to the waist. I could never wear something like that in public!"

His gaze fell lower, to the quick rise and fall of her small breasts. "A lot of women couldn't get away with it," he murmured. "But you could. You're small enough that you wouldn't need to wear a bra with it."

"Mr. Hart!" she exclaimed, jerking back.

His eyebrows arched. "I've been Callaghan for months and today I've already been Mr. Hart twice. What did I say?"

Her face was a flaming red. "You…you know what you said!"

He did, all at once, and he chuckled helplessly. He shook his head as he reached for the ignition and switched it on. "And I thought Mrs. Lewis was old-fashioned. You make her look like a hippie!"

She wrapped her arms over her chest, still shaken by the remark. "You mustn't go around saying things like that. It's indecent!"

He had to force himself not to laugh again. She was serious. He shouldn't tease her, but it was irresistible. She made him feel warm inside, when he'd been empty for years. He should have realized that he was walking slowly toward an abyss, but he didn't notice. He enjoyed having her around, spoiling her a little. He glanced sideways at her. "Put your belt on, honey."

*Honey!* She fumbled it into the lock at her side, glancing at him uncertainly. He never used endearments and she didn't like them. But that deep, rough voice made her toes curl. She could almost imagine him whispering that word under his breath as he kissed a woman.

She went scarlet. Why had she thought of that? And

if the thought wasn't bad enough, her eyes went suddenly to his hard mouth and lingered there in spite of her resolve. She wondered if that mouth could wreak the devastation she thought it could. She'd only been kissed a time or two, and never by anybody who knew how. Callaghan would know how, she was sure of it.

He caught her looking at him and one eyebrow went up. "And what sort of scandalous thoughts are going through that prudish mind now?" he taunted.

She caught her breath. "I don't know what you mean!"

"No?"

"No! And I do not have a prudish mind!"

"You could have fooled me," he said under his breath, and actually grinned.

"Hold your breath until you get any more apple butter with your biscuits," she muttered back. "And wait until you get another biscuit, too!"

"You can't starve me," he said smugly. "Rey and Leo will protect me."

"Oh, right, like they protected me! How could you do that? Carrying me out like a package, and them standing there singing like fools. I don't know why I ever agreed to work for such a loopy family!"

"Loopy? Us?"

"You! You're all crazy."

"What does that make you?" he murmured dryly. "You work for us."

"I need my head read!"

"I'll get somebody on it first thing."

She glanced at him sourly. "I thought you wanted me to quit."

"I already told you, not during roundup!" he reminded her. "Maybe when summer comes, if you're determined."

"I'm not determined. You're determined. You don't like me."

He pursed his lips, staring straight ahead. "I don't, do I?" he said absently. "But you're a fine housekeeper and a terrific cook. If I fired you, the others would stick me in a horse trough and hold me under."

"You destroyed the cake I baked for you," she recalled uneasily. "And you let your snake fall on me."

"That was Herman's own idea," he assured her. His face hardened. "The cake—you know why."

"I know now." She relented. "I'm sorry. I don't know what nice mothers are like, either, because I never had one. But if I had little kids, I'd make their birthdays so special," she said almost to herself, smiling. "I'd bake cakes and give them parties, and make ice cream. And they'd have lots and lots of presents." Her hand went involuntarily to the necklace he'd given her.

He saw that, and something warm kindled in his chest. "You like kids?" he asked without wanting to.

"Very much. Do you?"

"I haven't had much to do with them. I like Mack's toddler, though," he added. The foreman had a little boy two years old who always ran to Cag to be picked up. He always took something over for the child when he went to see Mack and his wife. Tess knew, although he never mentioned it.

She looked out the window. "I don't suppose I'll ever have kids of my own."

He scowled. "Why do you say that?"

She wrapped her arms around her chest. "I don't like...the sort of thing that you have to do to get them."

He stepped on the brakes so hard that the seat belt jerked tight and he stared at her intently.

She flushed. "Well, some women are cold!"

"How do you know that you are?" he snapped, hating himself for even asking.

She averted her gaze out the window. "I can't stand to have a man touch me."

"Really?" he drawled. "Then why did you gasp and stand there with your heartbeat shaking you when I slid my hand over your shoulder in the dress shop?"

Her body jerked. "I never!"

"You most certainly did," he retorted, and felt a wave of delight wash over him at the memory of her soft skin under his hands. It had flattered him, touched him, that she was vulnerable with him.

"It was… I mean, I was surprised. That's all!" she added belligerently.

His fingers tapped on the steering wheel as he contemplated her with narrowed eyes. "Something happened to you. What?"

She stared at him, stunned.

"Come on. You know I don't gossip."

She did. She moved restlessly against the seat. "One of my mother's lovers made a heavy pass at me," she muttered. "I was sixteen and grass green, and he scared me to death."

"And now you're twenty-two," he added. He stared at her even harder. "There aren't any twenty-two-year-old virgins left in America."

"Says who?" she shot at him, and then flushed as she felt herself fall right into the trap.

His lips pursed, and he smiled so faintly that she almost missed it.

"That being the case," he said in a soft, mocking tone, "how do you know that you're frigid?"

She was going to choke to death trying to answer that. She drew in an exasperated breath. "Can't we go home?"

She made the word sound soft, mysterious, enticing. He'd lived in houses all his life. She made him want a home. But it wasn't a thing he was going to admit just yet, even to himself.

"Sure," he said after a minute. "We can go home." He took his foot off the brake, put the truck in gear and sent it flying down the road.

It never occurred to him that taking her shopping had been the last thing on his mind this morning, or that his pleasure in her company was unusual. He was reclusive these days, stoic and unapproachable; except when Tess came close. She was vulnerable in so many ways, like the kitten they'd both adopted. Surely it was just her youth that appealed to him. It was like giving treats to a deprived child and enjoying its reactions.

Except that she trembled under his hands and he'd been years on his own. He liked touching her and she liked letting him. It was something he was going to have to watch. The whole situation was explosive. But he was sure he could handle it. She was a sweet kid. It wouldn't hurt if he spoiled her just a little. Of course it wouldn't.

## CHAPTER FOUR

THE BROTHERS, LIKE Tess and the rest of the staff, were worn to a frazzle by the time roundup was almost over.

Tess hadn't thought Cag meant it when he'd invited her to ride with him while he gathered strays, but early one morning after breakfast, he sent her to change into jeans and boots. He was waiting for her at the stable when she joined him there.

"Listen, I'm a little rusty," Tess began as she stared dubiously toward two saddled horses, one of whom was a sleek black gelding who pranced in place.

"Don't worry. I wouldn't put you on Black Diamond even if you asked. He's mine. This is Whirlwind," he said, nodding toward a pretty little red mare. "She's a registered quarter horse and smart as a whip. She'll take care of you." He summed her up with a glance, smiling at the blue windbreaker that matched her eyes and the Atlanta Braves baseball cap perched atop her red-gold curls.

"You look about ten," he mused, determined to put an invisible Off Limits sign on her mentally.

"And you look about—" she began.

He cut her off in midsentence. "Hop aboard and let's get started."

She vaulted easily into the saddle and gathered the reins loosely in her hands, smiling at the pleasure of being on a horse again. She hadn't ridden since her father's death.

He tilted his tan Stetson over his eyes and turned his mount expertly. "We'll go out this way," he directed, taking the lead toward the grassy path that wound toward the line camp in the distance. "Catch up."

She patted the horse's neck gently and whispered to her. She trotted up next to Cag's mount and kept the pace.

"We do most of this with light aircraft, but there are always a few mavericks who aren't intimidated by flying machines. They get into the brush and hide. So we have to go after those on horseback." He glanced at her jean-clad legs and frowned. "I should have dug you out some chaps," he murmured, and she noticed that he was wearing his own—bat-wing chaps with stains and scratches from this sort of work. "Don't ride into the brush like that," he added firmly. "You'll rip your legs open on the thorns."

"Okay," she said easily.

He set the pace and she followed, feeling oddly happy and at peace. It was nice riding with him like this across the wide, flat plain. She felt as if they were the only two people on earth. There was a delicious silence out here, broken only by the wind and the soft snorting of the horses and occasionally a distant sound of a car or airplane.

They worked through several acres of scrubland, flushing cows and calves and steers from their hiding places and herding them toward the distant holding pens. The men had erected several stockades in which to place the separated cattle, and they'd brought in a tilt-tray, so that the calves could be branded and ear-tagged.

The cows, identified with the handheld computer by the computer chips embedded in their tough hides, were either culled and placed in a second corral to be shipped out, or driven toward another pasture. The calves would be shipped to auction. The steers, already under contract, would go to their buyers. Even so far away from the ranch, there was tremendous organization in the operation.

Tess took off her Braves cap and wiped her sweating forehead on her sleeve.

Hardy, one of the older hands, grinned as he fetched up beside her on his own horse. "Still betting on them Braves, are you? They lost the pennant again last fall… that's two years in a row."

"Oh, yeah? Well, they won it once already," she reminded him with a smug grin. "Who needs two?"

He chuckled, shook his head and rode off.

"Baseball fanatic," Cag murmured dryly as he joined her.

"I'll bet you watched the playoffs last fall, too," she accused.

He didn't reply. "Hungry?" he asked. "We can get coffee and some stew over at the chuck wagon."

"I thought only those big outfits up in the Rockies still packed out a chuck wagon."

"If we didn't, we'd all go hungry here," he told her. "This ranch is a lot bigger than it looks."

"I saw it on the map in your office," she replied. "It sure covers a lot of land."

"You should see our spread in Montana," he mused. "It's the biggest of the lot. And the one that kept us all so busy a few weeks ago, trying to get the records on the computer."

She glanced back to where two of the men were working handheld computers. "Do all your cowboys know how to use those things?" she asked.

"Most of them. You'd be amazed how many college boys we get here between exams and new classes. We had an aeronautical engineer last summer and a professor of archaeology the year before that."

"Archaeology!"

He grinned. "He spent more time digging than he spent working cattle, but he taught us how to date projectile points and pottery."

"How interesting." She stretched her aching back. "I guess you've been to college."

"I got my degree in business from Harvard."

She glanced at him warily. "And I barely finished high school."

"You've got years left to go to college, if you want to."

"Slim chance of that," she said carelessly. "I can't work and go to school at the same time."

"You can do what our cowboys do—work a quarter and go to school a quarter." He fingered the reins gently. "In fact, we could arrange it so that you could do that, if you like. Jacobsville has a community college. You could commute."

The breath left her in a rush. "You'd let me?" she asked.

"Sure, if you want to."

"Oh, my goodness." She thought about it with growing delight. She could study botany. She loved to grow things. She might even learn how to cultivate roses and do grafting. Her eyes sparkled.

"Well?"

"I could study botany," she said absently. "I could learn to grow roses."

He frowned. "Horticulture?"

"Yes." She glanced at him. "Isn't that what college teaches you?"

"It does, certainly. But if you want horticulture, the vocational school offers a diploma in it."

Her face became radiant at the thought. "Oh, how wonderful!"

"What an expression," he mused, surprised at the pleasure it gave him. "Is that what you want to do, learn to grow plants?"

"Not just plants," she said. *"Roses!"*

"We've got dozens of them out back."

"No, not just old-fashioned roses. Tea roses. I want to do grafts. I want to…to create new hybrids."

He shook his head. "That's over my head."

"It's over mine, too. That's why I want to learn it."

"No ambition to be a professional of some sort?" he persisted. "A teacher, a lawyer, a doctor, a journalist?"

She hesitated, frowning as she studied his hard face. "I like flowers," she said slowly. "Is there something wrong with that? I mean, should I want to study something else?"

He didn't know how to answer that. "Most women do, these days."

"Sure, but most women don't want jobs working in a kitchen and keeping house and growing flowers, do they?" She bit her lip. "I don't know that I'd be smart enough to do horticulture…"

"Of course you would, if you want to do it," he said impatiently. His good humor seemed to evaporate as he stared at her. "Do you want to spend your life working in somebody else's kitchen?"

She shifted. "I guess I will," she said. "I don't want to get married, and I don't really see myself teaching kids or practicing medicine. I enjoy cooking and keeping house. And I love growing things." She glanced at him belligerently. "What's wrong with that?"

"Nothing. Not a damned thing."

"Now I've made you mad."

His hand wrapped around the reins. He didn't look at her as he urged his mount ahead, toward the chuck wagon where several cowboys were holding full plates.

He couldn't tell her that it wasn't her lack of ambition that disturbed him. It was the picture he had of her, surrounded by little redheaded kids digging in the rose garden. It upset him, unsettled him. He couldn't start thinking like that. Tess was just a kid, despite her age, and he'd better keep that in mind. She hadn't even started to live yet. She'd never known intimacy with a man. She was likely to fall headlong in love with the first man who touched her. He thought about that, about being the first, and it rocked him to the soles of his feet. He had to get his mind on something else!

They had a brief lunch with several of the cowboys. Tess let Cag do most of the talking. She ate her stew with a biscuit, drank a cup of coffee and tried not to notice the speculative glances she was getting. She didn't know that it was unusual for Cag to be seen in the company of a woman, even the ranch housekeeper. Certainly he'd never brought anyone female out to a roundup before. It aroused the men's curiosity.

Cag ignored the looks. He knew that having Tess along was innocent, so what did it matter what anyone else thought? It wasn't as if he was planning to drag her off into the brush and make love to her. Even as he thought it, he pictured it. His whole body went hot.

"We'd better get going," he said abruptly, rising to his feet.

Tess thanked the cook for her lunch, and followed Cag back to the horses.

They rode off toward the far pastures without a word being spoken. She wondered what she'd done to make Cag mad, but she didn't want to say anything. It might only make matters worse. She wondered if he was mad because she wanted to go back to school.

They left the camp behind and rode in a tense silence. Her eyes kept going to his tall, powerful body. He seemed part of the horse he rode, so comfortable and careless that he might have been born in the saddle. He had powerful broad shoulders and lean hips, with long legs that were sensuously outlined by the tight-fitting jeans he wore under the chaps. She'd seen plenty of rodeo cowboys in her young life, but none of them would have held a candle to Cag. He looked elegant even in old clothes.

He turned his head and caught her staring, then frowned when she blushed.

"Did you ever go rodeoing?" she asked to cover her confusion.

He shook his head. "Never had much use for it," he said honestly. "I didn't need the money, and I always had enough to do here, or on one of the other ranches in the combine."

"Dad couldn't seem to stay in one place for very long," she murmured thoughtfully. "He loved the rodeo circuit, but he didn't win very often."

"It wasn't much of a life for you, was it?" he asked. "It must have been hard to go to school at all."

She smiled. "My education was hit-and-miss, if that's what you mean. But there were these correspondence courses I took so I could get my high school diploma." She flushed deeper and glanced at him. "I know I'm not very educated."

He reined in at a small stream that crossed the wooded path, in the shade of a big oak tree, and let his horse drink, motioning her to follow suit. "It wasn't a criticism," he said. "Maybe I'm too blunt sometimes, but people always know where they stand with me."

"I noticed."

A corner of his mouth quirked. "You aren't shy about expressing your own opinions," he recalled. "It's refreshing."

"Oh, I learned to fight back early," she murmured. "Rodeo's a tough game, and some of the other kids I met were pretty physical when they got mad. I may not be big, but I can kick like a mule."

"I don't doubt it." He drew one long leg up and hooked it over the pommel while he studied her. "But despite all that male company, you don't know much about men."

This was disturbing territory. She averted her gaze to the bubbling stream at their feet. "So you said, when we went to the store." She remembered suddenly the feel of his hard fingers on her soft skin and her heart began to race.

His black eyes narrowed. "Didn't you ever go out on dates?"

Her lithe body shifted in the saddle. "These days, most girls don't care what they do and they're clued up about how to take care of themselves." She glanced at him and away. "It makes it rough for the few of us who don't think it's decent to behave that way. Men seem to expect a girl to give out on the first date and they get mad when she won't."

He traced a cut on his chaps. "So you stopped going out."

She nodded. "It seemed the best way. Besides," she murmured uncomfortably, "I told you. I don't like... that."

*"That?"*

He was going to worry the subject to death. "That," she emphasized. "You know, being grabbed and forcibly fondled and having a man try to stick his tongue down your throat!"

He chuckled helplessly.

"Oh, you don't understand!"

"In fact, I do," he replied, and the smile on his lips was full of worldly knowledge and indulgent amusement. "You were lucky that your would-be suitors didn't know any more than you did."

She frowned because she didn't understand.

His black eyes searched her face. "Tess, an experienced man doesn't grab. Ever. He doesn't have to. And French kisses need to be worked up to, very slowly."

Her heart was really going now. It shook the cotton blouse she was wearing. She stared at the chaps where Cag's long fingers were resting, and remembered the feel of his lean, strong hands.

"Embarrassed?" he asked softly.

She hesitated. Then she nodded.

His heart jumped wildly as he stared at her, unblinking. "And curious?" he added in a deep, slow drawl.

After a few seconds, she nodded again, but she couldn't make herself meet his eyes.

His hand clenched on the pommel of his saddle as he fought the hunger he felt to teach her those things, to satisfy her curiosity. His gaze fell to her soft mouth and he wanted it. It was crazy, what he was thinking. He couldn't afford a lapse like that. She was just a kid and she worked for him...

She heard the creak of leather as he swung down out of the saddle. After a minute, she felt his lean hands hard on her waist. He lifted her down from the horse abruptly and left the horses to drink their fill.

The sun filtered down to the ground in patterns through the oak leaves there, in the middle of nowhere, in the shelter of the trees where thick grass grew on the shallow banks of the stream and open pasture beyond the spot. The wind whipped around, but Tess couldn't hear it or the gurgle of the stream above the sound of her own heart.

His hands felt rough against her skin. They felt as if he wasn't quite in control, and when she looked up at him, she realized that he wasn't. His face was like steel. The only thing alive in it were those black Spanish eyes, the legacy of a noble Madrid ancestry.

She felt her knees wobble because of the way he was looking at her, his eyes bold on her body, as if he knew exactly what was under her clothing.

The thought of Callaghan Hart's mouth on her lips made her breath catch in her throat. She'd always been a little afraid of him, not because she thought he might hurt her, but because late at night she lay wondering how it would feel if he kissed her. She'd thought about it a lot lately, to her shame. He was mature, experienced, confident, all the things she wasn't. She knew she couldn't handle an affair with him. She was equally sure that he wouldn't have any amorous interest in a novice like her. She'd *been* sure, she amended. Because he was looking at her now in a way he'd never looked at her before.

Her cold hands pressed nervously into the soft cotton of his shirt, feeling the warmth and strength of his chest under it.

"Callaghan," she whispered uncertainly.

His hard lips parted. "Nobody else calls me that," he said tersely, dropping his gaze to her mouth. He liked the way she made his name sound, as if it had a sort of magic.

Her fingers spread. She liked the feel of warm muscle under the shirt, and the soft, spongy feel of thick hair behind the buttons. He was hairy there, she suspected.

He wasn't breathing normally. She could feel his heartbeat against her skin. Her hands pressed gingerly against him, to explore, hesitantly, the hardness of his chest.

He stiffened. His hands on her waist contracted. His breathing changed.

Her hands stilled immediately. She looked up into glittery black eyes. She didn't understand his reactions, never having experienced them before.

"You don't know anything at all, do you?" he asked tersely, and it sounded as if he was talking to himself. He looked down at her short-nailed, capable little hands resting so nervously on top of his shirt. "Why did you stop?"

"You got stiff," she said.

He lifted an eyebrow. "Stiff?"

He looked as if he was trying not to smile, despite the tautness of his face and body.

"You know," she murmured. "Tense. Like you didn't want me to touch you."

He let out a slow breath. His hands moved from her waist to cover her cold fingers and press them closer. They felt warm and cozy, almost comforting. They flattened her hands so that she could feel his body in every cell.

She moved her fingers experimentally where the buttons ran down toward his belt.

"Don't get ambitious," he said, stilling her hands. "I'm not taking off my shirt for you."

"As if I would *ever*...!" she burst out, embarrassed.

He smiled indulgently, studying her flushed face, her wide, bright eyes. "I don't care whether you would, ever, you're not going to. Lift your face."

"Why?" she expelled on a choked breath.

"You know why."

She bit her lip, hard, studying his face with worried eyes. "You don't like me."

"Liking doesn't have anything to do with this." He let go of her hands and gripped her elbows, lifting her easily within reach of his mouth. His gaze fell to it and his chest rose and fell roughly. "You said you were curious," he murmured at her lips. "I'm going to do something about it."

Her hands gripped his shirt, wrinkling it, as his mouth came closer. She could taste the coffee on his warm breath and she felt as if the whole world had stopped spinning, as if the wind had stopped blowing, while she hung there, waiting.

His hard lips just barely touched hers, brushing

lightly over the sensitive flesh to savor it. Her eyes closed and she held herself perfectly still, so that he wouldn't stop.

He lifted his head fractionally. She looked as if she couldn't bear to have him draw back. Whatever she felt, it wasn't fear.

He bent again. His top lip nudged under hers, and then down to toy with her lower lip. He felt her gasp. Apparently the kisses she'd had from other men hadn't been arousing. He felt her hands tighten on his shirt with a sense of pure arrogant pleasure.

He brought both lips down slowly over her bottom one, letting his tongue slide softly against the silky, moist inner tissue. She gasped and her mouth opened.

"Yes," he whispered as his own mouth opened to meet it, press into it, parting her lips wide so that he could cover them completely.

His arms reached down, enclosing, lifting, so that she was completely off the ground in a hungry, warm embrace that seemed to swallow her whole.

The kiss was hard, slow, insistent and delicious. She clasped her hands at the back of Cag's neck and clung to it, her mouth accepting his, loving the hard crush of it. When she felt his tongue slipping past her lips, she didn't protest. She opened her mouth for him, met the slow, velvety thrust with a husky little moan, and closed her eyes even tighter as the intimacy of the kiss made her whole body clench with pleasure.

It seemed a long time before he lifted his head and watched her dazed, misty eyes open.

He searched them in the heady silence of the glade. Nearby a horse whinnied, but he didn't hear it. His heart was beating in time with Tess's, in a feverish rush. He was feeling sensations he'd almost forgotten how to feel. His body was swelling, aching, against hers. He watched her face color and knew that she felt it and understood it.

He eased her back down onto her feet and let her move away a few inches. His eyes never left hers and he didn't let her go completely.

She looked as stunned as he felt. He searched her eyes as his big hand lifted and his fingers traced a blatant path down her breast to the hard tip.

She gasped, but she didn't try to stop him. She couldn't, and he knew it.

His hand returned to her waist.

She leaned her forehead against him while she got her breath back. She wondered if she should be embarrassed. She felt hot all over and oddly swollen. Her mouth was sore, but she wished his hard lips were still covering it. The sensations curling through her body were new and exciting and a little frightening.

"Was it just…a lesson?" she whispered, because she wanted to know.

His hands smoothed gently over her curly head. He stared past it, toward the stream where the horses were still drinking. "No."

"Then, why?"

His fingers slid into her curls. He sighed heavily. "I don't know."

Her eyes closed. She stood against him with the wind blowing all around them and thought that she'd never been so happy, or felt so complete.

He was feeling something comparable, but it disturbed him and made him angry. He hadn't wanted it to come to this. He'd always known, at some level, that it would be devastating to kiss her. This little redhead with her pert manner and fiery temper. She could bring him to his knees. Did she know that?

He lifted his head and looked down at her. She wasn't smiling, flirting, teasing, or pert. She looked as shattered as he felt.

He put her away from him, still holding her a little too tightly by the arms.

"Don't read anything into it," he said shortly.

Her breath was jerky. "I won't."

"It was just proximity," he explained. "And abstinence."

"Sure."

She wasn't humoring him. She really believed him. He was amazed that she didn't know how completely he'd lost control, how violently his body reacted to her. He frowned.

She shifted uneasily and moved back. His hands fell away. Her eyes met his and her thin brows wrinkled. "You won't...you won't tell the brothers?" she asked. She moved a shoulder. "I wouldn't want them to think I was, well, trying to... I mean, that I was flirting or chasing you or...anything."

"I don't think you're even real," he murmured half-absently as he studied her. "I don't gossip. I told you that. As if I'd start telling tales about you, to my own damned brothers, just because a kiss got a little out of hand!"

She went scarlet. She whirled away from him and stumbled down the bank to catch the mare's reins. She mounted after the second try, irritated that he was already comfortably in the saddle by then, watching her.

"As for the rest of it," he continued, as if there hadn't

been any pause between words, "you weren't chasing me. I invited you out here."

She nodded, but she couldn't meet his eyes. What she was feeling was far too explosive, and she was afraid it might show in her eyes.

Her embarrassment was almost tangible. He sighed and rode closer, putting out a hand to tilt up her chin.

"Don't make such heavy weather of a kiss, Tess," he said quietly. "It's no big deal. Okay?"

"Okay." She almost choked on the word. The most earthshaking event of her life, and it was no big deal. Probably to him it hadn't been. The way he kissed, he'd probably worked for years perfecting his technique. But she'd never been kissed like that, and she was shattered. Still, he wasn't going to know it. He didn't even like her, he'd said as much. It had been an impulse, and obviously it was one he already regretted.

"Where do we go next?" she asked with a forced smile.

He scowled. She was upset. He should never have touched her, but it had been irresistible. It had been pure delight to kiss her. Now he had to forget that he ever had.

"The next pasture," he said curtly. "We'll roust out whatever cattle wildlife we find and then call it a day. You're drooping."

"I guess I am, a little," she confessed. "It's hot."

In more ways than one, he thought, but he didn't dare say it aloud. "Let's go, then."

He rode off, leaving her to follow. Neither of them mentioned what had happened. By the end of the day, they only spoke when they had to. And by the next morning, Cag was glaring at her as if she were the reason for global warming. Everything was back to normal.

## CHAPTER FIVE

SPRING TURNED TO SUMMER. Cag didn't invite Tess to go riding again, but he did have Leo speak to her about starting horticulture classes in the fall.

"I'd really like to," she told Leo. "But will I still be here then?" she added on a nervous laugh. "Cag's worse than ever lately. Any day now, he's going to fire me."

"That isn't likely," Leo assured her, secretly positive that Cag would never let her leave despite his antagonism, because the older man cared too much about her. Oddly Tess was the only person who didn't seem to realize that.

"If I'm still here," she said. "I'd love to go to school."

"We'll take care of it. Cheer up, will you?" he added gently. "You look depressed lately."

"Oh, I'm not," she assured him, lying through her teeth. "I feel just fine, really!"

She didn't tell him that she wasn't sleeping well, because she lay awake nights remembering the way Cag had kissed her. But if she'd hoped for a repeat of that afternoon, it had never come. Cag was all but hostile to her since, complaining about everything from the way she dusted to the way she fastened his socks together in the drawers. Nothing she did pleased him.

Mrs. Lewis remarked dryly that he acted lovesick, and Tess began to agonize about some shadowy woman that he might be seeing on those long evenings when he left the ranch and didn't come home until midnight. He never talked about a woman, but then, he didn't gossip. And even his brothers knew very little about his private life. It worried Tess so badly that even her appetite suffered. How would she survive if Cag married? She didn't like thinking about him with another woman. In fact, she hated it. When she realized why, she felt even worse. How in the world was it that she'd managed to fall in love with a man who couldn't stand to be around her, a man who thought of her only as a cook and housekeeper?

What was she going to do about it? She was terrified that it might show, although she saw no signs of it in her mirror. Cag paid her no more attention than he paid the housecleaning. He seemed to find her presence irritating, though, most especially at mealtimes. She began to find reasons to eat early or late, so that she didn't have to sit at the table with him glaring at her.

Oddly that made things worse. He started picking at her, and not in any teasing way. It got so bad that Leo and Rey took him aside and called him on it. He thought Tess had put them up to it, and blamed her. She withdrew into herself and sat alone in her room at night crocheting an afghan while she watched old black-and-white movies on the little television set her father had given her for Christmas four years ago. She spent less time with the brothers than ever, out of self-defense. But Cag's attitude hurt. She wondered if he was trying to make her quit, even though it was his idea to get her into school in the fall quarter. Perhaps, she thought miserably, he meant her to live in at the school dormitory and quit her job. The thought brought tears to her eyes and made her misery complete.

IT WAS A beautiful summer day when haying got underway on the ranch to provide winter forage for the cattle. It hadn't rained for over a week and a half, and while the danger of drought was ever present, this was a necessary dry spell. The hay would rot in the field if it rained. Besides, it was a comfortable heat, unseasonably cool. Even so, it was hot enough for shorts.

Tess had on a pair of denim cutoffs that she'd made from a torn pair of jeans, and she was wearing socks and sneakers and a gray tank top. She looked young and fresh and full of energy, bouncing across the hayfield with the small red cooler in her hands. She hadn't wanted to go near Cag, but Leo had persuaded her that his older brother would be dying of thirst out there in the blazing sun with nothing to drink. He sent a reluctant Tess out to him with a cooler full of supplies.

Cag, driving the tractor that was scooping the hay into huge round bales, stopped and let the engine idle when he saw her coming toward him. He was alone in the field, having sent two other men into adjacent fields to bale hay in the same fashion. It was blazing hot in the sun, despite his wide-brimmed straw hat. He was bare-chested and still pouring sweat. He'd forgotten to bring anything along to drink, and he hadn't really expected anyone to think about sending him something. He smiled ruefully to himself, certain that Tess wouldn't have thought of it on her own. She was still too nervous of him to come this close willingly, especially considering the way he'd treated her since that unfortunate kiss in the pasture.

It wasn't that he disliked her. It was that he liked her far too much. He ached every time he looked at her, especially since he'd kissed her. He found himself thinking about it all the time. She was years younger, another generation. Some nice boy would come along and she'd go head over heels. He had to remember that and not let a few minutes of remembered pleasure blind him to reality. Tess was too young for him. Period.

He cut off the tractor and jumped down as she approached him. Her eyes seemed to flicker as they brushed his sweaty chest, thick with black hair that ran down into his close-fitting jeans.

He wiped his hand on a work cloth. "Brought survival gear, did you?" he asked.

"Just a couple of cans of beer and two sandwiches," she said tautly. "Leo asked me to."

"Naturally," he drawled sarcastically. "I'd hardly expect you to volunteer."

She bit her lower lip to keep from arguing with him. She was keenly aware of his dislike. She offered the cooler.

He took it from her, noticing how she avoided touching him as it changed hands.

"Go back along the path," he said, irritated by his own concern for her. "I've seen two big rattlesnakes since I started. They won't like the sun, so they'll be in a cool place. And that—" he indicated her shorts and sneakers "—is stupid gear to wear in a pasture. You should have on thick jeans and boots. Good God, you weren't even looking where your feet were!"

"I was watching the ravens," she said defensively, indicating two of them lighting and flying away in the field.

"They're after field mice." His narrowed black eyes cut into her flushed, averted face. "You're all but shaking. What the hell's wrong with you today?" he demanded.

Her eyes shot back up to his and she stepped back. "Nothing. I should go."

He realized belatedly that the sight of him without his shirt was affecting her. He didn't have to ask why. He already knew. Her hands had been shyly exploring his chest, even through the shirt, the day he'd kissed her, and she'd wanted to unfasten it. But she'd acted as if she couldn't bear to be near him ever since. She avoided him and it made him furious.

"Why don't you run along home?" he asked curtly. "You've done your duty, after all."

"I didn't mind."

"Hell!" He put the cooler down. "You can't be bothered to come within five feet of me unless somebody orders you to." He bit off the words, glaring at her. He was being unreasonable, but he couldn't help himself. "You won't bring me coffee in the office when I'm working unless the door's open and one of my brothers is within shouting distance. What do you expect, you scrawny little redhead, that the sight of you maddens me with such passion that I'm likely to ravish you on the floor? You don't even have a woman's body yet!" he muttered, his eyes on her small, pert breasts under the tank top.

She saw where he was looking and it wounded her. The whiplash of his voice hit her like a brick. She stared at him uncomprehendingly, her eyes wounded. "I never…never said…" she stammered.

"As if you could make me lose my head," he continued coldly, his voice like a sharp blade as his eyes went over her disparagingly.

Her face flamed and the eyes that met his were suddenly clouded not with anger, but with pain. Tears flooded them and she whirled with a sob, running in the direction from which she'd come.

She hated him! *Hated* him! He was the enemy. He'd never wanted her here and now he was telling her that she didn't even attract him. How obvious it was now that he'd only been playing with her when he kissed her. He didn't want her, or need her, or even like her, and she was dying of love for him! She felt sick inside. She couldn't control her tears or the sobs that broke from her lips as she ran blindly into the small sweep of thick hay that he hadn't yet cut.

She heard his voice, yelling something, but she was too upset to hear him. Suddenly her foot hit something that gave and she stopped dead, whirling at a sound like frying bacon that came from the ground beside her.

The ugly flat, venomous head reared as the tail that shot up from the coil rattled its deadly warning. A rattler—five feet long at least—and she'd stepped on it! Its head drew back ominously and she was frozen with fear, too confused to act. If she moved it would strike. If she didn't move it would strike. She could already feel the pain in her leg where the fangs would penetrate....

She was vaguely aware of a drumming sound like running, heavy footsteps. Through her tears she saw the sudden flash of something metallic go past her. The snake and its head abruptly parted company, and then long, powerful arms were around her, under her, lifting her to a sweat-glistening hard chest that was under her cheek.

"God!"

Cag's arms contracted. He was hurting her and she didn't care. Her arms tightened around his neck and she sobbed convulsively. He curled her against him in an ardent fever of need, feeling her soft breasts press hard into his bare, sweaty, hair-roughened chest as his face burrowed into her throat. She thought he trembled, but surely she imagined it. The terror came full force now that the threat was over, and she gave way to her misery.

They clung to each other in the hot sunlight with the sultry breeze wafting around them, oblivious to the man running toward them. Tess felt the warm, hard muscles in his back strain as she touched them, felt Cag's breath in her ear, against her hair. His cheek drew across hers and her nails dug into him. His indrawn breath was audible. His arms contracted again, and this time it wasn't comfort, it was a deep, dragging hunger that found an immediate response in her.

His face moved against hers jerkily, dragging down from her cheek, so that his lower lip slowly, achingly, began to draw itself right across her soft, parted mouth. Her breath drew in sharply at the exquisite feel of it. She wanted his lips on hers, the way they had been that spring day by the stream. She wanted to kiss him until her young body stopped aching.

He hesitated. His hand was resting at the edge of her breast and even as the embrace became hungry, she stopped breathing altogether as she felt his hard lips suddenly part and search for hers, felt the caressing pressure of those lean fingers begin to move up....

On the edge of the abyss, a barely glimpsed movement in the distance brought Cag's dark head up and he saw Leo running toward them. He was almost trembling with the need to take Tess's soft mouth, but he forced himself to breathe normally. All the hot emotion slowly drained out of his face, and he stared at his young brother as if he didn't recognize him for the first few seconds.

"What was it, a rattler?" Leo asked, panting for breath as he came up beside them.

Cag nodded his head toward the snake. It lay in two pieces, one writhing like mad in the hot sun. Between the two pieces was the big hunting knife that Cag always carried when he was working alone in the fields.

"Whew!" Leo whistled, shaking his head. "Pretty accurate, for a man who was running when he threw it. I saw you from the south field," he added.

"I've killed a few snakes in my time," Cag replied, and averted his eyes before Leo could ask if any of them had had two legs. "Here," he murmured to Tess, his voice unconsciously tender. "Are you all right?"

She sniffed and wiped her red eyes and nodded. She was embarrassed, because at the last, it hadn't been comfort that had brought them so close together. It was staggering after the things he said, the harshness of his manner before she'd stepped on the snake.

Cag put her down gingerly and moved back, but his turbulent eyes never left her.

"It didn't strike you?" he asked belatedly, and went on one knee to search over her legs.

"No," she faltered. The feel of those hard fingers on her skin made her weak. "No, I'm fine." She was looking down at him with eyes full of emotion. He was beautiful, she thought dazedly, and when he started to stand up again, her eyes lingered helplessly on that broad, sexy chest with its fine covering of hair. Her hand had touched it just as he put her down, and her fingers still tingled.

"Heavens, Tess!" Leo breathed, taking off his hat to wipe the sweat from his brow. "You don't run across a hayfield like that, without looking where you're going! When we cut hay, we always find half a dozen of the damned things!"

"It's not her fault," Cag said in a surprisingly calm voice. "I upset her."

She didn't look at Cag. She couldn't. She turned to Leo with a wan smile. "Could you walk me back, just to the track that leads up to the house?" she asked. "I'm a little shaky."

"Sure," he said gently. "I'll carry you, if you like."

"No, I can walk." She turned away. With her back to Cag she added carefully, "Thanks for what you did. I've never seen anybody use a knife like that. It would have had me just a second later."

Cag didn't say anything. He turned away and retrieved his knife, wiping it on his jeans before he stuck it back into the sheath on his belt. He stalked back toward the tractor. He never looked back.

"What did he do to upset you?" Leo asked when they were out of earshot.

"The usual things," she said with resignation in her voice. "I can't imagine why he doesn't fire me," she added. "First he said I could go in the spring, but we got too busy, then he said I could go in the summer. But here it is, and I'm still here."

He didn't mention that he had his own suspicions about that. Cag was in deep, and quite obviously fighting a defensive battle where Tess was concerned. But he'd seen the look on Cag's face when he was holding her, and dislike was not what it looked like to him.

"Did you see him throw the knife?" she asked, still awed by the skill of it. "Dad used to have a throwing knife and he could never quite get the hang of hitting the target. Neither could I. It's a lot harder than it looks. He did it running."

"He's a combat veteran," he said. "He's still in the reserves. Nothing about Cag surprises us anymore."

She glanced at him with twinkling eyes. "Did you really hit Turkey Sanders to keep Cag from doing it?"

"Dorie told you!" He chuckled.

"Yes. She said you don't let Cag get into fights."

"We don't dare. He doesn't lose his temper much, but when he does, it's best to get out of the line of fire."

"Yes, I know," she said uneasily, still remembering the birthday cake.

He glanced at her. "You've had a hard time."

"With him?" She shrugged. "He's not so bad. Not as bad as he was around Christmas," she added. "I guess I'm getting used to sarcasm and insults. They bounce off these days."

He made a rough sound under his breath. "Maybe he'll calm down eventually."

"It doesn't matter. I like my job. It pays well."

He laughed, sliding a friendly arm around her shoulders as they walked. "At least there are compensations."

Neither of them saw a pair of black eyes across the field glaring after them hotly. Cag didn't like that arm around Tess, not one bit. He was going to have something to say to Leo about it later.

Blissfully unaware, Leo stopped at the trail that led back to the house. "Okay now?" he asked Tess.

"Yes, thanks."

He studied her quietly. "It may get worse before it gets better, especially now," he said with some concern.

"What do you mean?"

"Never you mind," he replied, and his eyes held a secret amusement.

THAT EVENING, AFTER the brothers cleaned up and had supper, Cag motioned Leo into the study and closed the door.

"Something wrong?" Leo asked, puzzled by his brother's taciturn silence since the afternoon.

Cag perched himself on the edge of his desk and stared, unblinking, at the younger man.

"Something," he agreed. Now that he was facing the subject, he didn't want to talk about it. He looked as disturbed as he felt.

"It's Tess, isn't it?" Leo asked quietly.

"She's twenty-two," Cag said evenly, staring hard at his brother. "And green as spring hay. Don't hit on her."

It was the last thing Leo expected the older man to say. "Don't *what?*" he asked, just to make sure he wasn't hearing things.

Cag looked mildly uncomfortable. "You had your arm around her on the way out of the field."

Leo's dark eyes twinkled. "Yes, I did, didn't I?" He pursed his lips and glanced at his brother with pure calculation. "She's a soft little thing, like a kitten."

Cag's face hardened and his eyes became dangerous. "She's off limits. Got that?"

Leo lifted both eyebrows. "Why?"

"Because she's a virgin," Cag said through his teeth. "And she works for us."

"I'm glad you remembered those things this afternoon," Leo returned. "But it's a shame you'd forgotten all about them until you saw me coming toward you. Or are you going to try and convince me that you weren't about to kiss the breath out of her?"

Cag's teeth ground together. "I was comforting her!"

"Is *that* what you call it?" came the wry response. "Son of a gun. I'm glad I have you to tell me these things."

"I wasn't hitting on her!"

Leo held up both hands. "Of course not!"

"If she's too young for you, she's damned sure too young for me."

"Was I arguing?"

Cag unruffled a little. "Anyway, she wants to go to school and study horticulture in the fall. She may not want to stay on here, once she gets a taste of younger men."

Why, he really believed that, Leo thought, his attention diverted. Didn't he see the way Tess looked at him, the way she acted around him lately? Or was he trying not to see it?

"She won't have to wait for that to happen," Leo murmured. "We hired a new assistant sales manager last week, remember? Sandy Gaines?"

Cag scowled. "The skinny blond fellow?"

"Skinny, sure, but he seems to have plenty of charm when it comes to our Tess. He brought her a teddy bear from his last trip to St. Louis, and he keeps asking her out. So far she won't go."

Cag didn't want to think about Tess with another man, especially the new salesman. "She could do worse, I guess," he said despite his misgivings.

"You might ask her out yourself," Leo suggested carelessly.

Cag's dark eyes held a world of cynicism. "I'm thirty-eight and she works for me."

Leo only smiled.

Cag turned away to the fireplace and stared down at the gas logs with resignation. "Does it show?" he asked after a minute.

That he cared for her, he meant. Leo smiled affectionately. "Only to someone who knows you pretty well. She doesn't. You won't let her close enough," Leo added.

Broad shoulders rose and fell. His eyes lifted to the huge painting of a running herd of horses tearing across a stormy plain. A great-uncle had painted it. Its wildness appealed to the brothers.

"She's grass green," Cag said quietly. "Anybody could turn her head right now. But it wouldn't last. She's too immature for anything...serious." He turned and met his brother's curious eyes. "The thing is," he said curtly, "that I can't keep my head if I touch her."

"So you keep her carefully at a distance to avoid complications."

Cag hesitated. Then he nodded. He stuffed his hands into the pockets of his jeans and paced. "I don't know what else to do. Maybe if we get her into school this fall, it will help. I was thinking we might even get her a job somewhere else."

"I noticed," Leo said dryly. "And then you tell her to wait one more season. She's waited two already."

Cag's black eyes cut into him. "I haven't been serious about a woman since I was sent to the Middle East," he said through his teeth. "I've been pretty bitter. I haven't wanted my heart twisted out of my chest again. Then, she came along." He nodded in the general direction of the kitchen. "With her curly red hair and big blue eyes and that pert little boyish figure." He shook his head as if to clear the image from it. "Damn it, I ache just looking at her!" He whirled. "I've got to get her out of here before I do something about it!"

Leo studied his hand. "Are you sure you don't want to do something about it?" he asked softly. "Because she wants you to. She was shaking when you put her down."

Cag glared at him. "The snake scared her."

"*You* scared her," came the wry response. "Have you forgotten how to tell when a woman's aroused?"

"No, I haven't forgotten," he replied grimly. "And that's why she's got to go. Right now."

"Just hold on. There's no need to go rushing into anything," Leo counseled.

"Oh, for God's sake, it's just a matter of time, don't you see?" Cag groaned. "You can't hold back an avalanche!"

"Like that, is it?"

"Worse." Cag lowered his head with a hard sigh. "Never like this. Never."

Leo, who'd never felt what passed for love in the world, stared at his brother with compassion but no real understanding of what he was going through.

"She fits in around here," Leo murmured.

"Sure she does. But I'm not going to marry her!"

Leo's eyebrows lifted. "Why not? Don't you want kids?"

"Corrigan's got one."

"Kids of your own," Leo persisted with a grin. "Little boys with big feet and curly red hair."

Cag lifted a paperweight from the desk and tossed it deliberately in one hand.

Leo held up both hands in a defensive gesture. "Don't throw it. I'm reformed. I won't say another word."

The paperweight was replaced on the desk. "Like I said before, I'm too old for her. After all the other considerations have been taken into account, that one remains. Sixteen years is too much."

"Do you know Ted Regan?"

Cag scowled. "Sure. Why?"

"Do you know how much older he is than Coreen?"

Cag swallowed. "Theirs is a different relationship."

"Calhoun Ballenger and Abby?"

Cag glared at him.

"Evan and Anna Tremayne?"

The glare became a black scowl.

Leo shrugged. "Dig your own grave, then. You should hear Ted groan about the wasted years he spent keeping Coreen at bay. They've got a child of their own now and they're talking about another one in the near future. Silver hair and all, Ted's the happiest fellow I know. Coreen keeps him young."

"I'll bet people talked."

"Of course people talked. But they didn't care."

That grin was irritating. Cag turned away from him. He didn't dare think about kids with curly red hair. He was already in over his head and having enough trouble trying to breathe.

"One day, a young man will come along and sweep her off her feet."

"You've already done that, several times," Leo said pointedly. "Carrying her off to the store to buy new clothes, and just today, out of the path of a rattler."

"She doesn't weigh as much as a good sack of potatoes."

"She needs feeding up. She's all nerves lately. Especially when you're around."

Cag's big hands clenched in his pockets. "I want to move the heifers into the west pasture tomorrow. What do you think?"

"I think it's a week too soon."

The broad shoulders shrugged. "Then we'll wait one more week. How about the pastures on the bottoms?"

"We haven't had rain, but we will. If they flood, we'll have every cowboy on the place out pulling cows out of mud." His eyes narrowed. "You know all that better than I do."

"I'm changing the subject."

Leo threw up his hands. "All right. Don't listen to me. But Sandy Gaines means business. He's flirting with her, hard. He's young and personable and educated, and he wears nice suits and drives a red Corvette."

Cag glared at him. "She can see through clothes and a car, even a nice car."

"She's had digs and sarcasm and insults from you," Leo said and he was serious. "A man who tells her she's pretty and treats her gently might walk up on her blind side. She's warming to him a little. I don't like it. I've heard things about him."

"What sort of things?" Cag asked without wanting to.

"That he's fine until he gets his hands on a bottle of liquor, and then he's every woman's worst nightmare. You and I both know the type. We don't want our Tess getting into a situation she can't handle."

"She wouldn't tolerate that sort of behavior from a man," he said stiffly.

"Of course not, but she barely weighs a hundred pounds sopping wet! Or have you forgotten that she couldn't even get away from Herman, and he only outweighs her by ten pounds? Gaines is almost your size!"

Cag's teeth clenched. "She won't go out with him," he said doggedly. "She's got better sense."

THAT IMPRESSION LASTED only two more days. Sandy Gaines, a dark blond-haired, blue-eyed charmer, came by to discuss a new advertising campaign with the brothers and waylaid Tess in the hall. He asked her to a dance at the Jacobsville dance hall that Friday night and she, frustrated and hurt by Cag's sarcasm and coldness, accepted without hesitation.

# CHAPTER SIX

SANDY PICKED HER UP early for the dance in his low-slung used red Corvette. Cag was nearby and he watched them with cold eyes, so eaten up with jealousy that he could hardly bear it. She was wearing their dress, to top it all, the blue dress he'd helped her pick out when he'd taken her shopping. How could she wear it for that city dude?

"Get her home by midnight," he told Sandy, and he didn't smile.

"Sure thing, Mr. Hart!"

Sandy put Tess into the car quickly and drove off. Tess didn't even look at Cag. She was uncomfortably aware of the dress she had on, and why Cag glared at her. But he didn't want to take her anywhere, after all, so why should he object to her going out on a date? He didn't even like her!

"What's he, your dad?" Sandy drawled, driving far too fast.

"They all look out for me," she said stiffly.

Sandy laughed cynically. "Yeah? Well, he acts like you're his private stock." He glanced at her. "Are you?"

"Not at all," she replied with deliberate carelessness.

"Good." He reached for her hand and pressed it. "We're going to have a nice time. I've looked forward to this all week. You're a pretty little thing."

She smiled. "Thanks."

"Now you just enjoy yourself and don't worry about heavy-handed surrogate parents, okay?"

"Okay."

But it didn't work out that way. The first two dances were fun, and she enjoyed the music. But very quickly, Sandy found his way to the bar. After his second whiskey sour, he became another man. He held her too closely and his hands wandered. When he tried to kiss her, she struggled.

"Oh, no, you don't," he muttered when she tried to sidestep him. He caught her hand and pulled her out of the big structure by a side door. Seconds later, he pushed her roughly up against the wall in the dim light.

Before she could get a hand up, he was kissing her—horrible wet, invasive kisses that made her gag. She tasted the whiskey on his breath and it sickened her even further. His hands grasped her small breasts roughly, hurting, twisting. She cried out and fought him, trying to get away, but his hips levered down over hers with an obscene motion as he laughed, enjoying her struggles as she tried valiantly to kick him.

It was like that other time, when she was sixteen and she'd been at the mercy of another lecherous man. The memories further weakened her, made her sick. She tried to get her knee up, but she only gave him an opening that brought them even more intimately together and frightened her further. She was beating at his chest, raging at him, and his hand was in the neckline of her dress, popping buttons off in his drunken haste, when she felt the pressure against her body suddenly lessen.

There were muffled curses that stopped when Sandy was suddenly pushed up against the wall himself with one arm behind him and a mercilessly efficient hand at his neck, the thumb hard under his ear. Cag looked violent as Tess had rarely seen him. The hold was more than dangerous, it was professional. She didn't have the slightest doubt that he could drop the other man instantly if it became necessary.

"Move, and I'll break your neck," Cag said in a voice like hot steel. His black eyes cut to Tess and took in her disheveled clothing, her torn bodice. He jerked his head toward the ranch pickup that was parked just at the edge of the grass. "It's unlocked. Go and get inside."

She hesitated, sick and wobbly and afraid.

"Go on," Cag said softly.

She turned. She might have pleaded for Sandy, except that she didn't think he deserved having her plead for him. He might have... God only knew what he might have done if Cag hadn't shown up! She resisted the urge to kick him while Cag had him powerless, and she wobbled off toward the truck.

She was aware of dull thuds behind her, but she didn't turn. She went to the truck, climbed in and sat shivering until a cold, taciturn Cag joined her.

Before he got into the cab, he pulled off the denim shirt he was wearing over a black T-shirt and put it over her shoulders the wrong way. He didn't attempt to touch her, probably aware that she was sick enough of being touched at the moment.

"Get into that," he said as he fastened his seat belt, "and fasten your belt."

He reached for the ignition and she noticed that his knuckles were bleeding. As she struggled into the shoulder harness she glanced toward the barn and saw Sandy leaning against the wall, looking very weak.

"I couldn't make him stop," she said in a thin voice.

"I didn't expect him to…to get drunk. He seemed so nice. I never go out with big men usually—" Her voice broke. "Damn him! Oh, damn him! I never dreamed he'd be like *that!* He seemed like such a nice man!"

He glanced toward her with a face like black thunder, but he didn't speak. He put the truck in gear and drove her home.

The others were out for the evening. They were alone in the house. She started to go toward her room, but he turned her into the study and closed the door.

He seated her on the big black antique leather divan that graced the corner near the picture window and went to pour brandy into a snifter.

He came back and sat beside her, easing her cold, trembling hands around the bowl and offering it at her swollen lips. It stung and she hesitated, but he tilted it up again.

She let out a single sob and quickly controlled herself. "Sorry," she said.

"Why did you go out with him?"

"He flattered me," she said with pure self-disgust. "He was sweet to me and he seemed sort of boyish. I thought… I thought he'd be a perfect gentleman, the sort of man I'd never have to fight off. But he was different when we were alone. And then he started drinking."

"You're grass green," he muttered. "You can't size up men even now, can you?"

"I haven't dated much."

"I noticed."

She glanced up at his set features and then down into the brandy.

"Why haven't you?" he persisted.

She tried not to notice how sexy he looked in that

black T-shirt that clung to every muscle he had. He was big, lean, all powerful muscle and bristling vitality. It made her weak to look at him, and she averted her eyes.

"My mother came to see us one day, when I was sixteen," she said uneasily. "She wanted to see how much I'd grown up, she said." She shifted. "She brought her latest lover. He was a playboy with lots of money and apparently he saw that it irritated her when he paid me some attention, so he put on the charm and kept it up all day. After supper, she was miffed enough to take my dad off into another room. Dad was crazy about her, even then." She swallowed. "It made her lover furious and vengeful. He closed the door and before I knew what was happening, he locked it and threw me down onto the sofa. He tore my clothes and touched me…." She closed her eyes at the horrible memory. "It was like tonight, only worse. He was a big man and strong. I couldn't get away, no matter how hard I fought, and in the end I just screamed. My father broke in the door to get to him. I'll never forget what he said to that man, and my mother, before he threw them off the place. I never saw her again. Or wanted to."

Cag let out the breath he'd been holding. So many things made sense now. He searched her wan little face with feelings of possession. She'd had so much pain and fear from men. She probably had no idea that tenderness even existed.

"You're tied up in bad memories, aren't you, little one?" he asked quietly. "Maybe they need to be replaced with better ones."

"Do they?" Her voice was sad, resigned. She finished the brandy and Cag put the snifter on the table.

She started to get up, only to find him blocking her

way. He eased her back down onto the wide divan and slid down alongside her.

She gasped, wondering if she'd gotten out of the frying pan only to fall into the fire. She frantically put her hands against his broad chest and opened her mouth to protest, but his fingers touched it lightly as he lay beside her and arched over her prone body, resting his formidable weight on his forearm.

"There's nothing to be afraid of, Tess," he said quietly. "Whatever disagreements we've had, you know that I'd never hurt you physically. Especially after the ordeal you've just been through."

She knew, but she was still nervous of him. He was even more powerfully built than Sandy, and in this way, in an intimate way, he was also an unknown quantity.

While she was thinking, worrying, he bent and she felt the warm threat of his big body as his mouth drew softly over her eyes, closing the lids. It moved to her temples, her eyebrows. He kissed her closed eyes, his tongue lightly skimming the lashes. She jerked, and his lean hand eased under her nape, soothing her, calming her.

She had little experience, but she wasn't so naive that she couldn't recognize his. Every touch, every caress, was expert. He eased down so slowly that she only realized how close he really was when she moved and felt his warm, hard chest move with her. By then, she was a prisoner of her own sensual curiosity, sedated by the exquisite pleasure his mouth was giving her as it explored her face.

By the time he reached her lips, the feel and smell of him were already familiar. When his hard mouth eased her lips apart and moved into them, she felt the increased pressure of his chest against her breasts, and she stiffened with real fear.

He lifted away immediately, but only a breath. His black eyes searched her blue ones slowly.

"You still don't know me like this," he murmured, as if he were talking to himself as he studied her flushed face, understanding the fear he read in it. "You're afraid, aren't you?"

She swallowed. Her mouth felt dry as she looked at him. "I think I am," she whispered.

He smiled lazily and traced her lips with a lean forefinger. "Will you relax if I promise to go so far and stop?" he whispered.

"So...far?" she asked in a hushed tone, searching his black eyes curiously.

He nodded. He teased her lips apart and touched the inside of her lower lip with the tip of his finger. "We'll make a little love," he whispered as he bent. "And then you'll go to bed. Your own, not mine," he added with dry mischief.

Her fingers clenched and unclenched on the soft fabric of his undershirt, like a kitten kneading a new place to lie. She could hear her own breath sighing out against his mouth as it came closer.

"You don't like me," she breathed.

His thumb rubbed quite roughly over her mouth. "Are you sure? You must know that I want you!" he said, and it came out almost as a growl. "Taunting you was the only way I knew to keep you at arm's length, to protect you. I was a fool! I'm too old for you, but at least I'm not like that damned idiot who took you out tonight!"

Nothing got into her sluggish brain except those

three feverish words. "You want me?" she whispered as if it was some dark secret. She looked up at him with wonder and saw the muted ferocity in his eyes.

His hand was on her waist now and it contracted until it all but bruised. "Yes, Tess. Is it shocking to hear me say it?" His gaze fell to her mouth and lower, to the two little peaks that formed suddenly against the torn bodice of her dress and were revealed even under the thick fabric of his concealing shirt. "You want me, too," he whispered, bending. "I can see it...."

She wanted to ask how he knew, but the taste of his breath against her lips weakened her. She wanted him to kiss her. She wanted nothing more in the world. Her nails curled into his powerful chest and she felt him shiver again just as his mouth slowly, tenderly, eased down on her parted lips.

He drew back almost at once, only to ease down again as his lips toyed with hers, brushing lightly from the upper lip to the lower one, teasing and lifting away in a silence that smoldered. She felt the warm pressure increase from second to second, and the leisure of his movements reassured her. She began to relax. Her body lost its rigor and softened against him. After a few seconds of the lazy, tender pressure, her lips opened eagerly for him. She heard a soft intake of breath as he accepted the unspoken invitation with increasingly intimate movements of his hard mouth.

The spicy fragrance of his cologne surrounded her. She knew that as long as she lived, every time she smelled it, it would invoke these images of Cag lying against her on the leather divan in the muted light of the study. She would hear the soft creak of the leather as his body moved closer to her own; she would hear the faint ticking of the old-fashioned grandfather clock near the desk. Most of all, she would feel the hard warmth of Cag's mouth and the slow caress of his lean hands up and down her rib cage, making her body ache with new pleasures.

His head lifted and he looked at her again, this time reading with pinpoint accuracy the sultry look of her eyes, the faint pulse in her throat, the hard tips of her breasts rising against the slip that her half-open bodice revealed. Somewhere along the way, he'd unbuttoned his shirt that she was wearing and it was lying back away from her torn dress.

He traced the ragged edge of the fabric with returning anger. "Did it have to be this dress?" he groaned.

She winced. "You never seemed to look at me," she defended herself. "He wanted to take me out, and it was the nicest thing I had in my closet."

He sighed heavily. "Yes, I know." He smiled wryly. "I didn't think I could risk taking you out. But look what happened because I didn't."

"He was so drunk," she whispered hoarsely. "He would have forced me..."

"Not while there was a breath in my body," he returned intently.

"How did you know?" she asked suddenly.

He pushed a stray curl away from her cheek. "I don't know," he said, frowning as if it disturbed him. "Something I'd heard about Gaines bothered me. One of the men said that he was fine as long as there wasn't a bottle anywhere nearby, and another one mentioned a threatened lawsuit over a disastrous date. I remembered that you'd gone to the dance at the bar." He shrugged.

"Maybe it was a premonition. Thank God I paid attention to it."

"Yes." A thick strand of jet black hair had fallen onto his broad forehead. Hesitantly she reached up and pushed it back, her fingers lingering on its coolness.

He smiled because it was the first time that she'd voluntarily touched him.

She sought his eyes, sought permission. As if he understood the new feelings that were flaring up inside her, he drew her hand down to his chest and opened her fingers, pressing them there, firmly.

Her hand moved experimentally, pressing down and then curling into the thick hair she could feel under the soft fabric of his shirt.

Impatiently he lifted himself and peeled off the T-shirt, tossing it to the floor. He lay back down again beside her, curling his leg into hers as he guided her hand back to his chest.

She hesitated again. This was another step, an even bigger one.

"Even teenagers do this," he mused, smiling gently at her inhibitions. "It's perfectly permissible."

"Is it?" Her fingers touched him as if she expected them to be burned. But then they pressed into the thick pelt of hair and explored, fascinated by the size and breadth of his chest, the warmth and strength of it.

He arched with pure pleasure and laughed delightedly at the sensations she aroused. It had been a long time since a woman had touched him like that.

She smiled shyly, fascinated by his reaction. He seemed so stoic, so reserved, that this lack of inhibition was surprising.

"Men are like cats," he murmured. "We love to be stroked."

"Oh." She studied him as if he were an exhibit in a museum, curious about every single cell of his body.

"Feeling more secure now?" he asked softly. "More adventurous?"

"I'm not sure." She looked up at him, quizzically.

"Nothing heavy," he promised. His black eyes were softer than she'd ever seen them. "It's no news to me that you're a rank beginner."

"What are you…going to do?" she stammered, wide-eyed.

"Kiss you," he breathed, letting his gaze fall to her bare breasts.

"Th…there?" she gasped.

He touched her lightly, smiling at the expression on her taut face. "There," he whispered. He bent and drew his cheek softly over the bruised flesh, careful not to hurt her with the light pressure.

While she was trying to cope with so many new and shocking sensations, his mouth smoothed back over the soft, silky flesh and she felt it open. He tasted her flushed skin in a heated fever of need. Her hands curled up into his thick hair and she held him to her, whimpering softly with pleasure as she found herself drawing his face hungrily to where the flesh was very taut and sensitive.

"Here?" he whispered, hesitating.

"Oh…yes!" she choked.

His mouth opened obediently and he drew the hard nipple into it with a faint, soft suction that brought a sharp cry from her dry lips.

She thought she felt him tremble, and then he was

moving onto his back, breathing roughly as he carried her with him. He held her at his side, their legs intimately entangled, while he fought to get his breath back.

His skin was cool against her hot breasts where they were pressed together above the waist. Her cheek was against the hard muscle of his upper arm and she caught again that elusive spicy scent that clung to him.

Her hand eased onto the thick hair at his chest, but he caught it and held it a little roughly at her side.

"No," he whispered.

She didn't understand what she'd done wrong. A minute later, he got to his feet and bent to retrieve his undershirt. While he shrugged into it, she tugged up her bodice and tried to fasten it.

But when she would have gotten to her feet, he pressed her back down.

"Stay put," he said quietly. He turned and left the room.

She'd barely gotten her breathing calm when he was back, sitting down beside her with a cold can of beer in his hand.

He popped it open and took a sip before he pulled her up beside him and held it to her lips.

"I don't like beer," she murmured dazedly.

"I'm going to taste of it," he replied matter-of-factly. "If you swallow some, you won't find the taste so unpleasant when I kiss you."

Her heart jumped wildly.

He met her surprised expression with a smile. "Did you think we were finished?" he asked softly.

She blushed.

"I was getting too aroused," he murmured dryly. "And so were you. I'm not going to let it go that far."

She searched his hard face with open curiosity. "What does it feel like to you, when you kiss me like that?" she asked quickly, before she lost her nerve.

"How does it feel when I do it?"

"I don't know. Shivery. Hot. I never felt anything like that before."

He took a sip of the beer and looked down at her hungrily. "Neither did I," he said tersely. His eyes seemed to possess her as they ran like caressing hands all over her. "Your breasts are freckled," he said with an intimate smile and chuckled when she blushed. He held her face up to his and kissed her nose. "I'm not going to rush out to the nearest bar and gossip about it," he whispered when he saw the faint apprehension in her wide eyes. "It's a lover's secret—a thing we don't share with other people. Like the scar on my belly."

She frowned slightly. He tugged down the waistband of his jeans and drew her hand against him where a long, thick scar was just visible above his belt.

"It runs down to my groin," he said solemnly. "Fortunately, it missed the more…vital areas. But it was touch and go for a few days and the scar is never going to go away."

Her fingers lingered there. "I'm sorry you were hurt."

He held her hand to him and smiled. "This is something I haven't shown to anyone else," he told her. "Except my brothers."

It made sense then. She looked up into his eyes. "A… lover's secret," she whispered, amazed that she could think of him like that, so easily.

He nodded. He wasn't smiling. "Like the freckles on your breasts, just around the nipples."

She felt her breath gathering speed, like an old-time

steam engine. Her breasts felt tight, and not because of Sandy's rough handling. She frowned a little because it was uncomfortable and she still didn't quite understand it.

"We swell, both of us, when we're aroused," he said quietly, glancing at the small hand that had come up to rest a little gingerly against one taut nipple. "It's uncomfortable, isn't it?"

"Just…just a little." She felt like a child in a candy store, breathless with delight as she looked at him. "I liked…what you did," she whispered.

"So did I. Have a few sips of this and I'll do it again."

Her breath caught. She sipped and wrinkled her nose. He took two more huge swallows before he put the can on the table and came back to her.

He stretched out beside her and this time when he slid his leg in between both of hers, it wasn't shocking or frightening. It felt natural, right. His hands slid under her as he bent again to her mouth. Now the kisses weren't tentative and seeking. They were slow and insistent and arousing. They were passionate kisses, meant to drag a response from the most unwilling partner.

Tess found herself clinging to him as if she might drown, her nails biting into his nape, and every kiss was more intimate than the last, more demanding, more arousing, more complete.

When his powerful body eased completely down over hers, she didn't protest at all. Her arms slid around his waist, her legs parted immediately, and she melted into the leather under them, welcoming the hard crush of him, the sudden heat and swelling that betrayed his hunger.

"You can feel it, can't you?" he whispered intimately at her ear and moved a little, just to make sure she could.

"Cag…!"

"I want you so badly, Tess!" he whispered, and his mouth slid over her cheek and onto her lips. He bit at them with a new and staggering intimacy that set her body on fire. When his tongue eased into her mouth, she opened her lips to accept it. When he pressed her legs farther apart so that he could settle intimately between them, she arched into him. When he groaned and his hands found her breasts, she gave everything that she was into his keeping. He never thought he could draw back in time. He shook convulsively with the effort. He dragged his hips away and turned, lying on his back with Tess settled close against his side while he fought his own need, and hers.

"Don't…move!" he stated when she turned closer to him.

She stilled at once, half-heard bits of advice from a parade of motherly women coming back to her and making sudden sense.

She could feel Cag's powerful body vibrating with the hunger the kisses had built in it. He was like corded wood, breathing harshly. It fascinated her that he'd wanted her that much, when she was a rank beginner. He certainly wasn't!

When she felt him begin to relax, she let out a sigh of relief. She hadn't known what to do or say. Men in that condition were a mystery to her.

She felt his hand in her curly hair, holding her cheek to his chest. Under it, she heard the heavy, hard beat of his heart, like a fast drum.

"I haven't touched a woman since my fiancée threw me over," he said in a harsh tone.

Years ago. He didn't say it, but Tess knew that was what he was implying. She lifted her head and rose up, resting her hand on his shoulder to steady her as she searched his face. There was a hard flush along his high cheekbones, but his eyes were quiet, soft, full of mystery as they met hers.

"You want to know why I drew back."

She nodded.

He let go of her hair and touched her soft, swollen mouth with his. "You're a virgin."

He sounded so certain of it that she didn't bother to argue. It would have been pretty pointless at the moment, anyway.

"Oh. I see." She didn't, but it sounded mature.

He chuckled gently. "You don't know beans," he corrected. He moved suddenly, turning her over so that his body half covered hers and his eyes were inches from her own. His big hand caught her hip and curved it up into his intimately. The reaction of his body was fierce and immediate, and very stark. She flushed.

"I don't date anymore," he said, watching her mouth. "I don't have anything to do with women. This—" he moved her subtly against that part of him that was most obvious "—is delicious and heady and even a little shocking. I haven't felt it in a very long time."

Curiosity warred with embarrassment. "But I'm not experienced," she said.

He nodded. "And you think it should take an experienced woman to arouse me this much."

"Well, yes."

He bent and drew his lips over her open mouth in a

shivery little caress that made her breath catch. "It happens every time I touch you," he whispered into her lips. "An experienced woman would have realized immediately why I was so hostile and antagonistic toward you. It's taken you months."

He covered her mouth with his, kissing her as his hand slid back inside her dress and played havoc with her self-control. But it only lasted seconds. He got up abruptly and pulled her up with him, holding her a few inches away from him with steely hands at her waist.

"You have to go to bed. Alone. Right now," he said emphatically.

Her breath came in soft spurts as she looked up at him with her heart in her eyes.

He actually groaned and pulled her close, into a bearish embrace. He stood holding her, shivering as they pressed together.

"Dear God," he whispered poignantly, and it sounded reverent, almost a plea for divine assistance. "Tess, do you know how old I am?" he groaned at her ear. "We're almost a generation apart!"

Her eyes were closed. She was dreaming. It had all been a dream, a sweet, sensuous dream that she never wanted to end.

"I can still feel your mouth on my breasts when I close my eyes," she whispered.

He made another rough sound and his arms tightened almost to pain. He didn't know how he was going to let her go.

"Baby," he whispered, "this is getting dangerous."

"You never called me 'baby' before," she murmured.

"I was never this close to being your lover before," he whispered gruffly. His head lifted and his black eyes glittered down into her pale blue ones. "Not like this, Tess," he said roughly. "Not in a fever, because you've had a bad experience."

"You made love to me," she said, still dazed by the realization of how much their turbulent relationship had changed in the space of a few minutes.

"You wanted me to," he returned.

"Oh, yes," she confessed softly. Her lips parted and she watched, fascinated at the expression on his face when he looked down at them.

She reached up to him on tiptoe, amazed that it took such a tiny little tug to bring his hard mouth crashing passionately down onto her parted lips. He actually lifted her off the floor in his ardor, groaning as the kiss went on endlessly.

She felt swollen all over when he eased her back down onto her feet.

"This won't do," he said unsteadily. He held her by the shoulders, firmly. "Are you listening?"

"I'm trying to," she agreed, searching his eyes as if they held the key to paradise. His hands contracted.

"I want you, honey," he said curtly. "Want you badly enough to seduce you, do you understand?" His gaze fell to her waist and lingered there with the beginnings of shock. All at once, he was thinking with real hunger of little boys with curly red hair....

## CHAPTER SEVEN

"WHY ARE YOU looking at me like that?" Tess asked softly.

His hands contracted on her waist for an instant before he suddenly came to his senses and realized what he was thinking and how impossible it was. He closed his eyes and breathed slowly, until he got back the control he'd almost lost.

He put her away from him with an odd tenderness. "You're very young," he said. "I only meant to comfort you. Things just…got out of hand. I'm sorry."

She searched his eyes and knew that what they'd shared hadn't made a whit of difference to their turbulent relationship. He wanted her, all right, but there was guilt in his face. He thought she was too young for anything permanent. Or perhaps that was the excuse he had to use to conceal the real one—that he was afraid to get involved with a woman again because he'd been so badly hurt by one.

She dropped her gaze to his broad chest, watching its jerky rise and fall curiously. He wasn't unaffected by her. That was oddly comforting.

"Thanks for getting rid of the bad memory, anyway," she said in a subdued tone.

He hesitated before he spoke, choosing his words. "Tess, it wasn't only that," he said softly. "But you have to realize how things are. I've been alone for a long time. I let you go to my head." He took a long, harsh breath. "I'm not a marrying man. Not anymore. But you're a marrying woman."

She ground her teeth together. Well, that was plain enough. She looked up at him, red-cheeked. "I didn't propose! And don't get your hopes up, because I won't. Ever. So there."

He cocked his head, and for an instant something twinkled deep in his eyes. "Never? I'm devastated."

The humor was unexpected and it eased the pain of the awkward situation a little. She peeked up at him. "You're very attractive," she continued, "but it takes more than looks to make a marriage. You can't cook and you don't know which end of a broom to use. Besides that, you throw cakes at people."

He couldn't deny that. His firm mouth, still swollen from the hot kisses they'd shared, tugged up at the corners. "I missed you by a mile. In fact," he reminded her, "you weren't even in the room when I threw it."

She held up a hand. "I'm sorry. It's too late for excuses. You're right off my list of marriage prospects. I hope you can stand the shock."

He chuckled softly. "So do I." She was still flushed, but she looked less tormented than she had. "Are you all right now?" he asked gently.

She nodded and then said, "Yes. Thank you," she added, her voice softer than she intended it to be.

He only smiled. "He won't be back, in case you're worried about that," he added. "I fired him on the spot."

She drew in a breath. "I can't say I'm sorry about that. He wasn't what he seemed."

"Most men aren't. And the next time you accept a date, I want to know first."

She stared at him. "I beg your pardon?"

"You heard me. You may not consider me good husband material," he murmured, "but I'm going to look out for your interests just the same." He studied her seriously for a moment. "If I can't seduce you, nobody else can, either."

"Well, talk about sour grapes!" she accused.

"Count on it," he agreed.

"And what if I want to be seduced?" she continued.

"Not this week," he returned dryly. "I'll have to look at my calendar."

"I didn't mean you!"

His black eyes slid up and down her body in the torn dress that she'd covered with his shirt. "You did earlier," he murmured with a tender smile. "And I wanted to."

She sighed. "So did I. But I won't propose, even if you beg."

He shrugged powerful shoulders. "My heart's broken."

She chuckled in spite of herself. "Sure it is."

She turned and reached for the doorknob.

"Tess."

She glanced back at him. "Yes?"

His face was solemn, no longer teasing. "They told you about her, didn't they?"

He meant his brothers had told her about his doomed engagement. She didn't pretend ignorance. "Yes, they did," she replied.

"It was a long time ago, but it took me years to get over it. She was young, too, and she thought I was just what she wanted. But the minute I was out of sight, she found somebody else."

"And you think I would, too, because I'm not mature enough to be serious," she guessed.

His broad chest rose and fell. "That's about the size of it. You're pretty green, honey. It might be nothing more concrete than a good case of repressed lust."

"If that's my excuse, what's yours?" she asked with pursed lips. "Abstinence?"

"That's my story and I'm sticking to it like glue."

She laughed softly. "Coward."

He lifted one eyebrow. "You can write a check on that. I've been burned and I've got the scars to prove it."

"And I'm too young to be in love with you."

His heart jerked in his chest. The thought of Tess being in love with him made his head spin, but he had to hold on to his common sense. "That's right." His gaze went homing to her soft mouth and he could taste it all over again. He folded his arms over his broad chest and looked at her openly, without amusement or mockery. "Years too young."

"Okay. Just checking." She opened the door. A crash of thunder rumbled into the silence that followed. Seconds later, the bushes outside his window scratched against the glass as the wind raged.

"Are you afraid of storms?" he asked.

She shook her head. "Are you?"

"I'll tell you tomorrow."

She looked puzzled.

"You've spent enough time around livestock to know that thunderstorms play hell with cattle from time to time. We'll have to go out and check on ours if this keeps up. You can lie in your nice, soft dry bed and think about all of us getting soaked to the skin."

She thought about how bad summer colds could be. "Wear a raincoat," she told him.

He smiled at that affectionate concern, and it was in his eyes this time, too. "Okay, boss."

She grinned. "That'll be the day."

He lifted an eyebrow. "You're big on songs these days," he murmured. "That was one of Buddy Holly's. Want me to sing it to you?"

She realized belatedly which song he was talking about, and she shook her head. "No, thanks. It would upset the neighbors' dogs."

He glowered at her. "I have a good voice."

"Sure you do, as long as you don't use it for singing," she agreed. "Good night, Callaghan. Thanks again for rescuing me."

"I can't let anything happen to the family biscuit chef," he said casually. "We'd all starve."

She let him get away with that. He might not believe in marriage, but he was different after their ardent interlude. He'd never picked at her, teased her, before. Come to think of it, she'd never teased him. She'd been too afraid. That was ancient history now. She gave him one last shy, smiling glance and went out the door.

He stood where she left him, his eyes narrowed, his body still singing with the pleasure she'd given him. She was too young. His mind knew it. If he could only convince the rest of him…

SURPRISINGLY TESS SLEPT that night, despite the storms that rippled by, one after another. The memory of Cag's tender passion had all but blotted out the bad memories Gaines had given her. If only Cag wanted her on a permanent basis. At least they'd gotten past the awkwardness that followed that physical explosion of pleasure. It would make things easier for both of them.

She made breakfast the following morning and there was nobody to eat it. One of the men, wet and bedraggled looking, came to the back door to explain why breakfast went untouched.

It seemed that the high winds combined with drenching rain had brought down some huge old oak trees, right through several fences. While she slept soundly, in the outer pastures, cattle had gotten loose and had to be rounded up again, and the broken fences had to be mended. Half the outfit was soaked and all but frozen from the effort. The brothers had dragged in about daylight and fallen asleep, too tired even for their beloved biscuits.

It was almost noon before they came wandering into the kitchen. Breakfast had gone to the ranch dogs and the chickens, but she had beef and potatoes in a thick stew—with biscuits—waiting.

Rey and Leo smiled at her. To her astonishment, Cag gave her an openly affectionate glance as he sat down at the head of the table and reached for the coffeepot.

"It amazes me how you always keep food hot," Leo remarked. "Thanks, Tess. We were dead on our feet when we finally got back this morning."

"It was a rough night, I gather," she murmured as she ferried butter and jam to the table.

Leo watched her curiously. "We heard that you had one of your own," he said, regretting the careless remark when he saw her flush. "I'm sorry we didn't get our hands on Gaines before he ran for the border," he added, and the familiar, funny man she'd come to know suddenly became someone else.

"That goes double for me," Rey added grimly.

"Well, he had plenty of attention without counting on either of you," Cag remarked pleasantly. "I understand that he left tire marks on his way out in the early hours of the morning. The sniveling little weasel," he added.

"Amazing, isn't it, that Gaines actually walked away under his own steam," Leo told Rey.

Rey nodded. "And here we've been wasting our time saving people from him—" he indicated Cag "—for years."

"People don't need saving from me," Cag offered. "I'm not a homicidal maniac. I can control my temper," he added.

Leo pursed his lips. "Say, Tess, did the chocolate icing stain ever come completely off the wall…?"

She was fumbling with a lid that wouldn't come off, flustered from the whole conversation and wishing she could sink through the floor.

"Here, give me that," Cag said softly.

She gave it to him. Their hands touched and they looked at each other for just a second too long, something the brothers picked up on immediately.

Cag opened the jar and put it on the table while she went to get spoons.

"At least he's stopped throwing cakes at people," Rey remarked.

Cag lifted the jar of apple butter and looked at his brother intently.

Rey held up a hand and grinned sheepishly as he fell to eating his stew.

"If it's all right, I thought I'd go ahead and apply to the local technical school," Tess said quickly, before she lost her nerve. "For fall classes in horticulture, you know."

"Sure," Leo said. "Go ahead."

Cag lifted his gaze to her slender body and remembered how sweet it had been to hold in the silence of the study. He let his gaze fall back to his plate. He couldn't deter her. She didn't belong to him. She did need an occupation, something that would support her. He didn't like the idea of her keeping house for anyone else. She was safe here; she might not be in some other household. And if she went as a commuter, she could still work for the brothers.

"I could...live in the dormitory, if you want," she continued doggedly.

That brought Cag's head up. "Live in the dormitory? What the hell for?" he exclaimed.

His surprise took some of the gloom out of her heart. She clasped her hands tight in front of her, against her new jeans. "Well, you only said I could stay until summer," she said reasonably. "It's summer now. You didn't say anything about staying until fall."

Cag looked hunted. "You won't find another job easily in the fall, with all the high school seniors out grabbing them," he said curtly. He glanced back at his plate. "Stay until winter."

She wondered why Rey and Leo were strangling on their coffee.

"Is it too strong?" she asked worriedly, nodding toward the cups.

"Just...right." Leo choked, coughing. "I think I caught cold last night. Sorry. I need a tissue..."

"Me, too!" Rey exploded.

They almost knocked over their chairs in their rush

to get out of the room. Muffled laughter floated back even after the door had been closed.

"Idiots," Cag muttered. He looked up at Tess, and something brushed against his heart, as softly as a butterfly. He could hardly breathe.

She looked at him with eyes that loved him, and hated the very feeling. He wanted her to go, she knew he did, but he kept putting it off because he was sorry for her. She was so tired of being pitied by him.

"I don't mind living in the dormitory at school, if you want me to leave here," she repeated softly.

He got up from his chair and moved toward her. His big, lean hands rested on her shoulders and he looked down from his great height with quiet, wondering eyes. She was already like part of him. She made him bubble inside, as if he'd had champagne. The touch of her, the taste of her, were suddenly all too familiar.

"How would you manage to support yourself, with no job?" he asked realistically.

"I could get something part-time, at the school."

"And who'll bake biscuits for us?" he asked softly. "And worry about us when we're tired? Who'll remember to set the alarm clocks and remind me to clean Herman's cage? Who'll fuss if I don't wear my raincoat?" he added affectionately.

She shrugged. His hands felt nice. She loved their warmth and strength, their tenderness.

He tilted her chin up and searched her quiet eyes. Fires kindled deep in his body and made him hungry. He couldn't afford to indulge what he was feeling. Especially not here, in the kitchen, where his brothers could walk in any minute.

But while he was thinking it, his rebellious hands slid

up to frame her face and he bent, brushing his mouth tenderly over her soft lips.

"You shouldn't let me do this," he whispered.

"Oh, I'm not," she assured him softly. "I'm resisting you like crazy." She reached up to link her arms around his neck.

"Are you?" He smiled as he coaxed her lips under his and kissed her slowly.

She smiled against his mouth, lifting toward him. "Yes. I'm fighting like mad. Can't you tell?"

"I love the way you fight me...!"

The kiss became possessive, insistent, feverish, all in the space of seconds. He lifted her against him and groaned at the fierce passion she kindled in him so effortlessly.

Only the sound of booted feet heading their way broke them apart. He set her down gently and struggled to get back in his chair and breathe normally. He managed it, just.

Tess kept her back to the brothers until she could regain her own composure. But she didn't realize that her mouth was swollen and the softness in her eyes was an equally vivid giveaway.

Cag was cursing himself and circumstances under his breath for all he was worth. Having her here was going to be an unbearable temptation. Why hadn't he agreed to letting her live in at the school?

Because he ached for her, that was why. He was alive as he hadn't been in seven long years and the thought of going back into his shell was painful.

His black eyes settled on Tess and he wondered how he could ever have lived from day to day without looking at her at least once. He was getting a fixation on red curly hair and pale freckled skin. She was too young for him. He knew that, but he couldn't seem to keep his hands off her. He didn't know what he was going to do. If he didn't find something to occupy him, and quickly, he was going to end up seducing her. That would be the end of the world. The absolute end.

TESS BORROWED ONE of the ranch trucks the next morning after breakfast and drove herself to the campus of the Jacobsville Vocational-Technical School. The admissions office was easy to find. She was given forms to fill out, a course schedule for the fall quarter, and advice on financial assistance. From there, she went to the financial office and filled out more forms. It took until lunch to finally finish, but she had a sense of accomplishment by the time she left the campus.

On her way back to the ranch, she stopped in at the local café and had coffee and a sandwich while she did some thinking about her situation.

Cag said he didn't want her to move out, but did he really mean it, or was he just sorry for her? He liked kissing her, but he didn't want to keep doing it. He seemed not to be able to stop. Maybe, she thought, that was the whole problem. She made him forget all the reasons why he shouldn't get involved with her, every time he came close.

If she was gone, of course, he wouldn't get close enough to have his scruples damaged. But he'd said that he didn't want her to leave. It was a puzzle she couldn't seem to solve.

The sandwich tasted flat, although it was roast beef, one of her favorites. She put it down and stared at it without seeing.

"Thinking of giving it its freedom, huh?" Leo asked with a grin, and sat down across from her. He took off his hat, laid it on the chair beside him and gestured toward the sandwich. "I hate to tell you this, but there's absolutely no way known to science that a roast beef sandwich can be rejuvenated." He leaned forward conspiratorially. "Take it from a beef expert."

She chuckled despite her sadness. "Oh, Leo, you're just impossible," she choked.

"It runs in the family." He held up a hand and when the waitress came to see what he wanted, he ordered coffee.

"No lunch?" Tess asked.

He shook his head. "No time. I'm due at the Brewsters' in forty-five minutes for a business meeting over lunch. Rubber chicken and overdone potatoes, like last time," he muttered. He glanced at her. "I wish you were cooking for it instead of Brewster's daughter. She's pretty as a picture and I hear tell she had operatic aspirations, but she couldn't make canned soup taste good."

He sounded so disgusted that Tess smiled in spite of herself. "Are you going by yourself, or are the brothers going, too?"

"Just Cag and me. Rey escaped on a morning flight to Tulsa to close a land deal up there."

She lowered her eyes to the half-finished sandwich. "Does Cag like her... Miss Brewster?"

He hesitated. "Cag doesn't like women, period. I thought you knew."

"You said she was pretty."

"Like half a dozen other women who have fathers in the cattle business," he agreed. "Some of them can even cook. But as you know Cag gave up on women when he was thrown over for a younger man. Hell, the guy was only three years younger than him, at that. She used his age as an excuse. It wasn't, really. She just didn't want him. The other guy had money, too, and she did want him."

"I see."

He sipped coffee and pursed his lips thoughtfully. "I've told you before how Cag reacts to women most of the time," he reminded her. "He runs." He smiled. "Of course, he's been doing his best to run from you since last Christmas."

She looked at him with her heart in her eyes. "He has?" she asked.

"Sure! He wants you to go off to school so you'll remove temptation from his path. But he also wants you to stay at the ranch while you go to school, in case you run into any handsome eligible bachelors there. I think he plans to save you from them, if you do."

She was confused and it showed.

"He said," he related, "that you shouldn't be exposed to potential seducers without us to protect you."

She didn't know whether to laugh or cry.

He held up a hand when she started to speak. "He thinks you should commute."

"But he doesn't want me at the ranch, don't you see?" she asked miserably, running a hand through her short, curly hair. "He keeps leaving to get away from me!"

"Why would he leave if you weren't getting to him?" he asked reasonably.

"It's still a rotten way to live," she said pointedly. "Maybe if I go to school I'll meet somebody who'll think I'm old enough for them."

"Oh, that's just sour grapes," he murmured dryly.

"You have no idea *how* sour," she replied. "I give up. I can't spend the rest of my life hoping that he'll change his mind about me. He's had almost a year, and he hasn't changed a thing."

"He stopped throwing cakes," he said.

"Because I stopped baking them!"

He checked his watch and grimaced. "I'd love to stay here and talk recipes with you, but I'm late." He got up and smiled at her. "Don't brood, okay? I have a feeling that things are going to work out just fine."

That wasn't what she thought, but he was gone before she could put the thought into words.

# CHAPTER EIGHT

IT WAS INEVITABLE that Leo would bring up the matter of the Brewster girl's cooking the next day. Breakfast was too much of a rush, and they didn't get to come home for lunch. But when two of the three brothers and Tess sat down to supper, Leo let it fly with both barrels.

"That Janie Brewster isn't too bad-looking, is she?" Leo murmured between bites of perfectly cooked barbecued chicken. "Of course, she can ruin a chicken."

Cag glanced at him quickly, as if the remark puzzled him. Then he glanced at Tess's studiously down bent head and understood immediately what Leo was trying to do.

He took a forkful of chicken and ate it before he replied, "She'll never make a cook. Or even much of a wife," he added deliberately. "She knows everything."

"She does have a university degree."

"In psychology," Cag reminded him. "I got psychoanalyzed over every bite of food." He glanced at Tess. "It seems that I have repressed feelings of inadequacy because I keep a giant reptile," he related with a twinkle in his black eyes.

Tess's own eyes widened. "You do?"

He nodded. "And I won't eat carrots because I have some deep-seated need to defy my mother."

She put a napkin to her mouth, trying to ward off laughter.

"You forgot the remark she made about the asparagus," Leo prompted.

Cag looked uncomfortable. "We can forget that one."

"But it's the best one!" Leo turned to Tess. "She said that he won't eat asparagus because of associations with impo—"

"Shut up!" Cag roared.

Leo, who never meant to repeat the blatant sexual remark, only grinned. "Okay."

Tess guessed, quite correctly, that the word Cag had cut off was *impotence.* And she was in a perfect position to tell Leo that it certainly didn't apply to his older brother, but she wouldn't have dared.

As it was, her eyes met Cag's across the table, and she flushed at the absolutely wicked glitter in those black eyes, and almost upset her coffee.

Leo, watching the byplay, was affectionately amused at the two of them trying so hard not to react. There was a sort of intimate merriment between them, despite Cag's attempts to ward off intimacy. Apparently he hadn't been wholly successful.

"I've got a week's worth of paperwork to get through," Cag said after a minute, getting up.

"But I made dessert," Tess said.

He turned, surprised. "I don't eat sweets. You know that."

She smiled secretively. "You'll like this one. It isn't really a conventional dessert."

He pushed in his chair. "Okay," he said. "But you'll have to bring it to me in the office. How about some coffee, too?"

"Sure."

Leo put down his napkin. "Well, you do the hard stuff. I'm going down to Shea's Bar to see if I can find Billy Telford. He promised me faithfully that he was going to give me a price on that Salers bull we're after. He's holding us up hoping that he can get more from the Tremaynes."

"The Tremaynes don't run Salers cattle," Cag said, frowning.

"Yes, but that's because Billy's only just been deluging them with facts on the advantages of diversification." He shrugged. "I don't think they'll buy it, but Billy does. I'm going to see if I can't get him dru... I mean," he amended immediately, "get him to give me a price."

"Don't you dare," Cag warned. "I'm not bailing you out again. I mean it."

"You drink from time to time," Leo said indignantly.

"With good reason, and I'm quiet about it. You aren't. None of us have forgotten the last time you cut loose in Jacobsville."

"I'd just gotten my degree," Leo said curtly. "It was a great reason to celebrate."

"To celebrate, yes. Not to wreck the bar. And several customers."

"As I recall, Corrigan and Rey helped."

"You bad boys," Tess murmured under her breath.

Cag glanced at her. "I never drink to excess anymore."

"Neither do I. And I didn't say that I was going to get drunk," Leo persisted. "I said I was going to get *Billy* drunk. He's much more malleable when he's not sober."

Cag shook a finger at him. "Nothing he signs inebriated will be legal. You remember that."

Leo threw up both hands. "For heaven's sake!"

"We can do without that bull."

"We can't! He's a grand champion," Leo said with pure, naked hunger in his tone. "I never saw such a beautiful animal. He's lean and healthy and glossy, like silk. He's a sire worthy of a foundation herd. I want him!"

Cag exchanged an amused glance with Tess. "It's love, I reckon," he drawled.

"With all due respect to women," Leo sighed, "there is nothing in the world more beautiful than a pedigree bull in his prime."

"No wonder you aren't married, you pervert," Cag said.

Leo glared at him. "I don't want to marry the bull, I just want to own him! Listen, your breeding program is standing still. I have ideas. Good ideas. But I need that bull." He slammed his hat down on his head. "And one way or another, Billy's going to sell him to me!"

He turned and strode out the door, looking formidable and determined.

"Is it really that good a bull?" Tess asked.

Cag chuckled. "I suppose it is." He shook his head. "But I think Leo has ulterior motives."

"Such as?"

"Never you mind." He studied her warmly for a minute, approving of her chambray shirt and jeans. She always looked neat and feminine, even if she didn't go in for seductive dresses and tight-fitting clothes. "Bring your mysterious dessert on into the office when you get it ready. Don't forget the coffee."

"Not me, boss," she replied with a pert smile.

SHE PUT THE finishing touches on the elegant dessert and placed it on a tray with the cup of coffee Cag liked after supper. She carried the whole caboodle into the study, where he was hunched over his desk with a pencil in one hand and his head in the other, going over what looked like reams of figure-studded pages of paper.

He got up when she entered and took the tray from her, placing it on the very edge of the desk. He scowled.

"What is it?" he asked, nodding toward a saucer of what looked like white foam rubber with whipped cream on top.

"It's a miniature Pavlova," she explained. "It's a hard meringue with a soft center, filled with fresh fruit and whipped cream. It takes a long time to make, but it's pretty good. At least, I think it is."

He picked up the dessert fork she'd provided and drew it down through the dessert. It made a faint crunching sound. Intrigued, he lifted a forkful of the frothy-looking substance to his mouth and tasted it. It melted on his tongue.

His face softened. "Why, this is good," he said, surprised.

"I thought you might like it," she said, beaming. "It isn't really a sweet dessert. It's like eating a cloud."

He chuckled. "That's a pretty good description." He sat down in the big leather swivel chair behind his desk with the saucer in his hand. But he didn't start eating again.

He lifted his chin. "Come here."

"Who, me?" she asked.

"Yes, you."

She edged closer. "You said that I mustn't let you do things to me."

"Did I say that?" he asked in mock surprise.

"Yes, you did."

He held out the arm that wasn't holding the saucer. "Well, ignore me. I'm sure I was out of my mind at the time."

She chuckled softly, moving to the chair. He pulled her down onto his lap so that she rested against his broad chest, with his shoulder supporting her back. He dipped out a forkful of her dessert and held it to her lips.

"It's not bad, is it?" she asked, smiling.

He took a bite of his own. "It's unique. I'll bet the others would love it, too." He glanced down at her expression and lifted an eyebrow. "Mm-hmm," he murmured thoughtfully. "So you made it just for me, did you?"

She shifted closer. "You work harder than everybody else. I thought you deserved something special."

He smiled warmly at her. "I'm not the only hard worker around here. Who scrubbed the kitchen floor on her hands and knees after I bought her a machine that does it?"

She flushed. "It's a very nice machine. I really appreciate it. But it's better if you do it with a toothbrush. I mean, the dirt in the linoleum pattern just doesn't come up any other way. And I do like a nice kitchen."

He grimaced. "What am I going to do with you? A modern woman isn't supposed to scrub floors on her hands and knees. She's supposed to get a degree and take a corporate presidency away from some good old boy in Houston."

She snuggled close to him and closed her eyes, loving his warm strength against her. Her hand smoothed over his shirt just at the pocket, feeling its softness.

"I don't want a degree. I'd like to grow roses."

"So you said." He fed her another bite of the dessert, which left one for himself. Then he sat up to put the saucer on the desk and reach for the coffee.

"I'll get it." She slid off his lap and fixed the coffee the way he liked it.

He took it from her and coaxed her back onto his lap. It felt good to hold her like that, in the pleasant silence of the office. He shared the coffee with her, too.

Her hand rested on his while she sipped the hot liquid, staring up into eyes that seemed fascinated by her. She wondered at their sudden closeness, when they'd been at odds for such a long time.

He was feeling something similar. He liked holding her, touching her. She filled an empty place in him with joy and delight. He wasn't lonely when she was close to him.

"Why roses?" he asked when they finished the coffee and he put the cup back on the desk.

"They're old," she said, settling back down against his chest. "They have a nobility, a history. For instance, did you know that Napoleon's Empress Josephine was famous for her rose garden, and that despite the war with England, she managed to get her roses shipped through enemy lines?"

He chuckled. "Now how did you know about that?"

"It was in one of my gardening magazines. Roses are prehistoric," she continued. "They're one of the oldest living plants. I like the hybrids, too, though. Dad bought me a beautiful tea rose the last year we lived in Victoria. I guess it's still where I planted it. But the house was rented, and we weren't likely to have a permanent home after that, so I didn't want to uproot my rosebush."

He smoothed his fingers over her small, soft hand where it pressed over his pocket. His fingers explored her neat, short nails while his breath sighed out at her forehead, ruffling her hair.

"I never had much use for flowers. Our mother wasn't much of a gardener, either."

She leaned back against his shoulder so that she could see his face. He looked bitter.

Her fingers went up to his mouth and traced his hard, firm lips. "You mustn't try to live in the past," she said. "There's a whole world out there waiting to be seen and touched and lived in."

"How can you be so optimistic, after the life you've had?" he wanted to know.

"I'm an incurable optimist, I guess," she said. "I've seen so much of the ugly side of life that I never take any nice thing for granted. It's been great, living here, being part of a family, even though I just work for you."

His lips pursed against her exploring fingers. He caught them and nibbled absently at their tips while he looked down into her eyes. "I like the way you cook."

"I'm not pretty, though," she mused, "and I can't psychoanalyze you over the vegetables."

"Thank God."

She chuckled.

He tugged at a lock of her hair and searched her eyes. "Cute of Leo to bring up the asparagus." His eyes narrowed and his smile faded as he looked down at her with kindling desire. "You knew what he was going to say, didn't you?"

She nodded. Her heart was racing too fast to allow for speech.

"Well, it was interesting, having asparagus signify

impotence," he murmured dryly, smiling at her blush. "But we could have told Miss Brewster that the asparagus lied, couldn't we, Tess?" he drawled.

She hid her hot face against him, feeling his laughter as his chest rippled with it.

"Sorry," he said at her ear, bending to gather her even closer against him. "I shouldn't tease you. It's irresistible. I love the way you blush." His arms tightened and his face nuzzled against hers, coaxing it around so that his lips could find her soft mouth. "I love...so much about you, Tess," he growled against her lips.

She reached up to hold him while the kiss grew and grew, like a spark being fanned into a bonfire.

He lifted away from her for an instant, to search her eyes and look down at her soft, yielding body.

Without the slightest hesitation, his hand smoothed over the chambray shirt she was wearing and went right to her small breast, covering it boldly, teasing the nipple to immediate hardness with his thumb.

Her lips parted with the excitement he aroused, and he bent and took her soft sigh right into his mouth.

She didn't have the experience to know how rare this mutual delight was, but he did. It was pleasurable with some women, but with Tess, it was like walking through fireworks. He enjoyed every single thing about her, from the way she curled into him when he touched her to the way her mouth opened eagerly for his. It made him feel vaguely invincible.

He made a rough sound in his throat as his hand edged between them, feeling blindly for her shirt buttons. She wasn't coy about that, either. She lay submissively in his arms, letting him open the shirt, letting him unclip her bra and push it away.

She didn't have to tell him that she liked his gazing on her body. It was even in the way her breath caught and fluttered.

He touched her delicately, lifting his gaze to her face to watch the way she reacted to it.

It occurred to him that she might love him, must love him, to let him be so familiar with her body, which he knew instinctively was innocent.

His heart jumped up into his throat as he traced around one tight little pink nipple.

"What did you do for experience before I came along?" he murmured half-teasingly.

"I watched movies on cable," she said, her own voice breathless. She shivered and her short nails dug into his shoulder. "Callaghan, is it supposed to…do that?" she whispered.

"What?"

She bit her lip and couldn't quite look at him.

He bent to her mouth and liberated her lower lip with a soft, searching kiss. "It's supposed to make your body swell," he whispered into her lips. "Does it?"

She swallowed hard. "All over?"

"All over."

She nuzzled her face into his hot throat while his hands worked magic on her. "It makes me ache."

"It's supposed to do that, too."

He had the weight of her in one big palm and he bent his head to put his mouth, open, on the nipple.

She shivered again and he heard a tight sob pass her lips. He knew he was going to get in over his head, and it didn't seem to matter anymore.

With a rough curse, he suddenly got to his feet and stripped her out of the shirt and bra before he lifted her and, with his mouth hard on hers, carried her to the divan.

He stretched her out on it, yielding and openly hungry, and came down beside her, one long leg inserted boldly between both of hers.

"Do you have any idea how dangerous this is?" he ground out against her breasts.

Her hands were fumbling for buttons. "It isn't, because we aren't…doing anything," she whispered with deathbed humor as she forced the stubborn shirt buttons apart and pushed the fabric away from hard, warm, hair-covered muscles. "You are…so beautiful," she added in a hushed, rapt whisper as she touched him and felt him go tense.

His teeth clenched. "Tess…" He made her name sound like a plea for mercy.

"Oh, come here. Please!" She drew him down on her, so that her bare breasts merged with his hard chest. She held him close while they kissed hungrily, feeling his long legs suddenly shift so that he was between hers, pressing against her in a new and urgent way.

He lifted his head and looked into her eyes. His own were coal black, glittering with desire, his face drawn and taut.

She watched him openly, all too aware of his capability, and that he could lose his head right here and she wouldn't care.

He shifted against her deliberately, and his head spun with pleasure. He laughed, but without humor.

"If I'd ever imagined that a virgin—" he stressed the word in a harsh, choked tone "—could make an utter fool of me!"

Her hands had been sliding up and down the hard

muscles of his back with pure wonder. Now they stilled, uncertain. "A…fool?" she whispered.

"Tess, have you gone numb from the waist down?" he asked through his teeth. "Can't you feel what's happened to me?"

"Well…yes," she said hesitantly. "Isn't it normal?"

He laughed in spite of the stabbing ache she'd given him. "Baby, you haven't got a clue, have you?"

"Did I do something wrong?"

"No!" He eased down again, giving in to his need, and hers, but careful not to give her too much of his formidable weight. His mouth moved lazily over her forehead, down to close her wide, wounded eyes. "You haven't done anything wrong. I want you," he whispered tenderly.

"I want you, too," she whispered back shyly.

He sighed as if he had the weight of the world on him. One big, lean hand slid under her hips and lifted them slowly, sensually into the hard thrust of him, and held her there.

She stiffened suddenly and a tiny little cry crawled out of her tight throat as she registered the heat and power of him in such stark intimacy.

"When it gets this bad," he whispered at her ear, "a man will lie, cheat, steal, kill to get rid of it! If I had just a little less honor, I'd tell you anything that would get those jeans off you in the least possible time."

"Get my jeans off…!"

The shock in her voice broke the tension. He lifted his head and burst out laughing despite the urgency in his body when he saw her face.

"You don't imagine that we could make love *through* them?" he asked.

She was scarlet. And he was laughing, the animal! She hit his shoulder angrily. "You stop that!"

He chuckled helplessly, shifting suddenly to lie beside her on the wide leather divan. He pulled her against him and lay there fighting for breath and control, deliciously aware of her bare breasts pressing warmly against his rib cage.

"Just when I think I'll go mad, you act your age."

"I'm not a kid!" she protested.

He smoothed her ruffled hair lazily and his chest rose and fell in a long sigh while the urgency slowly passed out of his body. "Yes, you are," he contradicted, his voice soft and affectionate. "And if we keep doing this, eventually, blushes or not, you're coming out of those jeans."

"As if I'd let you!"

"You'd help me," he returned. "Tess, I haven't really tried to seduce you," he added quietly. "You're as hungry for me as I am for you, and I know tricks I haven't used yet."

She drank in the male smell of his body with pleasure. "Such as?"

"You really want to know?" He drew her close and whispered in her ear.

"Callaghan!"

He kissed her shocked face, closing her open mouth with warm, tender kisses. "You've got a lot to learn, and I ache to teach it to you," he said after a minute. "But you aren't geared for an affair, and I have far too many principles to seduce a woman who works for me." He sighed wearily and drew her closer, wrapping her up against him. "Good God, Tess, how did we ever get into this situation?"

"You insisted that I sit on your lap while you ate dessert," she replied reasonably.

"It happened long before that. Months ago. I fought you like mad to keep you at arm's length."

"It didn't work," she informed him.

"So I noticed."

He didn't speak again and neither did she for a long time. They lay in each other's arms in the silence of the study, listening to the muted sounds of the night outside the window.

"Do you want me to go?" she asked finally.

His arms contracted. "Sure," he replied facetiously. "Like I want to give up breathing."

That was reassuring. She felt the same way. But he still wasn't mentioning anything permanent. Even through the euphoria of lying half nude against him, she did realize that.

Finally he let go of her and got up from the divan, careful not to look at her as he fetched her shirt and bra and put them beside her.

"You'd better..." He gestured, not putting it into words.

She dressed quickly, watching his long back as he stood beside the desk, idly touching the papers on it.

She got to her feet at last and after a minute she went around him to get the tray.

"I'll take this back to the kitchen."

He nodded without speaking. He was too choked with conflicting emotions to put a single one of them into words.

But when she went to pick up the tray, his hand covered the back of hers, briefly.

"I've put off a conference that I meant to attend in

Kansas City," he said quietly. "I'm going to go. Rey will be back in the morning before I leave, and Leo will be here."

She looked up at him with wide, soft eyes in a face that made his heart ache.

He cursed softly. "Tess, it wouldn't work," he said through his teeth. "You know it wouldn't!"

She made a motion with her shoulders and lowered her revealing eyes so that he couldn't read what was in them. "Okay."

"You'll like school," he forced himself to say. "There will be boys your own age, nice boys, not like some of the toughs you meet on the rodeo circuit."

"Sure."

"You can commute," he added after a minute. "None of us want you to give up your job while you're going to school. And I'll make sure we aren't alone again, like this."

She swallowed the lump in her throat and even forced a smile. "Okay."

He watched her pick up the tray and go out of the room. When he finally closed the door behind her, it was like putting the finishing touches on a high wall. He actually winced.

## CHAPTER NINE

CAG WAS DRESSED in a lightweight gray vested suit the next morning when he came in to breakfast. His suitcase was packed and waiting by the front door, along with his silver belly Stetson. He looked elegant when he dressed up. Tess had to force herself not to stare at him too closely while she served the meal.

Rey had walked in, still dressed in a suit himself, just as Tess started to put breakfast down on the table. He, like Callaghan, would never win any beauty contests, but he paid for dressing. He looked elegant and faintly dangerous, in a sexy sort of way. Tess was glad she was immune to him, and wondered vaguely if there had ever been a special woman in his life.

"I feel like Cinderella before the ball," Leo muttered, glancing from one of his brothers to the other. He was in jeans and a blue-checked shirt and boots, his blond-streaked brown hair shining like gold in the ceiling light.

Cag didn't react, but Rey took him up on it, peering deliberately under the table to see if Leo was wearing a dress.

"Cute, cute," Leo drawled. He picked up his fork and stabbed the air toward his brother. "I meant figuratively speaking. I don't wear dresses."

"Good thing, with your hairy legs," Rey retorted. He glanced toward Cag. "You leaving?"

Cag nodded as he finished a mouthful of eggs and washed it down with coffee. "I'm going to that legislative cattlemen's conference in Kansas City. I decided that I'd better go. The journals don't keep us completely up-to-date on pending legislation, and I've heard some rumors I don't like about new regulations."

"I've heard those same rumors," Leo remarked.

"We have to start policing our own industry better," Cag said. "All the rules and regulations and laws in the world won't work without better enforcement." He looked up. "You should have kept your seat on the legislative committee at the state cattlemen's association."

"Hindsight is a fine thing," Leo agreed. "I had too much to do at the time."

"If they ask you again, take it."

"You bet I will." He glanced at Cag. "Why don't you do it?"

Cag smiled. "I've got more than I can do already, as you'll discover when you look at the paperwork in the study. I only got half the figures keyed into the computer. You'll need to take the rest down to Margie in the office and get her to finish."

"Sure."

Neither Leo nor Rey noticed that Tess had turned away to the sink deliberately, because she knew why Cag hadn't finished that paperwork. She didn't want the other two brothers to see her flush.

Cag noticed. He didn't look at her, though, because he'd become more readable lately where she was concerned. He finished his coffee and got up.

"Well, I'm off. I'll try to be back by next weekend.

You can reach me at the Airport Hilton in Kansas City if you need me."

"We won't," Leo said with a grin. "Have a good time."

Cag glanced involuntarily at Tess, thinking how empty life without her was going to be, even for a few days. He'd grown all too fond of that red curly head of hair and those heavenly blue eyes.

"Take care of Tess while I'm gone," he said, trying to make a joke of it and failing miserably.

"I'll take care of myself, thanks very much," she shot right back and forced a smile, so that he'd think it wasn't killing her to watch him walk out the door.

"You never told us how your application went," Leo said suddenly.

"Oh, I was accepted on the spot," Tess said. "They've scheduled me for three classes when fall quarter begins. I went to the financial aid office and applied for tuition, which they say I can get, and it will pay for my books."

Cag frowned. "You've already applied?"

"Yes," she said with determined brightness. "I start in three weeks. I can hardly wait."

"So I see." Cag finished his goodbyes, added a few things for his brothers to take care of while he was away and left without another word.

Tess wondered why he was irritated that she'd applied for admission to the vocational school, when he'd already said he wanted her to do it. She knew he hadn't changed his mind. His behavior was puzzling.

Cag was thinking the same thing as he slammed his hat on his head, picked up his suitcase, and went out the front door. He'd known she was applying, but now it was definite. He thought of her in his arms the night before, hungry for his kisses, and then he thought of all the young men she'd meet when she started classes. She might meet a young man who liked roses, too. He had visions of her youthful crush on him melting quickly away in the heat of a new romance, and it made him vaguely sick.

He'd tried not to get in over his head, but it looked as if he was only fooling himself. Tess had wormed her way under his skin, right where his heart was. He wondered how he'd ever imagined that he could make a little love to her and walk away. He'd never been quite so confused or worried in his life. He wanted Tess as he'd never wanted anything. But he was afraid that she was in love with love, not him, because he was the first man who'd ever been intimate with her even in a slight way. He couldn't forget the fiancée who'd dropped him for someone younger. He couldn't bear to go through that a second time.

He got into the ranch truck and drove toward the airport, but his heart wasn't in it. Tess was going to go away to school, and he was going to lose her. But not right away, he comforted himself. She'd still be living at the ranch. He'd have time to get himself sorted out. And it wasn't as if she was going to meet someone else at once. He had plenty of time. The thought comforted him, and he put that worry aside.

CAG WOULDN'T HAVE been quite so comforted if he'd seen the big black limousine that drew up in front of the Hart ranch house barely two hours after he'd left.

Rey and Leo had already gone out with the men to look over a new batch of bulls when someone rang the doorbell.

Tess wiped her hands on a kitchen towel and left the pots she'd been scrubbing in the sink when she went to answer it.

A tall, taciturn man in a suit, carrying a briefcase, was standing there.

"Miss Theresa Brady?" the man asked politely.

It was a shock to hear her given name. She'd been called Tess for so long that she'd all but forgotten that it was a contraction of Theresa.

"Yes," she said hesitantly.

He held out a hand. "I'm Clint Matherson," he said, shaking hands. "Your late mother's attorney."

Her hand went limp in his. "My...*late*...mother?"

"I'm sorry to tell you that your mother passed away almost a month ago in Singapore. It wasn't possible to get word to you until now. I found you through a detective agency, but I've been out of town and the message only reached me a week ago. I'm very sorry," he said belatedly.

She hadn't thought of her mother in years, and only then with regret. It might have been sad to lose her if she'd ever shown the slightest affection for her only child, but she hadn't.

"I didn't know where she was," Tess said honestly. "We hadn't communicated since I was sixteen."

"Yes, she, uh, made me aware of that. She left you a portfolio of stocks in a trading company out of Singapore," he added. "If we could sit down and discuss her will?"

"I'm sorry. Of course. Come into the living room, please."

He sat down in an armchair and laid out the documents on the spotless oak coffee table, moving her flower arrangement aside to make room for them.

"I can't tell you much about this company. Frankly the stocks are as much a surprise to you as they are to me. She didn't ask my advice before she sank her money into them. You did know that she married a wealthy Singapore importer six years ago?"

"No," Tess said stiffly. "As I said, we haven't corresponded."

"A pity," he replied. "She gave up drinking and led a fairly admirable life in her last years. She was widowed about the time she contracted cancer. Her illness perhaps changed her outlook somewhat. I understand that she had plans to ask you to come out and visit with her, but she never carried them out." He smiled thinly. "She told me she was ashamed of the way she'd treated you, Miss Brady, and not too hopeful of making amends."

Tess clasped her hands together on the knees of her jeans. "I would have listened, if she'd wanted to talk to me."

He shrugged. "Perhaps it's just as well. But time is a great healer." He indicated the documents. "I'll have these stocks checked out by the end of the week. I should be able to give you some idea of their current worth on the Asian market then. You can decide whether you'd rather keep them or sell them. There are a few odds and ends, like her jewelry, which will be sent on to me and I'll forward them to you."

The thought of having something, anything, of her mother's made her uneasy. "Wasn't there any other relative?"

"A stepdaughter who still lives in Singapore. But she was already provided for by her father's will."

"Wouldn't she like the jewelry?"

He was surprised. "Well, she was fond of your mother, I understand. They were good friends. Yes, I imagine she would like it. But it's yours, Miss Brady. You were a blood relative."

"I never felt like one," she replied stiffly. "I'd like the daughter to have the jewelry and the other…personal things." She glanced at him and away. "It's hard to put into words, but I don't really want anything of hers. Not even the stock."

"Ah, but you have no choice about that," he said, surprising her. "There's no provision if you don't accept it. There must be some goal you've set in life that it would help you achieve. I understand that you work as a housekeeper here since your father's untimely death. Wouldn't you like to be financially independent?"

That remark changed her life. If she had a little money of her own, Callaghan wouldn't have to keep her on here because he was sorry for her. It would give her some measure of independence, even if leaving Callaghan broke her heart.

"Yes, I would," she answered the lawyer. "And I'll accept the stock. Thank you."

He indicated the places her signature was required, closed the documents up in his briefcase, shook hands and promised to be in touch soon about the stock.

"How much do you think it could be worth?" she asked hesitantly when he was on the verge of leaving.

"Hard to tell. It was bought for eighty dollars a share, but that was last year."

"And how much was bought?"

He smiled musingly. "About a million dollars worth."

She was pale. Her hand found the door and held on for support. "Oh."

"So you see, you won't be dependent on other people for your livelihood. Your mother may have neglected you in life, but she didn't forget you at the end. That must be some comfort."

It wasn't, but she smiled and pretended that it was. She closed the door and leaned back against it. Everything had changed in the course of a few minutes. She was a woman of means. She could do what she pleased. But it would be without Callaghan Hart, and that was the hardest pill of all to swallow.

She told the brothers about her visitor at the supper table.

They were silent after she related the size of the inheritance, glancing at each other as if communicating in some mysterious fashion.

"I can still go to school, but I'll be able to support myself now," she told them. "And I guess," she added reluctantly, "I won't need to work. I'm sorry to leave, but we've known for a long time that Callaghan really would prefer to have another cook."

"Why don't you ever call him Cag, like we do?" Leo asked gently.

She stared at her coffee cup. "It never seemed comfortable, I guess."

They exchanged another mysterious glance.

"Well, we'll advertise as soon as Cag comes home and we have time to discuss what we want to do," Rey said. "We'll miss you, Tess. Especially your biscuits."

"Amen to that. A good biscuit chef is really hard to find in these liberated times. I guess we'll be eating them out of tins from now on."

"Now, now," Tess chided, "Dorie can bake biscuits and even real bread. I'll bet she won't mind keeping you supplied. But you'll find a cook. I know you will."

They looked at her silently. "She won't be you," Leo said, and he smiled wistfully.

TESS GOT USED to the idea of leaving in the days that followed. She was almost reconciled to it when Cag showed up late the next Friday afternoon. He looked tired and worn and unhappy until he saw Tess. His black eyes began to light up at once, and her heart ached, because it could have been so different if he'd loved her. She stood quietly in the kitchen when she wanted to fling herself into his arms and kiss him to death.

"Missed me?" he drawled.

She nodded, but she wouldn't look at him. "I've got to gather eggs. I forgot this morning. Welcome home," she said belatedly as she carried a small wicker basket out the back door.

"There you are!" Leo called, joining his brother in the kitchen. He clapped a hand on the taller man's shoulder. "How'd it go?"

"Fine. What's wrong with Tess?"

"What do you mean?"

Cag's eyes darkened. "She wouldn't look at me."

"Oh. Well, she's been unsettled since the lawyer came," Leo replied, carefully choosing his words. "Sudden wealth would do that to most people."

Cag's face lost a few shades of color. "Wealth?"

"Her mother died and left her a small fortune in stocks," he told the older man, watching with compassion the effect it had on him. "She says she'll be leaving as soon as we can hire a replacement. No need for her to work with a million dollars worth of stock, is there?"

Cag went to the sink and poured himself a glass of water that he didn't want, just to keep from groaning aloud. Tess had money. She was quitting. He'd thought he had time to work out his own feelings, and suddenly it was all up. She was leaving and he'd never see her again. She'd find somebody younger and get married and have babies. Tess would love having children of her own....

He put the glass down with a thud. "I've got things to do. How about those new bulls?"

"They came in, and I got Billy to sell me that Salers bull," he added smugly. "I've put him in a pasture all to himself with his own salt lick and a nice clean stall to keep him out of bad weather when it comes."

Cag didn't rise to the occasion which he would have only days before. He looked thoughtful and worried. Very worried.

"It won't be the same without Tess, will it?" Leo prompted gently.

Cag's face closed up completely. "I'll change and get back to the paperwork."

"Aren't you going to tell me how the conference went?"

"Later," Cag said absently. He walked out of the room without a backward glance.

HE ACTED ODDLY for the rest of the day. And he wasn't at the supper table.

"Said he had to go into town, God knows what for," Rey murmured as he buttered a flaky biscuit. "They pull in the sidewalks at six. He knows that."

"Maybe he's got something on his mind," Leo mused, watching Tess fuss over the chicken dish she was putting into a serving bowl.

Rey sighed. "Something big. He wasn't going toward Jacobsville," he added. "He was headed toward Shea's."

That brought Leo's head up. "He was?"

Tess finished putting food on the table, so preoccupied by Cag's reappearance that she couldn't put two thoughts together in any sort of order. It was much harder to leave than she'd even anticipated.

She missed the comment about Shea's Bar entirely, and she barely touched her own food. She cleaned up the kitchen, blind to the brothers' troubled glances, and went to bed early. She felt like it was the end of the world.

So DID CAG, who sat quietly at a corner table at Shea's Bar, drinking one whiskey highball after another until he was pleasantly numb and barely coherent.

No fool, he left the truck locked at the bar and took a cab back to the ranch. If the driver wondered at the identity of his overly quiet passenger, he didn't ask. He took the bills that were fumbled out of the cowhide wallet and drove away.

Cag managed to get through the living room without falling over anything, amazing considering the amount of whiskey he'd imbibed. He made it to his own room and even into the shower, an undertaking of mammoth proportions.

With his hair still damp and only a short robe covering his nudity, it occurred to him that he should ask Tess why the rush to get away from the ranch. That it was three in the morning didn't seem to matter. If she was asleep, why, she could just wake up and answer him.

He knocked at her door, but there was no answer. He opened it and walked in, bumping into a chair and the side table before he ever reached the bed.

He sat down on the side of it and noticed how hot the room was. She hadn't turned on the air conditioner, and then he remembered that his brothers had told him they'd shut the unit off temporarily while it was being worked on. No wonder it was so hot.

He reached out and pushed gently at Tess's shoulder under the cover. She moaned and kicked the cover away and he caught his breath. She was lying there just in her briefs, without any other covering, her beautiful little breasts bare and firm in the muted light of the security lamp outside her window.

He couldn't help himself. He reached out and traced those pretty breasts with the tips of his fingers, smiling when she arched and they went hard-tipped at once.

It seemed the most natural thing in the world to slide out of his robe and into bed beside her.

He turned her against his nude body, feeling her quiver softly and then ease closer to him. She felt like heaven in his arms. The feel of her soft, warm skin so intimately kindled a raging arousal in him.

He moved her onto her back and slid over her, his mouth gently smoothing across her lips until they parted and responded despite the sharp tang of whiskey on his breath.

Half-asleep, and sure that she was dreaming, her arms went under his and around him, her legs moved to admit him into an intimacy that made his head spin. He moved against her blindly, hungrily, urgently, his

mouth insistent on her mouth as he felt surges of pleasure breaking like waves inside him.

"Ca… Callaghan? Callaghan?" she whimpered.

"Yes, Tess…!" He caught her mouth again and his
hand went to her thigh, pulling her even closer, straining against the thin nylon barrier that was all that separated them.

If this was what he wanted, it was what she wanted,
too. She relaxed and gave in to the sweet, fierce sensations that came from the intimate contact with his
powerful body.

But even as his fingers sought her hips in a fierce
urgency, the liquor finally caught up with him. He gave
a soft, explosive sigh and a curse and suddenly went
limp on her, the full weight of his body pressing her
hard into the sheets.

She lay dazed, wondering exactly what had happened. Cag had no clothes on. She was wearing briefs,
but nothing more. Not being totally stupid, she realized that sex involved a little more contact than this,
but it was blatant intimacy, all the same. She shifted
experimentally, but nothing happened. He'd been very
aroused, but now he was relaxed all over.

She eased away a little and pushed. He went over
onto his back in a liquid sprawl and with a long sigh.

Curious, she sat up in bed and looked at him, surprised at how much she enjoyed the sight of him like
that. He might have been a warm statue for all the movement in him, but he was a delight even to her innocent
eyes. She smiled secretively as she studied him un-
ashamedly, thinking that for tonight he belonged to her,
even if he didn't want to. After all, she hadn't coaxed
him in here. He'd come of his own free will. He had

to feel something for her, if he'd had to go out and get himself drunk to express what he really wanted.

While she looked at him she weighed her options. She could leave him here and shoo him out first thing in the morning—unless, of course, he awoke in the same condition he'd just been in except sober. In which case, her innocence was really going to be gone. Or she could try to get him back to his room. That would be impossible. He was deadweight. She could call the brothers to help her—but that would create a scandal.

In the end, she curled up beside him, pulled the sheet over both of them and went to sleep in his arms. Let tomorrow take care of itself, she mused while she enjoyed the feel of all that latent strength so close against her nudity. She loved him. If this was all she could ever have, she was going to have this one night. Even if he never knew about it.

CAG FELT LITTLE HAMMERS at either side of his head. He couldn't seem to open his eyes to discover what was the sound that had disturbed him. He remembered drinking a glass of bourbon whiskey. Several glasses. He remembered taking a shower and falling into bed. He remembered....

His eyes flew open and he sat straight up. But instead of looking at the bare back beside him, covered just decently by a sheet, he scanned his own nudity to the door, where Rey and Leo were standing frozen in place.

He jerked the sheet over his hips, held his throbbing head and said, predictably, "How did I get in here?"

"You bounder," Leo murmured, so delighted by his brother's predicament that he had to bite his tongue to keep from smiling. Finally he'd got Cag just where he wanted him!

"That goes double for me," Rey said, acting disgusted as he glanced toward Tess's prone figure barely covered by the sheet. "And she works for us!"

"Not anymore," Leo said with pure confidence as he folded his arms over his chest. "Guess who's getting married?" He raised his voice, despite Cag's outraged look. "Tess? Tess! Wake up!"

She forced her eyes open, glanced at Cag and froze. As she pulled up the sheet to her chin, she turned and saw the brothers standing poker-faced in the doorway.

Then she did what any sane woman might do under the circumstances. She screamed.

## CHAPTER TEN

AN AWKWARD FEW minutes later, a cold sober and pole-axed Cag jerked into his robe and Tess retreated under the sheet until he left. He never looked at her, or spoke. She huddled into the sheet and wished she could disappear.

She felt terrible. Even though it wasn't her fault, any of it. She hadn't gone and climbed into bed with him, after all, and she certainly hadn't invited him into bed with her! When she'd dozed off, she'd been almost convinced that the whole episode had been a dream. Now it was more like a nightmare.

TESS WENT INTO the kitchen to make the breakfast that the brothers had found missing at its usual time. That was why they'd come looking for her, and how they knew Cag was in bed with her. She groaned as she realized what she was going to have to endure around the table. She decided beforehand that she'd eat her breakfast after they finished and keep busy in another part of the house until they were gone.

The meal was on the table when three subdued men walked into the kitchen and sat down. Tess couldn't look at any of them. She mumbled something about dusting the living room and escaped.

Not ten minutes later, Leo came looking for her.

She was cleaning a window that she'd done twice already. She couldn't meet his eyes.

"Was everything okay? I'm sorry if the bacon was a little overdone...."

"Nobody's blaming you for anything," he said, interrupting her quietly. "And Cag's going to do the right thing."

She turned, red-faced. "But he didn't do anything, Leo," she said huskily. "He was drunk and he got into the wrong bed, that's all. Nothing, absolutely nothing, went on!"

He held up a hand. "Cag doesn't know that nothing went on," he said, lowering his voice. "And you aren't going to tell him. Listen to me," he emphasized when she tried to interrupt, "you're the only thing that's going to save him from drying into dust and blowing away, Tess. He's alone and he's going to stay that way. He'll never get married voluntarily. This is the only way it will ever happen, and you know it."

She lifted her head proudly. "I won't trick him into marriage," she said curtly.

"I'm not asking you to. *We'll* trick him into it. You just go along."

"I won't," she said stubbornly. "He shouldn't have to marry me for something he didn't do!"

"Well, he remembers some of it. And he's afraid of what he can't remember, so he's willing to get married."

She was still staring at him with her eyes unblinking. "I love him!" she said miserably. "How can I ever expect him to forgive me if I let him marry me when he doesn't want to!"

"He does want to. At least, he wants to right now. Rey's gone for the license, you both go to the doctor in thirty minutes for a blood test and you get married Friday in the probate judge's office." He put a gentle hand on her shoulder. "Tess, if you love him, you have to save him from himself. He cares about you. It's so obvious to us that it's blatant. But he won't do anything about it. This is the only way he has a chance at happiness, and we're not letting him throw it away on half-baked fears of failure. So I'm sorry, but you're sort of the fall guy here. It's a gamble. But I'd bet on it."

"What about when he remembers, if he does, and we're already married?" she asked plaintively.

"That's a bridge you can cross when you have to." He gave her a wicked grin. "Besides, you need an insurance policy against anything that might…happen."

"Nothing's going to happen!" she growled, her fists clenched at her side.

"That's what you think," he murmured under his breath, smiling—but only after he'd closed the door between them. He rubbed his hands together with gleeful satisfaction and went to find his sibling.

It was like lightning striking. Everything happened too fast for Tess's protests to make any difference. She wanted to tell Cag the truth, because she hadn't been drunk and she remembered what had gone on. But somehow she couldn't get him to herself for five minutes in the three days that followed. Before she knew what was happening, she and Cag were in the probate judge's office with Corrigan and Dorie, Simon and Tira, Leo and Rey behind them, cheering them on.

Tess was wearing a white off-the-shoulder cotton dress with a sprig of lily of the valley in her hair in lieu of a veil, and carrying a small nosegay of flowers.

They were pronounced man and wife and Cag leaned down to kiss her—on the cheek, perfunctorily, even reluctantly. He looked more like a man facing an incurable illness than a happy bridegroom, and Tess felt more guilty by the minute.

They all went to a restaurant to have lunch, which Tess didn't taste. Afterward, Leo and Rey went on a hastily arranged business trip to California while Corrigan and Simon and their respective wives went to their own homes.

Cag put Tess into the Mercedes, which he drove for special occasions, and took her back to the ranch.

She wanted to tell him the truth, but the look on his face didn't invite confidences, and she was certain that it would only make things worse and get his brothers into big trouble if she confessed now.

She knew that nothing had happened that night, but if she slept with Cag, he was going to know it, too. Besides, sleeping with him would eliminate any ideas of an annulment. She'd been thinking about that all day, that she could give him his freedom before any more damage was done. She had to talk to him before tonight, before their wedding night.

It was almost time to put on dinner and she'd just started changing out of her wedding dress when the door opened and Cag came in, closing the door deliberately behind him.

In nothing but a bra and half-slip, she turned, brush in hand, to stare at him as if he were an apparition. He was wearing his jeans and nothing else. His broad chest was bare and there was a look in his black eyes that she didn't like.

"Cag, I have to tell you...."

Before she could get the rest of the sentence out, he had her up in his arms and he was kissing her. It wasn't like other kisses they'd shared, which had an affectionate, teasing quality to them even in passion. These were rough, insistent, arousing kisses that were a prelude to out-and-out seduction.

Tess didn't have the experience to save herself. A few feverish minutes later, she was twisting under him on the cover of the bed trying to help him get rid of the last little bit of fabric that concealed her from his eyes.

He was out of his jeans by then, and his mouth was all over her yielding body. He touched and tasted her in ways she'd never experienced, until she was writhing with hunger.

By the time he slid between her legs and began to possess her, she was so eager that the tiny flash of pain went almost unnoticed.

But not by Cag. He stopped at once when he felt the barrier give and lifted his head. His arms trembled slightly with the effort as he arched over her and put a rein on his desire long enough to search her wide, dazed eyes.

"I tried...to tell you," she stammered shakily when she realized why he was hesitating.

"If I could stop, I swear to God... I would!" he said in a hoarse, harsh whisper. He shuddered and bent to her mouth. "But it's too late! I'd rather die than stop!"

He kissed her hungrily as his body eased down and found a slow, sweet rhythm that brought gasps from the mouth he was invading. He felt her nails biting into his hips, pulling him, pleading, her whole body one long aching plea for satisfaction. She sobbed into his mouth as he gave her what she wanted in waves of sweet, hot ecstasy that built into a frightening crescendo just at the last.

She cried out and felt him shiver above her with the same exquisite delight she was feeling. Seconds later, he collapsed in her arms and she took the weight of him with joy, clinging as he fought to get his breath. His heartbeat shook both of them in the damp, lazy aftermath.

She felt his breath at her ear, jerky and hot. "Did I hurt you?" he asked.

"No. Oh, no," she breathed, burrowing closer.

Her body moved just slightly and his own clenched. It had been years. He'd ached for Tess, for the fulfillment she'd just given him. It was too soon, and he wasn't going to get over this subterfuge that had made him her husband, but just now his mind wasn't the part of his body that was in control.

He moved experimentally and heard her breath catch even as sharp pleasure rippled up his spine. No, he thought as he pulled her under him again, it wasn't too soon. It wasn't too soon at all!

It was dark when he got out of bed and pulled his jeans back on. Tess was lying in a damp, limp, spent sprawl on the cover where he'd left her. She looked up at him with dazed blue eyes, her face rosy in the aftermath of passion, her body faintly marked where his hands and his mouth had explored her. She was his. She belonged to him. His head lifted with unconscious, arrogant pride of possession.

"How was it?" he asked.

She couldn't believe he'd said anything so blatant to her after the lovemaking that had been nothing short of a revelation. She hadn't dreamed that her body was capable of such sensations as she'd been feeling. And he asked her that question with the same interest he'd have shown about a weather report.

She stared at him, confused.

"Was it worth a sham wedding?" he continued, wounded by her silence that had made him feel obliged to go through with a wedding he didn't want. She'd trapped him and he felt like a fool, no matter how sweet the bait had been.

She drew the cover back over her nudity, ashamed because of the way he was looking at her. He made her feel as if she'd done something terrible.

"You knew nothing happened that night," he continued quietly. "I didn't. I was too drunk to care what I did, but I remembered all too well that I lost my head the minute I touched you. For all I knew, I might have gone through with it. But you knew better, and you let me marry you in spite of it, knowing it wasn't necessary."

She clutched the coverlet. "I tried to tell you, but I couldn't seem to get you alone for five minutes," she murmured defeatedly.

"Of course you couldn't," he returned. His voice was as cold as his eyes. "I wasn't going to make matters worse by seducing you a second time."

"I thought it was your brothers…."

She didn't finish, but her face gave the game away. His eyes positively glittered. "My brothers? Of course. My brothers!" He glared down at her. "They were in on it, too, weren't they? No wonder they did their best to make me feel like a heel! Did you convince them to go along with the lie?"

She wanted to tell him that it had been Leo's idea in the first place, but what good would it do now? He was making it clear that he'd married her against his will and blamed her for making it necessary. Nothing she could say would be much of a defense.

Her silence only made him madder. He turned toward the door.

"Where…are you going? Do you want supper?"

He looked at her over one broad, bare shoulder. "I've had all I want. Of everything."

He went through the doorway and slammed the door behind him.

Tess dissolved into tears of misery. Well, she was married, but at what cost? If Cag had ever been close to loving her, he wasn't anymore. He hated her; she'd seen it in his eyes. She'd trapped him and he hated her.

She got up, feeling unusually stiff and sore in odd places, and went to take a shower. The sooner she could get back to normal, or nearly normal, the better.

She bathed and dressed in a neat flowered shirtwaist dress, combed her freshly washed and dried curly hair and went to the kitchen to make supper. But even as she went into the room, she heard one of the ranch trucks crank up and roar away in a fury.

Curious, she searched the house for Cag, even braving his own bedroom. His closet was still open and she caught a whiff of aftershave. She leaned against the doorjamb with a long sigh. So he'd run out, on their wedding night. Well, what did she expect, that he'd stay home and play the part of the loving husband? Fat chance, after the things he'd said.

She fixed herself a sandwich with some cold roast beef and drank a glass of milk. Then she waited for Cag to come home.

When he hadn't come back by midnight, she went

to her room and crawled into bed. She was certain that she lay awake for an hour, but she never heard him come in. She slept alone and miserable, still tingling with the memories of the past few hours. If only he'd loved her, just a little, she might have had hope. She had none, now.

By morning, she knew what she had to do. She went looking for Cag, to tell him she was leaving. She had the promise of her mother's legacy and a small savings account, plus last week's salary that she hadn't spent. She could afford a bus ticket and a cheap apartment somewhere, anywhere, out of Jacobsville.

It might have been just as well that Cag still hadn't come home. His room was empty, his bed hadn't been slept in. The brothers were still out of town and Mrs. Lewis wasn't coming again until the next week. Nobody would be here to say goodbye to her. But what did it matter? Cag had made his disgust and contempt very clear indeed. He wouldn't care if she left. She could get the divorce herself and have the papers sent to him. He didn't love her, so what reason was there to stay here and eat her heart out over a man who didn't want her?

She blushed a little as her mind provided vivid proof that it wasn't a case of his not wanting her physically. He'd been insatiable, inexhaustible. Perhaps that was why he left. Perhaps he was ashamed of how hungry he'd been for her, of letting her see that hunger. Her own inexperience had been her worst drawback, because she had no real knowledge of how men behaved after they'd soothed an ache. She didn't think a man in love would insult his new bride and leave her alone all night. Apparently he was still furious with her and in no mood to forgive what he saw as a betrayal of the worst kind.

Well, he needn't expect her to be sitting at home mourning his loss! She'd had enough of being alternately scorned, rejected and passionately kissed. He could find another object for his desires, like the non-cooking Miss Brewster! And she wished the woman joy of him. Such a narrow-minded, hard-nosed man deserved a woman who'd lead him around by the ear!

TESS PACKED, TOOK a long last look around the first real home she'd ever known and called a cab. She thought about leaving a note. But, after all, Cag hadn't left her one when he'd stayed out all night. He must have known that she'd be worried, but he hadn't cared about her feelings. Why should she care about his? Now it was her turn. But she was staying out much longer than a night.

She took the cab to the airport and walked into the terminal, staying only until the cab pulled away. She hailed another cab, climbed in and went to the bus station, just in case Cag tried to trace her. She wasn't going to make it easy for him! She bought a ticket for St. Louis and sat down to wait for the bus.

A plane ticket would have been nice, but she couldn't afford the luxury. She had to conserve her small store of cash. It would be enough to keep her for at least a week or two. After that, she could worry about getting enough to eat. But if she ran out of luck, there was always the shelter. Every city had one, full of compassionate people willing to help the down and out. If I ever get rich, she thought, I'll donate like crazy to keep those shelters open!

She *was* rich, she remembered suddenly, and bit her lip as she realized that she hadn't left the lawyer a forwarding address. She went to the nearest phone and, taking his card from her wallet, phoned and told his secretary that she was going out of town and would be in touch in a week or so. That business accomplished, she sat back down on one of the long benches and waited for the bus to arrive.

ST. LOUIS WAS HUGE. Tess noticed barges going down the wide Mississippi and thought how much fun it would be to live in a river town. She'd lived inland all her life, it seemed.

She found a small efficiency apartment and paid a week's rent in advance. Then she bought a newspaper and got a sandwich from a nearby deli and went back to her room to read and eat.

There weren't a lot of jobs available. She could wait, of course, and hope for something she could do that paid a nice salary. But her skills were limited, and cooking was her best one. It seemed like kindly providence that there was a cooking job available at a local restaurant; and it was nearby!

She went the very next morning just after daylight to apply. The woman who interviewed her was dubious when Tess told her how old she was, but Tess promised she could do the job, which turned out to be that of a pastry chef.

The woman, still skeptical but desperate to fill the position, gave Tess a probationary job. Delighted, she got into the apron and cap and got started.

By the end of the day, her employer was quite impressed and Tess was hired unconditionally.

She went back to her apartment tired but satisfied that things had worked out for her so quickly. She spared a thought for Cag. If he'd come home, he probably wondered where she was. She didn't dare expand on that theme or she'd be in tears.

Running away had seemed the answer to all her problems yesterday, but it wasn't so cut-and-dried today. She was in a strange city where she had no family or friends, in a lonely apartment, and all she had to show for it was a job. She thought of the brothers waiting patiently for their breakfast and nobody there to fix it. She thought of Cag and how happy she'd felt that night she'd taken him the special dessert in his study. Things had been magical and for those few minutes, they'd belonged together. But how soon it had all fallen apart, through no real fault of her own.

"I should have stayed," she said, thinking aloud. "I should have made him listen."

But she hadn't. Now she had to live with the consequences. She hoped they wouldn't be too bad.

CALLAGHAN DRAGGED BACK into the house a day and a half after he'd left it with his misery so visible that it shocked his brothers, who'd come back from their business trip to an ominously empty house.

They surged forward when he walked through the door.

"Well?" Leo prompted impatiently, looking past Cag to the door. "Where is she?"

Cag's tired mind took a minute to work that question out. "Where is she? What do you mean, where is she? She isn't here?" he exploded.

Rey and Leo exchanged worried glances as Cag pushed past them and rushed to Tess's room. It was empty. Her suitcase was gone, her clothes were gone, her shoes were gone. He looked over her dresser and on the bed, but there was no note. She hadn't left a trace. Cag's heart turned over twice as he realized what she'd done. She'd run away. She'd left him.

His big fists clenched by his sides. His first thought was that he was glad she'd gone; his life could get back to normal. But his second thought was that he felt as if half his body were missing. He was empty inside. Cold. Alone, as he'd never been.

He heard his brothers come up behind him.

"Her things are gone," he said without any expression in his voice.

"No note?" Leo asked.

Cag shook his head.

"Surely she left a note," Rey murmured. "I'll check the office."

He went back down the hall. Leo leaned against the wall and stared unblinking at his big brother.

"Gave her hell, did you?" he asked pointedly.

Cag didn't look at him. His eyes were on the open closet door. "She lied. She tricked me into marriage." He turned his black eyes on Leo. "You helped her do it."

"Helped her? It was my idea," he said quietly. "You'd never have married her if it was left up to you. You'd have gone through life getting older and more alone, and Tess would have suffered for it. She loved you enough to risk it. I'd hoped you loved her enough to forgive it. Apparently I was wrong right down the line. I'm sorry. I never meant to cause this."

Cag was staring at him. "It was your idea, not hers?"

Leo shrugged. "She didn't want any part of it. She said if you didn't want to marry her, she wasn't going to do anything that would force you to. I talked her into keeping quiet and then Rey and I made sure you didn't have much time to talk to each other before the wedding." His eyes narrowed. "All of us care about you, God knows why, you're the blooming idiot of the family. A girl like that, a sweet, kind girl with no guile about her, wants to love you and you kick her out the door." He shook his head sadly. "I guess you and Herman belong together, like a pair of reptiles. I hope you'll be very happy."

He turned and went back down the hall to find Rey.

Cag wiped his forehead with his sleeve and stared blindly into space. Tess was self-sufficient, but she was young. And on top of all his other mistakes, he'd made one that caused the others to look like minor fumbles. He hadn't used anything during that long, sweet loving. Tess could be pregnant, and he didn't know where she was.

## CHAPTER ELEVEN

TESS WAS ENJOYING her job. The owner gave her carte blanche to be creative, and she used it. Despite the aching hurt that Cag had dealt her, she took pride in her craft. She did a good job, didn't watch the clock and performed beautifully under pressure. By the end of the second week, they were already discussing giving her a raise.

She liked her success, but she wondered if Cag had worried about her. He was protective toward her, whatever his other feelings, and she was sorry she'd made things difficult for him. She really should call that lawyer and find out about her stock, so that she wouldn't have to depend on her job for all her necessities. And she could ask him to phone the brothers and tell them that she was okay. He'd never know where she was because she wasn't going to tell him.

SHE DID TELEPHONE Clint Matherson, the lawyer, who was relieved to hear from her because he had, indeed, checked out those stocks her mother had left her.

"I don't know quite how to tell you this," he said heavily. "Your mother invested in a very dubious new company, which had poor management and little operating capital from the very start. The owner was apparently a friend of hers. To get to the point, the stock is worthless. Absolutely worthless. The company has just recently gone into receivership."

Tess let out a long breath and smiled wistfully. "Well, it was nice while it lasted, to think that she did remember me, that I was independently wealthy," she told the lawyer. "But I didn't count on it, if you see what I mean. I have a job as a pastry chef in a restaurant, and I'm doing very well. If you, uh, speak to the Hart brothers…"

"*Speak* to them!" he exclaimed. "How I'd love to have the chance! Callaghan Hart had me on the carpet for thirty minutes in my own office, and I never got one word out. He left his phone number, reminded me that his brother was acting attorney general of our state and left here certain that I'd call him if I had any news of you."

Her heart leaped into her throat. Callaghan was looking for her? She'd wondered if he cared enough. It could be hurt pride, that she'd walked out on him. It could be a lot of things, none of which concerned missing her because he loved her.

"Did you tell him about the stock?" she asked.

"As I said, Miss Brady, I never got the opportunity to speak."

"I see." She saw a lot, including the fact that the attorney didn't know she was married. Her spirits fell. If Callaghan hadn't even mentioned it, it must not matter to him. "Well, you can tell them that I'm okay. But I'm not telling you where I am, Mr. Matherson. So Callaghan can make a good guess."

"There are still papers to be signed…" he began.

"Then I'll find a way to let you send them to me, through someone else," she said, thinking up ways and means of concealing her whereabouts. "Thanks, Mr. Matherson. I'll get back to you."

She hung up, secure in her anonymity. It was a big country. He'd never find her.

Even as she was thinking those comforting thoughts, Clint Matherson was reading her telephone number, which he'd received automatically on his Caller ID box and copied down while they were speaking. He thought what a good thing it was that Miss Brady didn't know how to disable that function, if she even suspected that he had it. He didn't smirk, because intelligent, successful attorneys didn't do that. But he smiled.

CALLAGHAN HADN'T SMILED for weeks. Leo and Rey walked wide around him, too, because he looked ready to deck anybody who set him off. The brothers had asked, just once, if Cag knew why Tess had left so abruptly and without leaving a note. They didn't dare ask again.

Even Mrs. Lewis was nervous. She was standing in for Tess as part-time cook as well as doing the heavy housework, but she was in awe of Callaghan in his black mood. She wasn't sure which scared her more, Cag or his scaly pet, she told Leo when Cag was out working on the ranch.

Always a hard worker, Cag had set new records for it since Tess's disappearance. He'd hired one private detective agency after another, with no results to date. A cabdriver with one of Jacobsville's two cab companies had been found who remembered taking her to the airport. But if she'd flown out of town, she'd done it under an assumed name and paid cash. It was impossible to find a clerk who remembered selling her a ticket.

Jacobsville had been thoroughly searched, too, but she wasn't here, or in nearby Victoria.

Callaghan could hardly tell his brothers the real reason that Tess had gone. His pride wouldn't let him. But he was bitterly sorry for the things he'd said to her, for the callous way he'd treated her. It had been a last-ditch stand to keep from giving in to the love and need that ate at him night and day. He wanted her more than he wanted his own life. He was willing to do anything to make amends. But Tess was gone and he couldn't find her. Some nights he thought he might go mad from the memories alone. She loved him, and he could treat her in such a way. It didn't bear thinking about. So he'd been maneuvered into marriage, so what? He loved her! Did it matter why they were married, if they could make it work?

But weeks passed with no word of her, and he had nightmares about the possibilities. She could have been kidnapped, murdered, raped, starving. Then he remembered her mother's legacy. She'd have that because surely she'd been in touch with…the lawyer! He could have kicked himself for not thinking of it sooner, but he'd been too upset to think straight.

Cag went to Matherson's office and made threats that would have taken the skin off a lesser man. She'd have to contact Matherson to get her inheritance. And when she did, he'd have her!

Sure enough, a few days after his visit there, the attorney phoned him.

He'd just come in from the stock pens, dirty and tired and worn to a nub.

"Hart," he said curtly as he answered the phone in his office.

"Matherson," came the reply. "I thought you might like to know that Miss Brady phoned me today."

Cag stood up, breathless, stiff with relief. "Yes? Where is she?"

"Well, I have Caller ID, so I got her number from the unit on my desk. But when I had the number checked out, it was a pay phone."

"Where?"

"In St. Louis, Missouri," came the reply. "And there's one other bit of helpful news. She's working as a pastry chef in a restaurant."

"I'll never forget you for this," Cag said with genuine gratitude. "And if you're ever in need of work, come see me. Good day, Mr. Matherson."

Cag picked up the phone and called the last detective agency he'd hired. By the end of the day, they had the name of the restaurant and the address of Tess's apartment.

Unwilling to wait for a flight out, Cag had a company Learjet pick him up at the Jacobsville airport and fly him straight to St. Louis.

It was the dinner hour by the time Cag checked into a hotel and changed into a nice suit. He had dinner at the restaurant where Tess worked and ordered biscuits.

The waiter gave him an odd look, but Cag refused to be swayed by offers of delicate pastries. The waiter gave in, shrugged and took the order.

"With apple butter," Cag added politely. He had experience enough of good restaurants to know that money could buy breakfast at odd hours if a wealthy customer wanted it and was willing to pay for the extra trouble.

The waiter relayed the order to Tess, who went pale and had to hold on to the counter for support.

"Describe the customer to me," she asked curtly.

The waiter, surprised, obliged her and saw the pale face go quite red with temper.

"He found me, did he? And now he thinks I'll cook him biscuits at this hour of the night!"

The assistant manager, hearing Tess's raised voice, came quickly over to hush her.

"The customer at table six wants biscuits and apple butter," the waiter said with resignation. "Miss Brady is unsettled."

"Table six?" The assistant manager frowned. "Yes, I saw him. He's dressed very expensively. If the man wants biscuits, bake him biscuits," he told Tess. "If he's influential, he could bring in more business."

Tess took off her chef's hat and put it on the counter. "Thank you for giving me the opportunity to work here, but I have to leave now. I make biscuits for breakfast. I don't make them for supper."

She turned and walked out the back door, to the astonishment of the staff.

The waiter was forced to relay the information to Cag, whose eyes twinkled.

"Well, in that case, I'll have to go and find her," he said, rising. "Nobody makes biscuits like Tess."

He left the man there, gaping, and went back to his hired car. With luck, he could beat Tess to her apartment.

And he did, with only seconds to spare as she got off the downtown bus and walked up the steps to her second-floor apartment.

Cag was standing there, leaning against the door. He

looked worn and very tired, but his eyes weren't hostile at all. They were…strange.

He studied her closely, not missing the new lines in her face and the thinner contours of her body.

"You aren't cut out for restaurant work," he said quietly.

"Well, I'm not doing it anymore, thanks to you. I just quit!" she said belligerently, but her heart was racing madly at the sight of him. She'd missed him so badly that her eyes ached to look at him. But he'd hurt her. The wound was still fresh, and the sight of him rubbed salt in it. "Why are you here?" she continued curtly. "You said you'd had enough of me, didn't you?" she added, referring to what he'd said that hurt most.

He actually winced. "I said a lot of stupid things," he replied slowly. "I won't expect you to overlook them, and I'll apologize for every one, if you'll give me a chance to."

She seemed to droop. "Oh, what's the point, Callaghan?" she asked wearily. "I left. You've got what you wanted all along, a house without me in it. Why don't you go home?"

He sighed. He'd known it wouldn't be easy. He leaned his forearm against the wall and momentarily rested his head there while he tried to think of a single reason that would get Tess back on the ranch.

"Mrs. Lewis can't make biscuits," he said. He glanced at her. "We're all starving to death on what passes for her cooking. The roses are dying," he added, playing every card he had.

"It's been so dry," she murmured. Blue eyes met his. "Haven't you watered them?"

He made a rough sound. "I don't know anything about roses."

"But they'll die," she said, sounding plaintive. "Two of them are old roses. Antiques. They're precious, and not because of the cost."

*"Well,"* he drawled, "if you want to save them, you better come home."

"Not with you there!" she said haughtily.

He smiled with pure self-condemnation. "I was afraid you'd feel that way."

"I don't want to come back."

"Too rich to bother with work that's beneath your new station?" he asked sarcastically, because he was losing and he couldn't bear to.

She grimaced. "Well, there isn't going to be any money, actually," she said. "The stocks are worthless. My mother made a bad investment and lost a million dollars." She laughed but it sounded hollow. "I'll always have to work for my living. But, then, I always expected to. I never really thought she'd leave anything to me. She hated me."

"Maybe she hated herself for having deserted you, did you think of that?" he asked gently. "She couldn't love you without having to face what she'd done, and live with it. Some people would rather be alone, than admit fault."

"Maybe," she said. "But what difference does it make now? She's dead. I'll never know what she felt."

"Would you like to know what I feel?" he asked in a different tone.

She searched his eyes coolly. "I already know. I'm much too young for you. Besides, I'm a weakness that you can't tolerate. And I lie," she added shortly. "You said so."

He stuck his hands deep into his pockets and stared at her with regret. "Leo told me the wedding was all his idea."

"Of course you'd believe your brother. You just wouldn't believe me."

His chest rose and fell. "Yes, that's how it was," he admitted, not bothering to lie about it. "I made you run away. Then I couldn't find you." His black eyes glittered. "You'll never know how that felt."

"Sure I know," she returned grimly. "It felt just the same as when you walked out the door and didn't come back all night!"

He leaned against the wall wearily. He'd avoided the subject, walked around it, worried it to death. Now here it was. He lifted his gaze to her face. "I wanted you too badly to come home," he said. "I couldn't have kept my hands off you. So I spent the night in the bunkhouse."

"Gee, thanks for saving me," she muttered.

He stood erect with one of those lightning moves that once had intimidated her. "I should have come home and ravished you!" he said shortly. "At least you'd still be there now. You'd have been too weak to walk when I got through with you!"

She caught her breath. "Well!"

He moved forward and took her by the shoulders. He shook her gently. "Listen, redhead, I love you!" he said through his teeth, and never had a man looked less loverlike. "I want you, I need you and you're going home with me or I'll…"

Her breath was suspended somewhere south of her collarbone. "Or you'll what?" she asked.

He eased her back against the door and bent to her mouth. "Or you'll get what you escaped when I left you that night."

She lifted her mouth to his, relaxing under his weight as he pinned her there and kissed her so hungrily that she moaned. She clung to him. The past weeks had been so empty, so lonely. Cag was here, in her arms, saying that he loved her, and it wasn't a dream!

After a few feverish seconds, he forced himself to lift away from her.

"Let's go inside," he said in a tortured voice.

She only nodded. She fumbled her key into the lock and apparently he closed and locked it behind them. He didn't even turn on a light. He picked her up, purse and all, and carried her straight into the bedroom.

"Amazing how you found this room so easily when you've never been in here before," she whispered shakily as he laid her on the bed and began to remove everything that was in the way of his hands.

"Nesting instinct," he whispered, his hands urgent.

"Is that what it is?" She reached up, pushing at his jacket.

"First things first," he murmured, resisting her hands. When he had her out of her clothes, he started on his own.

Minutes later, he was beside her in the bed, but he did nothing about it, except to pull her completely against him and wrap her up under the covers.

"Oh, dear God," he groaned reverently as he held her close. "Tess, I was so afraid that I'd lost you! I couldn't have borne it."

She melted into him, aware of the stark arousal of his body. But he wasn't doing anything about it.

"I don't like being alone," she replied, nuzzling her face against his warm, bare chest.

"You won't be, ever again." His hands smoothed over her back. One eased between them to lie gently against her stomach. "How are you feeling?" he asked suddenly.

She knew what he was asking. "I don't think I'm pregnant." She answered the question he hadn't put into words. "I'm tired a lot, but that could be work stress."

"But you could be."

She smiled against him. If this was a dream, she hoped she didn't wake up too soon. "I guess so." She sighed. "Why? Nesting instinct?"

He chuckled. "Yes. I'm thirty-eight. I'd love kids. So would you. You could grow them along with your precious roses."

She stiffened. "My roses! Oh, Cag…!"

His intake of breath was audible. "That's the first time you've ever shortened my name."

"You didn't belong to me before," she said shyly.

His arms tightened. "And now I do?"

She hesitated. "I hope so."

"I know so. And you belong to me." He moved so that she was on her back. "I've been rough with you. Even the first time. Tonight, it's going to be so slow and silky sweet that you won't know your name by the time I've satisfied you." He bent and touched his mouth with exquisite tenderness to her parted lips.

"How conceited," she teased daringly.

He chuckled with a worldliness she couldn't match. "And we'll see about that…."

It was unexpectedly tender this time, a feast of exquisite touches and rhythms that progressed far too slowly for the heat he roused in her slim young body.

She arched toward him and he retreated. He touched her and just as she trembled on the brink of ecstasy, he stopped touching her and calmed her. Then he started again.

On and on it went, so that time seemed to hang, suspended, around them. He taught her how to touch him, how to build the need and then deny it. She moaned with frustration, and he chuckled with pure joy.

When he heard her sob under the insistent pressure of his mouth, he gave in to the hunger. But even then, he resisted her clinging hands, her whispered pleadings.

"Make it last," he whispered at her open mouth, lazily moving against her. "Make it last as long as you can. When it happens, you'll understand why I won't let you be impatient."

She was shuddering already, throbbing. She met the downward motion of his hips with upward movements of her own, her body one long plea for satisfaction.

"It's so…good," she whispered, her words pulsing with the rhythm of his body, the same throb in her voice that was in her limbs. "So good…!"

"It gets better," he breathed. He moved sinuously against her, a new movement that was so arousing that she cried out and clung to him with bruising fingers. "There?" he whispered. "Yes. There. And here…."

She was sobbing audibly. Her whole body ached. It was expanding, tense, fearsome, frightening. She was never going to live through it. She was blind, deaf, dumb, so much a part of him that she breathed only through him.

He felt her frantic motions, heard the shuddering desire in her voice as she begged him not to stop. He obliged her with smooth, quick, deep motions that were like stabs of pure pleasure. She closed her eyes and her teeth ground together as the tension suddenly built to unbearable heights and she arched up to him with her last ounce of strength.

"Yes. Now. Now, finally, now!" he said tightly.

There was no time. She went over some intangible edge and fell, throbbing with pleasure, burning with it, so oblivious to her surroundings that she had no idea where she was. She felt the urge deep in her body, growing, swelling, exploding. At some level she was aware of a harsh groan from the man above her, of the fierce convulsion of his body that mirrored what was happening to hers.

She lost consciousness for a few precious seconds of unbearable pleasure, and then sobbed fiercely as she lost it even as it began.

He held her, comforted her. His mouth touched her eyes, her cheeks, her open mouth. Her body was still locked closely into his, and when she was able to open her eyes, she saw his pupils dilated, glittering with the remnants of passion.

"Do you know that I love you, after that," he whispered unsteadily, "or would you like to hear it a few dozen more times?"

She managed to shake her head. "I…felt it," she whispered back, and blushed as she realized just how close they were. "I love you, too. But you knew that already."

"Yes," he replied tenderly, brushing back her damp, curly hair. "I knew it the first time you let me touch you." He smiled softly at her surprise. "You were so very innocent, Tess. Not at all the sort of girl who'd permit liberties like that to just any man. It had to be love for you."

"It wasn't for you," she said quietly. "Not at first."

"Oh, yes, it was," he denied. His fingers lingered near her ear. "I started fighting you the day you walked into the kitchen. I wanted you so badly that I ached every time I looked at you." He smiled ruefully. "I was so afraid that you'd realize it."

"Why didn't you say so?" she asked.

His fingers contracted. "Because of the bad experience I had with a younger woman who threw me over because she thought I was too old for her." His shoulders moved. "You were even younger than she was at the time." His eyes were dark, concerned. "I was in over my head almost at once, and I thought I'd never be enough for you…"

"Are you nuts?" she gasped. "Enough for me? You're too *much* for me, most of the time! I can't match you. Especially like this. I don't know anything!"

"You're learning fast," he mused, looking down their joined bodies in the light from the night-light. "And you love like a poem," he whispered. "I love the way you feel in my arms like this. You make me feel like the best lover in the world."

"You are," she said shyly.

"Oh, no," he argued. "It's only because you don't have anyone to compare me with."

"It wouldn't matter," she said.

He touched her cheek gently. "I don't guess it would," he said then. "Because it's like the first time, every time I'm with you. I can't remember other women."

She hit him. "You'd better not!"

He grinned. "Love me?"

She pressed close. "Desperately."

"Try to get away again," he invited. "You're my wife. You'll never get past the first fence."

She traced a path on his shoulder and frowned. "I just thought of something. Where are your brothers?"

"Leo and Rey are in Denver."

"What are they doing in Denver?" she asked.

He sighed. "Getting away from me. I've been sort of hard to get along with."

"You don't say! And that's unusual?"

He pinched her lightly, making her squeal. "I'll be a model of courtesy starting the minute we get home. I promise."

Her arms curled around his neck. "When are we going home?"

He chuckled and moved closer, sensuous movements that began to have noticeable results. "Not right now...."

IT WAS TWO days later when they got back to the Hart ranch. And they still hadn't stopped smiling.

Tess had decided not to pursue her horticulture education just yet, because she couldn't leave Cag when she'd only just really found him. That could wait. So she had only one last tiny worry, about sleeping in the same room with an escaping Herman, although she loved Cag more than enough to tolerate his pet—in another bedroom.

But when she opened the door to Cag's room, which she would now share, the big aquarium was gone. She turned to Cag with a worried expression.

He put his arms around her and drew her close, glad that his brothers and Mrs. Lewis hadn't arrived just yet.

"Listen," he said softly, "remember that nesting instinct I told you I had?"

She nodded.

"Well, even the nicest birds don't keep a snake in the nest, where the babies are," he said, and his whole face smiled tenderly as he said it.

She caught her breath. "But you love him!"

"I love you more," he said simply. "I gave him to a friend of mine, who, coincidentally, has a female albino python. Speaking from experience, I can tell you that deep down any bachelor is far happier with a female of his own species than with any pet, no matter how cherished it is."

She touched his cheek lovingly. "Thank you."

He shrugged and smiled down at her. "I built the nest," he reminded her. "Now it's your turn."

"Want me to fill it, huh?"

He grinned.

She hugged him close and smiled against his broad chest. "I'll do my very best." Her heart felt full unto bursting. "Cag, I'm so happy."

"So am I, sweetheart." He bent and kissed her gently. "And now, there's just one more thing I need to make me the most contented man on earth."

She looked up at him expectantly, with a wicked gleam in her blue eyes. "Is there? What is it?" she asked suggestively.

"A pan of biscuits!" he burst out. "A great, big pan of biscuits! With apple butter!"

"You fraud! You charlatan! Luring me back here because of your stomach instead of your... Cag!"

He was laughing like a devil as he picked her up and tossed her gently onto the bed.

"I never said I wouldn't sing for my supper," he murmured dryly, and his hands went to his shirt buttons as he stood over her.

She felt breathless, joyful, absolutely gloriously loved. "In that case," she whispered, "you can have *two* pansful!"

BY THE TIME the brothers arrived that evening, Cag had already gone through half a panful. However, he seemed more interested in Tess than the food, anyway, so the brothers finally got their fill of biscuits after a long, dry spell.

"What are you two going to do when I build Tess a house like Dorie's got?" Cag asked them.

They looked horrified. Just horrified.

Rey put down his half-eaten biscuit and stared at Leo. "Doesn't that just beat all? Every time we find a good biscuit-maker, somebody goes and marries her and takes her away! First Corrigan, now him!"

"Well, they had good taste, you have to admit," Leo continued. "Besides, Tira can't bake at all, and Simon married her!"

"Simon isn't all that crazy about biscuits."

"Well, you do have a point there," Leo conceded.

Rey stared at Tess, who was sitting blatantly on her husband's lap feeding him a biscuit. He sighed. He'd been alone a long time, too.

"I'm not marrying anybody to get a biscuit," he said doggedly.

"Me, neither," Leo agreed, stuffing another one into his mouth. "Tell you what—" he pointed his apple butter spoon at Rey "—he can put up his house in the daytime and we'll take it down at night."

"You can try," Cag said good-naturedly.

"With our luck, we'll never find wives. Or if we do," Leo added dolefully, "they won't be able to cook at all."

"This is a great time to find a veteran housekeeper who can make bread," Cag stated. "Somebody who can take care of both of you when we move out."

"I can take care of myself," Rey muttered.

"So can I," Leo agreed.

"Be stubborn," Cag said. "But you'll change your tune one day."

"In a pig's eye!" they both said at once.

LATER, LYING IN Tess's soft arms, Cag remembered when he'd said the same things his brothers just had.

"They'll fall like kingpins one day," he told Tess as he smoothed her hair.

"If they're lucky," she agreed.

He looked down into her gentle eyes and he wasn't smiling. "If they're very lucky," he whispered. "Was I worth all the trouble, Tess?"

She nodded. "Was I?"

"You were never any trouble." He kissed her tenderly. "I'm sorry I gave you such a hard time."

"You're making up for it," she returned, pulling him down to her. "I'd rather have you than that million dollars, Cag," she breathed into his lips. "I'd rather have you than the whole world!"

If Cag hadn't been so busy following his newly acquired nesting instinct, he could have told her the same thing. But he was certain that she knew it already.

\* \* \* \* \*

# MATT

# CHAPTER ONE

THE MAN ON the hill sat on his horse with elegance and grace, and the young woman found herself staring at him. He was obviously overseeing the roundup, which the man at her side had brought her to view. This ranch was small by Texas standards, but around Jacobsville, it was big enough to put its owner in the top ten in size.

"Dusty, isn't it?" Ed Caldwell asked with a chuckle, oblivious to the distant mounted rider, who was behind him and out of his line of sight. "I'm glad I work for the corporation and not here. I like my air cool and unpolluted."

Leslie Murry smiled. She wasn't pretty. She had a plain, rather ordinary sort of face with blond hair that had a natural wave, and gray eyes. Her one good feature besides her slender figure was a pretty bow mouth. She had a quiet, almost reclusive demeanor these days. But she hadn't always been like that. In her early teens, Leslie had been flamboyant and outgoing, a live wire of a girl whose friends had laughed at her exploits. Now, at twenty-three, she was as sedate as a matron. The change in her was shocking to people who'd once known her. She knew Ed Caldwell from college in Houston. He'd graduated in her sophomore year, and she'd quit the following semester to go to work as a paralegal for his father's law firm in Houston. Things had gotten too

complicated there, and Ed had come to the rescue once
again. In fact, Ed was the reason she'd just been hired as
an executive assistant by the mammoth Caldwell firm.
His cousin owned it.

She'd never met Mather Gilbert Caldwell, or Matt as
he was known locally. People said he was a nice, easygoing man who loved an underdog. In fact, Ed said it
frequently himself. They were down here for roundup
so that Ed could introduce Leslie to the head of the corporation. But so far, all they'd seen was dust and cattle
and hardworking cowboys.

"Wait here," Ed said. "I'm going to ride over and find
Matt. Be right back." He urged his horse into a trot and
held on for dear life. Leslie had to bite her lip to conceal a smile at the way he rode. It was painfully obvious that he was much more at home behind the wheel
of a car. But she wouldn't have been so rude as to have
mentioned it, because Ed was the only friend she had
these days. He was, in fact, the only person around who
knew about her past.

While she was watching him, the man on horseback
on the hill behind them was watching her. She sat on a
horse with style, and she had a figure that would have
attracted a connoisseur of women—which the man on
horseback was. Impulsively he spurred his horse into
a gallop and came down the rise behind her. She didn't
hear him until he reined in and the harsh sound of the
horse snorting had her whirling in the saddle.

The man was wearing working clothes, like the other
cowboys, but all comparisons ended there. He wasn't
ragged or missing a tooth or unshaven. He was oddly
intimidating, even in the way he sat the horse, with

one hand on the reins and the other on his powerful denim-clad thigh.

Matt Caldwell met her gray eyes with his dark ones and noted that she wasn't the beauty he'd expected, despite her elegance of carriage and that perfect figure. "Ed brought you, I gather," he said curtly.

She'd almost guessed from his appearance that his voice would be deep and gravelly, but not that it would cut like a knife. Her hands tightened on the reins. "I… yes, he…he brought me."

The stammer was unexpected. Ed's usual sort of girl was brash and brassy, much more sophisticated than this shrinking violet here. He liked to show off Matt's ranch and impress the girls. Usually it didn't bother Matt, but he'd had a frustrating day and he was out of humor. He scowled. "Interested in cattle ranching, are you?" he drawled with ice dripping from every syllable. "We could always get you a rope and let you try your hand, if you'd like."

She felt as if every muscle in her body had gone taut. "I…came to meet Ed's cousin," she managed. "He's rich." The man's dark eyes flashed and she flushed. She couldn't believe she'd made such a remark to a stranger. "I mean," she corrected, "he owns the company where Ed works. Where I work," she added. She could have bitten her tongue for her artless mangling of a straightforward subject, but the man rattled her.

Something kindled in the man's dark eyes under the jutting brow; something not very nice at all. He leaned forward and his eyes narrowed. "Why are you really out here with Ed?" he asked.

She swallowed. He had her hypnotized, like a cobra

with a rabbit. Those eyes…those very dark, unyielding eyes…!

"It's not your business, is it?" she asked finally, furious at her lack of cohesive thought and this man's assumption that he had the right to interrogate her.

He didn't say a word. Instead, he just looked at her.

"Please," she bit off, hunching her shoulders uncomfortably. "You're making me nervous!"

"You came to meet the boss, didn't you?" he asked in a velvety smooth tone. "Didn't anyone tell you that he's no marshmallow?"

She swallowed. "They say he's a very nice, pleasant man," she returned a little belligerently. "Something I'll bet nobody in his right mind would dream of saying about you!" she added with her first burst of spirit in years.

His eyebrows lifted. "How do you know I'm not nice and pleasant?" he asked, chuckling suddenly.

"You're like a cobra," she said uneasily.

He studied her for a few seconds before he nudged his horse in the side with a huge dusty boot and eased so close to her that she actually shivered. He hadn't been impressed with the young woman who stammered and stuttered with nerves, but a spirited woman was a totally new proposition. He liked a woman who wasn't intimidated by his bad mood.

His hand went across her hip to catch the back of her saddle and he looked into her eyes from an unnervingly close distance. "If I'm a cobra, then what does that make you, cupcake?" he drawled with deliberate sensuality, so close that she caught the faint smoky scent of his breath, the hint of spicy cologne that clung to his lean, tanned face. "A soft, furry little bunny?"

She was so shaken by the proximity of him that she tried desperately to get away, pulling so hard on the reins that her mount unexpectedly reared and she went down on the ground, hard, hitting her injured left hip and her shoulder as she fell into the thick grass.

A shocked sound came from the man, who vaulted out of the saddle and was beside her as she tried to sit up. He reached for her a little roughly, shaken by her panic. Women didn't usually try to back away from him; especially ordinary ones like this. She fell far short of his usual companions.

She fought his hands, her eyes huge and overly bright, panic in the very air around her. "No…!" she cried out helplessly.

He froze in place, withdrawing his lean hand from her arm, and stared at her with scowling curiosity.

"Leslie!" came a shout from a few yards away. Ed bounced up as quickly as he could manage it without being unseated. He fumbled his way off the horse and knelt beside her, holding out his arm so that she could catch it and pull herself up.

"I'm sorry," she said, refusing to look at the man who was responsible for her tumble. "I jerked the reins. I didn't mean to."

"Are you all right?" Ed asked, concerned.

She nodded. "Sure." But she was shaking, and both men could see it.

Ed glanced over her head at the taller, darker, leaner man who stood with his horse's reins in his hand, staring at the girl.

"Uh, have you two introduced yourselves?" he asked awkwardly.

Matt was torn by conflicting emotions, the strongest

of which was bridled fury at the woman's panicky attitude. She acted as if he had plans to assault her, when he'd only been trying to help her up. He was angry and it cost him his temper. "The next time you bring a certifiable lunatic to my ranch, give me some advance warning," the tall man sniped at Ed. He moved as curtly as he spoke, swinging abruptly into the saddle to glare down at them. "You'd better take her home," he told Ed. "She's a damned walking liability around animals."

"But she rides very well, usually," Ed protested. "Okay, then," he added when the other man glowered at him. He forced a smile. "I'll see you later."

The tall man jerked his hat down over his eyes, wheeled the horse without another word and rode back up on the rise where he'd been sitting earlier.

"Whew!" Ed laughed, sweeping back his light brown hair uneasily. "I haven't seen him in a mood like that for years. I can't imagine what set him off. He's usually the soul of courtesy, especially when someone's hurt."

Leslie brushed off her jeans and looked up at her friend morosely. "He rode right up to me," she said unsteadily, "and leaned across me to talk with a hand on the saddle. I just…panicked. I'm sorry. I guess he's some sort of foreman here. I hope you don't get in trouble with your cousin because of it."

"That *was* my cousin, Leslie," he said heavily.

She stared at him vacantly. "That was Matt Caldwell?"

He nodded.

She let out a long breath. "Oh, boy. What a nice way to start a new job, by alienating the man at the head of the whole food chain."

"He doesn't know about you," he began.

Her eyes flashed. "And you're not to tell him," she returned firmly. "I mean it! I will not have my past paraded out again. I came down here to get away from reporters and movie producers, and that's what I'm going to do. I've had my hair cut, bought new clothes, gotten contact lenses. I've done everything I can think of so I won't be recognized. I'm not going to have it all dragged up again. It's been six years," she added miserably. "Why can't people just leave it alone?"

"The newsman was just following a lead," he said gently. "One of the men who attacked you was arrested for drunk driving and someone connected the name to your mother's case. His father is some high city official in Houston. It was inevitable that the press would dig up his son's involvement in your mother's case in an election year."

"Yes, I know, and that's what prompted the producer to think it would make a great TV movie of the week." She ground her teeth together. "That's just what we all need. And I thought it was all over. How silly of me," she said in a defeated tone. "I wish I were rich and famous," she added. "Then maybe I could buy myself some peace and privacy." She glanced up where the tall man sat silently watching the herding below. "I made some stupid remarks to your cousin, too, not knowing who he really was. I guess he'll be down in personnel first thing Monday to have me fired."

"Over my dead body," he said. "I may be only a lowly cousin, but I do own stock in the corporation. If he fires you, I'll fight for you."

"Would you really, for me?" she asked solemnly.

He ruffled her short blond hair. "You're my pal," he said. "I've had a pretty bad blow of my own. I don't want to get serious about anybody ever again. But I like having you around."

She smiled sadly. "I'm glad you can act that way about me. I can't really bear to be…" She swallowed. "I don't like men close to me, in any physical way. The therapist said I might be able to change that someday, with the right man. I don't know. It's been so long…"

"Don't sit and worry," he said. "Come on. I'll take you back to town and buy you a nice vanilla ice-cream cone. How's that?"

She smiled at him. "Thanks, Ed."

He shrugged. "Just another example of my sterling character." He glanced up toward the rise and away again. "He's just not himself today," he said. "Let's go."

Matt Caldwell watched his visitors bounce away on their respective horses with a resentment and fury he hadn't experienced in years. The little blond icicle had made him feel like a lecher. As if she could have appealed to him, a man who had movie stars chasing after him! He let out a rough sigh and pulled a much-used cigar from his pocket and stuck it in his teeth. He didn't light it. He was trying to give up the bad habit, but it was slow going. This cigar had been just recently the target of his secretary's newest weapon in her campaign to save him from nicotine. The end was still damp, in fact, despite the fact that he'd only arrived here from his office in town about an hour ago. He took it out of his mouth with a sigh, eyed it sadly and put it away. He'd threatened to fire her and she'd threatened to quit. She was a nice woman, married with two cute little kids. He couldn't let her leave him. Better the cigar than good help, he decided.

He let his eyes turn again toward the couple growing smaller in the distance. What an odd girlfriend Ed had latched onto this time. Of course, she'd let Ed touch her. She'd flinched away from Matt as if he was contagious. The more he thought about it, the madder he got. He turned his horse toward the bawling cattle in the distance. Working might take the edge off his temper.

ED TOOK LESLIE to her small apartment at a local boardinghouse and left her at the front door with an apology.

"You don't think he'll fire me?" she asked in a plaintive tone.

He shook his head. "No," he assured her. "I've already told you that I won't let him. Now stop worrying. Okay?"

She managed a smile. "Thanks again, Ed."

He shrugged. "No problem. See you Monday."

She watched him get into his sports car and roar away before she went inside to her lonely room at the top corner of the house, facing the street. She'd made an enemy today, without meaning to. She hoped it wasn't going to adversely affect her life. There was no going back now.

MONDAY MORNING, LESLIE was at her desk five minutes early in an attempt to make a good impression. She liked Connie and Jackie, the other two women who shared administrative duties for the vice president of marketing and research. Leslie's job was more routine. She kept up with the various shipments of cattle from one location to another, and maintained the herd records. It was exacting, but she had a head for figures and she enjoyed it.

Her immediate boss was Ed, so it was really a

peachy job. They had an entire building in downtown Jacobsville, a beautiful old Victorian mansion, which Matt had painstakingly renovated to use as his corporation's headquarters. There were two floors of offices, and a canteen for coffee breaks where the kitchen and dining room once had been.

Matt wasn't in his office much of the time. He did a lot of traveling because, aside from his business interests, he sat on boards of directors of other businesses and even on the board of trustees of at least one college. He had business meetings in all sorts of places. Once he'd even gone to South America to see about investing in a growing cattle market there, but he'd come home angry and disillusioned when he saw the slash and burn method of pasture creation that had already killed a substantial portion of rain forest. He wanted no part of that, so he turned to Australia instead and bought another huge ranching tract in the Northern Territory there.

Ed told her about these fascinating exploits, and Leslie listened with her eyes wide. It was a world she'd never known. She and her mother, at the best of times, had been poor before the tragedy that separated them. Now, even with Leslie's job and the good salary she made, it still meant budgeting to the bone so that she could afford even a taxi to work and pay rent on the small apartment where she lived. There wasn't much left over for travel. She envied Matt being able to get on a plane—his own private jet, in fact—and go anywhere in the world he liked. It was a glimpse inside a world she'd never know.

"I guess he goes out a lot," she murmured once when Ed had told her that his cousin was away in New York for a cattlemen's banquet.

"With women?" Ed chuckled. "He beats them off with a stick. Matt's one of the most hunted bachelors in South Texas, but he never seems to get serious about any one woman. They're just accessories to him, pretty things to take on the town. You know," he added with a faint smile, "I don't think he really likes women very much. He was kind to a couple of local girls who needed a shoulder to cry on, but that was as far as it went, and they weren't the sort of women to chase him. He's like this because he had a rough time as a child."

"How?" she asked.

"His mother gave him away when he was six."

Her intake of breath was audible. "Why?"

"She had a new boyfriend who didn't like kids," he said bluntly. "He wouldn't take Matt, so she gave him to my dad. He was raised with me. That's why we're so close."

"What about his father?" she asked.

"We...don't talk about his father."

"Ed!"

He grimaced. "This can't go any further," he said.

"Okay."

"We don't think his mother knew who his father was," he confided. "There were so many men in her life around that time."

"But her husband..."

"What husband?" he asked.

She averted her eyes. "Sorry. I assumed that she was married."

"Not Beth," he mused. "She didn't want ties. She didn't want Matt, but her parents had a screaming fit when she mentioned an abortion. They wanted him terribly, planned for him, made room for him in their house, took Beth and him in the minute he was born."

"But you said your father raised him."

"Matt has had a pretty bad break all around. Our grandparents were killed in a car wreck, and then just a few months later, their house burned down," he added. "There was some gossip that it was intentional to collect on insurance, but nothing was ever proven. Matt was outside with Beth, in the yard, early that morning when it happened. She'd taken him out to see the roses, a pretty strange and unusual thing for her. Lucky for Matt, though, because he'd have been in the house, and would have died. The insurance settlement was enough for Beth to treat herself to some new clothes and a car. She left Matt with my dad and took off with the first man who came along." His eyes were full of remembered outrage on Matt's behalf. "Grandfather left a few shares of stock in a ranch to him, along with a small trust that couldn't be touched until Matt was twenty-one. That's the only thing that kept Beth from getting her hands on it. When he inherited it, he seemed to have an instinct for making money. He never looked back."

"What happened to his mother?" she asked.

"We heard that she died a few years ago. Matt never speaks of her."

"Poor little boy," she said aloud.

"Don't make that mistake," he said at once. "Matt doesn't need pity."

"I guess not. But it's a shame that he had to grow up so alone."

"You'd know about that."

She smiled sadly. "I guess so. My dad died years ago. Mama supported us the best way she could. She wasn't very intelligent, but she was pretty. She used what she had." Her eyes were briefly haunted. "I haven't gotten over what she did. Isn't it horrible, that in a few seconds you can destroy your own life and several other peoples' like that? And what was it all for? Jealousy, when there wasn't even a reason for it. He didn't care about me—he just wanted to have a good time with an innocent girl, him and his drunk friends." She shivered at the memory. "Mama thought she loved him. But that jealous rage didn't get him back. He died."

"I agree that she shouldn't have shot him, but it's hard to defend what he and his friends were doing to you at the time, Leslie."

She nodded. "I know," she said simply. "Sometimes kids get the short end of the stick, and it's up to them to do better with their future."

All the same, she wished that she'd had a normal upbringing, like so many other kids had.

After their conversation, she felt sorry for Matt Caldwell and wished that they'd started off better. She shouldn't have overreacted. But it was curious that he'd been so offensive to her, when Ed said that he was the soul of courtesy around women. Perhaps he'd just had a bad day.

LATER IN THE WEEK, Matt was back, and Leslie began to realize how much trouble she'd landed herself in from their first encounter.

He walked into Ed's office while Ed was out at a meeting, and the ice in his eyes didn't begin to melt as he watched Leslie typing away at the computer. She hadn't seen him, and he studied her with profound, if prejudiced, curiosity. She was thin and not much above average height, with short blond hair that curled toward her face. Nice skin, but she was much too pale. He remembered her eyes most of all, wide and full of distaste as he came close. It amazed him that there was a woman on the planet who could find his money repulsive, even if he didn't appeal to her himself. It was new and unpleasant to discover a woman who didn't want him. He'd never been repulsed by a woman in his life. It left him feeling inadequate. Worse, it brought back memories of the woman who'd rejected him, who'd given him away at the age of six because she didn't want him.

She felt his eyes on her and lifted her head. Gray eyes widened and stared as her hands remained suspended just over the black keyboard.

He was wearing a vested gray suit. It looked very expensive, and his eyes were dark and cutting. He had a cigar in his hand, but it wasn't lit. She hoped he wasn't going to try to smoke it in the confined space, because she was allergic to tobacco smoke.

"So you're Ed's," he murmured in that deep, cutting tone.

"Ed's assistant," she agreed. "Mr. Caldwell…"

"What did you do to land the job?" he continued with a faintly mocking smile. "And how often?"

She wasn't getting what he implied. She blinked, still staring. "I beg your pardon?"

"Why did Ed bring you in here above ten other more qualified applicants?" he persisted.

"Oh, that." She hesitated. She couldn't tell him the real reason, so she told him enough of the truth to distract him. "I have the equivalent of an associate in arts degree in business and I worked as a paralegal for his father for four years in a law office," she said. "I might not have the bachelor's degree that was preferred, but I have experience. Or so Ed assured me," she added, looking worried.

"Why didn't you finish college?" he persisted.

She swallowed. "I had...some personal problems at the time."

"You still have some personal problems, Miss Murry," he replied lazily, but his eyes were cold and alert in a lean, hard face. "You can put me at the top of the list. I had other plans for the position you're holding. So you'd better be as good as Ed says you are."

"I'll give value for money, Mr. Caldwell," she assured him. "I work for my living. I don't expect free rides."

"Don't you?"

"No, I don't."

He lifted the cigar to his mouth, looked at the wet tip, sighed and slipped it back down to dangle, unlit in his fingers.

"Do you smoke?" she asked, having noted the action.

"I try to," he murmured.

Just as he spoke, a handsome woman in her forties with blond hair in a neat bun and wearing a navy-and-white suit, walked down the hall toward him.

He glared at her as she paused in the open door of Ed's office. "I need you to sign these, Mr. Caldwell. And Mr. Bailey is waiting in your office to speak to you about that committee you want him on."

"Thanks, Edna."

Edna Jones smiled. "Good day, Miss Murry. Keeping busy, are you?"

"Yes, ma'am, thank you," Leslie replied with a genuine smile.

"Don't let him light that thing," Edna continued, gesturing toward the cigar dangling in Matt's fingers. "If you need one of these—" she held up a small water pistol "—I'll see that you get one." She smiled at a fuming Matt. "You'll be glad to know that I've already passed them out to the girls in the other executive offices, Mr. Caldwell. You can count on all of us to help you quit smoking."

Matt glared at her. She chuckled like a woman twenty years younger, waved to Leslie, and stalked off back to the office. Matt actually started to make a comical lunge after her, but caught himself in time. It wouldn't do to show weakness to the enemy.

He gave Leslie a cool glance, ignoring the faint amusement in her gray eyes. With a curt nod, he followed Edna down the hall, the damp, expensive cigar still dangling from his lean fingers.

## CHAPTER TWO

FROM HER FIRST DAY on the job, Leslie was aware of Matt's dislike and disapproval of her. He piled the work on Ed, so that it would inevitably drift down to Leslie. A lot of it was really unnecessary, like having her type up old herd records from ten years ago, which had never been converted to computer files. He said it was so that he could check progress on the progeny of his earlier herd sires, but even Ed muttered when Leslie showed him what she was expected to do.

"We have secretaries to do this sort of thing," Ed grumbled as he stared at the yellowed pages on her desk. "I need you for other projects."

"Tell him," Leslie suggested.

He shook his head. "Not in the mood he's been in lately," he said with a rueful smile. "He isn't himself."

"Did you know that his secretary is armed?" she asked suddenly. "She carries a water pistol around with her."

Ed chuckled. "Matt asked her to help him stop smoking cigars. Not that he usually did it inside the building," he was quick to add. "But Mrs. Jones feels that if you can't light a cigar, you can't smoke it. She bought a water pistol for herself and armed the other secretaries, too. If Matt even lifts a cigar to his mouth in the executive offices, they shoot him."

"Dangerous ladies," she commented.

"You bet. I've seen…"

"Nothing to do?" purred a soft, deep voice from behind Ed. The piercing dark eyes didn't match the bantering tone.

"Sorry, Matt," Ed said immediately. "I was just passing the time of day with Leslie. Can I do anything for you?"

"I need an update on that lot of cattle we placed with Ballenger," he said. He stared at Leslie with narrowed eyes. "Your job, I believe?"

She swallowed and nodded, jerking her fingers on the keyboard so that she opened the wrong file and had to push the right buttons to close it again. Normally she wasn't a nervous person, but he made her ill at ease, standing over her without speaking. Ed seemed to be a little twitchy, himself, because he moved back to his own office the minute the phone rang, placing himself out of the line of fire with an apologetic look that Leslie didn't see.

"I thought you were experienced with computers," Matt drawled mockingly as he paused beside her to look over her shoulder.

The feel of his powerful body so close behind her made every muscle tense. Her fingers froze on the keyboard, and she was barely breathing.

With a murmured curse, Matt stepped back to the side of the desk, fighting the most intense emotions he'd ever felt. He stuck his hands deep into the pockets of his slacks and glared at her.

She relaxed, but only enough to be able to pull up the file he wanted and print it for him.

He took it out of the printer tray when it was finished

and gave it a slow perusal. He muttered something, and tossed the first page down on Leslie's desk.

"Half these words are misspelled," he said curtly.

She looked at it on the computer screen and nodded. "Yes, they are, Mr. Caldwell. I'm sorry, but I didn't type it."

Of course she hadn't typed it, it was ten years old, but something inside him wanted to hold her accountable for it.

He moved away from the desk as he read the rest of the pages. "You can do this file—and the others—over," he murmured as he skimmed. "The whole damned thing's illiterate."

She knew that there were hundreds of records in this particular batch of files, and that it would take days, not minutes or hours, to complete the work. But he owned the place, so he could set the rules. She pursed her lips and glanced at him speculatively. Now that he was physically out of range, she felt safe again. "Your wish is my command, boss," she murmured dryly, surprising a quick glance from him. "Shall I just put aside all of Ed's typing and devote the next few months to this?"

Her change of attitude from nervous kid to sassy woman caught him off guard. "I didn't put a time limit on it," Matt said curtly. "I only said, do it!"

"Oh, yes, sir," she agreed at once, and smiled vacantly.

He drew in a short breath and glared down at her. "You're remarkably eager to please, Miss Murry. Or is it just because I'm the boss?"

"I always try to do what I'm asked to do, Mr. Caldwell," she assured him. "Well, almost always," she amended. "Within reason."

He moved back toward the desk. As he leaned over to put down the papers she'd printed for him, he saw her visibly tense. She was the most confounding woman he'd ever known, a total mystery.

"What would you define as 'within reason'?" he drawled, holding her eyes.

She looked hunted. Amazing, that she'd been jovial and uninhibited just seconds before. Her stiff expression made him feel oddly guilty. He turned away. "Ed! Have you got my Angus file?" he called to his cousin through the open door to Ed's private office.

Ed was off the phone and he had a file folder in his hands. "Yes, sorry. I wanted to check the latest growth figures and projected weight gain ratios. I meant to put it back on your desk and I got busy."

Matt studied the figures quietly and then nodded. "That's acceptable. The Ballenger brothers do a good job."

"They're expanding, did you know?" Ed chuckled. "Nice to see them prospering."

"Yes, it is. They've worked hard enough in their lives to warrant a little prosperity."

While he spoke, Leslie was watching him covertly. She thought about the six-year-old boy whose mother had given him away, and it wrung her heart. Her own childhood had been no picnic, but Matt's upbringing had been so much worse.

He felt those soft gray eyes on his face, and his own gaze jerked down to meet them. She flushed and looked away.

He wondered what she'd been thinking to produce such a reaction. She couldn't have possibly made it plainer that she felt no physical attraction to him, so why the wide-eyed stare? It puzzled him. So many things about her puzzled him. She was neat and attractively dressed, but those clothes would have suited a dowager far better than a young woman. While he didn't encourage short skirts and low-cut blouses, Leslie was covered from head to toe; long dress, long sleeves, high neck buttoned right up to her throat.

"Need anything else?" Ed asked abruptly, hoping to ward off more trouble.

Matt's powerful shoulders shrugged. "Not for the moment." He glanced once more at Leslie. "Don't forget those files I want updated."

After he walked out, Ed stared after him for a minute, frowning. "What files?"

She explained it to him.

"But those are outdated," Ed murmured thoughtfully. "And he never looks at them. I don't understand why he has to have them corrected at all."

She leaned forward. "Because it will irritate me and make me work harder!" she said in a stage whisper. "God forbid that I should have time to twiddle my thumbs."

His eyebrows arched. "He isn't vindictive."

"That's what you think." She picked up the file Matt had left and grimaced as she put it back in the filing cabinet. "I'll start on those when I've finished answering your mail. Do you suppose he wants me to stay over after work to do them? He'd have to pay me overtime." She grinned impishly, a reminder of the woman she'd once been. "Wouldn't that make his day?"

"Let me ask him," Ed volunteered. "Just do your usual job for now."

"Okay. Thanks, Ed."

He shrugged. "What are friends for?" he murmured with a smile.

THE OFFICE WAS a great place to work. Leslie had a ball watching the other women in the executive offices lie in wait for Matt. His secretary caught him trying to light a cigar out on the balcony, and she let him have it from behind a potted tree with the water pistol. He laid the cigar down on Bessie David's desk and she "accidentally" dropped it into his half-full coffee cup that he'd set down next to it. He held it up, dripping, with an accusing look at Bessie.

"You told me to do it, sir," Bessie reminded him.

He dropped the sodden cigar back in the coffee and left it behind. Leslie, having seen the whole thing, ducked into the rest room to laugh. It amazed her that Matt was so easygoing and friendly to his other employees. To Leslie, he was all bristle and venom. She wondered what he'd do if she let loose with a water pistol. She chuckled, imagining herself tearing up Main Street in Jacobsville ahead of a cursing Matt Caldwell. It was such a pity that she'd changed so much. Before tragedy had touched her young life, she would have been very attracted to the tall, lean cattleman.

A few days later, he came into Ed's office dangling a cigar from his fingers. Leslie, despite her amusement at the antics of the other secretaries, didn't say a word at the sight of the unlit cigar.

"I want to see the proposal the Cattlemen's Association drafted about brucellosis testing."

She stared at him. "Sir?"

He stared back. She was getting easier on his eyes, and he didn't like his reactions to her. She was repulsed by him. He couldn't get past that because it destroyed his pride. "Ed told me he had a copy of it," he elaborated. "It came in the mail yesterday."

"Okay." She knew where the mail was kept. Ed tried to ignore it, leaving it in the in-box until Leslie dumped it on his desk in front of him and refused to leave until he dealt with it. This usually happened at the end of the week, when it had piled up and overflowed into the out-box.

She rummaged through the box and produced a thick letter from the Cattlemen's Association, unopened. She carried it back through and handed it to Matt.

He'd been watching her walk with curious intensity. She was limping. He couldn't see her legs, because she was wearing loose knit slacks with a tunic that flowed to her thighs as she walked. Very obviously, she wasn't going to do anything to call attention to her figure.

"You're limping," he said. "Did you see a doctor after that fall you took at my ranch?"

"No need to," she said at once. "It was only a bruise. I'm sore, that's all."

He picked up the receiver of the phone on her desk and pressed the intercom button. "Edna," he said abruptly, "set Miss Murry up with Lou Coltrain as soon as possible. She took a spill from a horse at my place a few days ago and she's still limping. I want her x-rayed."

"No!" Leslie protested.

"Let her know when you've made the appointment. Thanks," he told his secretary and hung up. His dark eyes met Leslie's pale ones squarely. "You're going," he said flatly.

She hated doctors. Oh, how she hated them! The doctor at the emergency room in Houston, an older man retired from regular practice, had made her feel cheap and dirty as he examined her and made cold remarks about tramps who got men killed. She'd never gotten over the double trauma of her experience and that harsh lecture, despite the therapists' attempts to soften the memory.

She clenched her teeth and glared at Matt. "I said I'm not hurt!"

"You work here. I'm the boss. You get examined. Period."

She wanted to quit. She wished she could. She had no place else to go. Houston was out of the question. She was too afraid that she'd be up to her ears in reporters, despite her physical camouflage, the minute she set foot in the city.

She drew a sharp, angry breath.

Her attitude puzzled him. "Don't you want to make sure the injury won't make that limp permanent?" he asked suddenly.

She lifted her chin proudly. "Mr. Caldwell, I had an...accident...when I was seventeen and that leg suffered some bone damage." She refused to think about how it had happened. "I'll always have a slight limp, and it's not from the horse throwing me."

He didn't seem to breathe for several seconds. "All the more reason for an examination," he replied. "You like to live dangerously, I gather. You've got no business on a horse."

"Ed said the horse was gentle. It was my fault I got thrown. I jerked the reins."

His eyes narrowed. "Yes, I remember. You were trying to get away from me. Apparently you think I have something contagious."

She could see the pride in his eyes that made him resent her. "It wasn't that," she said. She averted her gaze to the wall. "It's just that I don't like to be touched."

"Ed touches you."

She didn't know how to tell him without telling him everything. She couldn't bear having him know about her sordid past. She raised turbulent gray eyes to his dark ones. "I don't like to be touched by strangers," she amended quickly. "Ed and I have known each other for years," she said finally. "It's…different with him."

His eyes narrowed. He searched over her thin face. "It must be," he said flatly.

His mocking smile touched a nerve. "You're like a steamroller, aren't you?" she asked abruptly. "You assume that because you're wealthy and powerful, there isn't a woman alive who can resist you!"

He didn't like that assumption. His eyes began to glitter. "You shouldn't listen to gossip," he said, his voice deadly quiet. "She was a spoiled little debutante who thought Daddy should be able to buy her any man she wanted. When she discovered that he couldn't, she came to work for a friend of mine and spent a couple of weeks pursuing me around Jacobsville. I went home one night and found her piled up in my bed wearing a sheet and nothing else. I threw her out, but then she told everyone that I'd assaulted her. She had a field day with me in court until my housekeeper, Tolbert, was called to tell the truth about what happened. The fact that she lost the case should tell you what the jury thought of her accusations."

"The jury?" she asked huskily. Besides his problems with his mother, she hadn't known about any incident in his past that might predispose him even further to distrusting women.

His thin lips drew up in a travesty of a smile. "She had me arrested and prosecuted for criminal assault," he returned. "I became famous locally—the one black mark in an otherwise unremarkable past. She had the misfortune to try the same trick later on an oilman up in Houston. He called me to testify in his behalf. When he won the case, he had her prosecuted for fraud and extortion, and won. She went to jail."

She felt sick. He'd had his own dealings with the press. She was sorry for him. It must have been a real ordeal after what he'd already suffered in his young life. It also explained why he wasn't married. Marriage involved trust. She doubted he was capable of it any longer. Certainly it explained the hostility he showed toward Leslie. He might think she was pretending to be repulsed by him because she was playing some deep game for profit, perhaps with some public embarrassment in mind. He might even think she was setting him up for another assault charge.

"Maybe you think that I'm like that," she said after a minute, studying him quietly. "But I'm not."

"Then why act like I'm going to attack you whenever I come within five feet of you?" he asked coldly.

She studied her fingers on the desk before her, their short fingernails neatly trimmed, with a coat of colorless sheen. Nothing flashy, she thought, and that was true of her life lately. She didn't have an answer for him.

"Is Ed your lover?" he persisted coldly.

She didn't flinch. "Ask him."

He rolled the unlit cigar in his long fingers as he watched her. "You are one enormous puzzle," he mused.

"Not really. I'm very ordinary." She looked up. "I don't like doctors, especially male ones…"

"Lou's a woman," he replied. "She and her husband are both physicians. They have a little boy."

"Oh." A woman. That would make things easier. But she didn't want to be examined. They could probably tell from X-rays how breaks occurred, and she didn't know if she could trust a local doctor not to talk about it.

"It isn't up to you," he said suddenly. "You work for me. You had an accident on my ranch." He smiled mirthlessly. "I have to cover my bets. You might decide later on to file suit for medical benefits."

She searched his eyes. She couldn't really blame him for feeling like that. "Okay," she said. "I'll let her examine me."

"No comment?"

She shrugged. "Mr. Caldwell, I work hard for my paycheck. I always have. You don't know me, so I don't blame you for expecting the worst. But I don't want a free ride through life."

One of his eyebrows jerked. "I've heard that one before."

She smiled sadly. "I suppose you have." She touched her keyboard absently. "This Dr. Coltrain, is she the company doctor?"

"Yes."

She gnawed on her lower lip. "What she finds out, it is confidential, isn't it?" she added worriedly, looking up at him.

He didn't reply for a minute. The hand dangling the cigar twirled it around. "Yes," he said. "It's confidential. You're making me curious, Miss Murry. Do you have secrets?"

"We all have secrets," she said solemnly. "Some are darker than others."

He flicked a thumbnail against the cigar. "What's yours? Did you shoot your lover?"

She didn't dare show a reaction to that. Her face felt as if it would crack if she moved.

He stuck the cigar in his pocket. "Edna will let you

know when you're to go see Lou," he said abruptly, with a glance at his watch. He held up the letter. "Tell Ed I've got this. I'll talk to him about it later."

"Yes, sir."

He resisted the impulse to look back at her. The more he discovered about his newest employee, the more intrigued he became. She made him restless. He wished he knew why.

THERE WAS NO WAY to get out of the doctor's appointment. Leslie spoke briefly with Dr. Coltrain before she was sent to the hospital for a set of X-rays. An hour later, she was back in Lou's office, watching the older woman pore somberly over the films against a lighted board on the wall.

Lou looked worried when she examined the X-ray of the leg. "There's no damage from the fall, except for some bruising," she concluded. Her dark eyes met Leslie's squarely. "These old breaks aren't consistent with a fall, however."

Leslie ground her teeth together. She didn't say anything.

Lou moved back around her desk and sat down, indicating that Leslie should sit in the chair in front of the desk after she got off the examining table.

"You don't want to talk about it," Lou said gently. "I won't press you. You do know that the bones weren't properly set at the time, don't you? The improper alignment is unfortunate, because that limp isn't going to go away. I really should send you to an orthopedic surgeon."

"You can send me," Leslie replied, "but I won't go."

Lou rested her folded hands on her desk over the calendar blotter with its scribbled surface. "You don't know me well enough to confide in me. You'll learn, after you've been in Jacobsville a while, that I can be trusted. I don't talk about my patients to anyone, not even my husband. Matt won't hear anything from me."

Leslie remained silent. It was impossible to go over it again with a stranger. It had been hard enough to elaborate on her past to the therapist, who'd been shocked, to put it mildly.

The older woman sighed. "All right, I won't pressure you. But if you ever need anyone to talk to, I'll be here."

Leslie looked up. "Thank you," she said sincerely.

"You're not Matt's favorite person, are you?" Lou asked abruptly.

Leslie laughed without mirth. "No, I'm not. I think he'll find a way to fire me eventually. He doesn't like women much."

"Matt likes everybody as a rule," Lou said. "And he's always being pursued by women. They love him. He's kind to people he likes. He offered to marry Kitty Carson when she quit working for Dr. Drew Morris. She didn't do it, of course, she was crazy for Drew and vice versa. They're happily married now." She hesitated, but Leslie didn't speak. "He's a dish—rich, handsome, sexy, and usually the easiest man on earth to get along with."

"He's a bulldozer," Leslie said flatly. "He can't seem to talk to people unless he's standing on them." She folded her arms over her chest and looked uncomfortable.

So that's it, Lou thought, wondering if the young woman realized what her body language was giving away. Lou knew instantly that someone had caused those breaks in the younger woman's leg; very probably a man. She had reason to know.

"You don't like people to touch you," Lou said.

Leslie shifted in the chair. "No."

Lou's perceptive eyes went over the concealing garments Leslie wore, but she didn't say another word. She stood up, smiling gently. "There's no damage from the recent fall," she said gently. "But come back if the pain gets any worse."

Leslie frowned. "How did you know I was in pain?"

"Matt said you winced every time you got out of your chair."

Leslie's heart skipped. "I didn't realize he noticed."

"He's perceptive."

Lou prescribed an over-the-counter medication to take for the pain and advised her to come back if she didn't improve. Leslie agreed and went out of the office in an absentminded stupor, wondering what else Matt Caldwell had learned from her just by observation. It was a little unnerving.

WHEN SHE WENT BACK to the office, it wasn't ten minutes before Matt was standing in the doorway.

"Well?" he asked.

"I'm fine," she assured him. "Just a few bruises. And believe me, I have no intention of suing you."

He didn't react visibly. "Plenty have." He was irritated. Lou wouldn't tell him anything, except that his new employee was as closemouthed as a clam. He knew that already.

"Tell Ed I'll be out of the office for a couple of days," he said.

"Yes, sir."

He gave her a last look, turned and walked back out. It wasn't until Matt was out of sight that Leslie began to relax.

## CHAPTER THREE

THE NIGHTMARES CAME BACK that night. Leslie had even expected them, because of the visit to Dr. Lou Coltrain and the hospital's X-ray department. Having to wear high heeled shoes to work hadn't done her damaged leg any good, either. Along with the nightmare that left her sweating and panting, her leg was killing her. She went to the bathroom and downed two aspirin, hoping they were going to do the trick. She decided that she was going to have to give up fashion and wear flats again.

Matt noticed, of course, when he returned to the office three days later. His eyes narrowed as he watched her walk across the floor of her small office.

"Lou could give you something to take for the pain," he said abruptly.

She glanced at him as she pulled a file out of the metal cabinet. "Yes, she could, Mr. Caldwell, but do you really want a comatose secretary in Ed's office? Painkillers put me to sleep."

"Pain makes for inefficiency."

She nodded. "I know that. I have a bottle of aspirin in my purse," she assured him. "And the pain isn't so bad that I can't remember how to spell. It's just a few bruises. They'll heal. Dr. Coltrain said so."

He stared at her through narrowed, cold eyes. "You

shouldn't be limping after a week. I want you to see Lou again…"

"I've limped for six years, Mr. Caldwell," she said serenely. Her eyes kindled. "If you don't like the limp, perhaps you shouldn't stand and watch me walk."

His eyebrows arched. "Can't the doctors do anything to correct it?"

She glared at him. "I hate doctors!"

The vehemence of her statement took him aback. She meant it, too. Her face flushed; her eyes sparkled with temper. It was such a difference from her usual expression that he found himself captivated. When she was animated, she was pretty.

"They're not all bad," he replied finally.

"There's only so much you can do with a shattered bone," she said and then bit her lip. She hadn't meant to tell him that.

The question was in his eyes, on his lips, but it never made it past them. Just as he started to ask, Ed came out of his office and spotted him.

"Matt! Welcome back," he said, extending a hand. "I just had a call from Bill Payton. He wanted to know if you were coming to the banquet Saturday night. They've got a live band scheduled."

"Sure," Matt said absently. "Tell him to reserve two tickets for me. Are you going?"

"I thought I would. I'll bring Leslie along." He smiled at her. "It's the annual Jacobsville Cattlemen's Association banquet. We have speeches, but if you survive them, and the rubber chicken, you get to dance."

"Her leg isn't going to let her do much dancing," Matt said solemnly.

Ed's eyebrows lifted. "You'd be surprised," he said.

"She loves Latin dances." He grinned at Leslie. "So does Matt here. You wouldn't believe what he can do with a mambo or a rhumba, to say nothing of the tango. He dated a dance instructor for several months, and he's a natural anyway."

Matt didn't reply. He was watching the play of expressions on Leslie's face and wondering about that leg. Maybe Ed knew the truth of it, and he could worm it out of him.

"You can ride in with us," Matt said absently. "I'll hire Jack Bailey's stretch limo and give your secretary a thrill."

"It'll give me a thrill, too," Ed assured him. "Thanks, Matt. I hate trying to find a parking space at the country club when there's a party."

"That makes two of us."

One of the secretaries motioned to Matt that he had a phone call. He left and Ed departed right behind him for a meeting. Leslie wondered how she was going to endure an evening of dancing without ending up close to Matt Caldwell, who already resented her standoffish attitude. It would be an ordeal, she supposed, and wondered if she could develop a convenient headache on Saturday afternoon.

LESLIE HAD ONLY one really nice dress that was appropriate to wear to the function at the country club. The gown was a long sheath of shimmery silver fabric, suspended from her creamy shoulders by two little spaghetti straps. With it, she wore a silver-and-rhinestone clip in her short blond hair and neat little silver slippers with only a hint of a heel.

Ed sighed at the picture she made when the limousine pulled up in front of the boardinghouse where she was staying. She met him on the porch, a small purse clenched in damp hands, all aflutter at the thought of her first evening out since she was seventeen. She was terribly nervous.

"Is the dress okay?" she asked at once.

Ed smiled, taking in her soft oval face with its faint blush of lipstick and rouge, which was the only makeup she ever wore. Her gray eyes had naturally thick black lashes, which never needed mascara.

"You look fine," he assured her.

"You're not bad in a tux yourself," she murmured with a grin.

"Don't let Matt see how nervous you are," he said as they approached the car. "Somebody phoned and set him off just as we left my house. Carolyn was almost in tears."

"Carolyn?" she asked.

"His latest trophy girlfriend," he murmured. "She's from one of the best families in Houston, staying with her aunt so she'd be on hand for tonight's festivities. She's been relentlessly pursuing Matt for months. Some of us think she's gaining ground."

"She's beautiful, I guess?" she asked.

"Absolutely. In a way, she reminds me of Franny."

Franny had been Ed's fiancée, shot to death in a foiled bank robbery about the time Leslie had been catapulted into sordid fame. It had given them something in common that drew them together as friends.

"That must be rough," Leslie said sympathetically.

He glanced at her curiously as they approached the car. "Haven't you ever been in love?"

She shrugged, tugging the small faux fur cape closer

around her shoulders. "I was a late bloomer." She swallowed hard. "What happened to me turned me right off men."

"I'm not surprised."

He waited while the chauffeur, also wearing a tuxedo, opened the door of the black super-stretch limousine for them. Leslie climbed in, followed by Ed, and the door closed them in with Matt and the most beautiful blond woman Leslie had ever seen. The other woman was wearing a simple black sheath dress with a short skirt and enough diamonds to open a jewelry store. No point in asking if they were real, Leslie thought, considering the look of that dress and the very real sable coat wrapped around it.

"You remember my cousin, Ed," Matt drawled, lounging back in the leather seat across from Ed and Leslie. Small yellow lights made it possible for them to see each other in the incredibly spacious interior. "This is his secretary, Miss Murry. Carolyn Engles," he added, nodding toward the woman at his side.

Murmured acknowledgments followed his introduction. Leslie's fascinated eyes went from the bar to the phones to the individual controls on the air-conditioning and heating systems. It was like a luxury apartment on wheels, she thought, and tried not to let her amusement show.

"Haven't you ever been in a limousine before?" Matt asked with a mocking smile.

"Actually, no," she replied with deliberate courtesy. "It's quite a treat. Thank you."

He seemed disconcerted by her reply. He averted his head and studied Ed. His next words showed he'd forgotten her. "Tomorrow morning, first thing, I want

you to pull back every penny of support we're giving
Marcus Boles. Nobody, and I mean nobody, involves
me in a shady land deal like that!"

"It amazes me that we didn't see through him from
the start," Ed agreed. "The whole campaign was just a
diversion, to give the real candidate someone to shoot
down. He'll look like a hero, and Boles will take the fall
manfully. I understand he's being handsomely paid for
his disgrace. Presumably the cash is worth his reputa-
tion and social standing."

"He's got land in South America. I hear he's going
over there to live. Just as well," Matt added coldly. "If
he's lucky, he might make it to the airport tomorrow
before I catch up with him."

The threat of violence lay over him like an invisible mantle. Leslie shivered. Of the four people in that
car, she knew firsthand how vicious and brutal physical violence could be. Her memories were hazy, confused, but in the nightmares she had constantly, they
were all too vivid.

"Do calm down, darling," Carolyn told Matt gently.
"You're upsetting Ms. Marley."

"Murry," Ed corrected before Leslie could. "Strange,
Carolyn, I don't remember your memory being so poor."

Carolyn cleared her throat. "It's a lovely night, at
least," she said, changing the subject. "No rain and a
beautiful moon."

"So it is," Ed drawled.

Matt gave him a cool look, which Ed met with a va-
cant smile. Leslie was amused by the way Ed could look
so innocent. She knew him far too well to be fooled.

Matt, meanwhile, was drinking in the sight of Leslie in that formfitting dress that just matched her eyes.

She had skin like marble, and he wondered if it was as soft to the touch as it seemed. She wasn't conventionally pretty, but there was a quality about her that made him weak in the knees. He was driven to protect her, without knowing why he felt that way about a stranger. It irritated him as much as the phone call he'd fielded earlier.

"Where are you from, Ms. Murbery?" Carolyn asked.

"Miss Murry," Leslie corrected, beating Ed to the punch. "I'm from a little town north of Houston."

"A true Texan," Ed agreed with a grin in her direction.

"What town?" Matt asked.

"I'm sure you won't have heard of it," Leslie said confidently. "Our only claim to fame was a radio station in a building shaped like a ten-gallon hat. Very much off the beaten path."

"Did your parents own a ranch?" he persisted.

She shook her head. "My father was a crop duster."

"A what?" Carolyn asked with a blank face.

"A pilot who sprays pesticides from the air in a small airplane," Leslie replied. "He was killed…on the job."

"Pesticides," Matt muttered darkly. "Just what the groundwater table needs to—"

"Matt, can we forget politics for just one night?" Ed asked. "I'd like to enjoy my evening."

Matt gave him a measured glare with one eye narrowed menacingly. But he relaxed all at once and leaned back in his seat, to put a lazy arm around Carolyn and let her snuggle close to him. His dark eyes seemed to mock Leslie as if comparing her revulsion to Carolyn's frank delight in his physical presence.

She let him win this round with an amused smile.

Once, she might have enjoyed his presence just as much as his date was reveling in now. But she had more reason than most to fear men.

THE COUNTRY CLUB, in its sprawling clubhouse on a man-made lake, was a beautiful building with graceful arches and fountains. It did Jacobsville proud. But, as Ed had intimated, there wasn't a single parking spot available. Matt had the pager number of the driver and could summon the limousine whenever it was needed. He herded his charges out of the car and into the building, where the reception committee made them welcome.

There was a live band, a very good one, playing assorted tunes, most of which resembled bossa nova rhythms. The only time that Leslie really felt alive was when she could close her eyes and listen to music; any sort of music—classical, opera, country-western or gospel. Music had been her escape as a child from a world too bitter sometimes to stomach. She couldn't play an instrument, but she could dance. That was the one thing she and her mother had shared, a love of dancing. In fact, Marie had taught her every dance step she knew, and she knew a lot. Marie had taught dancing for a year or so and had shared her expertise with her daughter. How ironic it was that Leslie's love of dance had been stifled forever by the events of her seventeenth year.

"Fill a plate," Ed coaxed, motioning her to the small china dishes on the buffet table. "You could use a little more meat on those bird bones."

She grinned at him. "I'm not skinny."

"Yes, you are," he replied, and he wasn't kidding.

"Come on, forget your troubles and enjoy yourself. To-night, there is no tomorrow. Eat, drink and be merry."

*For tomorrow, you die,* came the finish to that admonishing verse, she recalled darkly. But she didn't say it. She put some cheese straws and finger sandwiches on a plate and opted for soda water instead of a drink.

Ed found them two chairs on the rim of the dance floor, where they could hear the band and watch the dancing.

The band had a lovely dark-haired singer with a hauntingly beautiful voice. She was playing a guitar and singing songs from the sixties, with a rhythm that made Leslie's heart jump. The smile on her face, the sparkle in her gray eyes as she listened to the talented performer, made her come alive.

From across the room, Matt noted the abrupt change in Leslie. She loved music. She loved dancing, too, he could tell. His strong fingers contracted around his own plate.

"Shall we sit with the Devores, darling?" Carolyn asked, indicating a well-dressed couple on the opposite side of the ballroom.

"I thought we'd stick with my cousin," he said carelessly. "He's not used to this sort of thing."

"He seems very much at home," Carolyn corrected, reluctantly following in Matt's wake. "It's his date who looks out of place. Good heavens, she's tapping her toe! How gauche!"

"Weren't you ever twenty-three?" he asked with a bite in his voice. "Or were you born so damned sophisticated that nothing touched you?"

She actually gasped. Matt had never spoken to her that way.

"Excuse me," he said gruffly, having realized his mistake. "I'm still upset by Boles."

"So...so I noticed," she stammered, and almost dropped her plate. This was a Matt Caldwell she'd never seen before. His usual smile and easygoing attitude were conspicuous for their absence tonight. Boles must really have upset him!

Matt sat down on the other side of Leslie, his eyes darkening as he saw the life abruptly drain out of her. Her body tensed. Her fingers on her plate went white.

"Here, Carolyn, trade places with me," Matt said suddenly, and with a forced smile. "This chair's too low for me."

"I don't think mine's much higher, darling, but I'll do it," Carolyn said in a docile tone.

Leslie relaxed. She smiled shyly at the other woman and then turned her attention back to the woman on the stage.

"Isn't she marvelous?" Carolyn asked. "She's from the Yucatán."

"Not only talented, but pretty, as well," Ed agreed. "I love that beat."

"Oh, so do I," Leslie said breathlessly, nibbling a finger sandwich but with her whole attention on the band and the singer.

Matt found himself watching her, amused and touched by her uninhibited joy in the music. It had occurred to him that not much affected her in the office. Here, she was unsure of herself and nervous. Perhaps she even felt out of place. But when the band was playing and the vocalist was singing, she was a different person. He got a glimpse of the way she had been, perhaps, before whatever blows of fate had made her so uneasy around him. He was intrigued by her, and not solely because she wounded his ego. She was a complex person.

Ed noticed Matt's steady gaze on Leslie, and he wanted to drag his cousin aside and tell him the whole miserable story. Matt was curious about Leslie, and he was a bulldozer when he wanted something. He'd run roughshod right over her to get his answers, and Leslie would retreat into the shell her experiences had built around her. She was just coming into the sunlight, and here was Matt driving her back into shadow. Why couldn't Matt be content with Carolyn's adoration? Most women flocked around him; Leslie didn't. He was sure that was the main attraction she held for his cousin. But Matt, pursuing her interest, could set her back years. He had no idea what sort of damage he could do to her fragile emotions.

The singer finished her song, and the audience applauded. She introduced the members of the band and the next number, a beautiful, rhythmic feast called "Brazil." It was Leslie's very favorite piece of music, and she could dance to it, despite her leg. She longed, ached, for someone to take her on the dance floor and let her show those stiff, inhibited people how to fly to that poignant rhythm!

Watching her, Matt saw the hunger in her eyes. Ed couldn't do those steps, but he could. Without a word, he handed Carolyn his empty plate and got to his feet.

Before Leslie had a chance to hesitate or refuse outright, he pulled her gently out of her seat and onto the dance floor.

His dark eyes met her shocked pale ones as he caught her waist in one lean, strong hand and took her left hand quite reverently into his right one.

"I won't make any sudden turns," he assured her. He nodded once, curtly, to mark the rhythm.

And then he did something remarkable.

Leslie caught her breath as she recognized his ability. She forgot to be afraid of him. She forgot that she was nervous to be held by a man. She was caught up in the rhythm and the delight of having a partner who knew how to dance to perfection the intricate steps that accompanied the Latin beat.

"You're good," Matt mused, smiling with genuine pleasure as they measured their quick steps to the rhythm.

"So are you." She smiled back.

"If your leg gives you trouble, let me know and I'll get you off the floor. Okay?"

"Okay."

"Then let's go!"

He moved her across the floor with the skill of a professional dancer and she followed him with such perfection that other dancers stopped and got out of the way, moving to the sidelines to watch what had become pure entertainment.

Matt and Leslie, enjoying the music and their own interpretation of it, were blind to the other guests, to the smiling members of the band, to everything except the glittering excitement of the dance. They moved as if they were bound by invisible strings, each to the other, with perfectly matching steps.

As the music finally wound down, Matt drew her in close against his lean frame and tilted her down in an elegant, but painful, finish.

The applause was thunderous. Matt drew Leslie upright again and noticed how pale and drawn her face was.

"Too much too soon," he murmured. "Come on. Off you go."

He didn't move closer. Instead, he held out his arm and let her come to him, let her catch hold of it where the muscle was thickest. She clung with both hands, hating herself for doing something so incredibly stupid. But, oh, it had been fun! It was worth the pain.

She didn't realize she'd spoken aloud until Matt eased her down into her chair again.

"Do you have any aspirin in that tiny thing?" Matt asked, indicating the small string purse on her arm.

She grimaced.

"Of course not." He turned, scanning the audience. "Back in a jiffy."

He moved off in the general direction of the punch bowl while Ed caught Leslie's hand in his. "That was great," he enthused. "Just great! I didn't know you could dance like that."

"Neither did I," she murmured shyly.

"Quite an exhibition," Carolyn agreed coolly. "But silly to do something so obviously painful. Now Matt will spend the rest of the night blaming himself and trying to find aspirin, I suppose." She got up and marched off with her barely touched plate and Matt's empty one.

"Well, she's in a snit," Ed observed. "She can't dance like that."

"I shouldn't have done it," Leslie murmured. "But it was so much fun, Ed! I felt alive, really alive!"

"You looked it. Nice to see your eyes light up again."

She made a face at him. "I've spoiled Carolyn's evening."

"Fair trade," he murmured dryly, "she spoiled mine

the minute she got into the limousine and complained
that I smelled like a sweets shop."

"You smell very nice," she replied.

He smiled. "Thanks."

Matt was suddenly coming back toward them, with
Lou Coltrain by the arm. It looked as if she were being
forcibly escorted across the floor and Ed had to hide
the grin he couldn't help.

"Well," Lou huffed, staring at Matt before she lowered her gaze to Leslie. "I thought you were dying,
considering the way he appropriated me and dragged
me over here!"

"I don't have any aspirin," Leslie said uneasily. "I'm
sorry…"

"There's nothing to be sorry about," Lou said instantly. She patted Leslie's hand gently. "But you've
had some pretty bad bruising and this isn't the sort
of exercise I'd recommend. Shattered bones are never
as strong, even when they're set properly—and yours
were not."

Embarrassed, Leslie bit her lower lip.

"You'll be okay," Lou promised with a gentle smile.
"In fact, exercise is good for the muscles that support
that bone—it makes it stronger. But don't do this again
for a couple of weeks, at least. Here. I always carry aspirin!"

She handed Leslie a small metal container of aspirin
and Matt produced another cup of soda water and stood
over her, unsmiling, while she took two of the aspirins
and swallowed them.

"Thanks," she told Lou. "I really appreciate it."

"You come and see me Monday," Lou instructed, her
dark eyes full of authority. "I'll write you a prescription

for something that will make your life easier. Not narcotics," she added with a smile. "Anti-inflammatories. They'll make a big difference in the way you get around."

"You're a nice doctor," she told Lou solemnly.

Lou's eyes narrowed. "I gather that you've known some who weren't."

"One, at least," she said in a cold tone. She smiled at Lou. "You've changed my mind about doctors."

"That's one point for me. I'll rush right over and tell Copper," she added, smiling as she caught her redheaded husband's eyes across the room. "He'll be impressed!"

"Not much impresses the other Dr. Coltrain," Matt told her after Lou was out of earshot. "Lou did."

"Not until he knew she had a whole closetful of Lionel electric trains," Ed commented with a chuckle.

"Their son has a lot to look forward to when he grows up," Matt mused. He glanced beside Leslie. "Where's Carolyn?"

"She left in a huff," Ed said.

"I'll go find her. Sure you'll be okay?" he asked Leslie with quiet concern.

She nodded. "Thanks for the aspirin. They really help."

He nodded. His dark eyes slid over her drawn face and then away as he went in search of his date.

"I've spoiled his evening, too, I guess," she said wistfully.

"You can't take credit for that," Ed told her. "I've hardly ever seen Matt having so much fun as he was when he was dancing with you. Most of the women around here can only do a two-step. You're a miracle on the dance floor."

"I love to dance," she sighed. "I always did. Mama was so light on her feet." Her eyes twinkled with fond memories. "I used to love to watch her when I was little and she danced with Daddy. She was so pretty, so full of life." The light went out of her eyes. "She thought I'd encouraged Mike, and the others, too," she said dully. "She…shot him and the bullet went through him, into my leg…"

"So that's how your leg got in that shape."

She glanced at him, hardly aware of what she'd been saying. She nodded. "The doctor in the emergency room was sure it was all my fault. That's why my leg wasn't properly set. He removed the bullet and not much else. It wasn't until afterward that another doctor put a cast on. Later, I began to limp. But there was no money for any other doctor visits by then. Mama was in jail and I was all alone. If it hadn't been for my best friend Jessica's family, I wouldn't even have had a home. They took me in despite the gossip and I got to finish school."

"I'll never know how you managed that," Ed said. "Going to school every day with the trial making headlines week by week."

"It was tough," she agreed. "But it made me tough, too. Fire tempers steel, don't they say? I'm tempered."

"Yes, you are."

She smiled at him. "Thanks for bringing me. It was wonderful."

"Tell Matt that. It might change him."

"Oh, he's not so bad, I think," she replied. "He dances like an angel."

He stared toward the punch bowl, where Matt was glancing toward him and Leslie. The dark face was harder than stone and Ed felt a tingle of apprehension when Matt left Carolyn and started walking toward them. He didn't like that easygoing stride of Matt's. The only time Matt moved that slowly was when he was homicidally angry.

## CHAPTER FOUR

LESLIE KNEW BY the look in Matt's eyes that he was furious. She thought his anger must be directed toward her, although she couldn't remember anything she'd done to deserve it. As he approached them, he had his cellular phone out and was pushing a number into it. He said something, then closed it and put it back in his pocket.

"I'm sorry, but we have to leave," he said, every syllable dripping ice. "It seems that Carolyn has developed a vicious headache."

"It's all right," Leslie said, and even smiled as relief swept over her that she hadn't put that expression on his handsome face. "I wouldn't have been able to dance again." Her eyes met Matt's shyly. "I really enjoyed it."

He didn't reply. His eyes were narrow and not very friendly. "Ed, will you go out front and watch for the car? I've just phoned the driver."

"Sure." He hesitated noticeably for a moment before he left.

Matt stood looking down at Leslie with an intensity that made her uncomfortable. "You make yourself out to be a broken stick," he said quietly. "But you're not what you appear to be, are you? I get the feeling that you used to be quite a dancer before that leg slowed you down."

She was puzzled. "I learned how from my mother," she said honestly. "I used to dance with her."

He laughed curtly. "Pull the other one," he said. He was thinking about her pretended revulsion, the way she constantly backed off when he came near her. Then, tonight, the carefully planned capitulation. It was an old trick that had been used on him before—backing away so that he'd give chase. He was surprised that he hadn't realized it sooner. He wondered how far she'd let him go. He was going to find out.

She blinked and frowned. "I beg your pardon?" she asked, genuinely puzzled.

"Never mind," he said with a parody of a smile. "Ed should be outside with the driver by now. Shall we go?"

He reached out a lean hand and pulled her to her feet abruptly. Her face was very pale at the hint of domination not only in his eyes, but the hold he had on her. It was hard not to panic. It reminded her of another man who had used domination; only that time she had no knowledge of how to get away. Now she did. She turned her arm quickly and pushed it down against his thumb, the weakest spot in his hold, freeing herself instantly as the self-defense instructor had taught her.

Matt was surprised. "Where did you learn that? From your mother?" he drawled.

"No. From my Tae Kwon Do instructor in Houston," she returned. "Despite my bad leg, I can take care of myself."

"Oh, I'd bet on that." His dark eyes narrowed and glittered faintly. "You're not what you seem, Miss Murry. I'm going to make it my business to find out the truth about you."

She blanched. She didn't want him digging into her past. She'd run from it, hidden from it, for years. Would she have to run some more, just when she felt secure?

He saw her frightened expression and felt even more certain that he'd almost been taken for the ride of his life. Hadn't his experience with women taught him how to recognize deceit? He thought of his mother and his heart went cold. Leslie even had a look of her, with that blond hair. He took her by the upper arm and pulled her along with him, noticing that she moved uncomfortably and tugged at his hold.

"Please," she said tightly. "Slow down. It hurts."

He stopped at once, realizing that he was forcing her to a pace that made walking painful. He'd forgotten about her disability, as if it were part of her act. He let out an angry breath.

"The damaged leg is real," he said, almost to himself. "But what else is?"

She met his angry eyes. "Mr. Caldwell, whatever I am, I'm no threat to you," she said quietly. "I really don't like being touched, but I enjoyed dancing with you. I haven't danced…in years."

He studied her wan face, oblivious to the music of the band, and the murmur of movement around them. "Sometimes," he murmured, "you seem very familiar to me, as if I've seen you before." He was thinking about his mother, and how she'd betrayed him and hurt him all those years ago.

Leslie didn't know that, though. Her teeth clenched as she tried not to let her fear show. Probably he had seen her before, just like the whole country had, her face in the tabloid papers as it had appeared the night they took her out of her mother's bloodstained apartment on a stretcher, her leg bleeding profusely, her sobs audible. But then her hair had been dark, and she'd been wearing glasses. Could he really recognize her?

"Maybe I just have that kind of face." She grimaced and shifted her weight. "Could we go, please?" she asked on a moan. "My leg really is killing me."

He didn't move for an instant. Then he bent suddenly and lifted her in his strong arms and carried her through the amused crowd toward the door.

"Mr.…Mr. Caldwell," she protested, stiffening. She'd never been picked up and carried by a man in her entire life. She studied his strong profile with fascinated curiosity, too entranced to feel the usual fear. Having danced with him, she was able to accept his physical closeness. He felt very strong and he smelled of some spicy, very exotic cologne. She had the oddest urge to touch his wavy black hair just over his broad forehead, where it looked thickest.

He glanced down into her fascinated eyes and one of his dark eyebrows rose in a silent question.

"You're…very strong, aren't you?" she asked hesitantly.

The tone of her voice touched something deep inside him. He searched her eyes and the tension was suddenly thick as his gaze fell to her soft bow of a mouth and lingered there, even as his pace slowed slightly.

Her hand clutched the lapel of his tuxedo as her own gaze fell to his mouth. She'd never wanted to be kissed like this before. When she'd been kissed during that horrible encounter, it had been repulsive—a wet, invading, lustful kiss that made her want to throw up.

It wouldn't be like that with Matt. She knew instinctively that he was well versed in the art of lovemaking, and that he would be gentle with a woman. His mouth was sensual, wide and chiseled. Her own mouth tin-

gled as she wondered visibly what it would feel like to
let him kiss her.

He read that curiosity with pinpoint accuracy and
his sharp intake of breath brought her curious eyes up
to meet his.

"Careful," he cautioned, his voice deeper than usual.
"Curiosity killed the cat."

Her eyes asked a question she couldn't form with
her lips.

"You fell off a horse avoiding any contact with me,"
he reminded her quietly. "Now you look as if you'd do
anything to have my mouth on yours. Why?"

"I don't know," she whispered, her hand contracting
on the lapel of his jacket. "I like being close to you,"
she confessed, surprised. "It's funny. I haven't wanted
to be close to a man like this before."

He stopped dead in his tracks. There was a faint vi-
bration in the hard arms holding her. His eyes lanced
into hers. His breath became audible. The arm under
her back contracted, bringing her breasts hard against
him as he stood there on the steps of the building, totally oblivious to everything except the ache that was
consuming him.

Leslie's body shivered with its first real taste of desire. She laughed shakily at the new and wonderful
sensations she was feeling. Her breasts felt suddenly
heavy. They ached.

"Is this what it feels like?" she murmured.

"What?" he asked huskily.

She met his gaze. "Desire."

He actually shuddered. His arms contracted. His
lips parted as he looked at her mouth and knew that
he couldn't help taking it. She smelled of roses, like

the tiny pink fairy roses that grew in masses around
the front door of his ranch house. She wanted him. His
head began to spin. He bent his dark head and bit at her
lower lip with a sensuous whisper.

"Open your mouth, Leslie," he whispered, and his
hard mouth suddenly went down insistently on hers.

But before he could even savor the feel of her soft
lips, the sound of high heels approaching jerked his head
up. Leslie was trembling against him, shocked and a
little frightened, and completely entranced by the unexpected contact with his beautiful mouth.

Matt's dark eyes blazed down into hers. "No more
games. I'm taking you home with me," he said huskily.

She started to speak, to protest, when Carolyn came
striding angrily out the door.

"Does she have to be carried?" the older woman
asked Matt with dripping sarcasm. "Funny, she was
dancing eagerly enough a few minutes ago!"

"She has a bad leg," Matt said, regaining his control.
"Here's the car."

The limousine drew up at the curb and Ed got out,
frowning when he saw Leslie in Matt's arms.

"Are you all right?" he asked as he approached them.

"She shouldn't have danced," Matt said stiffly as he
moved the rest of the way down the steps to deposit her
inside the car on the leather-covered seat. "She made
her leg worse."

Carolyn was livid. She slid in and moved to the other
side of Leslie with a gaze that could have curdled milk.
"One dance and we have to leave," she said furiously.

Matt moved into the car beside Ed and slammed
the door. "I thought we were leaving because you had
a headache," he snapped at Carolyn, his usual control

quite evidently gone. He was in a foul mood. Desire was frustrating him. He glanced at Leslie and thought how good she was at manipulation. She had him almost doubled over with need. She was probably laughing her head off silently. Well, she was going to pay for that.

Carolyn, watching his eyes on Leslie, made an angry sound in her throat and stared out the window.

To Ed's surprise and dismay, they dropped him off at his home first. He tried to argue, but Matt wasn't having that. He told Ed he'd see him at the office Monday and closed the door on his protests.

Carolyn was deposited next. Matt walked her to her door, but he moved back before she could claim a goodnight kiss. The way she slammed her door was audible even inside the closed limousine.

Leslie bit her lower lip as Matt climbed back into the car with her. In the lighted interior, she could see the expression on his face as he studied her slender body covetously.

"This isn't the way to my apartment," she ventured nervously a few minutes later, hoping he hadn't meant what he said just before they got into the limousine.

"No, it isn't, is it?" he replied dangerously.

Even as he spoke, the limousine pulled up at the door to his ranch house. He helped Leslie out and spoke briefly to the driver before dismissing him. Then he swung a frightened Leslie up into his arms and carried her toward the front door.

"Mr. Caldwell…" she began.

"Matt," he corrected, not looking at her.

"I want to go home," she tried again.

"You will. Eventually."

"But you sent the car away."

"I have six cars," he informed her as he shifted his light burden to produce his keys from the pocket of his slacks and insert one in the lock. The door swung open. "I'll drive you home when the time comes."

"I'm very tired." Her voice sounded breathless and high-pitched.

"Then I know just the place for you." He closed the door and carried her down a long, dimly lit hallway to a room near the back of the house. He leaned down to open the door and once they were through it, he kicked it shut with his foot.

Seconds later, Leslie was in the middle of a huge king-size bed, sprawled on the beige-brown-and-black comforter that covered it and Matt was removing her wrap.

It went flying onto a chair, along with his jacket and tie. He unbuttoned his shirt and slid down onto the bed beside her, his hands on either side of her face as he poised just above her.

The position brought back terrible, nightmarish memories. She stiffened all over. Her face went pale. Her eyes dilated so much that the gray of them was eclipsed by black.

Matt ignored her expression. He looked down the length of her in the clinging silver dress, his eyes lingering on the thrust of her small breasts. One of his big hands came up to trace around the prominent hard nipple that pointed through the fabric.

The touch shocked Leslie, because she didn't find it revolting or unpleasant. She shivered a little. Her eyes, wide and frightened, and a little curious, met his.

His strong fingers brushed lazily over the nipple and

around the contours of her breast as if the feel of her fascinated him.

"Do you mind?" he asked with faint insolence, and slipped one of the spaghetti straps down her arm, moving her just enough that he could pull the bodice away from her perfect little breast.

Leslie couldn't believe what was happening. Men were repulsive to her. She hated the thought of intimacy. But Matt Caldwell was looking at her bare breast and she was letting him, with no thought of resistance. She hadn't even had anything to drink.

He searched her face as his warm fingers traced her breast. He read the pleasure she was feeling in her soft eyes. "You feel like sun-touched marble to my hand," he said quietly. "Your skin is beautiful." His gaze traveled down her body. "Your breasts are perfect."

She was shivering again. Her hands clenched beside her head as she watched him touch her, like an observer, like in a dream.

He smiled with faint mockery when he saw her expression. "Haven't you done this before?"

"No," she said, and she actually sounded serious.

He discounted that at once. She was far too calm and submissive for an inexperienced woman.

One dark eyebrow lifted. "Twenty-three and still a virgin?"

How had he known that? "Well…yes." Technically she certainly was. Emotionally, too. Despite what had been done to her, she'd been spared rape, if only by seconds, when her mother came home unexpectedly.

Matt was absorbed in touching her body. His forefinger traced around the hard nipple, and he watched her body lift to follow it when he lifted his hand.

"Do you like it?" he asked softly.

She was watching him intensely. "Yes." She sounded as if it surprised her that she liked what he was doing.

With easy self-confidence, he pulled her up just a little and pushed the other strap down her arm, baring her completely to his eyes. She was perfect, like a warm statue in beautifully smooth marble. He'd never seen breasts like hers. She aroused him profoundly.

He held her by the upper part of her rib cage, his thumbs edging onto her breasts to caress them tenderly while he watched the expressions chase each other across her face. The silence in the bedroom was broken only by the sound of cars far in the distance and the sound of some mournful night bird outside the window. Closer was the rasp of her own breathing and her heart beating in her ears. She should be fighting for her life, screaming, running, escaping. She'd avoided this sort of situation successfully for six years. Why didn't she want to avoid Matt's hands?

Matt touched her almost reverently, his eyes on her hard nipples. With a faint groan, he bent his dark head and his mouth touched the soft curve of her breast.

She gasped and stiffened. His head lifted immediately. He looked at her and realized that she wasn't trying to get away. Her eyes were full of shocked pleasure and curiosity.

"Another first?" he asked with faint arrogance and a calculating smile that didn't really register in her whirling mind.

She nodded, swallowing. Her body, as if it was ignoring her brain, moved sensuously on the bed. She'd never dreamed that she could let a man touch her like this, that she could enjoy letting him touch her, after her one horrible experience with intimacy.

He put his mouth over her nipple and suckled her so insistently that she cried out, drowning in a veritable flood of shocked pleasure.

The little cry aroused Matt unexpectedly, and he was rougher with her than he meant to be, his mouth suddenly demanding on her soft flesh. He tasted her hungrily for several long seconds until he forced his mind to remember why he shouldn't let himself go in headfirst. He wanted her almost beyond bearing, but he wasn't going to let her make a fool of him.

He lifted his head and studied her flushed face clinically. She was enjoying it, but she needn't think he was going to let her take possession of him with that pretty body. He knew now that he could have her. She was willing to give in. For a price, he added.

She opened her eyes and lay there watching him with wide, soft, curious eyes. She thought she had him in her pocket, he mused. But she was all too acquiescent. That, he thought amusedly, was a gross miscalculation on her part. It was her nervous retreat that challenged him, not the sort of easy conquest with which he was already too familiar.

Abruptly he sat up, pulling her with him, and slid the straps of her evening dress back up onto her shoulders.

She watched him silently, still shocked by his ardor and puzzled at her unexpected response to it.

He got to his feet and rebuttoned his shirt, reaching for his snap-on tie and then his jacket. He studied her there, sitting dazed on the edge of his bed, and his dark eyes narrowed. He smiled, but it wasn't a pleasant smile.

"You're not bad," he murmured lazily. "But the fascinated virgin bit turns me right off. I like experience."

She blinked. She was still trying to make her mind work again.

"I assume that your other would-be lovers liked that wide-eyed, first-time look?"

Other lovers. Had he guessed about her past? Her eyes registered the fear.

He saw it. He was vaguely sorry that she wasn't what she pretended to be. He was all but jaded when it came to pursuing women. He hated the coy behavior, the teasing, the manipulation that eventually ended in his bedroom. He was considered a great catch by single women, rich and handsome and experienced in sensual techniques. But he always made his position clear at the outset. He didn't want marriage. That didn't really matter to most of the women in his life. A diamond here, an exotic vacation there, and they seemed satisfied for as long as it lasted. Not that there were many affairs. He was tired of the game. In fact, he'd never been more tired of it than he was right now. His whole expression was one of disgust.

Leslie saw it in his eyes and wished she could curl up into a ball and hide under the bed. His cold scrutiny made her feel cheap, just as that doctor had, just as the media had, just as her mother had…

He couldn't have explained why that expression on her face made him feel guilty. But it did.

He turned away from her. "Come on," he said, picking up her wrap and purse and tossing them to her. "I'll run you home."

She didn't look at him as she followed him down the length of the hall. It was longer than she realized,

and even before they got to the front door, her leg was
throbbing. Dancing had been damaging enough, without the jerk of his hand as they left the ballroom. But
she ground her teeth together and didn't let her growing discomfort show in her face. He wasn't going to
make her feel any worse than she already did by accusing her of putting on an act for sympathy. She went
past him out the door he was holding open, avoiding
his eyes. She wondered how things could have gone so
terribly wrong.

THE SPACIOUS GARAGE was full of cars. He got out the silver Mercedes and opened the door to let her climb inside, onto the leather-covered passenger seat. He closed
her door with something of a snap. Her fingers fumbled
the seat belt into its catch and she hoped he wouldn't
want to elaborate on what he'd already said.

She stared out the window at the dark silhouettes of
buildings and trees as he drove along the back roads
that eventually led into Jacobsville. She was sick about
the way she'd acted. He probably thought she was the
easiest woman alive. The only thing she didn't understand was why he didn't take advantage of it. The obvious reason made her even more uncomfortable. Didn't
they say that some men didn't want what came easily?
It was probably true. He'd been in pursuit as long as
she was backing away from him. What irony, to spend
years being afraid of men, running crazily from even
the most platonic involvement, to find herself capable of torrid desire with the one man in the world who
didn't want her!

He felt her tension. It was all too apparent that she

was disappointed that he hadn't played the game to its finish.

"Is that what Ed gets when he takes you home?" he drawled.

Her nails bit into her small evening bag. Her teeth clenched. She wasn't going to dignify that remark with a reply.

He shrugged and paused to turn onto the main highway. "Don't take it so hard," he said lazily. "I'm a little too sophisticated to fall for it, but there are a few rich single ranchers around Jacobsville. Cy Parks comes to mind. He's hell on the nerves, but he is a widower." He glanced at her averted face. "On second thought, he's had enough tragedy in his life. I wouldn't wish you on him."

She couldn't even manage to speak, she was so choked up with hurt. Why, she wondered, did everything she wanted in life turn on her and tear her to pieces? It was like tracking cougars with a toy gun. Just when she seemed to find peace and purpose, her life became nothing but torment. As if her tattered pride wasn't enough, she was in terrible pain. She shifted in the seat, hoping that a change of position would help. It didn't.

"How did that bone get shattered?" he asked conversationally.

"Don't you know?" she asked on a harsh laugh. If he'd seen the story about her, as she suspected, he was only playing a cruel game—the sort of game he'd already accused her of playing!

He glanced at her with a scowl. "And how would I know?" he wondered aloud.

She frowned. Maybe he hadn't read anything at all! He might be fishing for answers.

She swallowed, gripping her purse tightly.

He swung the Mercedes into the driveway of her boardinghouse and pulled up at the steps, with the engine still running. He turned to her. "How *would* I know?" he asked again, his voice determined.

"You seem to think you're an expert on everything else about me," she replied evasively.

His chin lifted as he studied her through narrowed eyes. "There are several ways a bone can be shattered," he said quietly. "One way is from a bullet."

She didn't feel as if she were still breathing. She sat like a statue, watching him deliberate.

"What do you know about bullets?" she asked shortly.

"My unit was called up during Operation Desert Storm," he told her. "I served with an infantry unit. I know quite a lot about bullets. And what they do to bone," he added. "Which brings me to the obvious question. Who shot you?"

"I didn't say... I was shot," she managed.

His intense gaze held her like invisible ropes. "But you were, weren't you?" he asked with shrewd scrutiny. His lips tugged into a cold smile. "As to who did it, I'd bet on one of your former lovers. Did he catch you with somebody else, or did you tease him the way you teased me tonight and then refuse him?" He gave her another contemptuous look. "Not that you refused. You didn't exactly play hard to get."

Her ego went right down to her shoes. He was painting her over with evil colors. She bit her lower lip. It was unpleasant enough to have her memories, but to have this man making her out to be some sort of nympho-maniac was painful beyond words. Her first real taste of tender intimacy had been with him, tonight, and he made it sound dirty and cheap.

She unfastened her seat belt and got out of the car with as much dignity as she could muster. Her leg was incredibly painful. All she wanted was her bed, her heating pad and some more aspirins. And to get away from her tormenter.

Matt switched off the engine and moved around the car, irritated by the way she limped.

"I'll take you to the door…!"

She flinched when he came close. She backed away from him, actually shivering when she remembered shamefully what she'd let him do to her. Her eyes clouded with unshed angry tears, with outraged virtue.

"More games?" he asked tersely. He hadn't liked having her back away again after the way she'd been in his bedroom.

"I don't…play games," she replied, hating the hic-cup of a sob that revealed how upset she really was. She clutched her wrap and her purse to her chest, accusing eyes glaring at him. "And you can go to hell!"

He scowled at the way she looked, barely hearing the words. She was white in the face and her whole body seemed rigid, as if she really was upset.

She turned and walked away, wincing inwardly with every excruciating step, to the front porch. But her face didn't show one trace of her discomfort. She held her head high. She still had her pride, she thought through a wave of pain.

Matt watched her go into the boardinghouse with more mixed, confused emotions than he'd ever felt. He remembered vividly that curious "Don't you know?" when he'd asked who shot her.

He got back into the Mercedes and sat staring through the windshield for a long moment before he started it. Miss Murry was one puzzle he intended to solve, and if it cost him a fortune in detective fees, he was going to do it.

# CHAPTER FIVE

LESLIE CRIED FOR what seemed hours. The aspirin didn't help the leg pain at all. There was no medicine known to man that she could take for her wounded ego. Matt had swept the floor with her, played with her, laughed at her naiveté and made her out to be little better than a prostitute. He was like that emergency room doctor so long ago who'd made her ashamed of her body. It was a pity that her first real desire for a man's touch had made her an object of contempt to the man himself.

Well, she told herself as she wiped angrily at the tears, she'd never make that mistake again. Matt Caldwell could go right where she'd told him to!

The phone rang and she hesitated to answer it. But it might be Ed. She picked up the receiver.

"We had a good laugh about you," Carolyn told her outright. "I guess you'll think twice before you throw yourself at him again! He said you were so easy that you disgusted him…!"

Almost shaking with humiliation, she put the receiver down with a slam and then unplugged the phone. It was so close to what Matt had already said that there was no reason not to believe her. Carolyn's harsh arrogance was just what she needed to make the miserable evening complete.

THE PAIN, COMBINED with the humiliation, kept her awake until almost daylight. She missed breakfast, not to mention church, and when she did finally open her eyes, it was to a kind of pain she hadn't experienced since the night she was shot.

She shifted, wincing, and then moaned as the movement caused another searing wave of discomfort up her leg. The knock on her door barely got through to her. "Come in," she said in a husky, exhausted tone.

The door opened and there was Matt Caldwell, unshaven and with dark circles under his eyes.

Carolyn's words came back to haunt her. She grabbed the first thing that came to hand, a plastic bottle of spring water she kept by the bed, and flung it furiously across the room at him. It missed his head, and Ed's, by a quarter of an inch.

"No, thanks," Ed said, moving in front of Matt. "I don't want any water."

Her face was lined with pain, white with it. She glared at Matt's hard, angry face with eyes that would have looked perfectly natural over a cocked pistol.

"I couldn't get you on the phone, and I was worried," Ed said gently, approaching her side of the double bed she occupied. He noticed the unplugged telephone on her bedside table. "Now I know why I couldn't get you on the phone." He studied her drawn face. "How bad is it?"

She could barely breathe. "Bad," she said huskily, thinking what an understatement that word was.

He took her thick white chenille bathrobe from the chair beside the bed. "Come on. We're going to drive you to the emergency room. Matt can phone Lou Coltrain and have her meet us there."

It was an indication of the pain that she didn't argue. She got out of bed, aware of the picture she must make in the thick flannel pajamas that covered every inch of her up to her chin. Matt was probably shocked, she thought as she let Ed stuff her into the robe. He probably expected her to be naked under the covers, conforming to the image he had of her nymphomania!

He hadn't said a word. He just stood there, by the door, grimly watching Ed get her ready—until she tried to walk, and folded up.

Ed swung her up in his arms, stopping Matt's instinctive quick movement toward her. Ed knew for a fact that she'd scream the house down if his cousin so much as touched her. He didn't know what had gone on the night before, but judging by the way Matt and Leslie looked, it had been both humiliating and embarrassing.

"I can carry her," he told Matt. "Let's go."

Matt glimpsed her contorted features and didn't hesitate. He led the way down the hall and right out the front door.

"My purse," she said huskily. "My insurance card…"

"That can be taken care of later," Matt said stiffly. He opened the back door of the Mercedes and waited while Ed slid her onto the seat.

She leaned back with her eyes closed, almost sick from the pain.

"She should never have gotten on the dance floor," Matt said through his teeth as they started toward town. "And then I jerked her up out of her chair. It's my fault."

Ed didn't reply. He glanced over the seat at Leslie with concern in his whole expression. He hoped she hadn't done any major damage to herself with that exhibition the night before.

Lou Coltrain was waiting in the emergency room as Ed carried Leslie inside the building. She motioned him down the hall to a room and closed the door behind Matt as soon as he entered.

She examined the leg carefully, asking questions that Leslie was barely able to answer. "I want X-rays," she said. "But I'll give you something for pain first."

"Thank you," Leslie choked, fighting tears.

Lou smoothed her wild hair. "You poor little thing," she said softly. "Cry if you want to. It must hurt like hell."

She went out to get the injection, and tears poured down Leslie's face because of that tender concern. She hardly ever cried. She was tough. She could take anything—near-rape, bullet wounds, notoriety, her mother's trial, the refusal of her parent to even speak to her…

"There, there," Ed said. He produced a handkerchief and blotted the tears, smiling down at her. "Dr. Lou is going to make it all better."

"For God's sake…!" Matt bit off angry words and walked out of the room. It was unbearable that he'd hurt her like that. Unbearable! And then to have to watch Ed comforting her…!

"I hate him," Leslie choked when he was gone. She actually shivered. "He laughed about it," she whispered, blind to Ed's curious scowl. "She said they both laughed about it, that he was disgusted."

"She?"

"Carolyn." The tears were hot in her eyes, cold on her cheeks. "I hate him!"

Lou came back with the injection and gave it, waiting for it to take effect. She glanced at Ed. "You might want to wait outside. I'm taking her down to X-ray my-self. I'll come and get you when we've done some tests."

"Okay."

He went out and joined Matt in the waiting room. The older man's face was drawn, tormented. He barely glanced at Ed before he turned his attention to the trees outside the window. It was a dismal gray day, with rain threatening. It matched his mood.

Ed leaned against the wall beside him with a frown. "She said Carolyn phoned her last night," he began. "I suppose that's why the phone was unplugged."

It was Matt's turn to look puzzled. "What?"

"Leslie said Carolyn told her the two of you were laughing at her," he murmured. "She didn't say what about."

Matt's face hardened visibly. He rammed his hands into his pockets and his eyes were terrible to look into.

"Don't hurt Leslie," Ed said suddenly, his voice quiet but full of venom. "She hasn't had an easy life. Don't make things hard on her. She has no place else to go."

Matt glanced at him, disliking the implied threat as much as the fact that Ed knew far more about Leslie than he did. Were they lovers? Old lovers, perhaps?

"She keeps secrets," he said. "She was shot. Who did it?"

Ed lifted both eyebrows. "Who said she was shot?" he asked innocently, doing it so well that he actually fooled his cousin.

Matt hesitated. "Nobody. I assumed...well, how else does a bone get shattered?"

"By a blow, by a bad fall, in a car wreck..." Ed trailed off, leaving Matt with something to think about.

"Yes. Of course." The older man sighed. "Dancing

put her in this shape. I didn't realize just how fragile she was. She doesn't exactly shout her problems to the world."

"She was always like that," Ed replied.

Matt turned to face him. "How did you meet her?"

"She and I were in college together," Ed told him. "We used to date occasionally. She trusts me," he added.

Matt was turning what he knew about Leslie over in his mind. If the pieces had been part of a puzzle, none of them would fit. When they first met, she avoided his touch like the plague. Last night, she'd enjoyed his advances. She'd been nervous and shy at their first meeting. Later, at the office, she'd been gregarious, almost playful. Last night, she'd been a completely different woman on the dance floor. Then, when he'd taken her home with him, she'd been hungry, sensuous, tender. Nothing about her made any sense.

"Don't trust her too far," Matt advised the other man. "She's too secretive to suit me. I thinks she's hiding something…maybe something pretty bad."

Ed didn't dare react. He pursed his lips and smiled. "Leslie's never hurt anyone in her life," he remarked. "And before you get the wrong idea about her, you'd better know that she has a real fear of men."

Matt laughed. "Oh, that's a good one," he said mockingly. "You should have seen her last night when we were alone."

Ed's eyes narrowed. "What do you mean?"

"I mean she's easy," Matt said with a contemptuous smile.

Ed's eyes began to glitter. He called his cousin a name that made Matt's eyebrows arch.

"Easy. My God!" Ed ground out.

Matt was puzzled by the other man's inexplicable be-havior. Probably he was jealous. His cell phone began to trill, diverting him. He answered it. He recognized Carolyn's voice immediately and moved away, so that Ed couldn't hear what he said. Ed was certainly acting strange lately.

"I thought you were coming over to ride with me this afternoon," Carolyn said cheerfully. "Where are you?"

"At the hospital," he said absently, his eyes on Ed's retreating back going through the emergency room doors. "What did you say to Leslie last night?"

"What do you mean?"

"When you phoned her!" Matt prompted.

Carolyn sounded vague. "Well, I wanted to see if she was better," she replied. "She seemed to be in a lot of pain after the dance."

"What else did you say?"

Carolyn laughed. "Oh, I see. I'm being accused of something underhanded, is that it? Really, Matt, I thought you could see through that phony vulnerabil-ity of hers. What did she tell you I said?"

He shrugged. "Never mind. I must have misunder-stood."

"You certainly did," she assured him firmly. "I wouldn't call someone in pain to upset them. I thought you knew me better than that."

"I do." He was seething. So now it seemed that Miss Murry was making up lies about Carolyn. Had it been to get even with him, for not giving in to her wiles? Or was she trying to turn his cousin against him?

"What about that horseback ride? And what are you doing at the hospital?" she added suddenly.

"I'm with Ed, visiting one of his friends," he said.

"Better put the horseback ride off until next weekend.
I'll phone you."

He hung up. His eyes darkened with anger. He
wanted the Murry woman out of his company, out of
his life. She was going to be nothing but trouble.

He repocketed the phone and went outside to wait
for Ed and Leslie.

A GOOD HALF HOUR LATER, Ed came out of the emergency
room with his hands in his pockets, looking worried.

"They're keeping her overnight," he said curtly.

"For a sore leg?" Matt asked with mild sarcasm.

Ed scowled. "One of the bones shifted and it's pressing on a nerve," he replied. "Lou says it won't get any
better until it's fixed. They're sending for an orthopedic
man from Houston. He'll be in this afternoon."

"Who's going to pay for that?" Matt asked coldly.

"Since you ask, I am," Ed returned, not intimidated
even by those glittery eyes.

"It's your money," the older man replied. He let out
a breath. "What caused the bone to separate?"

"Why ask a question when you already know the
answer?" Ed wanted to know. "I'm going to stay with
her. She's frightened."

He was fairly certain that even if Leslie could fake
pain, she couldn't fake an X-ray. Somewhere in the
back of his mind he found guilt lurking. If he hadn't
pulled her onto the dance floor, and if he hadn't jerked
her to her feet...

He turned away and walked out of the building without another word. Leslie was Ed's business. He kept telling himself that. But all the way home, his conscience
stabbed at him. She couldn't help being what she was.

Even so, he hadn't meant to hurt her. He remembered the tears, genuine tears, boiling out of her eyes when Lou had touched her hair so gently. She acted as if she'd never had tenderness in her life.

He drove himself home and tried to concentrate on briefing himself for a director's meeting the next day. But long before bedtime, he gave it up and drank himself into uneasy sleep.

THE ORTHOPEDIC MAN examined the X-rays and seconded Lou's opinion that immediate surgery was required. But Leslie didn't want the surgery. She refused to talk about it. The minute the doctors and Ed left the room, she struggled out of bed and hobbled to the closet to pull her pajamas and robe and shoes out of it.

In the hall, Matt came upon Ed and Lou and a tall, distinguished stranger in an expensive suit.

"You two look like stormy weather," he mused. "What's wrong?"

"Leslie won't have the operation," Ed muttered worriedly. "Dr. Santos flew all the way from Houston to do the surgery, and she won't hear of it."

"Maybe she doesn't think she needs it," Matt said.

Lou glanced at him. "You have no idea what sort of pain she's in," she said, impatient with him. "One of the bone fragments, the one that shifted, is pressing right on a nerve."

"The bones should have been properly aligned at the time the accident occurred," the visiting orthopedic surgeon agreed. "It was criminally irresponsible of the attending physician to do nothing more than bandage the leg. A cast wasn't even used until afterward!"

That sounded negligent to Matt, too. He frowned. "Did she say why not?"

Lou sighed angrily. "She won't talk about it. She won't listen to any of us. Eventually she'll have to. But in the meantime, the pain is going to drive her insane."

Matt glanced from one set face to the other and walked past them to Leslie's room.

She was wearing her flannel pajamas and reaching for the robe when Matt walked in. She gave him a glare hot enough to boil water.

"Well, at least you won't be trying to talk me into an operation I don't want," she muttered as she struggled to get from the closet to the bed.

"Why won't I?"

She arched both eyebrows expressively. "I'm the enemy."

He stood at the foot of the bed, watching her get into the robe. Her leg was at an awkward angle, and her face was pinched. He could imagine the sort of pain she was already experiencing.

"Suit yourself about the operation," he replied with forced indifference, folding his arms across his chest. "But don't expect me to have someone carry you back and forth around the office. If you want to make a martyr of yourself, be my guest."

She stopped fiddling with the belt of the robe and stared at him quietly, puzzled.

"Some people enjoy making themselves objects of pity to people around them," he continued deliberately.

"I don't want pity!" she snapped.

"Really?"

She wrapped the belt around her fingers and stared at it. "I'll have to be in a cast."

"No doubt."

"My insurance hasn't taken effect yet, either," she said with averted eyes. "Once it's in force, I can have the operation." She looked back at him coldly. "I'm not going to let Ed pay for it, in case you wondered, and I don't care if he can afford it!"

He had to fight back a stirring of admiration for her independent stance. It could be part of the pose, he realized, but it sounded pretty genuine. His dark blue eyes narrowed. "I'll pay for it," he said, surprising both of them. "It can come out of your weekly check."

Her teeth clenched. "I know how much this sort of thing costs. That's why I've never had it done before. I'd never be able to pay it back in my lifetime."

His eyes fell to her body. "We could work something out," he murmured.

She flushed. "No, we couldn't!"

She stood up, barely able to stand the pain, despite the painkillers they'd given her. She hobbled over to the chair, where her shoes were placed, and eased her feet into them.

"Where are you going?" he asked conversationally.

"Home," she said, and started past him.

He caught her up in his arms like a fallen package and carried her right back to the bed, dumping her on it gently. His arms made a cage as he looked down at her flushed face. "Don't be stupid," he said in a voice that went right through her. "You're no good to yourself or anyone else in this condition. You have no choice."

Her lips trembled as she fought to control the tears. She would be helpless, vulnerable. Besides, that surgeon reminded her of the man at the emergency room in Houston. He brought back unbearable shame.

The unshed tears fascinated Matt. She fascinated him. He didn't want to care about what happened to her, but he did.

He reached down and smoothed a long forefinger over her wet lashes. "Do you have family?" he asked unexpectedly.

She thought of her mother, in prison, and felt sick to her very soul. "No," she whispered starkly.

"Are both your parents dead?"

"Yes," she said at once.

"No brothers, sisters?"

She shook her head.

He frowned, as if her situation disturbed him. In fact, it did. She looked vulnerable and fragile and completely lost. He didn't understand why he cared so much for her well-being. Perhaps it was guilt because he'd lured her into a kind of dancing she wasn't really able to do anymore.

"I want to go home," she said harshly.

"Afterward," he replied.

She remembered him saying that before, in almost the same way, and she averted her gaze in shame.

He could have bitten his tongue for that. He shouldn't bait her when she was in such a condition. It was hitting below the belt.

He drew in a long breath. "Leave it to Ed to pick up strays, and make me responsible for them!" he muttered, angry because of her vulnerability and his unwanted response to it.

She didn't say a word, but her lower lip trembled and she turned her face away from him. Beside her hip, her hand was clenched so tightly that the knuckles were white.

He shot away from the bed, his eyes furious. "You're

having the damned operation," he informed her flatly. "Once you're healthy and whole again, you won't need Ed to prop you up. You can work for your living like every other woman."

She didn't answer him. She didn't look at him. She wanted to get better so that she could kick the hell out of him.

"Did you hear me?" he asked in a dangerously soft tone.

She jerked her head to acknowledge the question but she didn't speak.

He let out an angry breath. "I'll tell the others."

He left her lying there and announced her decision to the three people in the hall.

"How did you manage that?" Ed asked when Lou and Dr. Santos went back in to talk to Leslie.

"I made her mad," Matt replied. "Sympathy doesn't work."

"No, it doesn't," Ed replied quietly. "I don't think she's had much of it in her whole life."

"What happened to her parents?" he wanted to know.

Ed was careful about the reply. "Her father misjudged the position of some electrical wires and flew right into them. He was electrocuted."

He frowned darkly. "And her mother?"

"They were both in love with the same man," Ed said evasively. "He died, and Leslie and her mother still aren't on speaking terms."

Matt turned away, jingling the change in his pocket restlessly. "How did he die?"

"Violently," Ed told him. "It was a long time ago. But I don't think Leslie will ever get over it."

Which was true, but it sounded as if Leslie was still in love with the dead man—which was exactly what

Ed wanted. He was going to save her from Matt, whatever it took. She was a good friend. He didn't want her life destroyed because Matt was on the prowl for a new conquest. Leslie deserved something better than to be one of Matt's ex-girlfriends.

Matt glanced at his cousin with a puzzling expression. "When will they operate?"

"Tomorrow morning," Ed said. "I'll be late getting to work. I'm going to be here while it's going on."

Matt nodded. He glanced down the hall toward the door of Leslie's room. He hesitated for a moment before he turned and went out of the building without another comment.


LATER, ED QUESTIONED HER about what Matt had said to her.

"He said that I was finding excuses because I wanted people to feel sorry for me," she said angrily. "And I do not have a martyr complex!"

Ed chuckled. "I know that."

"I can't believe you're related to someone like that," she said furiously. "He's horrible!"

"He's had a rough life. Something you can identify with," he added gently.

"I think he and his latest girlfriend deserve each other," she murmured.

"Carolyn phoned while he was here. I don't know what was said, but I'd bet my bottom dollar she denied saying anything to upset you."

"Would you expect her to admit it?" she asked. She lay back against the pillow, glad that the injection they'd given her was taking effect. "I guess I'll be clumping around your office in a cast for weeks, if he doesn't find some excuse to fire me in the meantime."

"There is company policy in such matters," he said easily. "He'd have to have my permission to fire you, and he won't get it."

"I'm impressed," she said, and managed a wan smile.

"So you should be," he chuckled. He searched her eyes. "Leslie, why didn't the doctor set those bones when it happened?"

She studied the ceiling. "He said the whole thing was my fault and that I deserved all my wounds. He called me a vicious little tramp who caused decent men to be murdered." Her eyes closed. "Nothing ever hurt so much."

"I can imagine!"

"I never went to a doctor again," she continued. "It wasn't just the things he said to me, you know. There was the expense, too. I had no insurance and no money. Mama had to have a public defender and I worked while I finished high school to help pay my way at my friend's house. The pain was bad, but eventually I got used to it, and the limp." She turned quiet eyes to Ed's face. "It would be sort of nice to be able to walk normally again. And I will pay back whatever it costs, if you and your cousin will be patient."

He winced. "Nobody's worried about the cost."

"He is," she informed him evenly. "And he's right. I don't want to be a financial burden on anyone, not even him."

"We'll talk about all this later," he said gently. "Right now, I just want you to get better."

She sighed. "Will I? I wonder."

"Miracles happen all the time," he told her. "You're overdue for one."

"I'd settle gladly for the ability to walk normally," she said at once, and she smiled.

## CHAPTER SIX

THE OPERATION WAS over by lunchtime the following day. Ed stayed until Leslie was out of the recovery room and out of danger, lying still and pale in the bed in the private room with the private nurse he'd hired to stay with her for the first couple of days. He'd spoken to both Lou Coltrain and the visiting orthopedic surgeon, who assured him that Miss Murry would find life much less painful from now on. Modern surgery had progressed to the point that procedures once considered impossible were now routine.

He went back to work feeling light and cheerful. Matt stopped him in the hall.

"Well?" he asked abruptly.

Ed grinned from ear to ear. "She's going to be fine. Dr. Santos said that in six weeks, when she comes out of that cast, she'll be able to dance in a contest."

Matt nodded. "Good."

Ed answered a question Matt had about one of their accounts and then, assuming that Matt didn't want anything else at the moment, he went back to his office. He had a temporary secretary, a pretty little redhead who had a bright personality and good dictation skills.

Surprisingly, Matt followed him into his office and closed the door. "Tell me how that bone was shattered," he said abruptly.

Ed sat down and leaned forward with his forearms on his cluttered desk. "That's Leslie's business, Matt," he replied. "I wouldn't tell you, even if I knew," he added, lying through his teeth with deliberate calm.

He sighed irritably. "She's a puzzle. A real puzzle."

"She's a sweet girl who's had a lot of hard knocks," Ed told him. "But regardless of what you think you know about her, she isn't 'easy.' Don't make the mistake of classing her with your usual sort of woman. You'll regret it."

Matt studied the younger man curiously and his eyes narrowed. "What do you mean, I think she's 'easy'?" he asked, bristling.

"Forgotten already? That's what you said about her."

Matt felt uncomfortable at the words that he'd spoken with such assurance to Leslie. He glanced at Ed irritably. "Miss Murry obviously means something to you. If you're so fond of her, why haven't you married her?"

Ed smoothed back his hair. "She kept me from blowing my brains out when my fiancée was gunned down in a bank robbery in Houston," he said. "I actually had the pistol loaded. She took it away from me."

Matt's eyes narrowed. "You never told me you were that despondent."

"You wouldn't have understood," came the reply. "Women were always a dime a dozen to you, Matt. You've never really been in love."

Matt's face, for once, didn't conceal his bitterness. "I wouldn't give any woman that sort of power over me," he said in clipped tones. "Women are devious, Ed. They'll smile at you until they get what they want, then they'll walk right over you to the next sucker. I've seen too many good men brought down by women they loved."

"There are bad men, too," Ed pointed out.

Matt shrugged. "I'm not arguing with that." He smiled. "I would have done what I could for you, though," he added. "We have our disagreements, but we're closer than most cousins are."

Ed nodded. "Yes, we are."

"You really are fond of Miss Murry, aren't you?"

"In a big brotherly sort of way," Ed affirmed. "She trusts me. If you knew her, you'd understand how difficult it is for her to trust a man."

"I think she's pulling the wool over your eyes," Matt told him. "You be careful. She's down on her luck, and you're rich."

Ed's face contorted briefly. "Good God, Matt, you haven't got a clue what she's really like."

"Neither have you," Matt commented with a cold smile. "But I know things about her that you don't. Let's leave it at that."

Ed hated his own impotence. "I want to keep her in my office."

"How do you expect her to come to work in a cast?" he asked frankly.

Ed leaned back in his chair and grinned. "The same way I did five years ago, when I had that skiing accident and broke my ankle. People work with broken bones all the time. And she doesn't type with her feet."

Matt shrugged. Miss Murry had him completely confused. "Suit yourself," he said finally. "Just keep her out of my way."

That shouldn't be difficult, Ed thought ruefully. Matt certainly wasn't on Leslie's list of favorite people. He wondered what the days ahead would bring. It would be like storing dynamite with lighted candles.

LESLIE WAS OUT of the hospital in three days and back at work in a week. The company had paid for her surgery, to her surprise and Ed's. She knew that Matt had only done that out of guilt. Well, he needn't flay himself over what happened. She didn't really blame him. She had loved dancing with him. She refused to think of how that evening had ended. Some memories were best forgotten.

She hobbled into Ed's office with the use of crutches and plopped herself down behind her desk on her first day back on the job.

"How did you get here?" Ed asked with a surprised smile. "You can't drive, can you?"

"No, but one of the girls in my rooming house works in downtown Jacobsville and we're going to become a carpool three days a week. I'm paying my share of the gas and on her days off, I'll get a taxi to work," she added.

"I'm glad you're back," he said with genuine fondness.

"Oh, sure you are," she said with a teasing glance. "I heard all about Karla Smith when the girls from Mr. Caldwell's office came to see me. I understand she has a flaming crush on you."

Ed chuckled. "So they say. Poor girl."

She made a face. "You can't live in the past."

"Tell yourself that."

She put her crutches on the floor beside the desk, and swiveled back in her desk chair. "It's going to be a little difficult for me to get back and forth to your office," she said. "Can you dictate letters in here?"

"Of course."

She looked around the office with pleasure. "I'm glad I got to come back," she murmured. "I thought Mr. Caldwell might find an excuse to let me go."

"I'm Mr. Caldwell, too," he pointed out. "Matt's bark is worse than his bite. He won't fire you."

She grimaced. "Don't let me cause trouble between you," she said with genuine concern. "I'd rather quit..."

"No, you won't," he interrupted. He ruffled her short hair with a playful grin. "I like having you around. Besides, you spell better than the other women."

Her eyes lit up as she looked at him. She smiled back. "Thanks, boss."

Matt opened the door in time to encounter the affectionate looks they exchanged and his face hardened as he slammed it behind him.

They both jumped.

"Jehosophat, Matt!" Ed burst out, catching his breath. "Don't do that!"

"Don't play games with your secretary on my time," Matt returned. His cold dark eyes went to Leslie, whose own eyes went cold at the sight of him. "Back at work, I see, Miss Murry."

"All the better to pay you back for my hospital stay, sir," she returned with a smile that bordered on insolence.

He bit back a sharp reply and turned to Ed, ignoring her. "I want you to take Nell Hobbs out to lunch and find out how she's going to vote on the zoning proposal. If they zone that land adjoining my ranch as recreational, I'm going to spend my life in court."

"If she votes for it, she'll be the only one," Ed assured him. "I spoke to the other commissioners myself."

He seemed to relax a little. "Okay. In that case, you can run over to Houlihan's dealership and drive my new Jaguar over here. It came in this morning."

Ed's eyes widened. "You're going to let me drive it?"

"Why not?" Matt asked with a warm smile, the sort Leslie knew she'd never see on that handsome face.

Ed chuckled. "Then, thanks. I'll be back shortly!" He started down the hall at a dead run. "Leslie, we'll do those letters after lunch!"

"Sure," she said. "I can spend the day updating those old herd records." She glanced at Matt to let him know she hadn't forgotten his instructions from before her operation.

He put his hands in the pockets of his slacks and his blue eyes searched her gray ones intently. Deliberately he let his gaze fall to her soft mouth. He remembered the feel of it clinging to his parted lips, hungry and moaning…

His teeth clenched. He couldn't think about that. "The herd records can wait," he said tersely. "My secretary is home with a sick child, so you can work for me for the rest of the day. Ed can let Miss Smith handle his urgent stuff today."

She hesitated visibly. "Yes, sir," she said in a wooden voice.

"I have to talk to Henderson about one of the new accounts. I'll meet you in my office in thirty minutes."

"Yes, sir."

They were watching each other like opponents in a match when Matt made an angry sound under his breath and walked out.

Leslie spent a few minutes sorting the mail and looking over it. A little over a half hour went by before she realized it. A sound caught her attention and she looked up to find an impatient Matt Caldwell standing in the doorway.

"Sorry. I lost track of the time," she said quickly, putting the opened mail aside. She reached for her crutches and got up out of her chair, reaching for her pad and pen when she was ready to go. She looked up at Matt, who seemed taller than ever. "I'm ready when you are, boss," she said courteously.

"Don't call me boss," he said flatly.

"Okay, Mr. Caldwell," she returned.

He glared at her, but she gave him a bland look and even managed a smile. He wanted to throw things.

He turned, leaving her to follow him down the long hall to his executive office, which had a bay window overlooking downtown Jacobsville. His desk was solid oak, huge, covered with equipment and papers of all sorts. There was a kid leather–covered chair behind the desk and two equally impressive wing chairs, and a sofa, all done in burgundy. The carpet was a deep, rich beige. The curtains were plaid, picking up the burgundy in the furniture and adding it to autumn hues. There was a framed portrait of someone who looked vaguely like Matt over the mantel of the fireplace, in which gas logs rested. There were two chairs and a table near the fireplace, probably where Matt and some visitor would share a pot of coffee or a drink. There was a bar against one wall with a mirror behind it, giving an added air of spacious comfort to the high-ceilinged room. The windows were tall ones, unused because the

Victorian house that contained the offices had central air-conditioning.

Matt watched her studying her surroundings covertly. He closed the door behind them and motioned her into a chair facing the desk. She eased down into it and put her crutches beside her. She was still a little uncomfortable, but aspirin was enough to contain the pain these days. She looked forward to having the cast off, to walking normally again.

She put the pad on her lap and maneuvered the leg in the cast so that it was as comfortable as she could get it.

Matt was leaning back in his chair with his booted feet on the desk and his eyes narrow and watchful as he sketched her slender body in the flowing beige pantsuit she was wearing with a patterned scarf tucked in the neck of the jacket. The outside seam in the left leg of her slacks had been snipped to allow for the cast. Otherwise, she was covered from head to toe, just as she had been from the first time he saw her. Odd, that he hadn't really noticed that before. It wasn't a new habit dating from the night he'd touched her so intimately, either.

"How's the leg?" he asked curtly.

"Healing, thank you," she replied. "I've already spoken to the bookkeeper about pulling out a quarter of my check weekly..."

He leaned forward so abruptly that it sounded like a gunshot when his booted feet hit the floor.

"I'll take that up with bookkeeping," he said sharply. "You've overstepped your authority, Miss Murry. Don't do it again."

She shifted in the chair, moving the ungainly cast, and assumed a calm expression. "I'm sorry, Mr. Caldwell."

Her voice was serene but her hands were shaking on the pad and pen. He averted his eyes and got to his feet, glaring out the window.

She waited patiently with her eyes on the blank pad, wondering when he was going to start dictation.

"You told Ed that Carolyn phoned you the night before we took you to the emergency room and made some cruel remarks." He remembered what Ed had related about that conversation and it made him unusually thoughtful. He turned and caught her surprised expression. "Carolyn denies saying anything to upset you."

Her expression didn't change. She didn't care what he thought of her anymore. She didn't say a word in her defense.

His dark eyebrows met over the bridge of his nose. "Well?"

"What would you like me to say?"

"You might try apologizing," he told her coldly, trying to smoke her out. "Carolyn was very upset to have such a charge made against her. I don't like having her upset," he added deliberately and stood looking down his nose at her, waiting for her to react to the challenge.

Her fingers tightened around the pen. It was going to be worse than she ever dreamed, trying to work with him. He couldn't fire her, Ed had said, but that didn't mean he couldn't make her quit. If he made things difficult enough for her, she wouldn't be able to stay.

All at once, it didn't seem worth the effort. She was tired, worn-out, and Carolyn had hurt her, not the reverse. She was sick to death of trying to live from one day to the next with the weight of the past bearing down on her more each day. Being tormented by Matt Caldwell on top of all that was the last straw.

She reached for her crutches and stood up, pad and all.

"Where do you think you're going?" Matt demanded, surprised that she was giving up without an argument.

She went toward the door. He got in front of her, an easy enough task when every step she took required extreme effort.

She looked up at him, resigned and resentful. "Ed said you couldn't fire me without his consent," she said quietly. "But you can hound me until I quit, can't you?"

He didn't speak. His face was rigid. "Would you give up so easily?" he asked, baiting her. "Where will you go?"

Her gaze dropped to the floor. Idly she noticed that one of her flat-heeled shoes had a smudge of mud on it. She should clean it off.

"I said, where will you go?" Matt persisted.

She met his cold eyes. "Surely in all of Texas, there's more than one secretarial position available," she said. "Please move."

He did move, but not in the way she'd expected. He took the crutches away from her and propped them against the bookshelf by the door. His hands went on either side of her head. His dark eyes held a faint glitter as he studied her wan face, her soft mouth.

"Don't you dare," she said tightly.

He moved closer. He smelled of spice and aftershave and coffee. His breath was warm where it brushed her forehead. She could feel the warmth of his tall, fit body, and she remembered how it had felt to let him hold her and touch her in his bedroom.

He was remembering those same things, but not with pleasure. He hated the attraction he felt for this woman, whom he didn't, couldn't trust.

"You don't like being touched, you said," he reminded her as his lean hand suddenly smoothed over her shoulder.

Her indrawn breath was audible. She looked up at him with all her hidden vulnerabilities exposed. "Please don't do this," she whispered. "I'm no threat to Ed, or to you, either. Just…let me go. I'll vanish."

She probably would, and that wounded him. He was making her life miserable. Why did this woman arouse such bitter feelings in him, when he was the soul of kindness to most people with problems—especially physical problems, like hers.

"Ed won't like it," he said tersely.

"Ed doesn't have to know anything," she said dully. "You can tell him whatever you like."

"Is he your lover?"

"No."

"Why not? You don't mind if he touches you."

"He doesn't. Not…the way you do."

Her strained voice made him question his own cruelty. He lifted his hand away from her body and tilted her chin up so that he could see her eyes. They were turbulent, misty.

"How many poor fools have you played the innocent with, Miss Murry?" he asked coldly.

She saw the lines in his face, many more than his age should have caused. She saw the coldness in his eyes, the bitterness of too many betrayals, too many loveless years.

Unexpectedly she reached up and touched his hair, smoothing it back as Lou had smoothed hers back in an act of silent compassion.

It made him furious. His body pressed completely against hers, as if holding her prisoner.

Her face colored. It was like that night. It was the way Mike had behaved, twisting his body against her innocent one and laughing at her embarrassment. He'd said things, done things to her in front of his friends that still made her want to gag.

Matt's hand fell to her hip. She was stiff against him, frozen with painful memories of another man, another encounter, that had begun just this way. She'd thought she loved Mike until he made her an object of lustful ridicule, making fun of her innocence as he anticipated its delights for the enjoyment of his laughing friends, grouped around them as he forcibly stripped the clothes away from her body. He laughed at her small breasts, at her slender figure, and all the while he touched her insolently and made jokes about her most intimate places.

She was years in the past, reliving the torment, the shame, that had seen her spread-eagled on the wood floor with Mike's drug-crazed friends each holding one of her shaking limbs still while Mike lowered his nude body onto hers and roughly parted her legs...

Matt realized belatedly that Leslie was frozen in place like a statue with a white face and eyes that didn't even see him. He could hear her heartbeat, quick and frantic. Her whole body shook, but not with pleasure or anticipation.

Frowning, he let her go and stepped back. She shivered again, convulsively. Mike had backed away, too, to the sound of a firecracker popping loudly. But it hadn't been a firecracker. It had been a bullet. It went right through him, into Leslie's leg. He looked surprised. Leslie remembered his blue eyes as the life visibly went out of them, leaving them fixed and blank just before he fell heavily on her. There had been such a tiny hole in his back, compared to the one in his chest. Her mother was screaming, trying to fire again, trying to kill her. Leslie had seduced her own lover, she wanted to kill them both, and she was glad Mike was dead. Leslie would be dead, too!

Leslie remembered lying there naked on the floor, with a shattered leg and blood pouring from it so rapidly that she knew she was going to bleed to death before help arrived...

"Leslie?" Matt asked sharply.

He became a white blur as she slid down the wall into oblivion.

WHEN SHE CAME TO, Ed was bending over her with a look of anguished concern. He had a damp towel pressed to her forehead. She looked at him dizzily.

"Ed?" she murmured.

"Yes. How are you?"

She blinked and looked around. She was lying on the big burgundy leather couch in Matt's office. "What happened?" she asked numbly. "Did I faint?"

"Apparently," Ed said heavily. "You came back to work too soon. I shouldn't have agreed."

"But I'm all right," she insisted, pulling herself up. She felt nauseous. She had to swallow repeatedly before she was able to move again.

She took a slow breath and smiled at him. "I'm still a little weak, I guess, and I didn't have any breakfast."

"Idiot," he said, smiling.

She smiled back. "I'm okay. Hand me my crutches, will you?"

He got them from where they were propped against
the wall, and she had a glimpse of Matt standing there
as if he'd been carved from stone. She took the crutches
from Ed and got them under her arms.

"Would you drive me home?" she asked Ed. "I think
maybe I will take one more day off, if that's all right?"

"That's all right," Ed assured her. He looked across
the room. "Right, Matt?"

Matt nodded, a curt jerk of his head. He gave her one
last look and went out the door.

The relief Leslie felt almost knocked her legs from
under her. She remembered what had happened, but
she wasn't about to tell Ed. She wasn't going to cause
a breach between him and the older cousin he adored.
She, who had no family left in the world except the
mother who hated her, had more respect for family than
most people.

She let Ed take her home, and she didn't think about
what had happened in Matt's office. She knew that
every time she saw him from now on, she'd relive those
last few horrible minutes in her mother's apartment
when she was seventeen. If she'd had anyplace else to
go, she'd leave. But she was trapped, for the moment,
at the mercy of a man who had none, a victim of a past
she couldn't even talk about.

ED WENT BACK to the office determined to have it out
with Matt. He knew instinctively that Leslie's collapse
was caused by something the other man did or said, and
he was going to stop the treatment Matt was giving her
before it was too late.

It was anticlimactic when he got into Matt's office,

with his speech rehearsed and ready, only to find it empty.

"He said he was going up to Victoria to see a man about some property, Mr. Caldwell," one of the secretaries commented. "Left in a hurry, too, in that brand-new red Jaguar. We hear you got to drive it over from Houlihan's."

"Yes, I did," he replied, forcing a cheerful smile. "It goes like the wind."

"We noticed," she murmured dryly. "He was flying when he turned the corner. I hope he slows down. It would be a pity if he wrecked it when he'd only just gotten it."

"So it would," Ed replied. He went back to his own office, curious about Matt's odd behavior but rather relieved that the showdown wouldn't have to be faced right away.

# CHAPTER SEVEN

MATT WAS DOING almost a hundred miles an hour on the long highway that led to Victoria. He couldn't get Leslie's face out of his mind. That hadn't been anger or even fear in her gray eyes. It went beyond those emotions. She had been terrified; not of him, but of something she could see that he couldn't. Her tortured gaze had hurt him in a vulnerable spot he didn't know he had. When she fainted, he hated himself. He'd never thought of himself as a particularly cruel man, but he was with Leslie. He couldn't understand the hostility she roused in him. She was fragile, for all her independence and strength of will. Fragile. Vulnerable. Tender.

He remembered the touch of her soft fingers smoothing back his hair and he groaned out loud with self-hatred. He'd been tormenting her, and she'd seen right through the harsh words to the pain that lay underneath them. In return for his insensitivity, she'd reached up and touched him with genuine compassion. He'd rewarded that exquisite tenderness with treatment he wouldn't have offered to a hardened prostitute.

He realized that the speed he was going exceeded the limit by a factor of two and took his foot off the pedal. He didn't even know where the hell he was going. He was running for cover, he supposed, and laughed coldly at his own reaction to Leslie's fainting spell. All his life he'd been kind to stray animals and people down on their luck. He'd followed up that record by torturing a crippled young woman who felt sorry for him. Next, he supposed, he'd be kicking lame dogs down steps.

He pulled off on the side of the highway, into a lay-by, and stopped the car, resting his head on the steering wheel. He didn't recognize himself since Leslie Murry had walked into his life. She brought out monstrous qualities in him. He was ashamed of the way he'd treated her. She was a sweet woman who always seemed surprised when people did kind things for her. On the other hand, Matt's antagonism and hostility didn't seem to surprise her. Was that what she'd had the most of in her life? Had people been so cruel to her that now she expected and accepted cruelty as her lot in life?

He leaned back in the seat and stared at the flat horizon. His mother's desertion and his recent notoriety had soured him on the whole female sex. His mother was an old wound. The assault suit had made him bitter, yet again, despite the fact that he'd avenged himself on the perpetrator. But he remembered her coy, sweet personality very well. She'd pretended innocence and helplessness and when the disguise had come off, he'd found himself the object of vicious public humiliation. His name had been cleared, but the anger and resentment had remained.

But none of that excused his recent behavior. He'd overreacted with Leslie. He was sorry and ashamed for making her suffer for something that wasn't her fault. He took a long breath and put the car in gear. Well, he couldn't run away. He might as well go back to work. Ed would probably be waiting with blood in his eye, and he wouldn't blame him. He deserved a little discomfort.

ED DID READ HIM the riot act, and he took it. He couldn't deny that he'd been unfair to Leslie. He wished he could understand what it was about her that raised the devil in him.

"If you genuinely don't like her," Ed concluded, "can't you just ignore her?"

"Probably," Matt said without meeting his cousin's accusing eyes.

"Then would you? Matt, she needs this job," he continued solemnly.

Matt studied him sharply. "Why does she need it?" he asked. "And why doesn't she have anyplace to go?"

"I can't tell you. I gave my word."

"Is she in some sort of trouble with the law?"

Ed laughed softly. "Leslie?"

"Never mind." He moved back toward the door. He stopped and turned as he reached it. "When she fainted, she said something."

"What?" Ed asked curiously.

"She said, 'Mike, don't.'" He didn't blink. "Who's Mike?"

"A dead man," Ed replied. "Years dead."

"The man she and her mother competed for."

"That's right," Ed said. "If you mention his name in front of her, I'll walk out the door with her, and I won't come back. Ever."

That was serious business to Ed, he realized. He frowned thoughtfully. "Did she love him?"

"She thought she did," Ed replied. His eyes went cold. "He destroyed her life."

"How?"

Ed didn't reply. He folded his hands on the desk and just stared at Matt.

The older man let out an irritated breath. "Has it occurred to you that all this secrecy is only complicating matters?"

"It's occurred. But if you want answers, you'll have to ask Leslie. I don't break promises."

Matt muttered to himself as he opened the door and went out. Ed stared after him worriedly. He hoped he'd done the right thing. He was trying to protect Leslie, but for all he knew, he might just have made matters worse. Matt didn't like mysteries. God forbid that he should try to force Leslie to talk about something she only wanted to forget. He was also worried about Matt's potential reaction to the old scandal. How would he feel if he knew how notorious Leslie really was, if he knew that her mother was serving a sentence for murder?

ED WAS WORRIED ENOUGH to talk to Leslie about it that evening when he stopped by to see how she was.

"I don't want him to know," she said when Ed questioned her. "Ever."

"What if he starts digging and finds out by himself?" Ed asked bluntly. "He'll read everyone's point of view except yours, and even if he reads every tabloid that ran the story, he still won't know the truth of what happened."

"I don't care what he thinks," she lied. "Anyway, it doesn't matter now."

"Why not?"

"Because I'm not coming back to work," she said evenly, avoiding his shocked gaze. "They need a typist at the Jacobsville sewing plant. I applied this afternoon and they accepted me."

"How did you get there?" he asked.

"Cabs run even in Jacobsville, Ed, and I'm not totally penniless." She lifted her head proudly. "I'll pay your cousin back the price of my operation, however long it takes. But I won't take one more day of the sort of treatment I've been getting from him. I'm sorry if he hates women, but I'm not going to become a scapegoat. I've had enough misery."

"I'll agree there," he said. "But I wish you'd reconsider. I had a long talk with him…"

"You didn't tell him?" she exclaimed, horrified.

"No, I didn't tell him," he replied. "But I think you should."

"It's none of his business," she said through her teeth. "I don't owe him an explanation."

"I know it doesn't seem like it, Leslie," he began, "but he's not a bad man." He frowned, searching for a way to explain it to her. "I don't pretend to understand why you set him off, but I'm sure he realizes that he's being unfair."

"He can be unfair as long as he likes, but I'm not giving him any more free shots at me. I mean it, Ed. I'm not coming back."

He leaned forward, feeling defeated. "Well, I'll be around if you need me. You're still my best friend."

She reached out and touched his hand where it rested on his knee. "You're mine, too. I don't know how I'd have managed if it hadn't been for you and your father."

He smiled. "You'd have found a way. Whatever you're lacking, it isn't courage."

She sighed, looking down at her hand resting on his. "I don't know if that's true anymore," she confessed. "I'm so tired of fighting. I thought I could come to Jacobsville and get my life in order, get some peace. And the first man I run headlong into is a male chauvinist with a grudge against the whole female sex. I feel like I've been through the wringer backward."

"What did he say to you today?" he asked.

She blotted out the physical insult. "The usual things, most vividly the way I'd upset Carolyn by lying about her phone call."

"Some lie!" he muttered.

"He believes her."

"I can't imagine why. I used to think he was intelligent."

"He is, or he wouldn't be a millionaire." She got up. "Now go home, Ed. I've got to get some rest so I can be bright and cheerful my first day at my new job."

He winced. "I wanted things to be better than this for you."

She laughed gently. "And just think what a terrible world we'd have if we always got what we think we want."

He had to admit that she had a point. "That sewing plant isn't a very good place to work," he added worriedly.

"It's only temporary," she assured him.

He grimaced. "Well, if you need me, you know where I am."

She smiled. "Thanks."

HE WENT HOME and ate supper and was watching the news when Matt knocked at the door just before opening it and walking in. And why not, Ed thought, when Matt had been raised here, just as he had. He grinned at his cousin as he came into the living room and sprawled over an easy chair.

"How does the Jag drive?" he asked.

"Like an airplane on the ground," he chuckled. He stared at the television screen for a minute. "How's Leslie?"

He grimaced. "She's got a new job."

Matt went very still. "What?"

"She said she doesn't want to work for me anymore. She got a job at the sewing plant, typing. I tried to talk her out of it. She won't budge." He glanced at Matt apologetically. "She knew I wouldn't let you fire her. She said you'd made sure she wanted to quit." He shrugged. "I guess you did. I've known Leslie for six years. I've never known her to faint."

Matt's dark eyes slid to the television screen and seemed to be glued there for a time. The garment company paid minimum wage. He doubted she'd have enough left over after her rent and grocery bill to pay for the medicine she had to take for pain. He couldn't remember a time in his life when he'd been so ashamed of himself. She wasn't going to like working in that plant. He knew the manager, a penny-pinching social climber who didn't believe in holidays, sick days, or paid vacation. He'd work her to death for her pittance and complain because she couldn't do more.

Matt's mouth thinned. He'd landed Leslie in hell with his bad temper and unreasonable prejudice.

Matt got up from the chair and walked out the door without a goodbye. Ed went back to the news without much real enthusiasm. Matt had what he wanted. He didn't look very pleased with it, though.

AFTER A LONG NIGHT fraught with even more nightmares, Leslie got up early and took a cab to the manufacturing company, hobbling in on her crutches to the personnel office where Judy Blakely, the personnel manager, was waiting with her usual kind smile.

"Nice to see you, Miss Murry!"

"Nice to see you, too," she replied. "I'm looking forward to my new job."

Mrs. Blakely looked worried and reticent. She folded her hands in a tight clasp on her desk. "Oh, I don't know how to tell you this," she wailed. She grimaced. "Miss Murry, the girl you were hired to replace just came back a few minutes ago and begged me to let her keep her job. It seems she has serious family problems and can't do without her salary. I'm so sorry. If we had anything else open, even on the floor, I'd offer it to you temporarily. But we just don't."

The poor woman looked as if the situation tormented her. Leslie smiled gently. "Don't worry, Mrs. Blakely, I'll find something else," she assured the older woman. "It's not the end of the world."

"I'd be furious," she said, her eyes wrinkled up with worry. "And you're being so nice… I feel like a dog!"

"You can't help it that things worked out like this." Leslie got to her feet a little heavily, still smiling. "Could you call me a cab?"

"Certainly! And we'll pay for it, too," she said firmly. "Honestly, I feel so awful!"

"It's all right. Sometimes we have setbacks that really turn into opportunities, you know."

Mrs. Blakely studied her intently. "You're such a positive person. I wish I was. I always seem to dwell on the negative."

"You might as well be optimistic, I always think," Leslie told her. "It doesn't cost extra."

Mrs. Blakely chuckled. "No, it doesn't, does it?" She phoned the cab and apologized again as Leslie went outside to wait for it.

She felt desolate, but she wasn't going to make that poor woman feel worse than she already did.

She was tired and sleepy. She wished the cab would come. She eased down onto the bench the company had placed out front for its employees, so they'd have a place to sit during their breaks. It was hard and uncomfortable, but much better than standing.

She wondered what she would do now. She had no prospects, no place to go. The only alternative was to look for something else or go back to Ed, and the latter choice wasn't a choice at all. She could never look Matt Caldwell in the face again without remembering how he'd treated her.

The sun glinted off the windshield of an approaching car, and she recognized Matt's new red Jaguar at once. She stood up, clutching her purse, stiff and defensive as he parked the car and got out to approach her.

He stopped an arm's length away. He looked as tired and worn-out as she did. His eyes were heavily lined. His black, wavy hair was disheveled. He put his hands on his hips and looked at her with pure malice.

She stared back with something approaching hatred.

"Oh, what the hell," he muttered, adding something about being hanged for sheep, as well as lambs.

He bent and swooped her up in his arms and started walking toward the Jaguar. She hit him with her purse.

"Stop that," he muttered. "You'll make me drop you. Considering the weight of that damned cast, you'd probably sink halfway through the planet."

"You put me down!" she raged, and hit him again. "I won't go as far as the street with you!"

He paused beside the passenger door of the Jag and searched her hostile eyes. "I hate secrets," he said.

"I can't imagine you have any, with Carolyn shouting them to all and sundry!"

His eyes fell to her mouth. "I didn't tell Carolyn that you were easy," he said in a voice so tender that it made her want to cry.

Her lips trembled as she tried valiantly not to.

He made a husky sound and his mouth settled right on her misty eyes, closing them with soft, tender kisses.

She bawled.

He took a long breath and opened the passenger door, shifting her as he slid her into the low-slung vehicle. "I've noticed that about you," he murmured as he fastened her seat belt.

"Noticed...what?" she sobbed, sniffling.

He pulled a handkerchief out of his dress slacks and put it in her hands. "You react very oddly to tenderness."

He closed the door on her surprised expression and fetched her crutches before he went around to get in behind the wheel. He paused to fasten his own seat belt and give her a quick scrutiny before he started the powerful engine and pulled out into the road.

"How did you know I was here?" she asked when the tears stopped.

"Ed told me."

"Why?"

He shrugged. "Beats me. I guess he thought I might be interested."

"Fat chance!"

He chuckled. It was the first time she'd heard him

laugh naturally, without mockery or sarcasm. He shifted gears. "You don't know the guy who owns that little enterprise," he said conversationally, "but the plant is a sweatshop."

"That isn't funny."

"Do you think I'm joking?" he replied. "He likes to lure illegal immigrants in here with promises of big salaries and health benefits, and then when he's got them where he wants them, he threatens them with the immigration service if they don't work hard and accept the pittance he pays. We've all tried to get his operation closed down, but he's slippery as an eel." He glanced at her with narrowed dark eyes. "I'm not going to let you sell yourself into that just to get away from me."

"Let me?" She rose immediately to the challenge, eyes flashing. "You don't tell me what to do!"

He grinned. "That's better."

She hit her hand against the cast, furious. "Where are you taking me?"

"Home."

"You're going the wrong way."

"My home."

"No," she said icily. "Not again. Not ever again!"

He shifted gears, accelerated, and shifted again. He loved the smoothness of the engine, the ride. He loved the speed. He wondered if Leslie had loved fast cars before her disillusionment.

He glanced at her set features. "When your leg heals, I'll let you drive it."

"No, thanks," she almost choked.

"Don't you like cars?"

She pushed back her hair. "I can't drive," she said absently.

"What?"

"Look out, you're going to run us off the road!" she squealed.

He righted the car with a muffled curse and down-shifted. "Everybody drives, for God's sake!"

"Not me," she said flatly.

"Why?"

She folded her arms over her breasts. "I just never wanted to."

More secrets. He was becoming accustomed to the idea that she never shared anything about her private life except, possibly, with Ed. He wanted her to open up, to trust him, to tell him what had happened to her. Then he laughed to himself at his own presumption. He'd been her mortal enemy since the first time he'd laid eyes on her, and he expected her to trust him?

"What are you laughing at?" she demanded.

He glanced at her as he slowed to turn into the ranch driveway. "I'll tell you one day. Are you hungry?"

"I'm sleepy."

He grimaced. "Let me see if I can guess why."

She glared at him. His own eyes had dark circles. "You haven't slept, either."

"Misery loves company."

"You started it!"

"Yes, I did!" he flashed back at her, eyes blazing. "Every time I look at you, I want to throw you down on the most convenient flat surface and ravish you! How's that for blunt honesty?"

She stiffened, wide-eyed, and gaped at him. He pulled up at his front door and cut off the engine. He turned in his seat and looked at her as if he resented her intensely. At the moment, he did.

His dark eyes narrowed. They were steady, intimidating. She glared into them.

But after a minute, the anger went out of him. He looked at her, really looked, and he saw things he hadn't noticed before. Her hair was dark just at her scalp. She was far too thin. Her eyes had dark circles so prominent that it looked as if she had two black eyes. There were harsh lines beside her mouth. She might pretend to be cheerful around Ed, but she wasn't. It was an act.

"Take a picture," she choked.

He sighed. "You really are fragile," he remarked quietly. "You give as good as you get, but all your vulnerabilities come out when you've got your back to the wall."

"I don't need psychoanalysis, but thanks for the thought," she said shortly.

He reached out, noticing how she shrank from his touch. It didn't bother him now. He knew that it was tenderness that frightened her with him, not ardor. He touched her hair at her temple and brushed it back gently, staring curiously at the darkness that was more prevalent then.

"You're a brunette," he remarked. "Why do you color your hair?"

"I wanted to be a blonde," she replied instantly, trying to withdraw further against the door.

"You keep secrets, Leslie," he said, and for once he was serious, not sarcastic. "At your age, it's unusual. You're young and until that leg started to act up, you were even relatively healthy. You should be carefree. Your life is an adventure that's only just beginning."

She laughed hollowly. "I wouldn't wish my life even on you," she said.

He raised an eyebrow. "Your worst enemy," he concluded for her.

"That's right."

"Why?"

She averted her eyes to the windshield. She was tired, so tired. The day that had begun with such promise had ended in disappointment and more misery.

"I want to go home," she said heavily.

"Not until I get some answers out of you…!"

"You have no right!" she exploded, her voice breaking on the words. "You have no right, no right…!"

"Leslie!"

He caught her by the nape of the neck and pulled her face into his throat, holding her there even as she struggled. He smoothed her hair, her back, whispering to her, his voice tender, coaxing.

"What did I ever do to deserve you?" she sobbed. "I've never willingly hurt another human being in my life, and look where it got me! Years of running and hiding and never feeling safe…!"

He heard the words without understanding them, soothing her while she cried brokenly. It hurt him to hear her cry. Nothing had ever hurt so much.

He dried the tears and kissed her swollen, red eyes tenderly, moving to her temples, her nose, her cheeks, her chin and, finally, her soft mouth. But it wasn't passion that drove him now. It was concern.

"Hush, sweetheart," he whispered. "It's all right. It's all right!"

She must be dotty, she thought, if she was hearing endearments from Attila the Hun here. She sniffed and wiped her eyes again, finally getting control of herself.

She sat up and he let her, his arm over the back of her seat, his eyes watchful and quiet.

She took a steadying breath and slumped in the seat, exhausted.

"Please take me home," she asked wearily.

He hesitated, but only for a minute. "If that's what you really want."

She nodded. He started the car and turned it around.

HE HELPED HER to the front door of the boardinghouse, visibly reluctant to leave her.

"You shouldn't be alone in this condition," he said flatly. "I'll phone Ed and have him come over to see you."

"I don't need..." she protested.

His eyes flared. "The hell you don't! You need someone you can talk to. Obviously it isn't going to be your worst enemy, but then Ed knows all about you, doesn't he? You don't have secrets from him!"

He seemed to mind. She searched his angry face and wondered what he'd say if he knew those secrets. She gave him a lackluster smile.

"Some secrets are better kept," she said heavily. "Thanks for the ride."

"Leslie."

She hesitated, looking back at him.

His face looked harder than ever. "Were you raped?"

# CHAPTER EIGHT

THE WORDS CUT like a knife. She actually felt them. Her sad eyes met his dark, searching ones. "Not quite," she replied tersely.

As understatements went, it was a master stroke. She watched the blood drain out of his face, and knew he was remembering, as she was, their last encounter, in his office, when she'd fainted.

He couldn't speak. He tried to, but the words choked him. He winced and turned away, striding back to the sports car. Leslie watched him go with a curious emptiness, as if she had no more feelings to bruise. Perhaps this kind detachment would last for a while, and she could have one day without the mental anguish that usually accompanied her, waking and sleeping.

She turned mechanically and went slowly into the house on her crutches, and down the hall to her small apartment. She had a feeling that she wouldn't see much of Matt Caldwell from now on. At last she knew how to deflect his pursuit. All it took was the truth—or as much of it as she felt comfortable letting him know.

ED PHONED TO check on her later in the day and promised to come and see her the next evening. He did, arriving with a bag full of the Chinese take-out dishes she loved. While they were eating it, he mentioned that her job was still open.

"Miss Smith wouldn't enjoy hearing that," she teased lightly.

"Oh, Karla's working for Matt now."

She stared down at the wooden chopsticks in her hand. "Is she?"

"For some reason, he doesn't feel comfortable asking you to come back, so he sent me to do it," he replied. "He realizes that he's made your working environment miserable, and he's sorry. He wants you to come back and work for me."

She stared at him hard. "What did you tell him?"

"What I always tell him, that if he wants to know anything about you, he can ask you." He ate a forkful of soft noodles and took a sip of the strong coffee she'd brewed before he continued. "I gather he's realized that something pretty drastic happened to you."

"Did he say anything about it to you?"

"No." He lifted his gaze to meet hers. "He did go to the roadhouse out on the Victoria highway last night and wreck the bar."

"Why would he do something like that?" she asked, stunned by the thought of the straitlaced Mather Caldwell throwing things around.

"He was pretty drunk at the time," Ed confessed. "I had to bail him out of jail this morning. That was one for the books, let me tell you. The whole damned police department was standing around staring at him openmouthed when we left. He was only ever in trouble once, a woman accused him of assault—and he was cleared. His housekeeper testified that she'd been there the whole time and she and Matt had sent the baggage packing. But he's never treed a bar before."

She remembered the stark question he'd asked her and how she'd responded. She didn't understand why her past should matter to Matt. In fact, she didn't want to understand. He still didn't know the whole of it, and she was frightened of how he'd react if he knew. That wonderful tenderness he'd given her in the Jaguar had been actually painful, a bitter taste of what a man's love would be like. It was something she'd never experienced, and she'd better remember that Matt was the enemy. He'd felt sorry for her. He certainly wasn't in love with her. He wanted her, that was all. But despite her surprising response to his light caresses, complete physical intimacy was something she wasn't sure she was capable of responding to. The memories of Mike's vicious fondling made her sick. She couldn't live with them.

"Stop doing that to yourself," Ed muttered, dragging her back to the present. "You can't change the past. You have to walk straight into the future without flinching. It's the only way, to meet things head-on."

"Where did you learn that?" she asked.

"Actually I heard a televised sermon that caught my attention. That's what the minister said, that you have to go boldly forward and meet trouble head-on, not try to run away from it or hide." He pursed his lips. "I'd never heard it put quite that way before. It really made me think."

She sipped coffee with a sad face. "I've always tried to run. I've had to run." She lifted her eyes to his. "You know what they would have done to me if I'd stayed in Houston."

"Yes, I do, and I don't blame you for getting out while you could," Ed assured her. "But there's something I have to tell you now. And you're not going to like it."

"Don't tell me," she said with black humor, "someone from the local newspaper recognized me and wants an interview."

"Worse," he returned. "A reporter from Houston is down here asking questions. I think he's traced you."

She put her head in her hands. "Wonderful. Well, at least I'm no longer an employee of the Caldwell group, so it won't embarrass your cousin when I'm exposed."

"I haven't finished. Nobody will talk to him," he added with a grin. "In fact, he actually got into Matt's office yesterday when his secretary wasn't looking. He was only in there for a few minutes, and nobody knows what was said. But he came back out headfirst and, from what I hear, he ran out the door so fast that he left his briefcase behind with Matt cursing like a wounded sailor all the way down the hall. They said Matt had only just caught up with him at the curb when he ran across traffic and got away."

She hesitated. "When was this?"

"Yesterday." He smiled wryly. "It was a bad time to catch Matt. He'd already been into it with one of the county commissioners over a rezoning proposal we're trying to get passed, and his secretary had hidden in the bathroom to avoid him. That was how the reporter got in."

"You don't think he…told Matt?" she asked worriedly.

"No. I don't know what was said, of course, but he wasn't in there very long."

"But, the briefcase…"

"...was returned to him unopened," Ed said. "I know because I had to take it down to the front desk." He smiled, amused. "I understand he paid someone to pick it up for him."

"Thank God."

"It was apparently the last straw for Matt, though," he continued, "because it wasn't long after that when he said he was leaving for the day."

"How did you know he was in jail?"

He grimaced. "Carolyn phoned me. He'd come by her place first and apparently made inroads into a bottle of Scotch. She hid the rest, after which he decided to go and get his own bottle." He shook his head. "That isn't like Matt. He may have a drink or two occasionally, but he isn't a drinker. This has shocked everybody in town."

"I guess so." She couldn't help but wonder if it had anything to do with the way he'd treated her. But if he'd gone to Carolyn, perhaps they'd had an argument and it was just one last problem on top of too many. "Was Carolyn mad at him?" she asked.

"Furious," he returned. "Absolutely seething. It seems they'd had a disagreement of major proportions, along with all the other conflicts of the day." He shook his head. "Matt didn't even come in to work today. I'll bet his head is splitting."

She didn't reply. She stared into her coffee with dead eyes. Everywhere she went, she caused trouble. Hiding, running—nothing seemed to help. She was only involving innocent people in her problems.

Ed hesitated when he saw her face. He didn't want to make things even worse for her, but there was more news that he had to give her.

She saw that expression. "Go ahead," she invited.

"One more thing is all I need right now, on top of being crippled and jobless."

"Your job is waiting," he assured her. "Whenever you want to come in."

"I won't do that to him," she said absently. "He's had enough."

His eyes became strangely watchful. "Feeling sorry for the enemy?" he asked gently.

"You can't help not liking people," she replied. "He likes most everybody except me. He's basically a kind person. I just rub him the wrong way."

He wasn't going to touch that line. "The same reporter who came here had gone to the prison to talk to your mother," he continued. "I was concerned, so I called the warden. It seems…she's had a heart attack."

Her heart jumped unpleasantly. "Will she live?"

"Yes," he assured her. "She's changed a lot in six years, Leslie," he added solemnly. "She's reconciled to serving her time. The warden says that she wanted to ask for you, but that she was too ashamed to let them contact you. She thinks you can't ever forgive what she said and did to you."

Her eyes misted, but she fought tears. Her mother had been eloquent at the time, with words and the pistol. She stared at her empty coffee cup. "I can forgive her. I just don't want to see her."

"She knows that," Ed replied.

She glanced at him. "Have you been to see her?"

He hesitated. Then he nodded. "She was doing very well until this reporter started digging up the past. He was the one who suggested the movie deal and got that bit started." He sighed angrily. "He's young and ambitious and he wants to make a name for himself. The world's full of people like that, who don't care what damage they do to other peoples' lives as long as they get what they want."

She was only vaguely listening. "My mother...did she ask you about me?"

"Yes."

"What did you tell her?" she wanted to know.

He put down his cup. "The truth. There really wasn't any way to dress it up." His eyes lifted. "She wanted you to know that she's sorry for what happened, especially for the way she treated you before and after the trial. She understands that you don't want to see her. She says she deserves it for destroying your life."

She stared into space with the pain of memory eating at her. "She was never satisfied with my father," she said quietly. "She wanted things he couldn't give her, pretty clothes and jewelry and nights on the town. All he knew how to do was fly a crop-dusting plane, and it didn't pay much..." Her eyes closed. "I saw him fly into the electrical wires, and go down," she whispered gruffly. "I saw him go down!" Her eyes began to glitter with feeling. "I knew he was dead before they ever got to him. I ran home. She was in the living room, playing music, dancing. She didn't care. I broke the record player and threw myself at her, screaming."

Ed grimaced as she choked, paused, and fought for control. "We were never close, especially after the funeral," she continued, "but we were stuck with each other. Things went along fairly well. She got a job waiting tables and made good tips when she was working. She had trouble holding down a job because she slept so much. I got a part-time job typing when I was sixteen, to help out. Then when I'd just turned seventeen, Mike came into the restaurant and started flirting with her. He was so handsome, well-bred and had nice manners. In no time, he'd moved in with us. I was crazy about him, you know the way a young girl has crushes on older men. He teased me, too. But he had a drug habit that we didn't know about. She didn't like him teasing me, anyway, and she had a fight with him about it. The next day, he had some friends over and they all got high." She shivered. "The rest you know."

"Yes." He sighed, studying her wan face.

"All I wanted was for her to love me," she said dully. "But she never did."

"She said that," he replied. "She's had a lot of time to live with her regrets." He leaned forward to search her eyes. "Leslie, did you know that she had a drug habit?"

"She what?" she exclaimed, startled.

"Had a drug habit," he repeated. "That's what she told me. It was an expensive habit, and your father got tired of trying to support it. He loved her, but he couldn't make the sort of money it took to keep her high. It wasn't clothes and jewelry and parties. It was drugs."

She felt as if she'd been slammed to the floor. She moved her hands over her face and pushed back her hair. "Oh, Lord!"

"She was still using when she walked in on Mike and his friends holding you down," he continued.

"How long had she been using drugs?" she asked.

"A good five years," he replied. "Starting with marijuana and working her way up to the hard stuff."

"I had no idea."

"And you didn't know that Mike was her dealer, either, apparently."

She gasped.

He nodded grimly. "She told me that when I went to see her, too. She still can't talk about it easily. Now that she has a good grip on reality, she sees what her lifestyle did to you. She had hoped that you might be married and happy by now. It hurt her deeply to realize that you don't even date."

"She'll know why, of course," she said bitterly.

"You sound so empty, Leslie."

"I am." She leaned back. "I don't care if the reporter finds me. It doesn't matter anymore. I'm so tired of running."

"Then stand and deliver," he replied, getting to his feet. "Come back to work. Let your leg heal. Let your hair grow out and go back to its natural color. Start living."

"Can I, after so long?"

"Yes," he assured her. "We all go through periods of anguish, times when we think we can't face what lies ahead. But the only way to get past it is to go through it, straight through it. No detours, no camouflage, no running. You have to meet problems head-on, despite the pain."

She cocked her head and smiled at him with real affection. "Were you ever a football coach?"

He chuckled. "I hate contact sports."

"Me, too." She brushed her short hair back with her hands. "Okay. I'll give it a shot. But if your cousin gives me any more trouble…"

"I don't think Matt is going to cause you any more problems," he replied.

"Then, I'll see you on Thursday morning."

"Thursday? Tomorrow is just Wednesday…"

"Thursday," she said firmly. "I have plans for tomorrow."

AND SHE DID. She had the color taken out of her hair
at a local beauty salon. She took her contact lenses to
the local optometrist and got big-lensed, wire-framed
glasses to wear. She bought clothes that looked professional without being explicit.

Then, Thursday morning, cast and crutches notwith-
standing, she went back to work.

She'd been at her desk in Ed's office for half an hour
when Matt came in. He barely glanced at her, obviously
not recognizing the new secretary, and tapped on Ed's
door, which was standing open.

"I'm going to fly to Houston for the sale," he told
Ed. He sounded different. His deep voice held its usual
authority, but there was an odd note in it. "I don't suppose you were able to convince her to come back...why
are you shaking your head?"

Ed stood up with an exasperated sigh and pointed
toward Leslie.

Matt scowled, turning on his heel. He looked at her,
scowled harder, moved closer, peering into her upturned
face.

She saw him matching his memory of her with the
new reality. She wondered how she came off, but it was
far too soon to get personal.

His eyes went over her short dark hair, over the feminine but professional beige suit she was wearing with
a tidy patterned blouse, lingering on the glasses that
she'd never worn before in his presence. His own face
was heavily lined and he looked as if he'd had his own
share of turmoil since she'd seen him last. Presumably
he was still having problems with Carolyn.

"Good morning, Miss Murry," he murmured. His

eyes didn't smile at her. He looked as if his face was painted on.

That was odd. No sarcasm, no mockery. No insolent sizing up. He was polite and courteous to a fault.

If that was the way he intended to play it...

"Good morning, Mr. Caldwell," she replied with equal courtesy.

He studied her for one long moment before he turned back to Ed. "I should be back by tonight. If I'm not, you'll have to meet with the county commission and the zoning committee."

"Oh, no," Ed groaned.

"Just tell them we're putting up a two-story brick office building on our own damned land, whether they like it or not," Matt told him, "and that we can accommodate them in court for as many years as it takes to get our way. I'm tired of trying to do business in a hundred-year-old house with frozen pipes that burst every winter."

"It won't sound as intimidating if I say it."

"Stand in front of a mirror and practice looking angry."

"Is that how you did it?" Ed murmured dryly.

"Only at first," he assured the other man, deadpan. "Just until I got the hang of it."

"I remember," Ed chuckled. "Even Dad wouldn't argue with you unless he felt he had a good case."

Matt shoved his hands into his pockets. "If you need me, you know the cell phone number."

"Sure."

Still he hesitated. He turned and glanced at Leslie, who was opening mail. The expression on his face fascinated Ed, who'd known him most of his life. It wasn't a look he recognized.

Matt started out the door and then paused to look back at Leslie, staring at her until she lifted her eyes.

He searched them slowly, intently. He didn't smile. He didn't speak. Her cheeks became flushed and she looked away. He made an awkward movement with his shoulders and went out the door.

Ed joined her at her desk when Matt was out of sight. "So far, so good," he remarked.

"I guess he really doesn't mind letting me stay," she murmured. Her hands were shaking because of that long, searching look of Matt's. She clasped them together so that Ed wouldn't notice and lifted her face. "But what if that reporter comes back?"

He pursed his lips. "Odd, that. He left town yesterday. In a real hurry, too. The police escorted him to the city limits and the sheriff drove behind him to the county line."

She gaped at him.

He shrugged. "Jacobsville is a small, close-knit community and you just became part of it. That means," he added, looking almost as imposing as his cousin, "that we don't let outsiders barge in and start harassing our citizens. I understand there's an old city law still on the books that makes it a crime for anyone to stay in a local place of lodging unless he or she is accompanied by at least two pieces of luggage or a trunk." He grinned. "Seems the reporter only had a briefcase. Tough."

"He might come back with a trunk and two suitcases," she pointed out.

He shook his head. "It seems that they found another old law which makes it illegal for a man driving a rental car to park it anywhere inside the city limits. Strange, isn't it, that we'd have such an unusual ordinance."

Leslie felt the first ripple of humor that she'd experienced for weeks. She smiled. "My, my."

"Our police chief is related to the Caldwells," he explained. "So is the sheriff, one of the county commissioners, two volunteer firemen, a sheriff's deputy and a Texas Ranger who was born here and works out of Fort Worth." He chuckled. "The governor is our second cousin."

Her eyes widened. "No Washington connections?" she asked.

"Nothing major. The vice president is married to my aunt."

"Nothing major." She nodded. She let out her breath. "Well, I'm beginning to feel very safe."

"Good. You can stay as long as you like. Permanently, as far as I'm concerned."

She couldn't quite contain the pleasure it gave her to feel as if she belonged somewhere, a place where she was protected and nurtured and had friends. It was a first for her. Her eyes stung with moisture.

"Don't start crying," Ed said abruptly. "I can't stand it."

She swallowed and forced a watery smile to her lips. "I wasn't going to," she assured him. She moved her shoulders. "Thanks," she said gruffly.

"Don't thank me," he told her. "Matt rounded up the law enforcement people and had them going through dusty volumes of ordinances to find a way to get that reporter out of here."

*"Matt did?"*

He held up a hand as she started to parade her misgivings about what he might have learned of her past. "He doesn't know why the man was here. It was enough that he was asking questions about you. You're an employee. We don't permit harassment."

"I see."

She didn't, but that was just as well. The look Ed had accidentally seen on Matt's face had him turning mental cartwheels. No need to forewarn Leslie. She wasn't ever going to have to worry about being hounded again, not if he knew Matt. And he didn't believe for one minute that his cousin was flying all the way to Houston for a cattle sale that he usually wouldn't be caught dead at. The foreman at his ranch handled that sort of thing, although Leslie didn't know. Ed was betting that Matt had another reason for going to Houston, and it was to find out who hired that reporter and sent him looking for Leslie. He felt sorry for the source of that problem. Matt in a temper was the most menacing human being he'd ever known. He didn't rage or shout and he usually didn't hit, but he had wealth and power and he knew how to use them.

He went back into his office, suddenly worried despite the reassurances he'd given Leslie. Matt didn't know why the reporter was digging around, but what if he found out? He would only be told what the public had been told, that Leslie's mother had shot her daughter and her live-in lover in a fit of jealous rage and that she was in prison. He might think, as others had, that Leslie had brought the whole sordid business on herself by having a wild party with Mike and his friends, and he wouldn't be sympathetic. More than likely, he'd come raging back home and throw Leslie out in the street.

Furthermore, he'd have her escorted to the county line like the reporter who'd been following her.

He worried himself sick over the next few hours. He couldn't tell Leslie, when he might only be worrying for nothing. But the thought haunted him that Matt was every bit as dogged as a reporter when it came to ferreting out facts.

In the end, he phoned a hotel that Matt frequented when he was in Houston overnight and asked for his room. But when he was connected, it wasn't Matt who answered the phone.

"Carolyn?" Ed asked, puzzled. "Is Matt there?"

"Not right now," came the soft reply. "He had an appointment to see someone. I suppose he's forgotten that I'm waiting for him with this trolley full of food. I suppose it will be cold as ice by the time he turns up."

"Everything's all right, isn't it?"

"Why wouldn't it be?" she teased.

"Matt's been acting funny."

"Yes, I know. That Murry girl!" Her indrawn breath was audible. "Well, she's caused quite enough trouble. When Matt comes back, she'll be right out of that office, let me tell you! Do you have any idea what that reporter told Matt about her…?"

Ed hung up, sick. So not only did Matt know, but Carolyn knew, too. She'd savage Leslie, given the least opportunity. He had to do something. What?

ED DIDN'T EXPECT Matt that evening, and he was right. Matt didn't come back in time for the county commission meeting, and Ed was forced to go in his place. He held his own, as Matt had instructed him to, and got what he wanted. Then he went home, sitting on pins and needles as he waited for someone to call him—either Leslie, in tears, or Matt, in a temper.

But the phone didn't ring. And when he went into work the next morning, Leslie was sitting calmly at her desk typing the letters he'd dictated to her just before they closed the day before.

"How did the meeting go?" she asked at once.

"Great," he replied. "Matt will be proud of me." He hesitated. "He, uh, isn't in yet, is he?"

"No. He hasn't phoned, either." She frowned. "You don't suppose anything went wrong with the plane, do you?"

She sounded worried. Come to think of it, she looked worried, too. He frowned. "He's been flying for a long time," he pointed out.

"Yes, but there was a bad storm last night." She hesitated. She didn't want to worry, but she couldn't help it. Despite the hard time he'd given her, Matt had been kind to her once or twice. He wasn't a bad person; he just didn't like her.

"If anything had happened, I'd have heard by now," he assured her. His lips pursed as he searched for the words. "He didn't go alone."

Her heart stopped in her chest. "Carolyn?"

He nodded curtly. He ran a hand through his hair. "He knows, Leslie. They both do."

She felt the life ebb out of her. But what had she expected, that Matt would wait to hear her side of the story? He was the enemy. He wouldn't for one second believe that she was the victim of the whole sick business. How could she blame him?

She turned off the word processor and moved her chair back, reaching for her purse. She felt more defeated than she ever had in her life. One bad break after another, she was thinking, as she got to her feet a little clumsily.

"Hand me my crutches, Ed, there's a dear," she said steadily.

"Oh, Leslie," he groaned.

She held her hand out and, reluctantly, he helped her get them in place.

"Where will you go?" he asked.

She shrugged. "It doesn't matter. Something will turn up."

"I can help."

She looked up at him with sad resignation. "You can't go against your own blood kin, Ed," she replied. "I'm the outsider here. And one way or another, I've already caused too much trouble. See you around, pal. Thanks for everything."

He sighed miserably. "Keep in touch, at least."

She smiled. "Certainly I'll do that. See you."

He watched her walk away with pure anguish. He wished he could make her stay, but even he wouldn't wish that on her. When Matt came home, he'd be out for blood. At least she'd be spared that confrontation.

## CHAPTER NINE

LESLIE DIDN'T HAVE a lot to pack, only a few clothes and personal items, like the photograph of her father that she always carried with her. She'd bought a bus ticket to San Antonio, one of the places nosy reporters from Houston might not think to look for her. She could get a job as a typist and find another place to live. It wouldn't be so bad.

She thought about Matt, and how he must feel, now that he knew the whole truth, or at least, the reporter's version of it. She was sure that he and Carolyn would have plenty to gossip about on the way back home. Carolyn would broadcast the scandal all over town. Even if Leslie stopped working for Matt, she would never live down the gossip. Leaving was her only option.

Running away. Again.

Her hands went to a tiny napkin she'd brought home from the dance that she and Ed had attended with Matt and Carolyn. Matt had been doodling on it with his pen just before he'd pulled Leslie out of her seat and out onto the dance floor. It was a silly sentimental piece of nonsense to keep. On a rare occasion or two, Matt had been tender with her. She wanted to remember those times. It was good to have had a little glimpse of what love might have been like, so that life didn't turn her completely bitter.

She folded her coat over a chair and looked around to make sure she wasn't missing anything. She wouldn't have time to look in the morning. The bus would leave at 6:00 a.m., with or without her. She clumped around the apartment with forced cheer, thinking that at least she'd have no knowing, pitying smiles in San Antonio.

ED LOOKED UP as Matt exploded into the office, stopping in his tracks when he reached Leslie's empty desk. He stood there, staring, as if he couldn't believe what he was seeing.

With a sigh, Ed got up and joined him in the outer office, steeling himself for the ordeal. Matt was obviously upset.

"It's all right," he told Matt. "She's already gone. She said she was sorry for the trouble she'd caused, and that…"

"Gone?" Matt looked horrified. His face was like white stone.

Ed frowned, hesitating. "She said it would spare you the trouble of firing her," he began uneasily.

Matt still hadn't managed a coherent sentence. He ran his hand through his hair, disturbing its neat wave. He stuck his other hand into his pocket and went on staring at her desk as if he expected she might materialize out of thin air if he looked hard enough.

He turned to Ed. He stared at him, almost as if he didn't recognize him. "She's gone. Gone where?"

"She wouldn't tell me," he replied reluctantly.

Matt's eyes were black. He looked back at her desk and winced. He made a violent motion, pressed his lips together, and suddenly took a deep audible breath and with a furious scowl, he let out a barrage of nonstop curses that had even Ed gaping.

"…and I did *not* say she could leave!" he finished at the end.

Ed managed to meet those flashing eyes, but it wasn't easy. Braver men than he had run for cover when the boss lost his temper. "Now, Matt…"

"Don't you 'Now, Matt' me, dammit!" he raged. His fists were clenched at his sides and he looked as if he really wanted to hit something. Or someone. Ed took two steps backward.

Matt saw two of the secretaries standing frozen in the hall, as if they'd come running to find the source of the uproar and were now hoping against hope that it wouldn't notice them.

No such luck. "Get the hell back to work!" he shouted.

They actually ran.

Ed wanted to. "Matt," he tried again.

He was talking to thin air. Matt was down the hall and out the door before he could catch up. He did the only thing he could. He rushed back to his office to phone Leslie and warn her. He was so nervous that it took several tries and one wrong number to get her.

"He's on his way over there," Ed told her the minute she picked up the phone. "Get out."

"No."

"Leslie, I've never seen him like this," he pleaded. "You don't understand. He isn't himself."

"It's all right, Ed," she said calmly. "There's nothing more he can do to me."

"Leslie…!" he groaned.

The loud roar of an engine out front caught her attention. "Try not to worry," she told Ed, and put the receiver down on an even louder exclamation.

She got up, put her crutches in place and hobbled to open her door just as Matt started to knock on it. He paused there, his fist upraised, his eyes black in a face the color of rice.

She stood aside to let him in, with no sense of self-preservation left. She was as far down as she could get already.

He closed the door behind him with an ultracontrolled softness before he turned to look at her. She went back to her armchair and eased down into it, laying the crutches to one side. Her chin lifted and she just looked at him, resigned to more verbal abuse if not downright violence. She was already packed and almost beyond his reach. Let him do his worst.

Now that he was here, he didn't know what to do. He hadn't thought past finding her. He leaned back against the door and folded his arms over his chest.

She didn't flinch or avert her eyes. She stared right at him. "There was no need to come here," she said calmly. "You don't have to run me out of town. I already have my ticket. I'm leaving on the bus first thing in the morning." She lifted a hand. "Feel free to search if you think I've taken anything from the office."

He didn't respond. His chest rose and fell rhythmically, if a little heavily.

She smoothed her hand over the cast where it topped her kneecap. There was an itch and she couldn't get to it. What a mundane thing to think about, she told herself, when she was confronted with a homicidal man.

He was making her more nervous by the minute. She

shifted in the chair, grimacing as the cast moved awkwardly and gave her a twinge of pain.

"Why are you here?" she asked impatiently, her eyes flashing at him through her lenses. "What else do you want, an apology...?"

"An apology? Dear God!"

It sounded like a plea for salvation. He moved, for the first time, going slowly across the room to the chair a few feet away from hers, next to the window. He eased himself down into it and crossed his long legs. He was still scowling, watching, waiting.

His eyes were appraising her now, not cutting into her or mocking her. They were dark and steady and turbulent.

Her eyes were dull and lackluster as she averted her face. Her grip on the arm of the chair was painful. "You know, don't you?"

"Yes."

She felt as if her whole body contracted. She watched a bird fly past the window and wished that she could fly away from her problems. "In a way, it's sort of a relief," she said wearily. "I'm so tired...of running."

His face tautened. His mouth made a thin line as he stared at her. "You'll never have to run again," he said flatly. "There isn't going to be any more harassment from that particular quarter."

She wasn't sure she was hearing right. Her face turned back to his. It was hard to meet those searching eyes, but she did. He looked pale, worn.

"Why aren't you gloating?" she asked harshly. "You were right about me all along, weren't you? I'm a little tramp who lures men in and teases them...!"

"Don't!" He actually flinched. He searched for words

and couldn't manage to find anything to say to her. His guilt was killing him. His conscience had him on a particularly nasty rack. He looked at her and saw years of torment and self-contempt, and he wanted to hit something.

That expression was easily read in his dark eyes. She leaned her head back against the chair and closed her eyes on the hatred she saw there.

"Everybody had a different idea of why I did it," she said evenly. "One of the bigger tabloids even interviewed a couple of psychiatrists who said I was getting even with my mother for my childhood. Another said it was latent nymphomania…"

"Hell!"

She felt dirty. She couldn't look at him. "I thought I loved him," she said, as if even after all the years, she still couldn't believe it had happened. "I had no idea, none at all, what he was really like. He made fun of my body, he and his friends. They stretched me out like a human sacrifice and discussed…my…assets." Her voice broke. He clenched his hand on the arm of the chair.

Matt's expression, had she seen it, would have silenced her. As it was, she was staring blankly out the window.

"They decided Mike should go first," she said in a husky, strained tone. "And then they drew cards to see which of the other three would go next. I prayed to die. But I couldn't. Mike was laughing at the way I begged him not to do it. I struggled and he had the others hold me down while he…"

A sound came from Matt's tight throat that shocked her into looking at him. She'd never seen such horror in a man's eyes.

"My mother came in before he had time to—" she swallowed "—get started. She was so angry that she lost control entirely. She grabbed the pistol Mike kept in the table drawer by the front door and she shot him. The bullet went through him and into my leg," she whispered, sickened by the memory. "I saw his face when the bullet hit him in the chest from behind. I actually saw the life drain out of him." She closed her eyes. "She kept shooting until one of the men got the pistol away from her. They ran for their lives, and left us there, like that. A neighbor called an ambulance and the police. I remember that one of them got a blanket from the bedroom and wrapped me up in it. They were all…so kind," she choked, tears filling her eyes. "So kind!"

He put his face in his hands. He couldn't bear what he was hearing. He remembered her face in his office when he'd laughed at her. He groaned harshly.

"The tabloids made it look as if I'd invited what happened," she said huskily. "I don't know how a seventeen-year-old virgin can ask grown men to get high on drugs and treat her with no respect. I thought I loved Mike, but even so, I never did anything consciously to make him treat me that way."

Matt couldn't look at her. Not yet. "People high on drugs don't know what they're doing, as a rule," he said through his teeth.

"That's hard to believe," she said.

"It's the same thing as a man drinking too much alcohol and having a blackout," he said, finally lifting his head. He stared at her with dark, lifeless eyes. "Didn't I tell you once that secrets are dangerous?"

She nodded. She looked back out the window. "Mine was too sordid to share," she said bitterly. "I can't bear to be touched by men. By most men," she qualified. "Ed knew all about me, so he never approached me, that way. But you," she added quietly, "came at me like a bull in a pasture. You scared me to death. Aggression always reminds me of...of Mike."

He leaned forward with his head bowed. Even after what he'd learned in Houston already, he was unprepared for the full impact of what had been done to this vulnerable, fragile creature in front of him. He'd let hurt pride turn him into a predator. He'd approached her in ways that were guaranteed to bring back terrible memories of that incident in her past.

"I wish I'd known," he said heavily.

"I don't blame you," she said simply. "You couldn't have known."

His dark eyes came up glittering. "I could have," he contradicted flatly. "It was right under my nose. The way you downplayed your figure, the way you backed off when I came too close, the way you...fainted—" he had to force the word out "—in my office when I pinned you to the wall." He looked away. "I didn't see it because I didn't want to. I was paying you back," he said on a bitter laugh, "for having the gall not to fall into my arms when I pursued you."

She'd never imagined that she could feel sorry for Matt Caldwell. But she did. He was a decent man. Surely it would be difficult for him to face the treatment he'd given her, now that he knew the truth.

She smoothed her hands over her arms. It wasn't cold in the room, but she was chilled.

"You've never talked about it, have you?" he asked after a minute.

"Only to Ed, right after it happened," she replied.

"He's been the best friend in the world to me. When those people started talking about making a television movie of what had happened, I just panicked. They were all over Houston looking for me. Ed offered me a way out and I took it. I was so scared," she whispered. "I thought I'd be safe here."

His fists clenched. "Safe." He made a mockery of the very word.

He got to his feet and moved to the window, avoiding her curious gaze.

"That reporter," she began hesitantly. "He told you about it when he was here, didn't he?"

He didn't reply for a minute. "Yes," he said finally. "He had clippings of the story." She probably knew which ones, he thought miserably, of her being carried out on a stretcher with blood all over her. There was one of the dead man lying on the floor of the apartment, and one of her blond mother shocked and almost catatonic as policemen escorted her to the squad car.

"I didn't connect it when you told Ed you were going to Houston. I thought it was some cattle sale, just like you said," she remarked.

"The reporter ran, but he'd already said that he was working with some people in Hollywood trying to put together a television movie. He'd tried to talk to your mother, apparently, and after his visit, she had a heart attack. That didn't even slow him down. He tracked you here and had plans to interview you." He glanced at her. "He thought you'd be glad to cooperate for a percentage of the take."

She laughed hollowly.

"Yes, I know," he told her. "You're not mercenary.

That's one of the few things I've learned about you since you've been here."

"At least you found one thing about me that you like," she told him.

His face closed up completely. "There are a lot of things I like about you, but I've had some pretty hard knocks from women in my life."

"Ed told me."

"It's funny," he said, but he didn't look amused. "I've never been able to come to terms with my mother's actions—until I met you. You've helped me a lot—and I've been acting like a bear with a thorn in its paw. I've mistreated you."

She searched his lean, hard face quietly. He was so handsome. Her heart jumped every time she met his eyes. "Why did you treat me that way?" she asked.

He stuck his hand into his pocket. "I wanted you," he said flatly.

"Oh."

She wasn't looking at him, but he saw her fingers curl into the arm of the chair. "I know. You probably aren't capable of desire after what was done to you. Perhaps it's poetic justice that my money and position won't get me the one thing in the world I really want."

"I don't think I could sleep with someone," she agreed evenly. "Even the thought of it is…disgusting."

He could imagine that it was, and he cursed that man silently until he ran out of words.

"You liked kissing me."

She nodded, surprised. "Yes, I did."

"And being touched," he prompted, smiling gently at the memory of her reaction—astonishing now, considering her past.

She studied her lap. A button on her dress was loose. She'd have to stitch it. She lifted her eyes. "Yes," she said. "I enjoyed that, too, at first."

His face hardened as he remembered what he'd said to her then. He turned away, his back rigid. He'd made so damned many mistakes with this woman that he didn't know how he was going to make amends. There was probably no way to do it. But he could protect her from any more misery, and he was going to.

He rammed his hands into his pockets and turned. "I went to see that reporter in Houston. I can promise you that he won't be bothering you again, and there won't be any more talk of a motion picture. I went to see your mother, too," he added.

She hadn't expected that. She closed her eyes. She caught her lower lip in her teeth and bit it right through. The taste of blood steeled her as she waited for the explosion.

"Don't!"

She opened her eyes with a jerk. His face was dark and lined, like the downwardly slanted brows above his black eyes. She pulled a tissue from the box on the table beside her and dabbed at the blood on her lip. It was such a beautiful color, she thought irrelevantly.

"I didn't realize how hard this was going to be," he said, sitting down. His head bowed, he clasped his big hands between his splayed knees and stared at the floor. "There are a lot of things I want to tell you. I just can't find the right words."

She didn't speak. Her eyes were still on the blood-dotted tissue. She felt his dark eyes on her, searching, studying, assessing her.

"If I'd…known about your past…" he tried again.

Her head came up. Her eyes were as dead as stone. "You just didn't like me. It's all right. I didn't like you, either. And you couldn't have known. I came here to hide the past, not to talk about it. But I guess you were right about secrets. I'll have to find another place to go, that's all."

He cursed under his breath. "Don't go! You're safe in Jacobsville," he continued, his voice growing stronger and more confident as he spoke. "There won't be any more suspicious reporters, no more movie deals, no more persecution. I can make sure that nobody touches you as long as you're here. I can't…protect you anywhere else," he added impatiently.

Oh, that was just great, she thought furiously. Pity. Guilt. Shame. Now he was going to go to the opposite extreme. He was going to watch over her like a protective father wolf. Well, he could think again. She scooped up one of her crutches and slammed the tip on the floor. "I don't need protection from you or anybody else. I'm leaving on the morning bus. And as for you, Mr. Caldwell, you can get out of here and leave me alone!" she raged at him.

It was the first spark of resistance he'd seen in her since he arrived. The explosion lightened his mood. She wasn't acting like a victim anymore. That was real independence in her tone, in the whole look of her. She was healing already with the retelling of that painful episode in her life.

The hesitation in him was suddenly gone. So was the somber face. Both eyebrows went up and a faint light touched his black eyes. "Or what?"

She hesitated. "What do you mean, or what?"

"If I don't get out, what do you plan to do?" he asked pleasantly.

She thought about that for a minute. "Call Ed."

He glanced at his watch. "Karla's bringing him coffee about now. Wouldn't it be a shame to spoil his break?"

She moved restlessly in the chair, still holding on to the crutch.

He smiled slowly, for the first time since he'd arrived. "Nothing more to say? Have you run out of threats already?"

Her eyes narrowed with bad temper. She didn't know what to say, or what to do. This was completely unexpected.

He studied the look of her in the pretty blue-patterned housedress she was wearing, barefoot. She was pretty, too. "I like that dress. I like your hair that color, too."

She looked at him as if she feared for his sanity. Something suddenly occurred to her. "If you didn't come rushing over here to put me on the bus and see that I left town, why are you here?"

He nodded slowly. "I was wondering when you'd get around to that." He leaned forward, just as another car pulled up outside the house.

"Ed," she guessed.

He grimaced. "I guess he rushed over to save you," he said with resignation.

She glared at him. "He was worried about me."

He went toward the door. "He wasn't the only one," he muttered, almost to himself. He opened the door before Ed could knock. "She's all in one piece," he assured his cousin, standing aside to let him into the room.

Ed was worried, confused, and obviously puzzled

when he saw that she wasn't crying. "Are you all right?" he asked her.

She nodded.

Ed looked at her and then at Matt, curious, but too polite to start asking questions.

"I assume that you're staying in town now?" Matt asked her a little stiffly. "You still have a job, if you want it. No pressure. It's your decision."

She wasn't sure what to do next. She didn't want to leave Jacobsville for another town of strange people.

"Stay," Ed said gently.

She forced a smile. "I guess I could," she began. "For a while."

Matt didn't let his relief show. In a way he was glad Ed had shown up to save him from what he was about to say to her.

"You won't regret it," Ed promised her, and she smiled at him warmly.

The smile set Matt off again. He was jealous, and furious that he *was* jealous. He ran a hand through his hair again and glowered with frustration at both of them. "Oh, hell, I'm going back to work," he said shortly. "When you people get through playing games on my time, you might go to the office and earn your damned paychecks!"

He went out the door still muttering to himself, slammed into the Jaguar, and roared away.

Ed and Leslie stared at each other.

"He went to see my mother," she told him.

"And?"

"He didn't say a lot, except…except that there won't be any more reporters asking questions."

"What about Carolyn?" he asked.

"He didn't say a word about her," she murmured, having just remembered that Ed said Carolyn had gone to Houston with him. She grimaced. "I guess she'll rush home and tell the whole town about me."

"I wouldn't like to see what Matt would do about it, if she did. If he asked you to stay, it's because he plans to protect you."

"I suppose he does, but it's a shock, considering the way he was before he went out of town. Honestly, I don't know what's going on. He's like a stranger!"

"I've never heard him actually apologize," he said. "But he usually finds ways to get his point across, without saying the words."

"Maybe that was what he was doing," she replied, thinking back over his odd behavior. "He doesn't want me to leave town."

"That seems to be the case." He smiled at her. "How about it? You've still got a job if you want it, and Matt's taken you off the endangered list. You're safe here. Want to stay?"

She thought about that for a minute, about Matt's odd statement that she was safe in Jacobsville and she wouldn't be hounded anymore. It was like a dream come true after six years of running and hiding. She nodded slowly. "Oh, yes," she said earnestly. "Yes, I want to stay!"

"Then I suggest you put on your shoes and grab a jacket, and I'll drive you back to work, while we still have jobs."

"I can't go to work like this," she protested.

"Why not?" he wanted to know.

"It isn't a proper dress to wear on the job," she said, rising.

He scowled. "Did Matt say that?"

"I'm not giving him the chance to," she said. "From now on, I'm going to be the soul of conservatism at work. He won't get any excuses to take potshots at me."

"If you say so," he said with a regretful thought for the pretty, feminine dress that he'd never seen her wear in public. So much for hoping that Matt might have coaxed her out of her repressive way of dressing. But it was early days yet.

# CHAPTER TEN

FOR THE FIRST few days after her return to work, Leslie was uneasy every time she saw Matt coming. She shared that apprehension with two of the other secretaries, one of whom actually ripped her skirt climbing over the fence around the flower garden near the front of the building in a desperate attempt to escape him.

The incident sent Leslie into gales of helpless laughter as she told Karla Smith about it. Matt came by her office just as they were discussing it and stood transfixed at a sound he'd never heard coming from Leslie since he'd known her. She looked up and saw him, and made a valiant attempt to stop laughing.

"What's so funny?" he asked pleasantly.

Karla choked and ran for the ladies' room, leaving Leslie to cope with the question.

"Did you say something to the secretaries the other day to upset them?" she asked him right out.

He shifted. "I may have said a word or two that I shouldn't have," was all he'd admit.

"Well, Daisy Joiner just plowed through a fence avoiding you, and half her petticoat's still…out…there!" She collapsed against her desk, tears rolling down her cheeks.

She was more animated than he'd ever seen her. It lifted his heart. Not that he was going to admit it.

He gave her a harsh mock glare and pulled a cigar case out of his shirt pocket. "Lily-livered cowards," he muttered as he took out a cigar, flicked off the end with a tool from his slacks pocket, and snapped open his lighter with a flair. "What we need around here are secretaries with guts!" he said loudly, and flicked the lighter with his thumb.

Two streams of water hit the flame at the same time from different directions.

"Oh, for God's sake!" Matt roared as giggling, scurrying feet retreated down the hall.

"What were you saying about secretaries with guts?" she asked with twinkling gray eyes.

He looked at his drenched lighter and his damp cigar, and threw the whole mess into the trash can by Leslie's desk. "I quit," he muttered.

Leslie couldn't help the twinkle in her eyes. "I believe that was the whole object of the thing," she pointed out, "to make you quit smoking?"

He grimaced. "I guess it was." He studied her intently. "You're settling back in nicely," he remarked. "Do you have everything you need?"

"Yes," she replied.

He hesitated, as if he wanted to say something else and couldn't decide what. His dark eyes swept over her face, as if he were comparing her dark hair and glasses to the blond camouflage she'd worn when she first came to work for him.

"I guess I look different," she said a little self-consciously, because the scrutiny made her nervous. His face gave nothing away.

He smiled gently. "I like it," he told her.

"Did you need to see Ed?" she asked, because he still hadn't said why he was in Ed's office.

He shrugged. "It's nothing urgent," he murmured. "I met with the planning and zoning committee last night. I thought he might like to know how I came out."

"I could buzz him."

He nodded, still smiling. "Why don't you do that?"

She did. Ed came out of his office at once, still uncertain about Matt's reactions.

"Got a minute?" Matt asked him.

"Sure. Come on in." Ed stood aside to let the taller man stride into his office. He glanced back toward Leslie with a puzzled, questioning expression. She only smiled.

He nodded and closed the door, leaving Leslie to go back to work. She couldn't quite figure out Matt's new attitude toward her. There was nothing predatory about him lately. Ever since his return from Houston and the explosive meeting at her apartment, he was friendly and polite, even a little affectionate, but he didn't come near her now. He seemed to have the idea that any physical contact upset her, so he was being Big Brother Matt instead.

She should have been grateful. After all, he'd said often enough that marriage wasn't in his vocabulary. An affair, obviously, was out of the question now that he knew her past. Presumably affection was the only thing he had to offer her. It was a little disappointing, because Leslie had learned in their one early encounter that Matt's touch was delightful. She wished that she could tell him how exciting it was to her. It had been the only tenderness she'd ever had from a man in any physical respect, and she was very curious about that part of relationships. Not with just anyone, of course.

Only with Matt.

Her hands stilled on the keyboard as she heard footsteps approaching. The door opened and Carolyn came in, svelte in a beige dress that made the most of her figure, her hair perfectly coiffed.

"They said he let you come back to work here. I couldn't believe it, after what that reporter told him," the older woman began hotly. She gave Leslie a haughty, contemptuous stare. "That disguise won't do you any good, you know," she added, pausing to dig in her purse. She drew out a worn page from an old tabloid and tossed it onto Leslie's desk. It was the photo they'd used of her on the stretcher, with the caption, Teenager, Lover, Shot By Jealous Mother In Love Triangle.

Leslie just sat and looked at it, thinking how the past never really went away. She sighed wistfully. She was never going to be free of it.

"Don't you have anything to say?" Carolyn taunted.

Leslie looked up at her. "My mother is in prison. My life was destroyed. The man responsible for it all was a drug dealer." She searched Carolyn's cold eyes. "You can't imagine it, can you? You've always been wealthy, protected, safe. How could you understand the trauma of being a very innocent seventeen-year-old and having four grown men strip you naked in a drug-crazed frenzy and try to rape you in your own home?"

Amazingly Carolyn went pale. She hesitated, frowning. Her eyes went to the tabloid and she shifted uneasily. Her hand went out to retrieve the page just as the door to Ed's office opened and Matt came through it.

His face, when he saw Carolyn with the tearsheet in her hand, became dangerous.

Carolyn jerked it back, crumpled it, and threw it in the trash can. "You don't need to say anything," she said in a choked tone. "I'm not very proud of myself right now." She moved away from Leslie without looking at her. "I'm going to Europe for a few months. See you when I get back, Matt."

"You'd better hope you don't," he said in a voice like steel.

She made an awkward movement, but she didn't turn. She squared her shoulders and kept walking.

Matt paused beside the desk, retrieved the page and handed it to Ed. "Burn that," he said tautly.

"With pleasure," Ed replied. He gave Leslie a sympathetic glance before he went back into his office and closed the door.

"I thought she came to make trouble," she told Matt with evident surprise in her expression. Carolyn's abrupt about-face had puzzled her.

"She only knew what I mumbled the night I got drunk," he said curtly. "I never meant to tell her the rest of it. She's not as bad as she seems," he added. "I've known her most of my life, and I like her. She got it into her head that we should get married and saw you as a rival. I straightened all that out. At least, I thought I had."

"Thanks."

"She'll come back a different woman," he continued. "I'm sure she'll apologize."

"It's not necessary," she said. "Nobody knew the true story. I was too afraid to tell it."

He stuck his hands into his pockets and studied her.

His face was lined, his eyes had dark circles under them. He looked worn. "I would have spared you this if I could have," he gritted.

He seemed really upset about it. "You can't stop other people from thinking what they like. It's all right. I'll just have to get used to it."

"Like hell you will. The next person who comes in here with a damned tabloid page is going out right through the window!"

She smiled faintly. "Thank you. But it's not necessary. I can take care of myself."

"Judging by Carolyn's face, you did a fair job of it with her," he mused.

"I guess she's not really so bad." She glanced at him and away. "She was only jealous. It was silly. You never had designs on me."

There was a tense silence. "And what makes you think so?"

"I'm not in her league," she said simply. "She's beautiful and rich and comes from a good family."

He moved a step closer, watching her face lift. She didn't look apprehensive, so he moved again. "Not frightened?" he murmured.

"Of you?" She smiled gently. "Of course not."

He seemed surprised, curious, even puzzled.

"In fact, I like bears," she said with a deliberate grin.

That expression went right through him. He smiled. He beamed. Suddenly he caught the back of her chair with his hand and swiveled her around so that her face was within an inch of his.

"Sticks and stones, Miss Murry," he whispered softly, with a lazy grin, and brought his lips down very softly on hers.

She caught her breath.

His head lifted and his dark, quiet eyes met hers and held them while he tried to decide whether or not she was frightened. He saw the pulse throbbing at her neck and heard the faint unsteadiness of her breath. She was unsettled. But that wasn't fear. He knew enough about women to be sure of it.

He chuckled softly, and there was pure calculation in the way he studied her. "Any more smart remarks?" he taunted in a sensual whisper.

She hesitated. He wasn't aggressive or demanding or mocking. She searched his eyes, looking for clues to this new, odd behavior.

He traced her mouth with his forefinger. "Well?"

She smiled hesitantly. All her uncertainties were obvious, but she wasn't afraid of him. Her heart was going wild. But it wasn't with fear. And he knew it.

He bent and kissed her again with subdued tenderness.

"You taste like cigar smoke," she whispered impishly.

"I probably do, but I'm not giving up cigars completely, regardless of the water pistols," he whispered. "So you might as well get used to the taste of them."

She searched his dark eyes with quiet curiosity.

He put his thumb over her soft lips and smiled down at her. "I've been invited to a party at the Ballengers' next month. You'll be out of your cast by then. How about buying a pretty dress and coming with me?" He bent and brushed his lips over her forehead. "They're having a live Latin band. We can dance some more."

She wasn't hearing him. His lips were making her heart beat faster. She was smiling as she lifted her face to those soft kisses, like a flower reaching up to the sun. He realized that and smiled against her cheek.

"This isn't businesslike," she whispered.

He lifted his head and looked around. The office was empty and nobody was walking down the hall. He glanced back down at her with one lifted eyebrow.

She laughed shyly.

The teasing light in his eyes went into eclipse at the response that smile provoked in him. He framed her soft face in his big hands and bent again. This time the kiss wasn't light, or brief.

When she moaned, he drew back at once. His eyes were glittery with strong emotion. He let go of her face and stood up, looking down at her solemnly. He winced, as if he remembered previous encounters when he hadn't been careful with her, when he'd been deliberately cruel.

She read the guilt in his face and frowned. She was totally unversed in the byplay between men and women, well past the years when those things were learned in a normal way.

"I didn't mean to do that," he said quietly. "I'm sorry."

"It's all right," she stammered.

He drew in a long, slow breath. "You have nothing to be afraid of now. I hope you know that."

"I'm not frightened," she replied.

His face hardened as he looked at her. One hand clenched in his pocket. The other clenched at his side. She happened to look down and she drew in her breath at the sight of it.

"You're hurt!" she exclaimed, reaching out to touch

the abrasions that had crusted over, along with the swollen bruises that still remained there.

"I'll heal," he said curtly. "Maybe he will, too, eventually."

"He?" she queried.

"Yes. That yellow-backed reporter who came down here looking for you." His face tautened. "I took Houston apart looking for him. When I finally found him, I delivered him to his boss. There won't be any more problems from that direction, ever. In fact, he'll be writing obituaries for the rest of his miserable life."

"He could take you to court…"

"He's welcome, after my attorneys get through with him," he returned flatly. "He'll be answering charges until he's an old man. Considering the difference in our ages, I'll probably be dead by then." He paused to think about that. "I'll make sure the money's left in my estate to keep him in court until every penny runs out!" he added after a minute. "He won't even be safe when I'm six feet under!"

She didn't know whether to laugh or cry. He was livid, almost vibrating with temper.

"But you know what hurts the most?" he added, looking down into her worried eyes. "What he did still wasn't as bad as what I did to you. I won't ever forgive myself for that. Not if I live to be a hundred."

That was surprising. She toyed with her keyboard and didn't look at him. "I thought…you might blame me, when you knew the whole story," she said.

"For what?" he asked huskily.

She moved her shoulders restlessly. "The papers said it was my fault, that I invited it."

"Dear God!" He knelt beside her and made her look

at him. "Your mother told me the whole story," he
said. "She cried like a baby when she got it all out." He
paused, touching her face gently. "Know what she said?
That she'd gladly spend the rest of her life where she is,
if you could only forgive her for what she did to you."

She felt the tears overflowing. She started to wipe
them, but he pulled her face to his and kissed them away
so tenderly that they came in a veritable flood.

"No," he whispered. "You mustn't cry. It's all right.
I won't let anything hurt you ever again. I promise."

But she couldn't stop. "Oh, Matt…!" she sobbed.

All his protective instincts bristled. "Come here to
me," he said gently. He stood up and lifted her into his
arms, cast and all, and carried her down the deserted
hall to his office.

His secretary saw him coming and opened the door
for him, grimacing at Leslie's red, wet face.

"Coffee or brandy?" she asked Matt.

"Coffee. Make it about thirty minutes, will you? And
hold my calls."

"Yes, sir."

She closed the door and Matt sat down on the burgundy couch with Leslie in his lap, cradling her while
she wept.

He tucked a handkerchief into her hand and rocked
her in his arms, whispering to her until the sobs less-
ened.

"I'm going to replace the furniture in here," he murmured. "Maybe the paneling, too."

"Why?"

"It must hold some painful memories for you," he
said. "I know it does for me."

His voice was bitter. She recalled fainting, and coming to on this very couch. She looked up at him without malice or accusation. Her eyes were red and swollen, and full of curiosity.

He traced her cheek with tender fingers and smiled at her. "You've had a rough time of it, haven't you?" he asked quietly. "Will it do any good to tell you that a man wouldn't normally treat a woman, especially an innocent woman, the way those animals treated you?"

"I know that," she replied. "It's just that the publicity made me out to be little more than a call girl. I'm not like that. But it's what people thought I was. So I ran, and ran, and hid...if it hadn't been for Ed and his father, and my friend Jessica, I don't know what I would have done. I don't have any family left."

"You have your mother," he assured her. "She'd like to see you. If you're willing, I'll drive you up there, anytime you like."

She hesitated. "You do know that she's in prison for murder?" she asked.

"I know it."

"You're well-known here," she began.

"Oh, good Lord, are you trying to save me?" he asked with an exasperated sigh. "Woman, I don't give two hoots in hell for gossip. While they're talking about me, they're leaving some other person alone." He took the handkerchief and wiped her cheeks. "But for the record, most reporters keep out of my way." He pursed his lips. "I can guarantee there's one in Houston who'll run the next time he sees me coming."

It amazed her that he'd gone to that much trouble defending her. She lay looking at him with eyes like a cat's, wide and soft and curious.

They had an odd effect on him. He felt his body react

to it and caught his breath. He started to move her before she realized that he was aroused.

The abrupt rejection startled her. All at once she was sitting beside him on the couch, looking stunned.

He got up quickly and moved away, turning his back to her. "How would you like some coffee?" he asked gruffly.

She shifted a little, staring at him with open curiosity. "I… I would, thank you."

He went to the intercom, not to the door, and told his secretary to bring it in. He kept his back to Leslie, and to the door, even when Edna came in with the coffee service and placed it on the low coffee table in front of the sofa.

"Thanks, Edna," he said.

"Sure thing, boss." She winked at Leslie and smiled reassuringly, closing the door quietly behind her.

Leslie poured coffee into the cups, glancing at him warily. "Don't you want your coffee?"

"Not just yet," he murmured, trying to cool down.

"It smells nice."

"Yes, it does, but I've already had a little too much stimulation for the moment, without adding caffeine to the problem."

She didn't understand. He felt her eyes on his stiff back and with a helpless laugh, he turned around. To his amazement, and his amusement, she didn't notice anything wrong with him.

He went back to the couch and sat down, shaking his head as he let her hand him a cupful of fresh coffee.

"Is something wrong?" she asked.

"Not a thing in this world, baby doll," he drawled.

"Except that Edna just saved you from absolute ruin and you don't even know it."

Leslie stared into Matt's dancing eyes with obvious confusion.

"Never mind," he chuckled, sipping his coffee. "One day when we know each other better, I'll tell you all about it."

She sipped her coffee and smiled absently. "You're very different since you came back from Houston."

"I've had a bad knock." He put his cup down, but his eyes stayed on it. "I can't remember ever being grossly unfair to anyone before, much less an employee. It's hard for me, remembering some of the things I said and did to you." He grimaced, still not looking straight at her. "It hurt my pride that you'd let Ed get close, but you kept backing away from me. I never stopped to wonder why." He laughed hollowly. "I've had women throw themselves at me most of my adult life, even before I made my first million." He glanced at her. "But I couldn't get near you, except once, on the dance floor." His eyes narrowed. "And that night, when you let me touch you."

She remembered, too, the feel of his eyes and his hands and his mouth on her. Her breath caught audibly.

He winced. "It was the first time, wasn't it?"

She averted her eyes.

"I even managed to soil that one, beautiful memory." He looked down at his hands. "I've done so much damage, Leslie. I don't know how to start over, to begin again."

"Neither do I," she confessed. "What happened to me in Houston was a pretty bad experience, even if I'd been older and more mature when it happened. As it was, I gave up trying to go on dates afterward, because I connected anything physical with that one sordid incident. I couldn't bear it when men wanted to kiss me good-night. I backed away and they thought I was some sort of freak." Her eyes closed and she shuddered.

"Tell me about the doctor."

She hesitated. "He only knew what he'd been told, I guess. But he made me feel like trash." She wrapped both arms around her chest and leaned forward. "He cleaned the wound and bandaged my leg. He said that they could send me back to the hospital from jail for the rest."

Matt muttered something vicious.

"I didn't go to jail, of course, my mother did. The leg was horribly painful. I had no medical insurance and Jessica's parents were simple people, very poor. None of us could have afforded orthopedic surgery. I was able to see a doctor at the local clinic, and he put a cast on it, assuming that it had already been set properly. He didn't do X-rays because I couldn't afford any."

"You're lucky the damage could even be repaired," he said, his eyes downcast as he wondered at the bad luck she'd had not only with the trauma of the incident itself, but with its painful aftermath.

"I had a limp when it healed, but I walked fairly well." She sighed. "Then I fell off a horse." She shook her head.

"I wouldn't have had that happen for the world," he said, meeting her eyes. "I was furious, not just that you'd backed away from me, but that I'd caused you to hurt yourself. Then at the dance, it was even worse, when I realized that all those quick steps had caused you such pain."

"It was a good sort of pain," she told him, "because it led to corrective surgery. I'm really grateful about that."

"I'm sorry it came about in the way it did." He smiled at her new look. "Glasses suit you. They make your eyes look bigger."

"I always wore them until the reporter started trying to sell an idea for a television movie about what happened. I dyed my hair and got contacts, dressed like a dowager, did everything I could to change my appearance. But Jacobsville was my last chance. I thought if I could be found here, I could be tracked anywhere." She smoothed her skirt over the cast.

"You won't be bothered by that anymore," he said. "But I'd like to let my attorneys talk to your mother. I know," he said, when she lifted her head and gave him a worried look, "it would mean resurrecting a lot of unpleasant memories, but we might be able to get her sentence reduced or even get her a new trial. There were extenuating circumstances. Even a good public defender isn't as good as an experienced criminal lawyer."

"Did you ask her that?"

He nodded. "She wouldn't even discuss it. She said you'd had enough grief because of her."

She lowered her eyes back to her skirt. "Maybe we both have. But I hate it that she may spend the rest of her life in prison."

"So do I." He touched her hair. "She really is blond, isn't she?"

"Yes. My father had dark hair, like mine, and gray eyes, too. Hers are blue. I always wished mine were that color."

"I like your eyes just the way they are." He touched the wire rims of her frames. "Glasses and all."

"You don't have any problem seeing, do you?" she wondered.

He chuckled. "I have trouble seeing what's right under my nose, apparently."

"You're farsighted?" she asked, misunderstanding him.

He touched her soft mouth with his forefinger and the smile faded. "No. I mistake gold for tinsel."

His finger made her feel nervous. She drew back. His hand fell at once and he smiled at her surprise.

"No more aggression. I promise."

Her fascinated eyes met his. "Does that mean that you won't ever kiss me again?" she asked boldly.

"Oh, I will," he replied, delighted. He leaned forward. "But you'll have to do all the chasing from now on."

## CHAPTER ELEVEN

LESLIE SEARCHED HIS dark eyes slowly and then she began to smile. "Me, chase you?" she asked. He pursed his lips. "Sure. Men get tired of the chase from time to time. I think I'd like having you pursue me."

Mental pictures of her in a suit and Matt in a dress dissolved her in mirth. But the reversed relationship made her feel warm inside, as if she wasn't completely encased in ice. The prospect of Matt in her arms was exhilarating, even with her past. "Okay, but I draw the line at taking you to football games," she added, trying to keep things casual between them, just for the time being.

He grinned back. "No problem. We can always watch them on TV." The light in her eyes made him light-headed. "Feeling better now?" he asked softly.

She nodded. "I guess you can get used to anything when you have to," she said philosophically.

"I could write you a book on that," he said bitterly, and she remembered his past—his young life marked with such sadness.

"I'm sure you could," she agreed.

He leaned forward with the coffee cup still in his hands. He had nice hands, she thought absently, lean and strong and beautifully shaped. She remembered their touch on her body with delight.

"We'll take this whole thing one step at a time," he said quietly. "There won't be any pressure, and I won't run roughshod over you. We'll go at your pace."

She was a little reluctant. That one step at a time could lead anywhere, and she didn't like the idea of taking chances. He wasn't a marrying man and she wasn't the type for affairs. She did wonder what he ultimately had in mind for them, but she wasn't confident enough of this new relationship to ask. It was nice to have him like this, gentle and concerned and caring. She hadn't had much tenderness in her life, and she was greedy for it.

He glanced suddenly at the thin gold watch on his wrist and grimaced. "I should have been in Fort Worth an hour ago for a meeting with some stock producers." He glanced at her ruefully. "Just look at what you do to me," he murmured. "I can't even think straight anymore."

She smiled gently. "Good for me."

He chuckled, finished his coffee and put down the cup. "Better late than never, I suppose." He leaned down and kissed her, very softly. His eyes held a new, warm light that made her feel funny all over. "Stay out of trouble while I'm gone."

Her eyebrows rose. "Oh, that's cute."

He nodded. "You never put a foot wrong, did you?"

"Only by being stupid and gullible."

His dark eyes went even darker. "What happened wasn't your fault. That's the first idea we have to correct."

"I was madly infatuated for the first time in my life," she said honestly. "I might have inadvertently given him the idea…."

He put his thumb against her soft lips. "Leslie, what sort of decent adult man would accept even blatant signals from a teenager?"

It was a good question. It made her see what had happened from a different perspective.

He gave her mouth a long scrutiny before he abruptly removed his thumb and ruffled her short dark hair playfully. "Think about that. You might also consider that people on drugs very often don't know what they're doing anyway. You were in the wrong place at the wrong time."

She readjusted her glasses as they slipped further on her nose. "I suppose so."

"I'll be in Fort Worth overnight, but maybe we can go out to dinner tomorrow night?" he asked speculatively.

She indicated the cast. "I can see me now, clumping around in a pretty dress."

He chuckled. "I don't mind if you don't."

She'd never been on a real date before, except nights out with Ed, who was more like a brother than a boyfriend. Her eyes brightened. "I'd love to go out with you, if you mean it."

"I mean it, all right."

"Then, yes."

He grinned at her. "Okay."

She couldn't look away from his dark, soft eyes. It felt like electricity flowing between them. It was exciting to share that sort of intimate look. She colored. He arched an eyebrow and gave her a wicked smile.

"Not now," he said in a deep, husky tone that made her blush even more, and turned toward the door.

He opened it. "Edna, I'll be back tomorrow," he told his secretary.

"Yes, sir."

He didn't look back. The outer door opened and closed. Leslie got up with an effort and moved to the office door. "Do you want me to clean up in here?" she asked Edna.

The older woman just smiled. "Heavens, no. You go on back to work, Miss Murry. How's that leg feeling?"

"Awkward," she said, glowering at it. "But it's going to be nice not to limp anymore," she added truthfully. "I'm very grateful to Mr. Caldwell for having it seen to."

"He's a good man," his secretary said with a smile. "And a good boss. He has moods, but most people do."

"Yes."

Leslie clumped her way back down the hall to her office. Ed came out when he heard her rustling paper and lifted both eyebrows. "Feeling better?" he asked.

She nodded. "I'm a watering pot lately. I don't know why."

"Nobody ever had a better reason," he ventured. He smiled gently. "Matt's not so bad, is he?"

She shook her head. "He's not what I thought he was at first."

"He'll grow on you," he said. He reached for a file on his desk, brought it out and perched himself on the edge of her desk. "I need you to answer these. Feel up to some dictation?"

She nodded. "You bet!"

MATT CAME BACK late the next morning and went straight to Leslie when he arrived at the office. "Call Karla

Smith and ask if she'll substitute for you," he said abruptly. "You and I are going to take the afternoon off."

"We are?" she asked, pleasantly surprised. "What are we going to do?"

"Now there's a leading question," he said, chuckling. He pressed the intercom on her phone and told Ed he was swiping his secretary and then moved back while Leslie got Karla on the phone and asked her to come down to Ed's office.

It didn't take much time to arrange everything. Minutes later, she was seated beside Matt in the Jaguar flying down the highway just at the legal speed limit.

"Where are we going?" she asked excitedly.

He grinned, glancing sideways at the picture she made in that pretty blue-and-green swirl-patterned dress that left her arms bare. He liked her hair short and dark. He even liked her glasses.

"I've got a surprise for you," he said. "I hope you're going to like it," he added a little tautly.

"Don't tell me. You're taking me to see all the big snakes at the zoo," she said jokingly.

"Do you like snakes?" he asked unexpectedly.

"Not really. But that would be a surprise I wouldn't quite like," she added.

"No snakes."

"Good."

He slid into the passing lane and passed several other cars on the four-lane.

"This is the road to Houston," she said, noting a road sign.

"So it is."

She toyed with her seat belt. "Matt, I don't really like Houston."

"I know that." He glanced at her. "We're going to the prison to see your mother."

Her intake of breath was audible. Her hands clenched on her skirt.

He reached a lean hand over and gently pressed both of hers. "Remember what Ed says? Never back away from a problem," he said softly. "Always meet it head-on. You and your mother haven't seen each other in over five years. Don't you think it's time to lay rest to all the ghosts?"

She was uneasy and couldn't hide it. "The last time I saw her was in court, when the verdict was read. She wouldn't even look at me."

"She was ashamed, Leslie."

That was surprising. Her eyes met his under a frown. "Ashamed?"

"She wasn't taking huge amounts of drugs, but she was certainly addicted. She'd had something before she went back to the apartment and found you with her lover. The drugs disoriented her. She told me that she doesn't even remember how the pistol got into her hand, the next thing she knew, her lover was dead and you were bleeding on the floor. She barely remembers the police taking her away." His lips flattened. "What she does remember is coming back to her senses in jail and being told what she did. No, she didn't look at you during the trial or afterward. It wasn't that she blamed you. She blamed herself for being so gullible and letting herself be taken in by a smooth-talking, lying drug dealer who pretended to love her in return for a place to live."

She didn't like the memories. She and her mother had never been really close, but when she looked back, she remembered that she'd been standoffish and difficult, especially after the death of her father.

His hand contracted on both of hers. "I'm going to be right with you every step of the way," he said firmly. "Whatever happens, it won't make any difference to me. I only want to try to make things easier for you."

"She might not want to see me," she ventured.

"She wants to," he said grimly. "Very badly. She realizes that she might not have much time left."

She bit her lower lip. "I never realized she had heart trouble."

"She probably didn't, until she started consuming massive quantities of drugs. The human body can only take so much abuse until it starts rebelling." He glanced at her. "She's all right for now. She just has to take it easy. But I still think we can do something for her."

"A new trial would put a lot of stress on her."

"It would," he agreed. "But perhaps it isn't the sort of stress that would be damaging. At the end of that road, God willing, she might get out on parole."

Leslie only nodded. The difficult part lay yet ahead of her; a reunion that she wasn't even sure she wanted. But Matt seemed determined to bring it about.

IT WAS COMPLICATED to get into a prison, Leslie learned at once. There were all sorts of checkpoints and safety measures designed to protect visitors. Leslie shivered a little as they walked down the long hall to the room where visitors were allowed to see inmates. For her, the thought of losing her freedom was akin to fears of a lingering death. She wondered if it was that bad for her mother.

There was a long row of chairs at little cubicles, separated from the prisoners' side by thick glass. There was a small opening in the glass, which was covered with mesh wiring so that people could talk back and forth. Matt spoke to a guard and gestured Leslie toward one of the cubicles, settling her in the straight-backed chair there. Through the glass, she could see a closed door across the long room.

As she watched, aware of Matt's strong, warm hand on her shoulder, the door opened and a thin, drawn blond woman with very short hair was ushered into the room by a guard. She went forward to the cubicle where Leslie was sitting and lifted her eyes to the tense face through the glass. Her pale blue eyes were full of sadness and uncertainty. Her thin hands trembled.

"Hello, Leslie," she said slowly.

Leslie just sat there for a moment with her heart beating half to death. The thin, drawn woman with the heavily lined face and dull blue eyes was only a shadow of the mother she remembered. Those thin hands were so wasted that the blue veins on their backs stood out prominently.

Marie smiled with faint self-contempt. "I knew this would be a mistake," she said huskily. "I'm so sorry…" She started to get up.

"Wait," Leslie croaked. She grimaced. She didn't know what to say. The years had made this woman a stranger.

Matt moved behind her, both hands on her shoulders now, supporting her, giving her strength.

"Take your time," he said gently. "It's all right."

Marie gave a little start as she noticed that Matt was touching Leslie with some familiarity, and Leslie wasn't stiff or protesting. Her eyes connected with his dark ones and he smiled.

Marie smiled back hesitantly. It changed her lined, worn face and made her seem younger. She looked into her daughter's eyes and her own softened. "I like your boss," she said.

Leslie smiled back. "I like him, too," she confessed.

There was a hesitation. "I don't know where to start," she began huskily. "I've rehearsed it and rehearsed it and I simply can't find the words." Her pale eyes searched Leslie's face, as if she was trying to recall it from the past. She winced as she compared it with the terror-stricken face she'd seen that night so long ago. "I've made a lot of mistakes, Leslie. My biggest one was putting my own needs ahead of everybody else's. It was always what *I* wanted, what *I* needed. Even when I started doing drugs, all I thought about was what would make me happy." She shook her head. "Selfishness carries a high price tag. I'm so sorry that you had to pay such a high price for mine. I couldn't even bear to look at you at the trial, after the tabloids came out. I was so ashamed of what I'd subjected you to. I thought of you, all alone, trying to hold your head up with half the state knowing such intimate things about our lives…" She drew in a slow, unsteady breath and she seemed to slump. "I can't even ask you to forgive me. But I did want to see you, even if it's just this once, to tell you how much I regret it all."

The sight of her pinched face hurt Leslie, who hadn't realized her mother even felt remorse. There had been no communication between them. She knew now that Matt had been telling the truth about her mother's silence. Marie was too ashamed to face her, even now.

It eased the wound a little. "I didn't know about the drugs," Leslie blurted out abruptly.

Her tone brought Marie's eyes up, and for the first time, there was hope in them. "I never used them around you," she said gently. "But it started a long time ago, about the time your father...died." The light in her eyes seemed to dim. "You blamed me for his death, and you were right. He couldn't live up to being what I wanted him to be. He couldn't give me the things I thought I deserved." She looked down at the table in front of her. "He was a good, kind man. I should have appreciated him. It wasn't until he died that I realized how much he meant to me. And it was too late." She laughed hollowly. "From then on, everything went downhill. I didn't care anymore, about myself or you, and I went onto harder drugs. That's how I met Mike. I guess you figured out that he was my supplier."

"Matt did," Leslie corrected.

Marie lifted her eyes to look at Matt, who was still standing behind Leslie. "Don't let them hurt her anymore," she pleaded gently. "Don't let that reporter make her run anymore. She's had enough."

"So have you," Leslie said unexpectedly, painfully touched by Marie's concern. "Matt says...that he thinks his attorneys might be able to get you a new trial."

Marie started. Her eyes lit up, and then abruptly shifted. "No!" she said gruffly. "I have to pay for what I did."

"Yes," Leslie said. "But what you did..." She hesitated. "What you did was out of shock and outrage, don't you see? It wasn't premeditated. I don't know much about the law, but I do know that intent is everything. You didn't plan to kill Mike."

The older woman's sad eyes met Leslie's through the glass. "That's generous of you, Leslie," she said quietly. "Very generous, considering the notoriety and grief I caused you."

"We've both paid a price," she agreed.

"You're wearing a cast," her mother said suddenly. "Why?"

"I fell off a horse," Leslie said and felt Matt's hands contract on her shoulders, as if he was remembering why. She reached up and smoothed her hand over one of his. "It was a lucky fall, because Matt got an orthopedic surgeon to operate on my leg and put it right."

"Do you know how her leg was hurt?" the other woman asked Matt with a sad little smile.

"Yes," he replied. His voice sounded strained. The tender, caressing action of Leslie's soft fingers on his hand was arousing him. It was the first time she'd touched him voluntarily, and his head was reeling.

"That's another thing I've had on my conscience for years," the smaller woman told her daughter. "I'm glad you had the operation."

"I'm sorry for the position you're in," Leslie said with genuine sympathy. "I would have come to see you years ago, but I thought… I thought you hated me," she added huskily, "for what happened to Mike."

"Oh, Leslie!" Marie put her face in her hands and her shoulders shook. She wept harshly, while her daughter sat staring at her uncomfortably. After a minute, she wiped the tears from her red, swollen eyes. "No, I didn't hate you! I never blamed you!" Marie said brokenly. "How could I hate you for something that was never your fault? I wasn't a good mother. I put you at risk the minute I started using drugs. I failed you terribly. By letting Mike move in, I set you up for what he and his friends did to you. My poor baby," she choked. "You were so very young, so innocent, and to have men treat you…that way—" She broke off. "That's why I couldn't ask you to come, why I couldn't write or phone. I thought you hated *me!*"

Leslie's fingers clenched around Matt's on her shoulder, drawing strength from his very presence. She knew she could never have faced this without him. "I didn't hate you," she said slowly. "I'm sorry we couldn't talk to each other, at the trial. I…did blame you for Dad," she confessed. "But I was so young when it happened, and you and I had never been particularly close. If we had…"

"You can't change what was," her mother said with a wistful smile. "But it's worth all this if you can forgive me." Her long fingers moved restlessly on the mesh wiring. Her pained eyes met Leslie's. "It means everything if you can forgive me!"

Leslie felt a lump in her throat as she looked at her mother and realized the change in her. "Of course I can." She bit her lip. "Are you all right? Is your health all right?"

"I have a weak heart, probably damaged by all the drugs I took," Marie said without emphasis. "I take medicine for it, and I'm doing fine. I'll be all right, Leslie." She searched the younger woman's eyes intently. "I hope you're going to be all right, too, now that you aren't being stalked by that reporter anymore. Thank you for coming to see me."

"I'm glad I did," Leslie said, and meant it sincerely. "I'll write, and I'll come to see you when I can. Meanwhile, Matt's lawyers may be able to do something for you. Let them try."

There was a hesitation while the other woman exchanged a worried look with Matt.

Both his hands pressed on Leslie's shoulders. "I'll take care of her," he told Marie, and knew that she understood what he was saying. Nobody would bother Leslie again, as long as there was a breath in his body. He had power and he would use it on her daughter's behalf. She relaxed.

"All right, then," she replied. "Thank you for trying to help me, even if nothing comes of it."

Matt smiled at her. "Miracles happen every day," he said, and he was looking at Leslie's small hand caressing his.

"You hold on to him," the older woman told Leslie fervently. "If I'd had a man like that to care about me, I wouldn't be in this mess today."

Leslie flushed. Her mother spoke as if she had a chance of holding on to Matt, and that was absurd. He might feel guilt and sympathy, even regret, but her mother seemed to be mistaking his concern for love. It wasn't.

Matt leaned close to Leslie and spoke. "It's rather the other way around," Matt said surprisingly, and he didn't smile. "Women like Leslie don't grow on trees."

Marie smiled broadly. "No, they don't. She's very special. Take care of yourself, Leslie. I… I do love you, even if it doesn't seem like it."

Leslie's eyes stung with threatening tears. "I love you, too, Mama," she said in a gruff, uneasy tone. She could barely speak for the emotion she felt.

The other woman couldn't speak at all. Her eyes

were bright and her smile trembled. She only nodded. After one long look at her daughter, she got up and went to the door.

Leslie sat there for a minute, watching until her mother was completely out of sight. Matt's big hands contracted on her shoulders.

"Let's go, sweetheart," he said gently, and pressed a handkerchief into her hands as he shepherded her out the door.

That tenderness in him was a lethal weapon, she thought. It was almost painful to experience, especially when she knew that it wasn't going to last. He was kind, and right now he was trying to make amends. But she'd better not go reading anything into his actions. She had to take one day at a time and just live for the present.

SHE WAS QUIET all the way to the parking lot. Matt smoked a cigar on the way, one hand in his pocket, his eyes narrow and introspective as he strode along beside Leslie until they reached the car. He pushed a button on his electronic controller and the locks popped up.

"Thank you for bringing me here," Leslie said at the passenger door, her eyes full of gratitude as they lifted to his. "I'm really glad I came, even if I didn't want to at first."

He stayed her hand as she went to open the door and moved closer, so that she was standing between his long, muscular body and the door. His dark eyes searched hers intently.

His gaze fell to her soft mouth and the intensity of the look parted her lips. Her pulse raced like mad. Her reaction to his closeness had always been intense, but she could almost feel his mouth on her body as she looked up at him. It was frightening to feel such wanton impulses.

His eyes lifted and he saw that expression in her soft, dazed gray eyes. The muscles in his jaw moved and he seemed to be holding his breath.

Around them, the parking lot was deserted. There was nothing audible except the sound of traffic and the frantic throb of Leslie's pulse as she stared into Matt's dark, glittery eyes.

He moved a step closer, deliberately positioning his body so that one long, powerful leg brushed between her good leg and the bulky cast on the other one.

"Matt?" she whispered shakily.

His eyes narrowed. His free hand went to her face and spread against her flushed cheek. His thumb nudged at her chin, lifting it. His leg moved against her thighs and she gasped.

There was arrogance not only in the way he touched her, but in the way he looked at her. She was completely vulnerable when he approached her like this, and he must surely know it, with his experience of women.

"So many women put on an act," he murmured conversationally. "They pretend to be standoffish, they tease, they provoke, they exaggerate their responses. With you, it's all genuine. I can look at you and see everything you're thinking. You don't try to hide it or explain it. It's all right there in the open."

Her lips parted. It was getting very hard to breathe. She didn't know what to say.

His head bent just a little, so that she could feel his breath on her mouth. "You can't imagine the pleasure it gives me to see you like this. I feel ten feet tall."

"Why?" she whispered unsteadily.

His mouth hovered over hers, lightly brushing, teasing. "Because every time I touch you, you offer yourself up like a virgin sacrifice. I remember the taste of your breasts in my mouth, the soft little cries that pulsed out of you when I pressed you down into the mattress under my body." He moved against her, slowly and deliberately, letting her feel his instant response. "I want to take your clothes off and ease inside your body on crisp, white sheets…" he whispered as his hard mouth went down roughly on her soft lips.

She made a husky little cry as she pictured what he was saying to her, pictured it, ached for it. Of all the outrageous, shocking things to say to a woman…!

Her nails bit into his arms as she lifted herself against his arousal and pushed up at his mouth to tempt it into violence. The sudden whip of passion was unexpected, overwhelming. She moaned brokenly and her legs trembled.

He groaned harshly. For a few seconds, his mouth devoured her own. He had to drag himself away from her, and when he did, his whole body seemed to vibrate. There was a flush high on his cheekbones, and his eyes glittered.

She loved the expression on his face. She loved the tremor of the arms propped on either side of her head. Her chin lifted and her eyes grew misty with pleasure.

"Do you like making me this way?" he asked gruffly.

"Yes," she said, something wild and impulsive rising in her like a quick tide. She looked at the pulse in his throat, the quick rhythmic movement of his shirt under the suit he was wearing. Her eyes dropped boldly down his body to the visible effect of passion on him.

His intake of breath was audible as he watched her

eyes linger on him, there. His whole body shook convulsively, as if with a fever.

Her eyes went back to his. It was intimate, to look at him this way. She could feel his passion, taste it.

Her hands went to his chest and rested against his warm muscles through the shirt, feeling the soft cushion of hair under it. He wasn't trying to stop her, and she remembered what he'd said to her in his office, that she was going to have to do all the running. Well, why not? She had to find out sooner or later what the limits of her capability were. Now seemed as good a time as any, despite their surroundings. Shyly, involuntarily, her nervous hands slid down to his belt and hesitated.

His jaw clenched. He was helpless. Did she know? Her hands slowly moved over the belt and down barely an inch before they hesitated again. His heavy brows drew together in a ferocious scowl as he fought for control.

He seemed to turn to stone. There was not a trace of emotion on his lean, hard face, but his eyes were glittering wildly.

"Go ahead if you want to. But if you touch me there," he said in a choked, harsh tone, "I will back you into this car, push your skirt up, and take you right here in the parking lot without a second's hesitation. And I won't give a damn if the entire staff of the prison comes out to watch!"

## CHAPTER TWELVE

THE TERSE THREAT brought Leslie to her senses. She went scarlet as her hands jerked back from his body. "Oh, good Lord!" she said, horrified at what she'd been doing.

Matt closed his eyes and leaned his forehead against hers. It was damp with sweat and he shuddered with helpless reaction even as he laughed at her embarrassment.

She could barely get her own breath, and her body felt swollen all over. "I'm sorry, Matt, I don't know what got into me!"

The raging desire she'd kindled was getting the best of him. He'd wanted her for such a long time. He hadn't even thought of other women. "Leslie, I'm fairly vulnerable, and you're starting something both of us know you can't finish," he added huskily.

"I'm…not sure that I can't," she said, surprising both of them. She felt the damp warmth of his body close to hers and marveled at his vulnerability.

His eyes opened. He lifted his head slowly and looked down at her, his breath on her mouth. "If you have a single instinct for self-preservation left, you'd better get in the car, Leslie."

"Okay," she agreed breathlessly, her heart in her eyes as she looked at him with faint wonder.

She got in on the passenger side and fastened her seat belt. He came around to the driver's side and got into the car.

Her hands were curling in on the soft material of her purse and she looked everywhere except at him. She couldn't believe what she'd done.

"Don't make such heavy weather of it," he said gently. "I did say that you'd have to do the chasing, after all."

She cleared her throat. "I think I took it a little too literally."

He chuckled. The sound was deep and pleasant as the powerful car ate up the miles toward Jacobsville. "You have definite potential, Miss Murry," he mused, glancing at her with indulgent affection. "I think we're making progress."

She stared at her purse. "Slow progress."

"That's the best kind." He changed gears and passed a slow-moving old pickup truck. "I'll drop you by your house to change. We're going out on the town tonight, cast and all."

She smiled shyly. "I can't dance."

"There's plenty of time for dancing when you're back on your feet," he said firmly. "I'm going to take care of you from now on. No more risks."

He made her feel like treasure. She didn't realize she'd spoken aloud until she heard him chuckle.

"That's what you are," he said. "My treasure. I'm going to have a hard time sharing you even with other people." He glanced at her. "You're sure there's nothing between you and Ed?"

"Only friendship," she assured him.

"Good."

He turned on the radio and he looked more relaxed

than she'd ever seen him. It was like a beginning. She had no idea where their relationship would go, but she was too weak to stop now.

THEY WENT OUT to eat, and Matt was the soul of courtesy. He opened doors for her, pulled out chairs for her, did all the little things that once denoted a gentleman and proved to her forcefully that he wasn't a completely modern man. She loved it. Old-world courtesy was delicious.

They went to restaurants in Jacobsville and Victoria and Houston in the weeks that followed, and Matt even phoned her late at night, just to talk. He sent her flowers at the boardinghouse, prompting teasing remarks and secret smiles from other residents. He was Leslie's fellow, in the eyes of Jacobsville, and she began to feel as if her dreams might actually come true—except for the one problem that had never been addressed. How was she going to react when Matt finally made love to her completely? Would she be able to go through with intimacy like that, with her past?

It haunted her, because while Matt had been affectionate and kind and tender with her, it never went beyond soft, brief kisses in his car or at her door. He never attempted to take things to a deeper level, and she was too shy from their encounter at the prison parking lot to be so bold again.

THE CAST CAME OFF just before the Ballengers' party to which all of Jacobsville was invited. Leslie looked at her unnaturally pale leg with fascination as Lou Coltrain coaxed her into putting her weight on it for the first time without the supporting cast.

She did, worried that it wouldn't take her weight, while Matt stood grim-faced next to Lou and worried with her.

But when she felt the strength of the bone, she gasped. "It's all right!" she exclaimed. "Matt, look, I can stand on it!"

"Of course you can," Lou chuckled. "Dr. Santos is the best, the very best, in orthopedics."

"I'll be able to dance again," she said.

Matt moved forward and took her hand in his, lifting it to his mouth. "*We'll* be able to dance again," he corrected, holding her eyes with his.

Lou had to stifle amusement at the way they looked together, the tall dark rancher and the small brunette, like two halves of a whole. That would be some marriage, she thought privately, but she kept her thoughts to herself.

LATER, MATT CAME to pick her up at her apartment. She was wearing the long silver dress with the spaghetti straps, and this time without a bra under it. She felt absolutely vampish with her contacts back in and her hair clean and shining. She'd gained a little weight in the past few weeks, and her figure was all she'd ever hoped it would be. Best of all, she could walk without limping.

"Nice," he murmured, smiling as they settled themselves into the car. "But we're not going to overdo things, are we?"

"Whatever you say, boss," she drawled.

He chuckled as he cranked the car. "That's a good start to the evening."

"I have something even better planned for later," she said demurely.

His heart jumped and his fingers jerked on the steering wheel. "Is that a threat or a promise?"

She glanced at him shyly. "That depends on you."

He didn't speak for a minute. "Leslie, you can only go so far with a man before things get out of hand," he began slowly. "You don't know much about relationships, because you haven't dated. I want you to understand how it is with me. I haven't touched another woman since I met you. That makes me more vulnerable than I would be normally." His eyes touched her profile and averted to the highway. "I can't make light love to you anymore," he said finally, his voice harsh. "The strain is more than I can bear."

Her breath caught. She smoothed at an imaginary spot on her gown. "You want us to…to go on like we are."

"I do not," he said gruffly. "But I'm not going to put any pressure on you. I meant what I said about letting you make the moves."

She turned the small purse over in her hands, watching the silver sequins on it glitter in the light. "You've been very patient."

"Because I was very careless of you in those first weeks we knew each other," he said flatly. "I'm trying to show you that sex isn't the basis of our relationship."

She smiled. "I knew that already," she replied. "You've taken wonderful care of me."

He shrugged. "Penance."

She grinned, because it wasn't. He'd shown her in a hundred nonverbal ways how he felt about her. Even the other women in the office had remarked on it.

He glanced at her. "No comment?"

"Oh, I'm sorry, I was just thinking about something."

"About what?" he asked conversationally.

She traced a sequin on the purse. "Can you teach me how to seduce you?"

The car went off the road and barely missed a ditch before he righted it, pulled onto the shoulder and flipped the key to shut off the engine.

He gaped at her. "What did you say?"

She looked up at him in the dimly lit interior where moonlight reflected into the car. "I want to seduce you."

"Maybe I have a fever," he murmured.

She smiled. She laughed. He made her feel as if she could do anything. Her whole body felt warm and uninhibited. She leaned back in her seat and moved sinuously in the seat, liking the way the silky fabric felt against her bare breasts. She felt reckless.

His gaze fell to the fabric against which her hard nipples were distinctly outlined. He watched her body move and knew that she was already aroused, which aroused him at once.

He leaned over, his mouth catching hers as his lean hand slipped under the fabric and moved lazily against her taut breasts.

She moaned and arched toward his fingers, pulling them back when he would have removed them. Her mouth opened under his as she gave in to the need to experience him in a new way, in a new intimacy.

"This is dangerous." He bit off the words against her mouth.

"It feels wonderful," she whispered back, pressing his hand to her soft skin. "I want to feel you like this. I want to touch you under your shirt…"

He hadn't realized how quickly he could get a tie and a shirt out of the way. He pulled her across the console and against him, watching her pert breasts bury themselves in the thick hair that covered his chest. He moved her deliberately against it and watched her eyes grow languid and misty as she experienced him.

His mouth opened hers in a sensual kiss that was as explicit as lovemaking. She felt his tongue, his lips, his teeth, and all the while, his chest moved lazily against her bare breasts. His hand went to the base of her spine and moved her upon the raging arousal she'd kindled. He groaned harshly, and she knew that he wouldn't draw back tonight. The strange thing, the wonderful thing, was that she wasn't afraid.

A minute later, he forced his head up and looked at her, lying yielding and breathless against him. He touched her breasts possessively before he lifted his eyes to search hers. "You aren't afraid of me like this," he said huskily.

She drew in a shaking breath. "No. I'm not."

His eyes narrowed as he persisted. "You want me."

She nodded. She touched his lips with fingers that trembled. "I want you very much. I like the way you feel when you want me," she whispered daringly, the surprise of it in her expression as she moved restlessly against him. "It excites me to feel it."

He groaned out loud and closed his eyes. "For God's sake, honey, don't say things like that to me!"

Her fingers moved down to his chest and pressed there. "Why not? I want to know if I can be intimate with you. I have to know," she said hesitantly. "I've never been able to want a man before. And I've never felt anything like this!" She looked up into his open, curious eyes. "Matt, can we...go somewhere?" she whispered.

"And make love?" he asked in a tone that suggested he thought she was unbalanced.

Her expression softened. "Yes."

He couldn't. His brain told him he couldn't. But his stupid body was screaming at him that he certainly could! "Leslie, sweetheart, it's too soon…"

"No, it isn't," she said huskily, tracing the hair on his chest with cool fingers. "I know you don't want anything permanent, and that's okay. But I…"

The matter-of-fact statement surprised him. "What do you mean, I don't want anything permanent?"

"I mean, you aren't a marrying man."

He looked puzzled. He smiled slowly. "Leslie, you're a virgin," he said softly.

"I know that's a drawback, but we all have to start somewhere. You can teach me how," she said stubbornly. "I can learn."

"No!" he said softly. "It's not that at all." His eyes seemed to flicker and then burn like black coals. "Leslie, I don't play around with virgins."

Her mind wasn't getting this at all. She felt dazed by her own desire. "You don't?"

"No, I don't," he said firmly.

"Well, if you'll cooperate, I won't be one for much longer," she pointed out. "So there goes your last argument, Matt." She pressed deliberately closer to him, as aware as he was that his body was amazingly capable.

He actually flushed. He pushed away from her and moved her back into her own seat firmly, pulling up the straps of her dress with hands that fumbled a little. He looked as if she'd hit him in the head with something hard.

Puzzled, she fiddled with her seat belt as he snapped his own into place.

He looked formidably upset. He started the car with subdued violence and put it in gear, his expression hard and stoic.

As the Jaguar shot forward, she slanted a glance at him. It puzzled her that he'd backed away from her. Surely he wasn't insulted by her offer? Or maybe he was.

"Are you offended?" she asked, suddenly self-conscious and embarrassed.

"Heavens, no!" he exclaimed.

"Okay." She let out a relieved sigh. She glanced at him. He wouldn't look at her. "Are you sure you aren't?"

He nodded.

She wrapped her arms around her chest and stared out the windshield at the darkened landscape, trying to decide why he was acting so strangely. He certainly wasn't the man she thought she knew. She'd been certain that he wanted her, too. Now she wasn't.

The Jaguar purred along and they rode in silence. He didn't speak or look at her. He seemed to be deep in thought and she wondered if she'd ruined their budding relationship for good with her wanton tendencies.

It wasn't until he turned the car down a dirt road a few miles from the ranch that she realized he wasn't going toward the Ballengers' home.

"Where are we?" she asked when he turned down an even narrower dirt road that led to a lake. Signposts pointed to various cabins, one of which had Caldwell on it. He pulled into the yard of a little wood cabin in the woods, facing the lake, and cut off the engine.

"This is where I come to get away from business," he told her bluntly. "I've never brought a woman here."

"You haven't?"

His eyes narrowed on her flushed face. "You said you wanted to find out if you could function intimately. All right. We have a place where we won't be disturbed, and I'm willing. More than willing. So there's no reason to be embarrassed," he said quietly. "I want you every bit as badly as you want me. I have something to use. There won't be any risk. But you have to be sure this is what you really want. Once I take your virginity, I can't give it back. There's only one first time."

She stared at him. Her whole body felt hot at the way he was looking at her. She remembered the feel of his mouth on her breasts and her lips parted hungrily. But it was more than just hunger. He knew it.

She lifted her face to his and brushed a breathless little kiss against his firm chin. "I wouldn't let any other man touch me," she said quietly. "And I think you know it."

"Yes. I know it." He knew something else, as well; he knew that it was going to be a beginning, not an affair or a one-night stand. He was going to be her first man, but she was going to be his last woman. She was all he wanted in the world.

He got out and led her up the steps onto the wide porch where there was a swing and three rocking chairs. He unlocked the door, ushered her inside and locked it again. Taking her hand in his, he led her to the bedroom in back. There was a huge king-size bed in the room. It was covered by a thick comforter in shades of beige and red.

For the first time since she'd been so brazen with

him, reality hit her like a cold cloth. She stood just inside the doorway, her eyes riveted on that bed, as erotic pictures of Matt without clothing danced in her thoughts.

He turned to her, backing her up against the closed door. He sensed her nervousness, her sudden uncertainty.

"Are you afraid?" he asked somberly.

"I'm sorry, I guess I am," she said with a forced smile.

His lean hands framed her face and he bent and kissed her eyelids. "This may be your first time. It isn't mine. By the time we end up on that bed, you'll be ready for me, and fear is the very last thing you're going to feel."

He bent to her mouth then and began to kiss her. The caresses were tender and slow, not arousing. If anything, they comforted. She felt her fear of him, of the unknown, melt away like ice in the hot sun. After a few seconds, she relaxed and gave in to his gentle ardor.

At first it was just pleasant. Then she felt him move closer and his body reacted at once to hers.

He caught his breath as he felt the sudden surge of pleasure.

Her hands smoothed up his hard thighs, savoring the muscular warmth of them while his mouth captured hers and took possession of it a little roughly, because she was intensifying the desire that was already consuming him.

His body began to move on her, slow and caressing, arousing and tantalizing. Her breasts felt heavy. Her nipples were taut, and the friction of the silky cloth against them intensified the sensations he was kindling in her body, the desire she was already feeling.

His knee edged between both her legs in the silky dress and the slow movement of his hips made her body clench.

His hands went between them, working deftly on the tiny straps of her dress while he kissed her. It wasn't until she felt the rough hair of his chest against her bare breasts that she realized both of them were uncovered from the waist up.

He drew away a little and looked down at her firm, pretty little breasts while he traced them with his fingers.

"I'd like to keep you under lock and key," he murmured gruffly. "My own pretty little treasure," he added as his head bent.

She watched his mouth take her, felt the pleasure of warm lips on her body. She liked the sight of his mouth over her nipple, that dark, wavy hair falling unruly onto his broad forehead while his heavy eyebrows met and his eyes closed under the delicious whip of passion. She held his head to her body, smoothing the hair at his nape, feeling it cool and clean under her fingers.

When he finally lifted his head, she was leaning back against the door for support. Her eyes were misty with desire, her body trembled faintly with the force of it. She looked at him hungrily, with all the barriers down at last. Other men might repulse her, but she wanted Matt. She loved the feel of his hands and his eyes and his mouth on her body. She wanted to lie under him and feel the delicious pressure of his body against and over and inside her own. She wanted it so badly that she moaned softly.

"No second thoughts?" he asked gently.

"Oh, no! No second thoughts, Matt," she whispered, adoring him with her eyes.

With a slow, secret smile, he began to divest her of the dress and the remaining piece of clothing, leaving her standing before him with her body unveiled, taut with passion.

She was shy, but his hands soon made a jumble of her embarrassment. She felt her body jerk rhythmically as he suckled her breasts. It was so sweet. It was paradise.

When he eased her down onto the huge bed, she lay back against the pillows, totally yielding, and watched his evening clothes come off little by little. He watched her while he undressed, laughing softly, a sensual predatory note in his deep voice. She moved helplessly on the coverlet, her entire being aflame with sensations she'd never known. She could barely wait. She felt as if she was throbbing all over, burning with some unknown fire that threatened to consume her, an ache that was almost painful.

Her eyes widened when the last piece of fabric came away from his powerful body and her breath caught.

He liked that expression. He turned away just for a minute, long enough to extricate a packet from his wallet. He sat down beside her, opened it, and taught her matter-of-factly what to do with it. She fumbled a little, her eyes incredibly wide and fascinated and a little frightened.

"I won't hurt you," he said gently, searching her eyes. "Women have been doing this for hundreds of thousands of years. You're going to like it, Leslie. I promise you are."

She lay back, watching him with wide gray eyes full of curiosity as he slid alongside her.

His dark head bent to her body and she lay under him like a creamy, blushing sacrifice, learning the different ways she responded to his touch. He laughed when she arched up and moaned. He liked the way she opened to him, the way her breath rasped when his mouth slid tenderly over her belly and the soft, inner skin of her thighs. He made a sensual meal of her there on the pretty, soft comforter, while the sound of rain came closer outside the window, the moonlit night clouding over as a storm moved above the cabin.

She hadn't known that physical pleasure could be so devastating. She watched him touch and taste her, with eyes equally fascinated and aroused by some of the things he did to her.

Her shocked exclamation pulled an amused laugh from him. "Am I shocking you? Don't you read books and watch movies?" he asked as he poised just above her.

"It isn't…the same," she choked, arching as his body began to tease hers, her long legs shifting eagerly out of his way as he moved down against her.

Her hands were clenched beside her head, and he watched her eyes dilate as his hips shifted tenderly and she felt him against her in a shattering new intimacy. She gasped, looking straight into his dark eyes. "I… never dreamed…!"

"No words on earth could describe how this feels," he murmured, his breath rasping as he hesitated and then moved down again, tenderly. "You're beautiful, Leslie. Your body is exquisite, soft and warm and enticing. I love the way your skin feels under my mouth."

His breath caught as he moved closer and felt her body protest at the invasion. He paused to search over her flushed, drawn face. "I'm becoming your lover," he whispered huskily, drawing his body against hers sensuously to deepen his possession. "I'm going inside you. Now."

His face became rigid with control, solemn as he met her eyes and pushed again, harder, and watched her flinch. "I know. It's going to hurt a little, in spite of everything," he said softly. "But not for long. Do you still want me?"

"More than anything…in the world!" she choked, lifting her hips toward his in a sensual invitation. "It's all right." She swallowed. Impulsively she looked down and her mouth fell open. She couldn't have imagined watching, even a day before. "Matt…!" she gasped.

Her eyes came back up to his. His face looked as if every muscle in it was clenched. "It feels like my first time, too," he said a little roughly. His hands slid under her head, cradling it as he shifted slightly and then pushed once more.

Her pretty body lifted off the bed. It seemed to ripple as he moved intimately into closer contact. "I never thought…we could talk…while we did something so intimate," she whispered back, gasping when he moved again and pleasure shot through her. "Yes…oh, yes, please do…that!" she pleaded huskily, clutching at his shoulders.

"Here, like this?" he asked urgently, and moved again.

Her tiny cry was affirmation enough. He eased down on her, his eyes looking straight into hers as he began a rhythm that combined tension with exquisite pleasure and fleeting, burning pain.

His eyes dilated as he felt the barrier. He shivered. His body clenched. He'd never had an innocent woman. Leslie was totally out of his experience. He hadn't thought about how it would feel until now. Primitive thoughts claimed his mind, ancestral memories perhaps that spoke of an ancient age when this would have been a rite of passage.

She was feeling something very similar as her body yielded to the domination of his. The discomfort paled beside the feelings that were consuming her. Glimpses of unbelievable pleasure were mingling with the stinging pain. Past it, she knew, lay ecstasy.

He kissed her hungrily as his lean, fit body moved on her in the silence of the cabin. Suddenly rain pounded hard outside the curtained window, slamming into the roof, the ground, the trees. The wind howled around the corner. There was a storm in him, too, as he lay stretched tight with desire, trying to hold back long enough to let Leslie share what he knew he would feel.

"I've never been so hungry," he bit off against her mouth. His hands contracted under her head, tangling in her hair. His body shuddered. "I'm going to have to hurt you. I can't wait any longer. It's getting away from me. I have to have you…now!"

Her legs moved sensuously against his, loving the faint abrasion of the hair that covered his. "Yes!" she said huskily, her eyes full of wonder. "I want it. I want… it with you."

One lean hand went to her upper thigh. His lips flattened. He looked straight into her eyes as his hand suddenly pinned her hips and he thrust down fiercely.

She cried out, grimacing, writhing as she felt him deep in her body, past a stinging pain that engulfed her.

He stilled, holding her in place while he gave her body time to adjust, his eyes blazing with primitive triumph. His gaze reflected pride and pleasure and possession.

"Yes," he said roughly. "You're part of me and I'm part of you. Now you belong to me, completely."

Her eyes mirrored her shocked fascination. She moved a little and felt him move with her. She swallowed, and then swallowed again, her breath coming in soft jerks as she adjusted to her first intimacy. She loved him. The feel of him was pure delight. She was a woman. She could be a woman. The past was dying already and she was whole and sensuous and fully capable. Her smile was brilliant with joyful self-discovery.

She pulled his head down to hers and kissed him hungrily. The pain had receded and now she felt a new sensation as his hips moved. There were tiny little spasms of pleasure. Her breath came raggedly as she positioned herself to hold on to them. Her nails bit into the hard muscle of his upper arms.

His dark eyes were full of indulgent amusement as he felt her movements. She hesitated once, shy. "Don't stop," he whispered. "I'll do whatever you want me to do."

Her lips parted. It wasn't the answer she'd expected.

He bent and kissed her eyelids again, his breath growing more ragged by the minute. "Find a position that gives you what you need," he coaxed. "I won't take my pleasure until you've had yours."

"Oh, Matt," she moaned, unbearably touched by a generosity that she hadn't expected.

He laughed through his desire, kissing her face tenderly. "My own treasure," he whispered. "I wish I could make it last for hours. I want you to blush when you're sixty, remembering this first time. I want it to be perfect for you."

The pleasure was building. It was fierce now, and she was no longer in control of her own body. It lifted up to Matt's and demanded pleasure. She was totally at the mercy of her awakened passion, blind with the need for fulfillment. She became aware of a new sort of tension that was lifting her fiercely to meet every quick, downward motion of his lean hips, that stretched her under his powerful body, that made her pulse leap with delicious throbs of wild delight.

He watched her body move and ripple, watched the expression on her face, in her wide, blind eyes, and smiled. "Yes," he murmured to himself. "Now you understand, don't you? You can't fight it, or deny it, or control it…" He stopped abruptly.

"No! Please, don't…stop!" Her choked cry was followed by frantic, clinging hands that pulled at him.

He eased down again, watching as she shivered. "I'm not going to stop," he whispered softly. "Trust me. I only want to make it as good as it can be for you."

"It feels…wonderful," she said hoarsely. "Every time you move, it's like…like electric shocks of pleasure."

"And we've barely started, baby," he whispered. He shifted his hips, intensifying her cries. She was completely yielded to him, open to him, wanton. He'd never dreamed that it would be like this. His head began to spin with the delight his body was taking from hers.

She curled her long legs around his powerful ones

and lifted herself, gasping when it brought a sharp stab of pleasure.

His hand swept down her body. His face hardened as he began to increase the pressure and the rhythm. She clung to him, her mouth on his throat, on his chest, his chin, wherever she could reach, while he gave in to his fierce hunger and threw away his control.

She'd never dreamed how it would be. She couldn't get close enough, or hold on tight enough. She felt him in every cell of her body. She was ardent, inciting him, matching his quick, hard movements, her back lifting to promote an even closer contact.

She whispered things to him, secret, erotic things that drove him to sensual urgency. She was moaning. She could hear her frantic voice pleading, hear the sound their movements made on the box springs, feel the power and heat of him as her body opened for him and clenched with tension that begged for release.

She whispered his name and then groaned it, and then repeated it in a mad, hoarse little sound until the little throbs of pleasure became one long, aching, endless spasm of ecstasy that made her blind and deaf under the fierce, demanding thrust of his body. She cried out and shivered in the grip of it, her voice throbbing like her body. She felt herself go off the edge of the world into space, into a red heat that washed over every cell in her body.

When she was able to think again, she felt his body shake violently, heard the harsh groan at her ear as he, too, found ecstasy.

He shuddered one last time and then his warm strong body relaxed and she felt it push hers deeper into the mattress. His mouth was at her throat, pressing hungrily. His lips moved all over her face, touching and lifting in a fever of tenderness.

Her dazed eyes opened and looked up into his. He was damp with sweat, as she was. His dark eyes smiled with incredible gentleness into hers.

She arched helplessly and moaned as the pleasure washed over her again.

"More?" he whispered, and his hips moved obligingly, so that the sweet stabs of delight came again and again and again.

She sobbed helplessly afterward, clinging to him as she lay against his relaxed body.

His hand smoothed over her damp hair. He seemed to understand her shattered response, as she didn't.

"I don't know why I'm bawling my head off," she choked, "when it was the closest to heaven I've ever been."

"There are half a dozen technical names for it," he murmured drowsily. "It's letdown blues. You go so high that it hurts to come down."

"I went high," she murmured with a smile. "I walked on the moon."

He chuckled. "So did I."

"Was…was it all right?" she asked suddenly.

He rolled her over on her back and looked down into her curious face. "You were the best lover I've ever had," he said, and he wasn't teasing. "And you will be, from now on, the only woman I ever have."

"Oh, that sounds serious," she murmured.

"Doesn't it, though?" His dark eyes went over her like an artist's brush committing beauty to canvas. He touched her soft breasts with a breathlessly tender caress. "I won't be able to stop, you know," he added con-versationally.

"Stop?"

"This," he replied. "It's addictive. Now that I've had you, I'll want you all the time. I'll go green every time any other man so much as looks at you."

It sounded as if he was trying to tell her something, and she couldn't decide what it was. She searched his dark eyes intently.

He smiled with indulgent affection. "Do you want the words?"

"Which words?" she whispered.

He brushed his lips over hers with incredible, breathless tenderness. "Marry me, Leslie."

## CHAPTER THIRTEEN

HER GASP WAS AUDIBLE. It was more than she'd dared hope for when she came in here with him. He chuckled at her expression.

"Did you think I was going to ask you to come out to the ranch and live in sin with me?" he teased with twinkling eyes. His hand swept down over her body possessively. "This isn't enough. Not nearly enough."

She hesitated. "Are you sure that you want something, well, permanent?"

His eyes narrowed. "Leslie, if I'd been a little more reckless, you'd have something permanent. I wanted very badly to make you pregnant."

Her face brightened. "Did you, really? I thought about it, too, just at the end."

He smoothed back her hair and found himself fighting the temptation to start all over again with nothing between them.

"We'll have children," he promised her. "But first we'll build a life together, a secure life that they'll fall into very naturally."

She was fascinated by the expression on his face. It was only just dawning on her that he felt more than a fleeting desire for her body. He was talking about a life together, children together. She knew very little about true relationships, but she was learning all the time.

"Heavy thoughts?" he teased.

"Yes." She smoothed her fingers over his lean cheek.

"Care to share them?" he murmured.

"I was thinking how sweet it is to be loved," she whispered softly.

He lifted an eyebrow. "Physically loved?"

"Well, that, too," she replied.

He smiled quizzically. "Too?"

"You'd never have taken me to bed unless you loved me," she said simply, but with conviction. "You have these strange old-world hang-ups about innocence."

"Strange, my foot!"

She smiled up at him complacently. "Not that I don't like them," she assured him. The smile faded as she searched his dark eyes. "It was perfect. Just perfect. And I'm glad I waited for you. I love you, Matt."

His chest rose and fell heavily. "Even after the way I've treated you?"

"You didn't know the truth," she said. "And even if you were unfair at first, you made all sorts of restitution. I won't have a limp anymore," she added, wide-eyed. "And you gave me a good job and looked out for me..."

He bent and kissed her hungrily. "Don't try to make it sound better than it was. I've been an ogre with you. I'm only sorry that I can't go back and start over again."

"None of us can do that," she said. "But we have a second chance, both of us. That's something to be thankful for."

"From now on," he promised her solemnly, "everything is going to be just the way you want it. The past has been hard for me to overcome. I've distrusted women for so long, but with you I've been able to forget what my mother did. I'll cherish you as long as I live."

"And I'll cherish you," she replied quietly. "I thought I would never know what it was to be loved."

He frowned a little, drawing her palm to his lips. "I never thought I would, either. I was never in love before."

She sighed tenderly. "Neither was I. And I never dreamed it would be so sweet."

"I imagine it's going to get better year after year," he ventured, toying with her fingers.

Her free hand slid up into his dark hair. "Matt?"

"What?"

"Can we do that again?"

He pursed his lips. "Are you sure that you can?" he asked pointedly.

She shifted on the coverlet and grimaced with the movement. "Well, maybe not. Oh, dear."

He actually laughed, bending to wrap her up against him and kiss her with rough affection. "Come here, walking wounded. We'll have a nice nap and then we'll go home and make wedding plans." He smoothed down her wild hair. "We'll have a nice cozy wedding and a honeymoon anywhere you want to go."

"I don't mind if we don't go anywhere, as long as I'm with you," she said honestly.

He sighed. "My thoughts exactly." He glanced down at her. "You could have had a conventional wedding night, you know."

She smoothed her hand over his hair-roughened chest. "I didn't know that you'd want to marry me. But just the same, I had to know if I could function intimately with you. I wasn't sure, you see."

"I am," he said with a wicked grin.

She laughed heartily. "Yes, so am I, now, but it was

important that I knew the truth before things went any further between us. I knew it was difficult for you to hold back, and I couldn't bear the thought of letting you go. Not that I expected you to want to marry me," she added ruefully.

"I wanted to marry you the first time I kissed you," he confessed. "Not to mention the first time I danced with you. It was magic."

"For me, too."

"But you had this strange aversion to me and I couldn't understand why. I was a beast to you. Even Ed said it wasn't like me to treat employees that badly. He read me the riot act and I let him."

"Ed's nice."

"He is. But I'm glad you weren't in love with him. At first, I couldn't be sure of the competition."

"Ed was a brotherly sort. He still is." She kissed his chest. "But I love you."

"I love you, too."

She laid her cheek against the place she'd kissed and closed her eyes. "If the lawyers can help my mother, maybe she'll be out for the first christening."

"At least for the second," he agreed, and smiled as his arms closed warm and protective around her, drawing her closer. It was the safest she'd ever been in her life, in those warm, strong arms in the darkness. The nightmares seemed to fade into the shadows of reality that they'd become. She would walk in the light, now, unafraid. The past was over, truly over. She knew that it would never torment her again.

MATT AND LESLIE were married in the local Presbyterian church, and the pews were full all the way to the back. Leslie thought that every single inhabitant of Ja-cobsville had shown up for the wedding, and she wasn't far wrong. Matt Caldwell had been the town's foremost bachelor for so long that curiosity brought people for miles around. All the Hart boys showed up, including the state attorney general, as well as the Ballengers, the Tremaynes, the Jacobs, the Coltrains, the Dever-ells, the Regans and the Burkes. The turnout read like the local social register.

Leslie wore a white designer gown with a long train and oceans of veiling and lace. The women in the of-fice served as maids and matrons of honor, and Luke Craig acted as Matt's best man. There were flower girls and a concert pianist. The local press was invited, but no out of town reporters. Nobody wrote about Leslie's tragic past, either. It was a beautiful ceremony and the reception was uproarious.

Matt had pushed back her veil at the altar with the look of a man who'd inherited heaven. He smiled as he bent to kiss her, and his eyes were soft with love, as were her own.

They held hands all through the noisy reception on the lawn at Matt's ranch, where barbecue was the order of the day.

Leslie had already changed clothes and was walking among the guests when she came upon Carolyn Engles unexpectedly.

The beautiful blonde came right up to her with a genuine smile and a present in her hands.

"I got this for you, in Paris," Carolyn said with vis-ible hesitation and self-consciousness. "It's sort of a peace offering and an apology, all in one."

"You didn't have to do this," Leslie stammered.

"I did." She nodded toward the silver-wrapped present. "Open it."

Leslie pulled off the paper with helpless excitement, puzzled and touched by the other woman's gesture. She opened the velvet box inside and her breath caught. It was a beautiful little crystal swan, tiny and perfect.

"I thought it was a nice analogy," Carolyn murmured. "You've turned out to be a lovely swan, and nobody's going to hurt you when you go swimming around in the Jacobsville pond."

Impulsively Leslie hugged the older woman, who laughed nervously and actually blushed.

"I'm sorry for what I did that day," Carolyn said huskily. "Really sorry. I had no idea…"

"I don't hold grudges," Leslie said gently.

"I know that." She shrugged. "I was infatuated with Matt and he couldn't see me for dust. I went a little crazy, but I'm myself again now. I want you both to be very happy."

"I hope the same for you," Leslie said with a smile.

Matt saw them together and frowned. He came up beside Leslie and placed an arm around her protectively.

"Carolyn brought this to me from Paris," Leslie said excitedly, showing him the tiny thing. "Isn't it beautiful?"

Matt was obviously puzzled as he exchanged looks with Carolyn.

"I'm not as bad as you think I am," Carolyn told him. "I really do hope you'll be happy. Both of you."

Matt's eyes smiled. "Thank you."

Carolyn smiled back ruefully. "I told Leslie how sorry I was for the way I behaved. I really am, Matt."

"We all have periods of lunacy," Matt replied. "Otherwise, nobody in his right mind would ever get into the cattle business."

Carolyn laughed delightedly. "So they say. I have to go. I just wanted to bring Leslie the peace offering. You'll both be on my guest list for the charity ball, by the way."

"We'll come, and thank you," Matt returned.

Carolyn nodded, smiled and moved away toward where the guests' cars were parked.

Matt pulled his new wife closer. "Surprises are breaking out like measles."

"I noticed." She linked her arms around his neck and reached up to kiss him tenderly. "When everybody goes home, we can lock ourselves in the bedroom and play doctor."

He chuckled delightedly. "Can we, now? Who gets to go first?"

"Wait and see!"

He turned her back toward their guests with a grin that went from ear to ear. "Lucky me," he said, and he wasn't joking.

THEY WOKE THE next morning in a tangle of arms and legs as the sun peered in through the gauzy curtains. Matt's ardor had been inexhaustible, and Leslie had discovered a whole new world of sensation.

She rolled over onto her back and stretched, uninhibited by her nudity. Matt propped himself on an elbow and looked at her with eyes full of love and possession.

"I never realized that marriage would have so many fringe benefits," she murmured. She stretched again. "I don't know if I have enough strength to walk after last night."

"If you don't, I'll carry you," he said with a loving smile. He reached over to kiss her lazily. "Come on, treasure. We'll have a nice shower and then we'll go and find some breakfast."

She kissed him back. "I love you."

"Same here."

"You aren't sorry you married me, are you?" she asked impulsively. "I mean, the past never really goes away. Someday some other reporter may dig it all back up again."

"It won't matter," he said. "Everybody's got a skeleton or two. And no, I'm not sorry I married you. It was the first sensible thing I've done in years. Not to mention," he added with a sensual touch of his mouth to her body, "the most pleasurable."

She laughed. "For me, too." Her arms pulled him down to her and she kissed him heartily.

HER MOTHER DID get a new trial, and her sentence was shortened. She went back to serve the rest of her time with a light heart, looking forward to the day when she could get to know her daughter all over again.

As for Leslie, she and Matt grew closer with every passing day and became known locally as "the love-birds," because they were so rarely seen apart.

Matt's prediction about her mother's release came true, as well. Three years after the birth of their son, Leslie gave birth to a daughter who had Matt's dark hair and, he mused, a temper to match his own. He had to fight tears when the baby was placed in his arms. He loved his son, but he'd wanted a little girl who looked like his own treasure, Leslie. Now, he told her, his life was complete. She echoed that sentiment with all her heart. The past had truly been laid to rest. She and Matt had years of happiness ahead of them.

Most of Jacobsville showed up for the baby's christening, including a small blond woman who was enjoying her first days of freedom. Leslie's mother had pride of place in the front pew. Leslie looked from Matt to her mother, from their three-year-old son to the baby in her arms. Her gray eyes, when they lifted to Matt's soft, dark ones, were radiant with joy. Dreams came true, she thought. Dreams came true.

\* \* \* \* \*

## SPECIAL EXCERPT FROM

**HQN**

*As teenagers, they couldn't get enough of each other. So when Sunny Dalton returns to her hometown of Lone Star Ridge, Texas, and is reunited with Shaw Jameson, the sparks they both assumed had long fizzled out are quickly reignited. But too many old secrets lay hidden below the surface, threatening the happily-ever-after they've never given up on...*

*Read on for a sneak peek at*
Tangled Up in Texas,
*the first book in Lone Star Ridge from*
USA TODAY *bestselling author Delores Fossen.*

Shaw looked up when he heard the sound of the approaching vehicle. Not coming from behind but rather ahead—from the direction of the ranch. It was a dark blue SUV barreling toward him, and it screeched to a stop on the other side of the intimate apparel he'd found lying on the road.

Because of the angle of the morning sunlight and the SUV's tinted windshield, Shaw couldn't see the driver, but he sure as heck saw the woman who stepped from the passenger's side.

Talk about a gut punch of surprise. The biggest surprise of the morning, and that was saying something considering the weird underwear on the road.

Sunny Dalton.

She was a blast from the past and a tangle of memories. And here she was walking toward him like a siren in her snug jeans and loose gray shirt.

And here he was on the verge of drooling.

Shaw did something about that and made sure he closed his mouth, but he knew it wouldn't stay that way. Even though Sunny and he were no longer teenagers, his body just steamed up whenever he saw her.

Sunny smiled at him. However, he didn't think it was so much from steam but rather a sense of polite frustration.

"Shaw," she said on a rise of breath.

Her voice was smooth and silky. Maybe a little tired, too. Even if Shaw hadn't seen her in a couple of years, he was pretty sure that was fatigue in her steel blue eyes.

She'd changed her hair. It was still a dark chocolate brown, but it no longer hung well past her shoulders. It was shorter in a nonfussy sort of way, which would have maybe looked plain on most women. On Sunny, it just framed that amazing face.

And Shaw knew his life was about to get a whole lot more complicated.

*Don't miss*
Tangled Up in Texas *by Delores Fossen,*
*available March 2020 wherever*
*HQN Books and ebooks are sold!*

HQNBooks.com

PHDFEXP0320

# *Love Harlequin romance?*

## DISCOVER.

Be the first to find out about promotions,
news and exclusive content!

Facebook.com/HarlequinBooks

Twitter.com/HarlequinBooks

Instagram.com/HarlequinBooks

Pinterest.com/HarlequinBooks

ReaderService.com

## EXPLORE.

Sign up for the Harlequin e-newsletter and
download a free book from any series at
**TryHarlequin.com**

## CONNECT.

Join our Harlequin community to
share your thoughts and connect
with other romance readers!
**Facebook.com/groups/HarlequinConnection**

HSOCIAL2020